D1337067

GOD OF VENGEANCE

GOD OF VENGEANCE

Giles Kristian

BANTAM PRESS

LONDON · TORONTO · SYDNEY · AUCKLAND · JOHANNESBURG

TRANSWORLD PUBLISHERS
61–63 Uxbridge Road, London W5 5SA
A Random House Group Company
www.transworldbooks.co.uk

First published in Great Britain
in 2014 by Bantam Press
an imprint of Transworld Publishers

A CIP catalogue record for this book
is available from the British Library.

ISBNs 9780593066188 (cased)
9780593066195 (tpb)

Addresses for Random House Group Ltd companies outside the UK
can be found at: www.randomhouse.co.uk
The Random House Group Ltd Reg. No. 954009

The Random House Group Limited supports the Forest Stewardship Council® (FSC®),
the leading international forest-certification organisation. Our books carrying the
FSC label are printed on FSC®-certified paper. FSC is the only forest-certification
scheme supported by the leading environmental organisations, including
Greenpeace. Our paper procurement policy can be found
at www.randomhouse.co.uk/environment

Typeset in 11/14½pt Meridian by
Kestrel Data, Exeter, Devon.
Printed and bound in Great Britain by
Clays Ltd, Bungay, Suffolk.

2 4 6 8 10 9 7 5 3 1

MIX
Paper from
responsible sources
FSC® C016897

God of Vengeance is for Phil, Pietro and Drew, with whom I rowed the Dragon Harald Fairhair.

SIGURD HARALDARSON'S WORLD, SOUTH-WEST NORWAY, AD 785

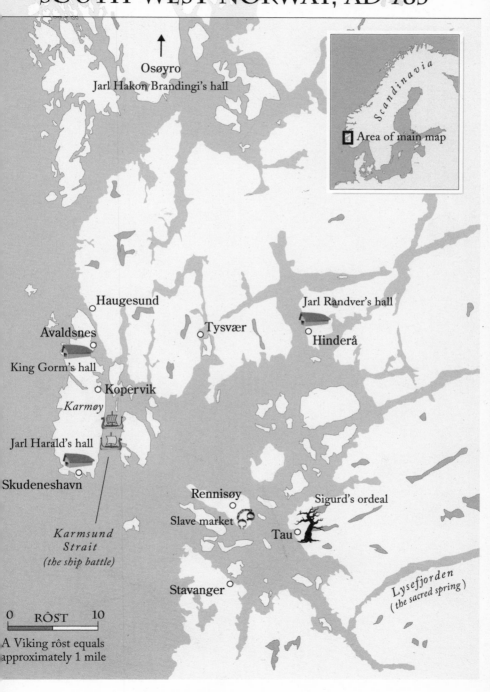

↑

Osøyro
Jarl Hakon Brandingi's hall

Scandinavia

Area of main map

Haugesund

Jarl Randver's hall

Avaldsnes

Tysvær

Hinderå

King Gorm's hall

Kopervik

Karmøy

Jarl Harald's hall

Skudeneshavn

Rennisøy

Sigurd's ordeal

Slave market

Tau

*Karmsund
Strait
(the ship battle)*

Stavanger

*Lysefjorden
(the sacred spring)*

0   RÔST   10

A Viking rôst equals
approximately 1 mile

I know that I hung
On a wind-rocked tree
Nine whole nights,
With a spear wounded,
And to Óðin offered
Myself to myself;
On that tree
Of which no one knows
From what root it springs.

Óðin's Rune-Song

PROLOGUE

AD775, Avaldsnes, Norway

THE WOODS WERE SILENT BUT THE MEN WERE NOT. THEY PROGRESSED slowly and with care. No sudden movements. Round-shouldered like wolves, heads pulled in, eyes half closed so that their whites would not betray them. And yet every other footfall snapped a twig or disturbed the pine litter, making the guilty one curse inwardly and hold still as a rock to see if the bull elk would bolt.

For now at least the creature stood upwind and unaware, its hide dappled pale gold in the late morning sunlight threading through the trees.

Three hunters had broken off from the group. Two men and a boy, and all of them carrying spears, the boy's one and a half times his own height, its haft almost too thick for his hand to grasp, though he had not dropped it all day. If he had learnt anything in his seven years it was that you did not drop your spear in woods where boar might be foraging. Or where an injured wolf might linger. You especially did not drop it in front of your father or the king, no matter how white your knuckles or how much your fingers ached.

They should have waited for the men with bows perhaps. The dogs too. But kings and jarls were not good at waiting and now

11

the king turned around and grinned at the boy, putting a thick finger to his lips, his copper beard bristling in the breeze. Then he gestured to the boy's father to skirt round to the right of the glade and the boy knew this was doing his father a great honour and pride bloomed hot in his chest. For once the king made to cast his spear the elk would sense it and take off eastward, and Jarl Harald would hurl his own spear and bring the creature down.

So the boy held still now, his heart beating in his ears, his stomach knotted with the thrill of it all. He would sooner die than be the one to scare the beast off now and ruin their casts.

The bull is magnificent, he thought, trying to be as still as his brothers had taught him, each measured breath rich with the sweet, pungent scent of tree bark and pine resin and the moss that crept up the lower trunks. All around him bracken quivered in the shadows. Something scuttled across an ancient animal track near by, and far behind them a dog's bark echoed off the trees, but the boy kept his eyes on the elk, hoping his gaze could somehow hold it there, as though his eyes could bind the beast to the spot as Gleipnir, the dwarf-forged chain, had held the mighty wolf.

Then, shielding the gesture with his own body, the king waved a hand at the boy behind him, inviting him to be the one to throw the first spear. The boy blinked. Swallowed. They had been out since before dawn and this was the first worthy prey they had found and now he would have the honour of casting first. And if there was another thing he had learnt in his seven years it was that you did not miss when a man with a torc at his neck the thickness of your wrist invited you to launch your spear. Every day the boy practised with sword and shield but never with a spear so thick he could barely grip it.

He nodded to the king and the king nodded back. He would have acknowledged his father too and made sure of where he was, but he would not allow himself to tear his thoughts from the elk.

'Even before you throw, see the spear in your mind, flying straight and true,' his brother Sorli had told him, and no doubt

Sorli had been told it by Sigmund, who had heard it from Thorvard, which was the way of it with brothers. 'See the spear pass through the elk's flesh and drive into its heart. Only when you have spun this picture in the eye of your mind should you make the throw.'

And so the boy spun the picture of it now as he eased his leading foot forward, making up ground and preparing to put all of his seven years behind the throw.

But the bull had many more years in him than the boy and suddenly he hauled up his great head and sniffed the air. He was a giant. Over seven feet tall at the shoulder and then there was his great head and the antlers which themselves spanned a distance much greater than the boy's height. The beast's hackles rose as he lowered that great head and flattened his ears, and the boy was close enough now to see the flies buzzing near his muzzle and hear the crunch of his teeth working through the tough plants he had rooted up.

Now!

The boy made three quick strides and on the fourth step hurled the spear and it flew, arcing slightly before striking the bull in its right hind quarters but not hard enough to stay in the flesh, as the bull roared and turned and galloped off through the trees.

Towards the boy's father.

Harald gave a roar to rival the bull's as he cast his own spear, the iron blade streaking like lightning, but somehow the beast swerved, too limber for its great size, and the jarl's spear gouged a red streak along its neck but flew on into the trees.

'Thór's arse!' Harald yelled, as the bull plunged off, snapping branches and twigs and vanishing deep into the pine wood.

But the king was laughing, great booming peals that echoed off the trunks and bent him double, hands on his knees, his spear stuck in the earth beside him.

'What is so funny?' the boy's father called, an angry flush beneath his golden beard, for he had missed and that was bad enough without his host laughing about it.

Still laughing, the king straightened and came over to the boy, putting an arm around his shoulders, at which the boy straightened and puffed up his chest and tried to grow a year's worth in a heartbeat.

'It's your boy, Harald!' the king said. 'By the gods he's got a throw on him! I swear that proud bull shit himself when he saw young Sigurd's face.'

The boy did not know if he was being complimented or if the king was making fun of him. He tried to smile but could feel that it was all teeth and nothing else, and then his father burst into laughter too and between the two men the sound was like the roar of the sea.

'I would not like to get on your bad side, boy!' the king said, giving his shoulder a shake that made his brain rattle in its skull.

But the boy was still thinking about the bull elk. About how he had failed to bring it down. Next time the spear would pierce the flesh, he told himself. Next time he would be stronger.

'I don't know about you, Harald, but I am thirsty,' the king said, pulling his spear from the earth.

'I am always thirsty,' Harald said, as the rest of the hunting party drew nearer, the men eager to catch up with their lords and the dogs barking with the bull elk's scent in their noses.

Sigurd gathered up his own spear and his father pointed at the blade.

'See the blood there, boy?' Harald said. 'That was a good throw. Better than mine.'

And with that they turned north to make their way back to King Gorm's hall and the mead that awaited them there.

And somehow the spear in the boy's hand no longer felt too big.

CHAPTER ONE

AD785, Skudeneshavn, Norway

THE JARL RAN HIS FINGERS THROUGH THE SCRAPS OF GRISTLE AND white knuckles of bone on the platter before him. Then, his hand gleaming, he raised it to the rings of twisted silver which sat below the muscle of his left arm and rubbed the grease between metal and skin. A grin spread within his beard, growing broader still when one of the rings began to shift enough for him to wedge a thick thumb between the snarling beast heads that had for a year or more closed the circle.

'This for the man who puts Olaf on his arse!' he roared and was answered by the pounding of hands on the pine planks of the mead table as he pulled the ring from his own flesh and held it aloft, its greasy lustre catching the flicker of oil lamps before he slammed it down beside his trencher. 'We need to give Hagal some new stories, eh! He has been giving us the same tales for years and thinks that simply changing the names is enough to fool us!'

Everyone laughed at that apart from Hagal 'Crow-Song' who flushed crimson beneath his neat fair beard and muttered some half-hearted defence.

'He thinks we don't know he is serving the same scraps over

and over,' Harald roared, the huge silver brooch that pinned the cloak on his right shoulder glinting in the flamelight, 'but what *he* doesn't know is that while he is farting out of his mouth, we are sleeping.' Folk crowed and hammered palms against the mead bench and the poor skald batted the air with a hand and put his horn to his mouth.

'Don't break any necks, Olaf!' Harald warned with a glistening finger and woven brows.

Without turning to see if there were any challengers – for there always were – Olaf shrugged his broad shoulders and clambered out from the mead bench, brushing crumbs from the tunic stretched over the barrel of his chest. He put his drinking horn to his full lips and downed its contents to a din of cheers and table-thumping that all but shook the timbers of Eik-hjálmr, the jarl's hall.

'Take your time, Olaf! You will live many years with the humiliation of what is about to happen,' Sorli said, grinning at his friends who hoisted their mead horns in appreciation of Sorli's boasting. Men and women fumbled in the darker corners and dogs growled over scraps.

'Ha!' Olaf exclaimed, upending the mead horn on his head to show that it was empty, then flinging it at a dark-haired thrall who caught it with practised ease.

'You'll be making friends with the mice and the dogs soon enough, old man,' Sorli said, stirring the new floor reeds with a foot and almost unbalancing with the doing of it. 'Remember that one, Crow-Song!' he called over to the skald, who curled his lip, beyond caring now.

Sigurd raised his own drinking horn to his lips and mumbled a curse into it. Beside him his friend Svein shook his head, the thick braids of red hair swishing like reefing ropes on a sail. 'Your brother has pissed away his senses,' he said, then grinned. 'But we will get a laugh out of it, hey!'

Sigurd nodded half-heartedly. He was in no mood for laughter, as anyone around him would have known. And yet he would stay to watch his elder brother attempt to make good boasts that had often filled Eik-hjálmr the way breath fills the sky.

'You should look away now, boy,' Sorli barked at Harek who was conspicuous amongst all those grizzled growling men for his beardless face but more so for his hair which was white as ale froth and smooth as a girl's. 'I don't want you seeing your old father dropped on his arse in front of his friends.' Sorli frowned, scratching amongst his thick, golden hair which, when hanging loose as it was now, had earned him the byname Baldr because men and women both thought that Sorli resembled that most fair-faced god. But Baldr son of Óðin was also said to be the wisest of the gods and that, Sigurd thought, was where the similarity ended.

Harek did not look away, instead humouring Sorli with a gentle smile and nod. Then he looked at his mother who sat cradling Harek's infant brother, though all you could see of the bairn was a shock of hair as white as Harek's sticking from the blanket like cotton grass. His mother rolled her eyes, shook her head and went back to cooing in little Eric's ear.

'I'm ready, boy,' Olaf said, shoving men aside who were gathering in the middle of the hall to watch the match. 'No tears now. Your father and brothers are watching.' Olaf winked at Sigurd and Sigurd could not help but grin at the man who was his father's closest friend and sword-brother. It was strange, Sigurd thought as he climbed up to stand on the mead bench for a better view, how he wanted Olaf to answer Sorli's crowing with a serving of floor rushes, and yet also wanted his brother to give a good account of himself, perhaps even surprise them all by dumping Olaf on his rear.

'Don't embarrass us, brother,' Thorvard called out, raising his mead horn, his wolf's grin doing nothing to disguise the sincerity of the command.

As the eldest of the brothers Thorvard took family honour more seriously than any of them but for their father perhaps, and Sigurd suspected that if Sorli were beaten too easily then Thorvard would feel duty-bound to challenge Olaf himself and salvage what he could of the family pride.

'Hey, Asgot!' Slagfid bellowed, his voice rolling through the hall like thunder above the din. 'Who is going to win? What do your runes say?' But the godi ignored Jarl Harald's champion, perhaps the only man but for Harald himself in that hall who would dare address him thus, and sat like a cloud threatening rain to the right of the jarl's high seat.

'You and Asgot make for shit company tonight,' Svein told Sigurd, taking the deer-antler comb on its thong around his neck and pulling its teeth through the beginnings of the red beard of which he was so proud. How many times in Sigurd's seventeen years had he heard his friend claim to be descended from the thunder god Thór himself? 'Is it the godi's bag of bones that has you as sour as a woman sailing the red river?'

A great cheer went up as Olaf and Sorli slammed into one another like bull deer during the rut and grappled.

'You know that isn't it,' Sigurd said.

Sorli slipped Olaf's grasp and swung a fist but missed and the men cheered as Olaf glanced round the hall and asked if anyone had seen where that punch landed.

'We'll get our chance,' Svein said. 'If there's one thing you can count on it's that with old Biflindi as king there will be more fights than there are bristles on Thór's ball sack.'

Olaf cracked a fist into Sorli's temple and the younger man staggered backwards but kept his feet.

'You and I will have years to make our fame,' Svein went on, gesturing to a thrall to refill his drinking horn. 'We'll wear our swords down to stubs,' he added, then gave a mischievous grin that suggested he had also meant the swords in their breeks.

'But not tomorrow,' Sigurd said, the bitterness of it working into him like iron rot into a helmet. He had trained with sword, axe and shield since he had been strong enough to hold them, and yet still he must stay behind while his three brothers and their father went into the steel-storm.

'Ah, drink up!' Svein said, thumping his mead horn against Sigurd's so that liquid spilled over the lip and splashed onto the shoulder of a man who was enjoying the fight too much to notice. Not that he would have picked a quarrel with Svein, Sigurd supposed, for Svein was already built like a troll. Given a handful more years he would be a red-haired, red-bearded giant, perhaps even bigger than his father, Styrbiorn, who sat with a beard full of mead and a lap full of wench across the hall, paying no interest to the fight whatever.

Sigurd drank.

'That's better,' Svein said, dragging the back of his hand across his mouth and giving a great belch that all but brought tears to Sigurd's eyes. And just then Olaf ducked underneath Sorli's leading arm, throwing his left shoulder into the younger man's chest and rolling across him so that he took Sorli's arm between both of his own and bent the hand back on itself, forcing Sorli to his knees lest his wrist be snapped.

Helpless, Sorli barked a curse and Olaf had the better of him enough to stretch out one arm and give a gaping yawn.

'Fuck!' a man named Aud exclaimed in the open doorway, still tightening his belt over his huge belly after a trip to the cesspit. 'I missed it.'

'Not much to miss,' another replied.

'Anyone else?' Olaf asked, his gaze raking over the gathering like a smith's tongs through hot coals. Several men called out or stepped forward but when they saw Thorvard press through the throng they stopped out of respect for him, and not just because he was the jarl's son, either.

'I will fight you, Uncle!' Sigurd heard himself call and this raised some laughter but not much. 'And if I beat you then I will earn my place aboard *Reinen* tomorrow.'

This threw Olaf off balance more than any man had ever done in Eik-hjálmr and he looked over at his jarl, but Harald was too busy frowning at Sigurd. Hagal the skald wasn't frowning though. The challenge had hooked him from his gloom like a fish from the dark and he clambered up onto the bench to get a clear view, spilling mead with the flurry of it.

'Sit down, boy!' Harald called to Sigurd, wafting fingers that gleamed with silver rings. 'I have seen one son made a fool of, for all that that is like wetting water. I will not have you on your knees too.'

'Let him fight!' a man yelled.

'Aye, he's got the makings of a good fighter, I've seen him and Svein working with spears. Let him have a swing at it!' someone else shouted.

Olaf scratched his bird's-nest beard and looked at Jarl Harald. 'I won't hurt him,' he said. 'So long as he doesn't tickle me.' He turned his broad smile on Sigurd. 'I can't abide tickling,' he said.

'Let him try, Father,' Sigurd's other brother Sigmund put in, standing on a mead bench beside the hearth, a pretty thrall under each arm. White teeth flashed in his golden beard. 'If he can beat Olaf then he'll be a useful man in the steel-storm tomorrow.' Sigurd nodded to him in thanks and Sigmund nodded back.

'No, Sigurd,' Thorvard said. Their brother's handsome face was carved in granite now. 'Go back to your sulking. This is my fight.' *Do not embarrass us all* is what Sigurd heard.

Sigurd burnt inside. All eyes were on him. Even Var and Vogg his father's two house hounds had called a truce over a fleshy bone and were looking up at him with red-rimmed eyes. This was not the first time Sigurd had asked his father to allow him to stand in the shieldwall but it was the first time he had asked in front of his friends and every sword- or spear-bearing man in the village. With a feeling like a ship's anchor plunging to the sea bed he knew his humiliation would be complete were his father to deny him now. Perhaps Harald knew this too, or else perhaps he decided that his youngest son needed to learn a valuable lesson about growing into a man. Whatever it was, Harald nodded then, and to Sigurd that simple gesture was sweeter than any mead he had tasted.

Thorvard swore, shrugged his huge shoulders and shook his head, stepping back to show that he withdrew his challenge.

Svein tapped a finger against his own head. 'You are mad,

Sigurd,' he said. 'The only time Olaf's been beaten was after too much mead when he fell asleep standing up before the fight even started.'

'That might happen again,' Sigurd suggested.

'And Asgot might pull some good portents out of a bull's arse,' his friend countered.

Sigurd curled his lip as an admission that neither was likely.

'All right then, you run along and have fun,' Svein said, batting the air with a big hand. 'I'll be over to scrape you off the floor when it's done.'

Sigurd drained his mead horn and gave it to his friend who was muttering something under his breath, then he turned and walked into the same space in which his older, stronger, more experienced brother had failed only moments before.

'Be gentle with Olaf, Sigurd!' Sigmund called above the clamour. 'When you're that old it takes time getting up off the floor and we have a fight tomorrow.'

This got a table-hammering and laughter like the rolling surf upon the shore, though all of them knew Olaf was as strong as an ox and a fighter in his prime. Olaf himself did not dignify it with a response, instead leaning in to Sigurd close enough that Sigurd could smell the mead on his breath and the pork grease in his beard. 'You sure about this, lad?' he asked in a low voice through lips still spread wide for the crowd.

Sigurd hoisted one eyebrow. 'I told her I would make you yowl like a kicked dog,' he said.

Olaf's eyes widened. 'Told who?' His smile contracted into a cat's arse in the bush of his beard.

'Her,' Sigurd replied, nodding towards Eik-hjálmr's door, and when Olaf looked round Sigurd kicked him in the bollocks. Olaf's eyes bulged like a fish's hauled from the depths and down he went, first onto his knees then falling over onto his side, hands thrust between his legs. For a moment Sigurd stood above the man, staring down at him as the men around them railed in outrage or laughed or acclaimed Sigurd as the new champion of Eik-hjálmr, the thunder of it so loud in that hall that Sigurd could not hear Olaf yowling though he could see the shape of it on his mouth.

And in the midst of this tumult Sigurd recalled the story of the hero Beowulf, so often breathed and bellowed by skalds beside Eik-hjálmr's hearth. For just as the monster Grendel was drawn by the din of men carousing in King Hrothgar's hall, so a shadow was coming to Skudeneshavn with the next day's dawn, for all that those around Sigurd this night drank and feasted and fought as though they would live for ever.

He looked through the throng and caught Thorvard's eye and his brother gave him an almost imperceptible nod that was the highest praise Sigurd could hope for or expect.

'Father, the ring?' Sigmund bellowed through the din. 'My little brother deserves his spoils.'

'Aye, give the lad his prize!' Orn Beak-Nose called. 'Seeing Uncle on his arse is worth that ring and more.'

Harald shook his head and slammed a big hand onto the arm ring before him. 'Not for that. The boy needs to learn respect.'

Others agreed with this and Sigmund bawled at them, sweeping his mead horn through the fug. Sigurd ignored them all, offering his hand to help Olaf to his feet. But Olaf growled an obscenity and so Sigurd shrugged and turned to walk back to his bench where Svein was waiting with two brimming horns and a grin as wide as a mead-hall door.

'You've ruined his night then,' Svein said. 'No notch for old Olaf.'

'But his wife will thank you for a good sound sleep,' a lad named Aslak said through a mouthful of bread. 'If Olaf doesn't spend all night scratching in the reeds looking for his balls.'

'There was no honour in that, Sigurd,' a man named Vigdis said, his greying brows knitted above disapproving eyes. 'You striplings mock the gods with your disrespect.' He shook his head at Sigurd. 'As the jarl's son you should know better.'

Svein and Aslak knew better than to nettle the older man further and so held their tongues, but Sigurd held Vigdis's eye.

'I know how to win,' he said, 'and that is enough for Óðin.'

The man shook his head again and went back to his food, and Svein, Aslak and Sigurd shared the sort of look that comes so easily to young men who hear what their elders say as rocks hear the river gushing over them.

The clamour rolled on as a stout man named Alfdis helped Olaf up and Jarl Harald's champion Slagfid swaggered into the circle, rumbling a challenge to anyone drunk enough to take him on. And beyond that smoke-seasoned haven of pine and oak the Valkyries were riding the night, their presence felt by all those grizzled, drunken boasters though mentioned by none. Tomorrow, then, the storm of swords. Dragon against dragon out in the Karmsund Strait.

The red war.

Sigurd felt the fury knotting in his gut like a spitting serpent but he fought to subdue it lest he draw every eye to the quarrel. He had come down to the harbour – the allotted gathering place – dressed for war in his thick woollen coat which reached to mid-thigh and was belted at the waist, woollen breeks and his greaves made from iron strips fastened to leather straps; a gift from the man he had kicked in the bollocks the night before. He did not own a sword, for his father said he must earn such a weapon, but he had brought his spear which was a better thing for a ship fight anyhow.

Not that he would get the chance to use it now.

'I made the challenge and everyone under that roof heard the terms, Father,' he said, his rage threatening to consume him. 'Did I not win?'

The jarl raised an eyebrow. 'What a noble victory that was.' He made a deep *umm* in his throat. 'You are lucky Olaf did not flay you alive and beat you with your own thigh bones,' he said, glancing at Olaf who nevertheless shot Sigurd a sympathetic look as he tied the helmet thongs in the snarl of his beard.

'So you will go back on it? Like a fox skulking back to his hole?' Sigurd dared.

'Careful, boy,' Harald growled.

Leading his pony by the bridle as he made to leave Skudenes-havn, Hagal Crow-Song stopped to take in the scene.

The jarl looked like a god of war on that jetty, the red dawn light across the black water like a bloodstain and glinting on the iron rings of his brynja. 'Besides, what would your mother say?' He nodded and Sigurd turned to look at Grimhild who stood on the grass-tufted rocks with Sigurd's younger sister Runa and all the other women, their faces harder set than their menfolk's as they watched them prepare themselves for battle.

Even war gods fear their wives, then, Sigurd reflected sourly.

'She is already warping my ear for taking three sons into the same fight,' Harald went on. 'If I took you too she would make what you did to Olaf look like a kiss on the cheek.' He frowned. 'Look now! Her eyes are into us like cat's claws.'

'The wind is good, Harald, and the men are ready,' Olaf called from where he stood on the jetty by *Reinen*'s prow.

Harald raised a hand and nodded, then barked at his thralls to hurry up with bringing all the spears they could carry down from Eik-hjálmr to load onto his ships: two longships of seventy-five feet, and a shorter karvi with thirteen pairs of oars. *Reinen*, the *Reindeer*, was Harald's best ship and well named, men thought, for she was broad and yet fast, as worthy to ride the sea road as a proud bull reindeer was to strut across the uplands east of Karmøy. Sigurd had often imagined the day he would stand aboard *Reinen* armed for battle amongst a fellowship of warriors.

'I will be careful, Father,' he said, knowing it was the same as spitting into driving rain.

'Ha!' Harald almost smiled at that. 'None of my sons knows the meaning of that.' Then, loud enough for Grimhild to hear: 'As your jarl I forbid it. As your father I forbid it. There is no more to say.'

'Don't worry, little brother,' Sigmund said, coming up and slapping Sigurd on the shoulder. His hair was braided for battle, his helmet was under one arm and he was one of the few men wearing mail. 'I'll try to spare some of the whoresons so that you will have someone to kill when Mother finally lets you fly the nest,' he said, smiling and waving at Grimhild and Runa. 'Tonight we get drunk, hey?'

But Sigurd was watching Harald's champion, Slagfid, carry the great set of reindeer antlers to *Reinen*'s bow. When the ship cast off, slipping into the fjord far enough away from Skudeneshavn not to upset the land spirits, they would mount the snarling beast head at the prow and Slagfid would set those antlers either side of the creature's eyes. As the man who would fight at the prow that day it was Slagfid's honour to mount those antlers in their iron sockets and, thus prepared for battle, *Reinen* and Slagfid both would strike fear into the enemy.

Sigurd felt a strong hand grip his shoulder and turned to look into his father's eyes. 'Your time will come, Sigurd,' Harald said. 'A warrior must master patience just as he masters the sword and shield.'

'I may be of use to you, Father, if things go against us,' Sigurd said, gripping his spear as tightly as he yet gripped the hope of changing the jarl's mind. 'Asgot said that you should not fight today, that the omens are bad. Another spear can only help.'

'That old crow's omens are always bad,' Harald said. 'If I listened to every cast of his runes I would never leave my hall.' The jarl turned to his men now, spread as they were across the jetty, the surrounding rocks and some already at their places aboard *Reinen*, Harald's second ship *Sea-Eagle*, and the short karvi which was named *Little-Elk*. All of them hefted shields, spears and axes, some wore iron helmets but most had leather skull caps or even fur hats for the protection they provided, though these men would be sweating soon enough.

'Men of Skudeneshavn!' Men could no more ignore Harald's voice than they could ignore a long-axe in a killer's hands, and it boomed out across the still water of the harbour and surged across the rocks like surf. 'We have been called out to fight for King Gorm, to whom we have pledged fealty and whose high seat we are oath-sworn to protect. Biflindi's lands to the east have been threatened by Jarl Randver. And our king is not happy about it.' There was a flash of teeth then in Harald's fair beard. 'That dog Randver has slipped his leash and his appetite has outgrown him. Today we whip the hound!'

The men cheered at that and those who carried spears banged the shafts against their shields and it was like an echo of King Gorm's byname Biflindi, meaning 'shield-shaker'. Even Hagal the skald seemed to be lifted like an eagle on a warm wind, despite how the jarl had teased him the night before.

'With the king's own men and those bondsmen he will have rounded up we will have the advantage of numbers.' Harald hawked and spat a wad of phlegm onto the slick decking of the jetty. 'But do not underestimate Jarl Randver for he is the kind that will wait until you are looking the other way and then bite your arse. Besides which, you know as well as I that bóndi more often than not run off back to their farms as soon as the first spears are thrown.'

'That's why Biflindi is fighting Randver at sea!' Slagfid roared from *Reinen*'s prow, 'because the goat-fucking bóndi can't run away if they're on a ship.'

Men cheered that rare wit from Harald's chosen prow man and more than ever Sigurd burnt to be one of them, a sword-brother going into a fight, instead of the jarl's youngest son who must stay behind with the women and the boys and the old men.

'See my son Sigurd here!' Harald exclaimed. 'Brave Týr himself could not be more eager to fight with us today!' Harald threw a brawny arm around Sigurd and pulled him into his chest, against the brynja's polished iron rings. 'I am lucky that all my sons are wolves. They thirst for the blood of our enemies!' Sigurd could smell the mead on his father's breath. A man needed mead or ale in his belly before he gave himself to the steel-storm, or else, Olaf had told him once, thoughts of blades slicing into flesh will send a man mad. 'The lad will fight amongst us soon enough.'

Then the jarl released Sigurd and turned his gaze on Asgot who was snarling at six thralls as they hauled on the halter of an ox, trying to bring it down to the water. The godi was dressed in animal skins and had bones plaited in his long, wolf-grey hair, and some of the women near by clutched their broods a little closer as if they feared Asgot might steal the children for some dark purpose.

'The Allfather craves blood, too!' Harald called, 'and we shall let him drink.' All eyes were turned to the godi and the ox, which was bellowing pitifully, either because it could smell the sea and feared it, or more likely because it had seen the wicked-sharp knife in Asgot's hand and had enough clever in it to know what was coming.

Asgot raised the knife in one claw-like hand, pointing the blade to the sky. 'Óðin, accept this offering. Show us your favour and together we will turn the sea red with the traitor's blood.' With that he stepped behind one of the thralls holding the ox's halter, threw an arm around the young man's face, hauled his head back and sliced open his throat in a crimson spray.

The women gasped as the thrall fell to his knees clutching the savage, blood-spitting wound and Harald's warriors beat their shields with spears and swords and the ox roared as the stink of blood filled its flaring nostrils.

'He was a good thrall,' Sigmund said above the clamour. Men were chanting 'Óðin' and the young thrall lay on the rocks, gore-drenched, wide-eyed and spluttering.

'He was,' Jarl Harald agreed, 'but the omens were bad. Today I would rather have the Allfather's favour and one less slave. Leave the beast, Asgot,' he called, then turned to Sigurd. 'Have them slaughter it properly, Sigurd. We will eat it at our victory feast.'

'Yes, Father,' Sigurd said, watching the godi drag the dead thrall towards the sea, his blood smearing the rocks. Then Asgot dropped the body into the plunging surf where it floated, limbs buffeted this way and that, its bloodless face turned up to the sky, the eyes bulged with the surprise of being dead.

Asgot looked at Harald and Sigurd, pulling the braids of his beard through his gore-slick hands so that those hair ropes wicked the blood and made him look even more feral. 'It is no bad thing to remember Njörd, too, before a sea fight,' he said and Harald nodded in agreement and put on his helmet which was a thing that would make even a king envious. Forged of the finest steel, it boasted many decorated panels of polished silver plate, and a high crest of bronze that came down to a raven's face, the creature's beak dividing two thick eyebrows of brass. Below these were eye guards and a nasal that made the wearer look like one of the Æsir come down from Asgard, and Sigurd had never seen anything more beautiful.

'He who stands with me this day to feed the wolf and the raven is my brother!' the jarl bellowed.

Olaf raised his spear. 'Harald!' he roared. 'Harald!' Then more than one hundred warriors took up the chant, 'Harald! Harald!', the din of it filling the new day, carrying to the gods like the call of the Gjallarhorn announcing the beginning of Ragnarök, the final battle, and Sigurd felt the thrill of it thrum in his blood like wind through a ship's rigging.

'Good luck, brother,' Sigurd said to Sigmund who was tying the thong of his own helmet beneath his golden-bearded chin.

'I will tell you all about it tonight, little brother,' he said with a grin, then turned to join the others boarding *Reinen*, *Sea-Eagle* and *Little-Elk*. Harald and five of his best warriors took up positions at *Reinen*'s bow and the rest seated themselves on their sea chests which served as row benches, as the spruce oars were taken from their trees and handed out. Mooring ropes were untied and at the command of *Reinen*'s helmsman, Thorald, those on the port side used their oars to push the ship out from the berth.

Wives and daughters came onto the jetty now and called out their farewells, wishing their menfolk good luck and commanding them to be careful, and the men mumbled their replies or simply waved or nodded, reluctant to be singled out amongst their sword-brothers.

In the time it takes to sharpen a knife all three ships were out in the deep water, heading east into the Skude Fjord towards the sun, their oars dipping and rising neatly for there was not much wind for sails, besides which Harald knew it was no bad thing to keep the men busy before a fight.

For a while the folk of Skudeneshavn watched them go, many touching Thór's hammers and other amulets and charms at their necks and muttering to the gods to bring their husbands, fathers and sons safely back from this day's bloodletting.

'I'm coming with you, Sigurd,' Sigurd's sister said, appearing beside him as he stared after *Reinen* as though strength of will alone would carry his body over the sea to land on the deck like a raven, would stand him beside his brothers Thorvard, Sorli and Sigmund.

'Did you hear me, brother? I'm coming to watch it,' Runa said.

Sigurd nodded to her then turned to Svein. 'We will have to hurry or it might be over before we get there.'

Svein shook his head. 'I told Thorvard not to kill any of the toad's arseholes until we found a nice spot with a good view.'

Someone whistled and they turned to see Aslak waiting up in the long grass of the bluff overlooking the harbour. He had brought the ponies, as Sigurd had asked. One extra by the looks.

'I told him I was coming, too,' Runa said before Sigurd could ask the question.

'I knew you would,' Svein said, smiling.

Sigurd might have guessed it too, though he was not sure that his younger sister should watch the battle with them, being only fourteen and too young for such things. He was about to say as much when their mother, who was amongst the other women leaving the jetty, called for Runa to walk back up to the village with her.

Even after five children, and four of them boys, Grimhild still owned a beauty that turned men's heads, but now her face was drawn tight as a ship's knot with the worry of seeing her husband and sons go off to fight for their king.

'Runa!' she called again. 'Come, girl! We have much to prepare for the men's return.'

'I want to go with Sigurd,' Runa called back. Her golden hair hung in two long braids and Sigurd knew that his sister was enjoying being able to show it off while she still could. In another year she would be of marriageable age and would have to cover her silken tresses. Yet her being too young for marriage did not stop men looking at Runa the way they looked at silver.

'You are coming home with me, daughter!' Grimhild said, her face flushing now at her daughter's defiance.

'Let her come, Mother,' Sigurd said, suddenly determined that Runa should go with them. He had had his fill of being told how things would be. 'She'll be fine with us.'

Grimhild frowned and Sigurd turned to Runa. 'Just keep walking,' he hissed. 'She won't want to make a big thing of it in front of her friends.'

'There's work to be done,' their mother protested, but Sigurd, who blamed his mother for his not being aboard *Reinen*, saw a chance to challenge her now and took Runa's hand in his own. And he did not need to look behind them to know the thunder that was on their mother's face, though no peal rolled after them. It was a pathetic piece of impudence, the kind that would have earned him a backhander from his father had Harald been there, and he felt the shame of it as they climbed the shingle-strewn track up to Aslak and the waiting ponies.

'Thank you,' Runa said, but Sigurd said nothing. He had other things to think about now as he nodded to Aslak and the four of them turned their mounts north to take the coastal track up towards Kopervik and beyond that Avaldsnes. For somewhere in between the two settlements they would look out and see the fleets of King Gorm Shield-Shaker and the rebel Jarl Randver come together in the appointed place. The two fleets would bind themselves together with ropes and grappling hooks, men and shields crammed in the thwarts.

So that the killing could begin.

CHAPTER TWO

BY THE TIME THEY CAME TO THE PLACE THEY WERE SWEAT-SHEENED and the ponies were lathered. The sun had passed overhead and now sat high in the western sky like a golden shield hung below the gabled roof of Valhöll, Óðin's hall of the slain, and Aslak said it was a good day for a fight.

'Not when there are arrows in the sky,' Sigurd replied, grimacing at the thought of a shaft streaking out of the sun's glare to bury itself in a man's eye socket.

'Then a man just keeps his shield up and his head down,' Svein suggested helpfully, at which Runa asked, a wry smile on her lips, if Svein had learnt all this from the many battles he had fought in.

But it was no easy thing to take the edge off Svein's eagerness, especially when he was talking of fighting, and now he turned his smile on all three of them. 'You will know sure enough when I have stood in the skjaldborg, Runa,' he said, dreaming of the shieldwall, 'for the skalds will be singing of it for a year after.' He tugged his fledgling beard. 'And the women will blush redder than these hairs whenever I am near.'

'Talking of skalds, I thought Hagal would be here,' Aslak said. 'It's not like him to miss a fight.'

Svein nodded. 'The gods know he needs some new threads to weave into his tales,' he said.

'Why would he need to see the thing with his own eyes when he can make it all up from the comfort of some wench's lap?' Sigurd put in. Still, Aslak had hit the nail square. It was unlike the skald to miss with his own eyes the makings of a saga tale which he could sell in a hundred mead halls throughout the land.

They had ridden the fifteen or so rôsts as fast as they could and, far from anyone whose land they rode across questioning them, some offered them ale or food and one karl brought out a bucket of water for the horses, because men knew who Sigurd was, especially when Svein reminded them. And they respected Jarl Harald enough to do whatever they could to help his son watch him and King Gorm put Jarl Randver back in his place. Which would be in a haugr, a dark burial mound, covered in earth and worms if he were lucky, but at the bottom of the fjord, draped in cold sea wrack and picked at by crabs if he were not.

'I hope all this lot are here to cheer for Biflindi,' Aslak said, for they four from Skudeneshavn were not the only folk who had come from all over Karmøy to watch the fight.

'They had better be,' Svein rumbled loud enough for a group of five lads near by to hear. 'For anyone cheering that sheep's dropping Jarl Randver will find himself ten feet that way wishing he were a bird,' he said, hurling a pebble over the bluff. 'Or maybe a fish.'

Groups had come north from Kopervik, south from King Gorm's fortress at Avaldsnes and east from Åkra, Ferkingstad and from several other villages, all of them eager to glut their eyes with the spectacle of a ship battle. And what a sight met them now as they gathered at the edge of the pine and birch wood on the bluff overlooking the Karmsund Strait which divided Karmøy from the mainland. Since Sigurd was a boy he had heard men say that the thunder god Thór waded those straits every morning on his way to Yggdrasil, the tree of life.

He will be wading through blood tomorrow morning, Sigurd thought.

Their bows pointing east towards the mainland, *Reinen*, *Sea-Eagle* and *Little-Elk* had their sails up now, their thwarts bristling with warriors and blades as their skippers, helmsmen and the skeleton crews manning the sails sought to bring them into line with King Gorm's seven other dragon-prowed ships. It was slow, laborious work because there was very little wind to speak of and what there was had to be caught on the sails and used wisely and patiently. But this, along with the calm sheltered waters of the strait, made conditions perfect for a ship fight, which was why the two sides had agreed to meet at the place.

'Even a fart's worth of wind can make a ship fight all but impossible,' Harald had told Sigurd once. 'You have as much chance of lashing boats together in a wind or current as you have of getting your wife to sit arse beside arse with a pretty young thrall and be happy about it.'

Yet, Shield-Shaker and Jarl Harald would need more than a still day and a sleeping sea to be sure of a victory here and Sigurd looked for signs amongst the rebel ships that Randver was an unfit overreaching jarl, but found none. The man's ships looked neat and clean and his crews looked able.

'Now I see why Jarl Randver was happy enough to fight in the shadow of Avaldsnes,' Sigurd said, for all men knew that it was those fighting nearer their home that most often had the victory. 'He has a lot of ships for a piss-in-the-wind upstart jarl. Maybe there is more to the man.'

'Aye, he has the ships but does he know how to use them?' Svein asked, though not even he would deny that six ships, four of them easily as big as if not bigger than *Reinen*, was more than anyone expected to see turn out against the king.

'The sheep turd has more money and men than your father,' Aslak said, giving voice to what they were all thinking as he fingered the iron Thór's hammer at his neck. 'Last year's raiding has filled his sea chests with silver and his head with ambition.'

'Still, six ships will not be enough,' Sigurd said, fixing on his sister's eyes because she was beginning to look afraid. 'Shield-Shaker has fought many ship battles. He would not be a king if he had not won most, if not all of them. And my father has sea-luck and the Allfather's own talent for war.'

The others mumbled their agreement at that and the white knot of Runa's hand relaxed a little around the silver pendant of Freyja which Sigurd knew was inside it, hot and clammy against her palm.

Outnumbered as he was, Jarl Randver was expected to lash his ships together side by side to form a great raft and wait to be attacked. Sigurd knew this tactic allowed a greater concentration of fighting power within a small space and enabled men to move from one boat to another as and when the advantage might be gained. And yet Jarl Randver's ships, sails down and oars shipped now, were barely shouting distance from each other and it was Jarl Harald who had drawn his three vessels close, like a man reining in his hounds. It was *his* crews that were busy with hooks and ropes.

'Your father is making a raft then,' Svein said, and from his frown and Aslak's face it was clear they thought this a strange scheme from Harald given how things stood.

'Why is he doing that, Sigurd?' Runa asked, unnerved by her friends' dark expressions.

For a while Sigurd watched his father's ship but eventually he grinned. 'Because he has done all this before and knows the ebb and flow of it,' he said. Only by putting himself in Harald's place had the answer come into Sigurd's mind, bright as a hooked mackerel glittering to the surface. 'With the king's ships holding off over there, *Sea-Eagle* and *Little-Elk* are vulnerable,' he said. 'If they remained separate Randver's ships would isolate them like wolves stalking a small deer, and take them. Lashing them together with *Reinen* gives my father a floating stronghold he can easily defend. He will draw the rebels in like crows on a fleshy bone and then the king will come.' His blood ran hot with the thought of it. 'Together they will smash that arse welt and be ship-rich for the trouble of it.'

Svein and Aslak nodded at this, grinning at their jarl's sea-craft. And yet Sigurd felt an unease gnawing at his guts like a rat on a coiled rope. Because once his father's three craft were lashed together and surrounded, if things went badly it would be no easy thing in the fray to separate them and let them fly.

Still, Shield-Shaker had seven other ships and by rights those ships should beat Randver's six even if Jarl Harald had stayed in his hall that morning. Sigurd clung to this thought, watching the two fleets which had set themselves up like pieces on a tafl board.

'Jarls are good at tafl,' he said under his breath, 'but kings are better.' The day would go well and the rebels would either yield or they would die.

King Gorm's men were cheering now, rousing themselves to the coming butchery, the sound of it drifting up to those gathered on the bluff. Sigurd and the others were right at the edge overlooking the rocky shoreline and the skerries out there in the Karmsund Strait, their arms anchored round birch trees that had themselves made a precarious stand on the sloping edge. Below them within a pebble's throw was a shingle beach upon which a knot of fishermen stood, their faces seaward but doubtless as wide-eyed as everyone else. Sigurd guessed they had been out in the strait when they had noticed two fleets bearing down on them. He imagined the curses that must have flown around those skiffs like shrieking gulls, so that the boats were now hauled up on the stones and the men's fishing was interrupted.

Five of King Gorm's longships, including Shield-Shaker's own ship *Hríð-visundr* – *Storm-Bison* – were strung out in a line now off Jarl Harald's port side, but two other ships were coming round *Reinen*'s stern to protect Harald's steerboard side.

'You were right, Sigurd. Your father means to draw them in and start the fight,' Aslak said, 'and hopefully it will be Jarl Randver himself who will take the bait.' He made hooks of his hands, the fingers clutching each other, to make his point. 'When they are grappled with Gorm's ships and the fighting is thick, those other two coming round will come together like stones and crush the traitor like a louse.'

Sigurd nodded, for Aslak had it right. 'It is a good plan,' he said.

His father would have the honour of being the first to blood the enemy and King Gorm would no doubt reward him for it afterwards. Loyal men earned silver on such days as this.

'Here they come!' one of the other young men on the bluff yelled. Perhaps his own father was aboard one of the king's ships, too. If so his stomach was no doubt twisting over itself now like Sigurd's was.

'It's *Fjord-Wolf*, Jarl Randver's ship!' someone else called. 'I have seen it before. That is the jarl standing there at the stern-post.'

'Aye, where it is safest,' an old man put in, spitting in disgust.

Sigurd did not know if the man standing at the sternpost of the breakaway ship was Randver, but he was dressed in mail and wearing a rich helmet and so it was entirely possible. And if so Sigurd did not blame the jarl for starting the fight at the stern, for all that it was not saga-worthy, because were Randver to die in the first spear and arrow exchange, not much would come of his ambition.

'It does not matter where he is standing,' Svein said, 'for my father can throw a spear twice the length of that ship. Jarl Randver would be better off back at Hinderå hiding under his mead table if he wanted to stay where it is safest!' He grinned. 'Though if the wind was right he would not be safe even there.'

'Which ship is your father on, lad?' the greybeard asked, rheumy eyes all squint and water as he willed them to be young and far-seeing again.

'He's the prow man on *Sea-Eagle*, that longship off *Reinen*'s steerboard,' Svein announced.

'Aah, then he must be a big 'un like you,' the greybeard said. 'I was a prow man once.'

Svein and Aslak shared a look that the old man's old eyes did not miss and he batted the air with a hand as if to say what did young men know anyway? And Sigurd was glad that the greybeard had not asked on which ship Aslak's father was. Olvir Quick-Spear had been killed in the last fight Jarl Harald had been obliged into because of his oath to King Gorm, and no one likes being reminded that their father rots in an earth mound outside the village. Not even if they live again in the next world, drinking and feasting in the Allfather's hall, as Olvir Quick-Spear surely did.

Sigurd's muscles had begun to thrum now, the blood in his veins seeming to bubble, the fame-thirst in his heart demanding to be slaked. The ash shaft of the spear in his right hand whispered to him, pleaded to be taken down into the fray where it could rip and rend and fulfil its purpose. But Sigurd must deny the spear as he himself had been denied, the pain of that still smouldering somewhere in him.

A hand clapped him on the back. 'There they go,' Svein said, as down in the strait the arrows streaked from ship to ship now that Jarl Randver's fleet had come within range of Jarl Harald's. These arrows would cause little harm to either side, though, for men had their shields up and those limewood planks now began to sprout feathered shafts.

Harald's men were still lashing his vessels together as Jarl Randver's ship came within range for the strongest men on either side to hurl their spears, which often had some good effect because a good spear with good muscle behind it could crack a shield and leave a man defenceless, at least until a new one could be taken up.

Randver's other ships were backing oars now, giving their jarl room to manoeuvre, to bring his prow, which bristled with his best warriors, up to *Reinen*'s prow where Slagfid stood with a spear in one hand, his great long-axe in the other and his helmet glinting in the sun. It was no easy thing, not even on a sleeping sea, to get those prows kissing, but Randver's oarsmen knew their work and Sigurd's hand clutched the spear tighter still as the thump of the bows carried up to them on the bluff and a great roar from both crews filled the still day.

Randver's prow man was too eager to make his fame and as he lowered his shield, pulling back his arm to hurl a hand axe, Slagfid cast his spear with the speed and fury of Thór's lightning and it ripped through the prow man's throat in a spray of gore, embedding in the shield of the man behind.

'Slagfid!' Svein roared as those on the bluff cheered and Jarl Harald's men beat their swords, spears and axes against their shields with pride for their champion. The dead man was hauled away and the warrior who took his place was wise to keep his shield high, but Slagfid had killed more men than were on Randver's ship and this would be simply one more. Gripping the huge axe in two hands he reared up like a bear, bringing the axe over his head in a great, death-promising arc, and the blade sliced into the warrior's shield, the lower horn cleaving the shield in two, the upper horn cutting through the man's collar bone and tearing down into his breast and trunk, splitting him like oak.

They cheered again, and then again when Slagfid hooked the next man's shield and leant back, hauling him over the top strake into the sea where he flailed, crushed between the ships' bellies. But Sigurd held his tongue and looked to *Fjord-Wolf*'s stern because he knew what would happen then if Jarl Randver was any type of leader at all. Sure enough the jarl was striding forward now, flanked by retainers with shields raised before him as he sought to let the sight of him raise his men to greater deeds.

The other men at the prows were jabbing with spears and probing with long-axes and some archers were climbing up onto the sheer strakes to loose their arrows from deadly range, but it was Slagfid who was doing the real killing. And yet Randver's other ships were like hounds desperate to get their teeth into the prey and one of them came alongside *Little-Elk*, hauling in their port-side oars quickly before the hulls banged together and Randver's men shot arrows and hurled spears as others threw grappling hooks into *Little-Elk*'s thwarts. These men put the rope around their backs and pulled with all their strength, bringing the ships together in the hope that their weight of numbers would see them clear *Little-Elk*'s decks.

But *Little-Elk*'s crew had other ideas and they presented a wall of shields the length of the karvi, a second row thrusting spears over heads and through the gaps. Asgot the godi was aboard her and he was as good with a spear as he was with the runes. Her skipper, a man named Solveig, was probably as old as the greybeard up there on the bluff but he was a solid fighting man who had earned Harald's trust. The chances were Solveig would need help from *Reinen* at some point, but he would not ask for it before it was absolutely needed and Harald knew it. If Harald could kill Randver before that happened he might win the battle before King Gorm even had to draw his sword.

Back in the pine wood behind them a raven was croaking and Sigurd felt Svein's eyes on him because Svein knew Sigurd attached meaning to such things. But Sigurd kept his eyes riveted on the battle below them and Svein let the thing go before giving it voice. Yet the raven kept up its protest, a gurgling croak rising in pitch that had Sigurd thumbing the runes he had etched into his spear's shaft. Not that the spell, a charm to make the spear fly straight and true, would do much to ward off the ill-omen that Sigurd heard in the bird's call, tangled like a sharp fish hook in a ball of twine. Not unless he could spear the bird itself, which Asgot would tell him was the same thing as spitting in Óðin's one eye.

And yet the gods favoured Harald and King Gorm still, for Slagfid had cracked another skull and the dead were piling up at *Fjord-Wolf*'s prow. Olaf was beside the champion now, thrusting his spear at enemy shields, knocking men back into their companions whilst further back men on both sides yelled encouragement and waited their turn to enter the fray.

On *Reinen*'s port side *Little-Elk* was holding its own, the shield-walls evenly matched, but on the steerboard side the men of *Sea-Eagle* were enduring a steel-storm from the crews of two more of Randver's longships which had rowed into position, one prow on to *Sea-Eagle*, the other coming alongside and grappling the vessels together even as Harald's men took axes to the ropes or tried to fend the ship off with oars.

Wielding his own hafted axe, Svein's father Styrbiorn was a giant at *Sea-Eagle*'s prow, looming there like Thór himself, roaring his challenge at the enemy stuffed in the thwarts of the prow coming at him head on.

Svein reached out again, clamping a great hand on Sigurd's shoulder, and Sigurd winced at the strength in it but he did not pull away as his friend growled encouragement at his father in the strait below.

'Your father is as good as Slagfid,' Sigurd said, which might have been true had Styrbiorn not too often been too drunk to stand so that no one really knew how useful he was in a fight any more. Not that anyone, Slagfid included, would have the balls to tell Styrbiorn that. Since Svein's mother Sibbe had died the only thing that could pull a smile out of Styrbiorn was mead or murder.

He killed the first man cleanly enough, with an overhead swing similar to Slagfid's but using the heel of the axe rather than the blade to crush the helmeted head of the man opposite. Now, though, it seemed he could hear his son cheering him on from the cliff above, or perhaps it was Loki who was whispering in his ear the promise of great saga tales, for Styrbiorn pissed all caution into the wind and clambered up onto the sheer strake, his left arm wrapped round *Sea-Eagle*'s prow beast, his right hand gripping the long-axe low on the shaft. With incredible strength – and no little balance for a drunkard, Sigurd thought – he stepped along the sheer strake and, roaring, scythed the axe round in a great horizontal arc, the blunt side hammering into a man's shield and knocking him and others down in a heap of chaos. Then he brought the axe up and over for another swing, this time deftly spinning the haft in his hand so that the blade flew first, slicing a man's head from his neck and seeing others cower down behind their shields.

Those on the cliff roared their approval, none louder than Svein himself, and those aboard *Sea-Eagle* hammered their shields to let *Reinen*'s crew know that they were not alone in this fight.

'I have never seen such a thing!' the greybeard exclaimed.

Neither had Sigurd ever heard of such. It was the stuff of fireside tales, but so was the next part of it, for all worthwhile tales have their sour parts. Styrbiorn should have climbed down then and got behind a shield for a breath or two and been happy with the fame he had woven for himself. Instead the blood-lust was on him and maybe too much mead was in him for he brought the axe round in another big loop but this time the shaft hit *Sea-Eagle*'s prow beast, snagged on the creature's pointed ear perhaps, and before Styrbiorn could correct the swing a man at the other prow reached out and thrust a spear into his belly.

Styrbiorn doubled over and his comrades managed to pull him back into the thwarts and Svein's hands clawed into his flaming red hair.

'Damned whoresons,' the greybeard muttered, shaking his head, and Sigurd wanted to tell Svein that perhaps it was not a serious wound and he looked at Aslak who shook his head. For there had been enough muscle and fear in that spear thrust to stop a charging boar. That had been clear even from the top of the bluff and from the giant's grunt that had carried across the water even above the battle din. Besides which, Styrbiorn did not wear a brynja because he could not afford to have one made that would fit his massive frame.

Perhaps that was the raven's omen, Sigurd thought, for the bird had stopped its croaking now. Styrbiorn had woven his last piece of fame as he came to the end which the Norns had spun for him. Either way it was a savage blow for *Sea-Eagle* whose men were stunned at losing their prow man so early in the fight. Wielding Styrbiorn's big axe, a fearsome fighter named Erlend muscled up to the prow and looked good for it, cleaving an arm off at the shoulder and doing Styrbiorn proud until an arrow took him in the face and he tipped over the side before the others could grab hold of him.

Randver's men were like hounds with the blood scent in

their noses now and they surged forward and Sigurd knew that trouble was coming because the men of the other enemy ship, lashed to *Sea-Eagle*'s steerboard side, had seen their fellows doing well at the prow and success begets success.

'Jarl Harald must send men to help *Sea-Eagle*,' Aslak said.

Sigurd shook his head. 'Not yet,' he muttered.

'Why not? And why don't the king's ships help?' Runa asked, teeth worrying at her bottom lip, fingers of one hand peeling the white bark from the birch she clung to, and it was a good question, so good that Sigurd did not know the answer. Yet the fear in his sister's eyes compelled him to say something.

'Those two ships are waiting either until all Randver's men are committed to the fight with *Sea-Eagle* or until the first of them spill onto *Sea-Eagle*'s deck, for that will leave the enemy's ship spear-light and Biflindi's men will take it easily.' Runa nodded and Aslak pursed his lips because it was almost a good answer. But Sigurd knew it was an answer as thin as mist and would dissipate at any moment when one of them asked why King Gorm's five other ships further off had not fully engaged with Randver's remaining two. Those held their formations in the strait off the port side of *Little-Elk* and Harald's raft of boats, raining arrows on each other but holding their distance. Sigurd could think of no reason why Biflindi's five had not overrun those two ships by now, or why he had not sent one of his dragons to savage the longship alongside *Little-Elk*.

Harald sent a knot of men over to *Little-Elk* perhaps at Solveig's request, perhaps not. Then the jarl gestured at a man beside him who Sigurd knew to be Yngvar because of his black-painted shield and Yngvar went over to *Reinen*'s side, took up his horn and blew a long note north up the strait towards Avaldsnes.

'The king must come now,' Svein said, those jaw-tight words his first since seeing his father fall.

Sigurd nodded, though in his mind he still heard the rising croak of the raven in the pine wood, the sound like a mockery of the horn which Yngvar was blowing repeatedly.

And King Gorm did not come.

'Look!' one of the youths from Kopervik exclaimed, pointing down to the two longships Shield-Shaker had sent round Jarl Harald's stern to protect *Sea-Eagle*'s steerboard side.

'Not before time,' the greybeard said, turning his sunken eyes on Sigurd. 'He's left your father in the fire too long already.'

'Ha! I'll wager you wouldn't say that to King Gorm's face, old man,' another youth said.

'And why not, youngen?' the old man asked. 'As you can see I'd be long dead before Shield-Shaker got around to sending someone to kill me.'

This might have got a few laughs had things been going better down in the strait. A warrior named Haki had stepped into Slagfid's place at the prow now to give Harald's champion a chance to catch his breath, for axe work will have muscles screaming and a man puffing like nothing else. But though Haki, Olaf, Thorvard and the others were holding Randver's crew at bay, the rebel jarl's other crews were pressing their advantage. In making his floating bulwark Harald had drawn the enemy in so that now four of Randver's six ships were committed. All King Gorm had to do was either deal with Randver's remaining two or at least keep them out of it while he took Randver's ship at the stern, cleared its deck and thus put an end to it.

The two allied ships had rowed round *Reinen*'s stern, but instead of coming alongside those two dragons that were attacking *Sea-Eagle* they manoeuvred up to that ship, whose crew were yelling at King Gorm's men to get into the fight.

'Óðin's bollocks,' Svein said, as the first arrows streaked from Shield-Shaker's ships into *Reinen* and *Sea-Eagle*'s thwarts.

'Treachery!' the greybeard yelled. 'You can never trust a king.' He looked over at Sigurd but Sigurd could not take his eyes from the scene below. 'Your father is a dead man now, youngen. Best get back to your kin quick as you can.'

'It's not over yet, you old goat,' Aslak said. 'Not while Slagfid still fights.'

Sigurd spat a curse and hoped the Allfather heard it, for such treachery was lower than a worm's belly and Óðin should not

see it played out. And yet Óðin loved chaos. Had Asgot not told
Sigurd that a thousand times? *Little-Elk* was on its own now
and holding its own too, and that was largely down to being
so much smaller than the ship lashed against it, for its warriors
were concentrated over a smaller area which enabled them to
present a shieldwall three men deep. But exposed out there on
the steerboard side of Jarl Harald's raft *Sea-Eagle* was doomed
and everyone knew it. For the most important thing now was to
preserve Jarl Harald, which meant his best warriors must stay
with him aboard *Reinen* lest they be overrun by Jarl Randver's
hearthmen from *Fjord-Wolf*.

Sea-Eagle's skipper Gudrod was at the centre of the shieldwall
bristling his longship's side, jabbing a spear at those who sought
to climb aboard his ship. But men were falling in that rampart
now and the gaps could not be plugged. Sigurd and his friends
were watching men they had known all their lives die, hacked
and stabbed, falling into the thwarts, and Sigurd growled at
Runa to look no more but she refused.

Then Gudrod went down from a spear thrust and one of
Randver's brave warriors saw his chance. His shield before him,
he threw himself over the top strakes into *Sea-Eagle*, forcing
the breach, and though he undoubtedly died a heartbeat later
those behind plunged after him. Once a shieldwall is broken
like that it nearly always spells disaster, so Sigurd had been told
by Olaf who, in the maw of it at his prow, must have known
what was happening aboard *Reinen*'s sister ship, though he
could do nothing about it. Thorvard was still in the thick of it
too, fighting like a champion, but now Harald came to the prow
himself bringing Sigmund and Sorli, so that Sigurd felt pride
bloom in his chest at the sight of his brothers wading into the
steel-storm, refusing to accept that they were beaten.

Seeing his jarl striding into the carnage, Slagfid stormed
back to his place at the prow and, leaving his axe with Haki,
worked with an enormous boar spear, thrusting and cutting,
his skill matched only by his strength. When Randver's men
saw Harald's champion back amidst the blood-fray they raised

their shields and pulled heads back into shoulders and a youth near Sigurd exclaimed that Jarl Randver looked like a berserker as he frothed and fumed at his warriors to show more steel and less limewood.

'We can still win this,' Aslak said. 'If the king sides with Harald and brings his ships across.'

'Fool, boy! The king wants the fishes feasting on Jarl Harald tonight!' the greybeard said, pointing at the king's two ships that were raining their arrow storm on Harald's floating fort. 'They've carved that ambition clear as runes on a standing stone.'

'Those ships have sided with Randver, that is plain, old man,' Sigurd said, 'but that is not to say that Biflindi himself is with the rancid pig's bladder. The king fights on. See.'

'You call that fighting, lad?' the greybeard said. 'Pah! My wife puts more into it when she scolds me for being drunk or looking too long at some pretty young thing.'

Sigurd felt the grimace on his face but did not bite back, because he knew the old goat saw the truth of it even with those withered eyes. The arrow fight going on between those seven ships was perhaps more dangerous than a hailstorm but not by much. It was a show, like a leashed dog growling at another passing by.

'See how far they've drifted,' Aslak observed and Sigurd nodded.

'There's more current in that sea than you would know to look at it,' he said, for Harald's raft of ships and Randver's lashed to it, having sat in the middle of the strait when the battle started, had now been brought much nearer the shore. 'They will have to cut themselves free soon. All of them,' Sigurd said, 'or risk being smashed on the rocks.'

'Then Father can escape?' Runa suggested, 'if they cut the ropes?' There was a spear-blade's glint of hope in her blue eyes.

'Aye, that'll be the only thing that saves your men now, girl,' the greybeard said, 'but old Njörd has already forsaken them, I am sure of it. He gives thin hope but not the wind or waves that Jarl Harald needs.'

'Any more talk from you, old man, and we will see how your warped bones fare against the rocks,' Sigurd growled. Aslak flapped his arms at the old man who must have seen enough steel in Sigurd's eyes to believe it was no empty threat for he shuddered, hitched lips back from rotting teeth and held his tongue.

'Bollocks,' Svein said as a cheer went up from Randver's men, for the shieldwall on *Sea-Eagle* had suddenly shattered like a clay pot dropped on a rock and the rebel jarl's warriors were winning, clearing the deck and washing it in the blood of Harald's hirðmen. Some of those fought on, trying to link up with their sword-brothers in twos and threes, but more of the enemy were spilling into the thwarts and it was clear that *Sea-Eagle* was lost. Men were hacked apart and speared in the back as they tried to scramble over the sheer strake onto *Reinen*, whose men thrust spears or hefted shields to try to protect those seeking refuge.

Over on the port side *Little-Elk* was a scene of butchery too. The enemy had somehow come aboard at the stern and, with her shieldwall thinned to face this new threat, gaps were not being filled and Randver's weight of numbers was telling. The scales had tipped and there was no bringing it back now.

Sigurd tasted bile in his mouth, could feel it rising from his stomach and burning as it came. The men from Skudeneshavn were being slaughtered and he could do nothing.

'Get back to your people, boy,' the greybeard said, risking Sigurd's wrath. 'You need to tell them what is coming. Give them a chance to scarper. For you can mark my words this foul thing won't end here.'

Sigurd thrust his spear down amongst the birch roots and strode towards the old man whose eyes bulged like boiled eggs. 'I told you to hold your tongue,' he growled, grabbing fistfuls of the man's tunic and hauling him through the long grass to the edge of the bluff so that they could both see the white water churning against the rocks below.

Then Sigurd saw the fishermen and their boat up on the shingle.

'I meant no harm!' the old man whined.

'Sigurd! Let him go!' Runa screamed. And the others watched, wide-eyed but closed-mouthed but for Svein who had seen his father killed already and so had no care for an old prattler who should have kept his lips together.

Still gripping the man, Sigurd had already forgotten him. In the strait the battle raged, the ring of steel on steel, the thump of blades against shields, the shrieks of the wounded and the roars of warriors, but in his mind Sigurd heard the rising croak of the raven that had watched from the pine wood.

He threw the old man to the ground. 'What is the quickest way down from here?' he asked him.

'There's a path beyond that rock,' the old man said, pointing a trembling hand. 'Leads right down to the water's edge.'

Sigurd nodded and turned to Svein and Aslak. 'Are you coming?' he asked. They looked at each other and nodded, and before the old man had even climbed back to his feet the three of them were tearing across the bluff, then scrambling down the worn narrow track towards the sea.

When they reached the shore the four fishermen turned and stood, two of them pulling knives from their belts, their nerves honed to an edge by what they had seen in the strait.

'Give me your boat,' Sigurd said, striding up to them, Svein at his right shoulder, Aslak at his left.

One of the men laughed though there was no mirth in it.

'Fuck off, boy,' another growled, waving his knife through the air.

Sigurd spun the spear in his hands and thrust, striking the man square on his forehead with the butt end and dropping him. The other three stepped backwards leaving their senseless companion lying on the wet shingle.

'That's Jarl Harald's son,' a man said and brows arched above round eyes.

'Take it,' a leathery-skinned fisherman said, nodding towards their small boat.

Sigurd nodded and turned his back on them, going over to the boat from which seagulls took off screeching, their feast of fish guts disturbed. They pulled it down into the still water of the sheltered cove and when the boat was in two feet of sea they climbed in, Aslak giving it a shove for good measure before he sprang aboard.

'I'll do it,' Svein said, placing himself in the middle, taking up both oars and setting them in their locks, his back to the open fjord. Sigurd looked up at the bluff and saw Runa, her hair bright as gold in the afternoon sun, and he waved at her but she kept both fists and the silver Freyja pendant against her breast. Then Sigurd turned and knelt at the bow, watching the battle rage beyond the skerry-guarded cove as Svein hauled back on the oars, his great strength pulling the boat away from the shore.

'What are you scheming, Sigurd?' Aslak asked as Svein's long strokes took them past the rocks out into the strait. 'We cannot do much with one spear.'

'Just be ready,' Sigurd said, standing up on the step, using his spear to balance as the battle din grew louder. Somewhere amongst the chaos a man screamed. Yngvar was still blowing his horn now and then, when he wasn't fighting for his life. Sigurd heard splashes as warriors fell into the sea, their ringed brynjas taking them down to the sea bed before they realized they were dead. *Sea-Eagle* was lost, its thwarts full of Jarl Randver's men, some of whom Sigurd could see stooped, stripping Harald's dead perhaps whilst others joined those who were now clearing *Reinen*'s deck. But even standing, Sigurd struggled to see over the ships' sides and it was only when he caught sight of his father's helmet, its panels of polished silver plate glinting in the sun, that he knew *Reinen* was lost too. For Harald had been driven back to the raised platform at *Reinen*'s stern and now stood a little forward of the tiller, his sons Sorli and Sigmund beside him, shields raised. Slagfid was there too, the champion's shoulders sagging with exhaustion now, though his shield was high and his great, worm-looped blade yet promised death to all who faced him.

'Faster, Svein,' Sigurd growled and Svein obeyed, shoulder

muscles billowing with each stroke, the veins in his neck corded like walrus-skin ropes as he took them ever closer to *Reinen*'s stern, making sure to keep a good distance from the two ships attacking her and also from *Sea-Eagle*, which now thronged with Jarl Randver's warriors.

Then Sigurd saw a small shieldwall stepping backwards along the port side and caught sight of Olaf barking commands at this last knot of Harald's household warriors. Thorvard was amongst them too, blood-spattered and grimacing as he defended their meagre shield rampart against the weight of the attack bearing down on them.

'*Little-Elk* has broken off!' Aslak called, which was something at least, and Sigurd saw the frenzied panic in that ship, heard the clump of oars as men took them up from the deck and pushed the staves out through the ports and began to row her away from the slaughter whilst Randver's men showered her with arrows. Sigurd could almost hear Asgot spitting curses and invoking the gods to come down from Valhöll and piss on the worm Jarl Randver.

Yngvar lay dead over *Reinen*'s sheer strake, still clutching the horn as though even now they hoped King Gorm would come to fight at their shoulder, but there was no sign of Biflindi and it was too late now anyway.

'Father! Sorli!' Sigurd called but the battle din was so loud that they could not hear him, or if they could they were too embroiled in the fray to take notice. With *Little-Elk* pulling away from the slaughter and *Sea-Eagle* already taken, Jarl Randver was able to set all of his warriors against those few of Jarl Harald's hearthmen still holding their ground at *Reinen*'s stern. More hooks thunked against ships' ribs and thwarts, more ropes were passed to Randver's men already brimming Harald's deck so that this floating platform now belonged to the rebel . . . but for some two spear-lengths of oak deck upon which the great warrior in the glittering, raven-beaked helmet held dominion with his best warriors and those of his own blood. Sigmund, who was a great fighter, ran two steps and jumped, thrusting his sword down behind an enemy's shield and into his neck, then he slammed his shield into the dying man's own and leapt back into his own shieldwall, a wolf's grin on his face. Sigurd's chest filled with pride at his brother's skill and daring even as he knew all hope was lost.

Now another horn blew, this one Jarl Randver's, and Sigurd saw that the rebel meant to offer terms to his defeated enemy. But Harald roared that Randver was a rancid goat's turd and the treacherous cunny snot of a slobbering whore and his men thumped their swords and spears against their shields to echo the insult and acclaim their defiance.

For a moment Randver's men seemed unsure what their jarl wanted of them but Harald made their minds up for them by taking a spear from Sorli and hurling it with such strength that it pierced a warrior's shield and pinned his arm to his chest, raising a cheer from those aboard *Reinen* who knew they would soon sit with their ancestors in Óðin's hall and drink to this moment.

The rebels' shieldwall stretched right across *Reinen*'s deck and must have been five men deep, a tide of steel and flesh that would drive Sigurd's father and his brave men into the sea or see them butchered in a sea of their own blood on the oak boards. Both sides roared as the skjaldborgs struck and the sword song played for the amusement of the Æsir. But Jarl Harald's men were pushed back foot by foot until they were level with the tiller and crammed beneath the great sternpost where the resin-sheened sheer strakes were carved with runes and gripping beasts.

Slagfid beat a man's shield down and Thorvard plunged his sword into the man's face, the blade erupting from the skull in a gleam of bone shards and blood. The man fell and Sorli burst forward into the gap, hacking his hand axe into a warrior's face and cleaving off his jaw before jumping back into his own shieldwall as quick as a lightning strike. But now some of Randver's men aboard the ship lashed to *Reinen*'s port side were loosing arrows and these shafts streaked into Harald's men who could not have their shields in two places at once, though three or four turned and tried to raise a rampart against this new threat. *Reinen*'s helmsman Thorald took an arrow in his neck and clutching at the thing dropped over the side and vanished. Then Harald staggered forward and Sigurd saw a feathered shaft jutting from his shoulder, though the rings of his brynja had taken the force and he made a show of standing tall again and rolling his shoulders.

'What do we do?' Aslak called, his face ashen, wide eyes appalled by what they were witnessing. 'They'll come for us soon enough.'

Sigurd did not answer. He stood swaying with the fishing boat, watching his father's and his brothers' last moments, and he could not tear his eyes away. A spear blade plunged into Aud's eye and he screamed, his shield arm falling so that the same spear struck again, opening his great belly, and Sigurd saw the glistening rope of his guts spring loose to thump on the deck. Olaf was barking commands, encouraging men to keep their shields overlapping and their heads down. Slagfid was growling at the enemy to come and die on his sword and Sigurd's brothers were shoulder to shoulder now, defiance coming off them like the stink of blood. But they were trapped and had barely the room to use their swords and it seemed that they would be tipped into the sea like discarded fish guts and would all get drowning deaths, which was something a man feared more than almost anything.

Perhaps that thought was too sour for Sorli, who surged forward, slamming his shield into the enemy rampart and throwing up his arm, reversing the blade to hack into the back of a man who was too tightly pressed to do anything about it. And with this the rest of Harald's men came spitting fury and contempt, throwing themselves at the enemy with their last strength. They were cut down, savaged by sword, spear and axe, and Sigurd yelled at Svein to row them even closer to *Reinen*'s stern. Svein said nothing but the oars plunged and the boat moved and Aslak sat in the stern keeping his protests behind a barricade of gritted teeth.

'The jarl! Protect the jarl!' someone yelled and Sigurd knew his father had been cut down though he had not seen the act.

'Vigdis!' Sigurd called, recognizing the warrior for the bear skin he wore, and Vigdis turned to look over the side, the eyes beneath his helmet's rim bulging when they saw Sigurd and his friends.

'Fuck off, boy!' Vigdis shouted. 'Get back to the village!' Vigdis, who had told Sigurd there was no honour in how he had beaten Olaf the night before, possessed enough honour now to hurl himself at the enemy lest they notice Sigurd, and Sigurd cursed as the man disappeared from sight.

Then Sigurd saw Alfdis where Vigdis had been and he called to him and Alfdis was similarly shocked to see him but Sigurd gave the man no time to speak.

'The jarl!' Sigurd yelled, pointing back into the fishing boat, and Alfdis understood without a moment's hesitation and nodded. Sigurd's heart hammered against his chest and he feared he was too late but then Alfdis and a man named Jorund came to the side and slung in between them was the jarl, wounded but alive. But then Alfdis was cut down and a big man raised his axe to finish the jarl, when Olaf appeared, thrusting his sword into the man's armpit to cleave his heart. He hauled the sword free in a gout of bright blood and turned his own gore-stained face to Sigurd, teeth white against the mess.

'No!' Harald yelled, his wits returning as Olaf took a hold of his other arm and pushed him to the side. Even wounded, his own blood slathered across his brynja, the jarl was strong enough to fight Olaf and Jorund while the rest of his men hacked and slashed and were being slaughtered behind him. Then Sigurd heard a splash and looked over to see Sorli in the water, flailing in his mail, and up on *Reinen* Thorvard looking down long enough to see that Sigurd had sight of their brother whom he had knocked into the water. Then Thorvard turned and stormed into the blood-fray and Sigurd saw a spear take him in the side as another man hacked into his neck with a hand axe. Two arrows took Jorund, one in the neck, the other in his thigh, and he fell over the side to sink in the dark sea. Aslak took a rope from the bilge and cast one end out to Sorli who grabbed it and pulled himself towards the boat.

'Olaf!' Sigurd yelled, but Olaf was doing what he could and somehow he managed to muscle his jarl to the side and with a great effort lifted him over, the jarl fighting in vain, and now with Svein's help Sigurd reached up and took hold of his father and the three of them fell back into the thwarts in a tangle of limbs. Olaf turned back to the fight, snatching up his sword, resolved to die with the others, when a spear struck his shoulder and he staggered backwards, his legs hitting *Reinen*'s side so that he toppled over the sheer strake and hit with a great splash.

Sigurd scrambled back to the bow and held out his spear and Olaf had enough sense left in him to take hold of it so that Sigurd could pull him in.

'Row!' Sigurd screamed and Svein was up and had the oars in the water, his broad shoulders and thickly muscled arms pulling the boat away from the slaughter even as Olaf clung on to the side and Sigurd clung on to Olaf and Aslak did what he could to keep Harald down lest the jarl try to jump back aboard *Reinen* to be cut down with his hearthmen.

'Hold on, Olaf,' Sigurd said, as he saw Slagfid still hewing men down and two or three other men fighting to the last.

One of whom was Sigmund his brother.

CHAPTER THREE

SVEIN ROWED, THE OARS ALL BUT SNAPPING WITH THE FORCE OF IT AS their blades pulled against the sea. Sigurd and Aslak managed to pull Olaf into the boat and he lay half drowned in the bilge, beard and brynja glistening with brine, his chest puffing like bellows. Similarly waterlogged but standing up in the boat, Sorli was spitting fury, his beard flecked with curses hurled back at Thorvard whose last act had been to throw his brother overboard. His eyes full of tears or salt water, Sorli railed at his brother for denying him his place in that last stand. He kicked the boat's strakes and yanked his blond braids and screamed at Thorvard who was past hearing now, and Sigurd did not try to calm him for Sorli was lost to the here and now and the best thing was to leave him alone.

Jarl Harald looked like a man dragged from his burial mound with the smell of Sæhrímnir the best of meats in his nose and the voices of his ancestors in his ears. His eyes were rivets fixed on the murder which was now two good spear-throws off their stern. His hands gripped the side of the boat like white claws. He had not laid eyes on Sigurd yet and Sigurd was glad for it, though he knew the moment must come.

A cheer went up from Jarl Randver's men, which could only mean that the last of Harald's warriors was dead, cut down on his lord's ship, his blood running across the oak planks with that of his sword-brothers, and Sigurd felt as though he was at sea in a storm, his head spinning and his thoughts in the whirl-pool of it.

'My sons,' Harald muttered, the words barely strong enough to ruffle his blood-specked golden beard. 'My sons.'

'The king betrayed us,' Olaf growled. There was blood in his hair and in the rings of his brynja but he paid it no heed. 'That putrid swine's bladder left us to be mauled.'

Sigurd realized he was still clutching the spear, knuckles white against the rune-carved ash. His guts felt as heavy as a quern stone and yet his heart was thumping like the hare that has seen the hawk. His brothers Sigmund and Thorvard were dead. Slagfid who was unbeatable, a warrior who had put fear in his enemy's bellies and whose boasts had seeped into Eik-hjálmr's beams like hearth smoke, was slaughtered. Svein's father Styrbiorn was gone, and Haki and Gudrod and so many more. Harald's finest warriors and retainers were corpses now, their weapons and warrior rings, their brynjur and helmets being pulled from their ripped bodies, while the ragged survivors drifted off like feathers from a fox-killed bird.

'Little-Elk!' Aslak called and Sigurd followed the line of his outstretched arm and saw the karvi off their bow. She was being rowed southwards, Solveig her helmsman and skipper wisely hugging the coast where Jarl Randver's ships might not dare to follow for fear of their plunder-heavy hulls striking the rocks now that the tide was slackening.

Olaf bellowed over to the karvi and Solveig had his oarsmen hold water until Svein could row them up to the ship and the men could climb aboard. Sigurd saw the relief in the men of Little-Elk's faces when they saw their jarl alive, and Asgot the godi, his beard braids sticky with blood, gnarred his thanks to the Allfather for giving them this one floating timber in the wreck of that day.

They left the fishing boat to drift where it would and the survivors, some twenty-nine men all told, rowed or watched the ships out in the Karmsund Strait or kept a lookout for rocks and skerries just below the surface as old Solveig carried his beaten jarl south, bound for Skudeneshavn. Sigurd remembered Runa but when he looked up he saw no sign of her amongst the few folk still gathered on the bluff and Aslak suggested that she was already riding home to bring news of the events to the village.

'We should not have left her,' Sigurd said.

'What choice did we have?' Aslak said, which was true enough. Still, Sigurd hoped that Runa knew that their father and Sorli were alive and that at least some of Skudeneshavn's menfolk had survived Jarl Randver and King Gorm's treachery and were even now coming home.

'They are not interested in us,' Olaf announced when he was certain that their enemies were not coming after them. He was looking back out into the strait the way a man looks at his family on the rocks when he is going off raiding, as though he wanted to go back as much as go on.

'Why would they be?' Jarl Harald said. 'They have my ships. They have killed my sons and my champion.' There was an arrow wound in his shoulder but he seemed unaware of it. 'They have broken me,' he murmured.

'Biflindi will pay in blood for this,' Sorli said, pushing his tunic sleeve up to examine the vicious-looking purple stain spreading on his left forearm. 'We will flay the skin from his back and cut off his balls.'

'And how will we do that, boy?' Harald asked, the words seeping from the twist of his lips. 'My sword-brothers are corpses. I am left with dregs, old men and boys.' Sigurd felt the sting of this, knew the barb of it bit into the pride of those at the oars now who kept their eyes down rather than meet their jarl's and see the anguish there. Harald stood on the steerboard side looking out at the ships he no longer owned. Farther off, King Gorm's longships were heading north again back to his base at Avaldsnes, his part in the thing over, the king content it seemed to let Randver keep the spoils. 'Óðin has washed his hands of me,' Harald said. He looked at Asgot who was on his knees scattering runes across the deck. 'You told me not to fight today. I should have listened.'

Asgot studied the stones before him and pursed his lips, then looked up at his jarl, his eyes as sharp and black as flint. 'One-Eye's hand is still in this, Harald. You would not be standing here otherwise. This blood is as the first drop in a pail before a storm. Óðin has set up the pieces on the tafl board and now rubs his hands at the thought of the game.'

'If old One-Eye wanted me to play this game he should have left me with more men,' Harald snarled and Asgot raised an eyebrow at that as he gathered up the rune stones to cast them again.

The sun was in the west and cloud-sheathed by the time they had rowed the protected waters east of Karmøy south and round the peninsula back to Skudeneshavn's safe harbour. The quayside bustled with folk come to see if their men were living or lost and Sigurd called to a friend of his mother to ask if Runa had beaten *Little-Elk* home. She had, at which news he sighed with relief and muttered thanks to the goddess Freyja.

As they moored up, Sigurd saw relief flood his mother's eyes when she caught sight of Harald, though she tempered that joy in respect for those women who could not see their husbands and lovers in *Little-Elk*'s thwarts. Neither did the jarl seem in the least happy to be alive. He was a brooding, sour presence amongst his milling people and they kept out of his way. But what Sigurd saw on his father, heavier than his fine brynja and his blood-slick helmet, was shame. It clung to the jarl, rounding his square shoulders and hooding eyes that would not fix on Grimhild's. Then she hammered her fists into his mail-clad chest, tears springing from her eyes now, and Sigurd knew his father must have whispered to her of their loss, given hard words to what her eyes had already told her. Harald stood there like a rock as Grimhild beat his chest and tore her nails on the bloodied rings of his brynja and moaned with such sorrow that others looked away. Then Harald pulled her against him, so that her iron-muffled cries were all but lost amongst the dark tide of woe rolling across the folk of Skudeneshavn.

Sigurd took Runa in his own arms and Sorli was left like a standing stone looking out to sea and a thousand gulls could not have made such a pity of shrieking as that which filled the still dusk as *Little-Elk* rocked gently against the jetty.

Sigurd felt Runa's body trembling in his arms, thrumming like a ship's rigging in strong wind, and he did not have the words to soothe her but then Olaf came up to them and laid a firm hand on Sigurd's shoulder.

'We must prepare, Sigurd. Get eyes on the strait. Bury our silver.' His eyes were rivet-sharp and his lip was hitched back from his teeth. 'There is every chance Jarl Randver will come here to finish the job. That is what I would do.'

Sigurd nodded, keen to do anything that would take him away from that place.

'Maybe the king will come himself,' Svein suggested, blinking at the water in his eyes, the big jaw bones beneath his beard clenching like a hand in the cold.

Olaf shook his head. 'Whatever Biflindi's part in this ill thing he will not want to be seen attacking his own oath-sworn men. Not unless he wants every jarl with spears and ships to doubt his word from now till Ragnarök.' He spat into the tufted grass. 'But that shit Randver will come and kill us with a smile on his face so we need to be ready.'

'I'll set watches,' Sigurd said. 'If Jarl Randver comes we'll gut him in front of his men.'

Olaf nodded but it lacked conviction. 'Make sure there's dry wood in the beacon and take the loudest horns you can find. If Randver comes I want you to wake the gods, lad.' He grimaced. 'With all this wailing a hundred men could land in the bay and we wouldn't hear them.'

Sigurd turned but Olaf gripped his arm to stop him. 'Give them spears. Even the youngens. If the whoreson comes he'll come to end it. There'll be no mercy. No terms.'

Sigurd glanced at his mother still wrapped in Jarl Harald's

arms, and at the other wet knots of wailing women. Let Randver come, he thought, gathering that possibility around himself like a cloak. He has killed Sigmund and Thorvard, so let him come and we will soak this night with blood.

Then he turned his back on them all and went to tell the young men of Skudeneshavn that only blood, not tears, would avenge their fathers. And Svein and Aslak went with him.

He set them in twos and threes on the high ground overlooking the strait and the Skudeneshavn fjord, then he, Svein and Aslak spent the night on a ridge looking north across the pastures of Hillesland whose blanket of buttercups glowed brightly in twilight. Full dark would not come again for two months, which meant that if a war band came it would not come unseen. But Jarl Randver and his men did not come that night and in the morning Sigurd returned to his father's hall and Olaf sent other men to the lookout posts.

'I should have come with you. Anything would have been better than spending the night here,' Sorli murmured into his mead horn, staring into the glowing embers of the hearthfire. Sigurd glanced around the hall at the women wreathed in smoke and misery and those of Harald's men who had survived but had lost friends and oarmates and pride.

Sigurd blinked the sting out of tired eyes, glad to have spent the night out on the hill rather than in that dark, bitter place. 'Where is Father?'

Sorli's gaze did not leave the last flame-licked sticks that resembled serpents now, their scaled hides pulsing with heat, grey to red to grey. 'With Asgot somewhere. And the gods,' he said. 'Trying to unpick the knot of this bad thing.' Sorli was still in his gore-spattered brynja, their enemies' blood clotted black in the rings, the spear shaft behind him stained with it.

Sigurd's own spear lay amongst the rushes beside him, its blade clean, the rune-etched shaft mocking him for he had not stood beside his brothers nor laid a single man low with it.

'Fucking Thorvard.' The words escaped Sorli's mouth like a dog's growl, the handsomeness of his face ruined by it.

'Do not speak ill of your brother, boy,' Olaf said, chewing a hunk of bread and looking into the same dying fire whose flames whispered a different saga to every eye.

'Do not tell me what to do, Uncle,' Sorli said, glaring at Olaf. 'He pushed me over the side. He took my honour from me and now here I sit with boys and old men and those who fled the fight.'

There were some murmurs and growls from the men of *Little-Elk* at that, though none was prepared to make any more out of it.

Olaf cocked an eyebrow, a deep hum stirring in his throat. 'You're a fool, Sorli,' he said, gesturing to a thrall to fill his cup. 'You think Thorvard was trying to shame you?'

Sorli was working a thumb into the palm of his right hand to loosen tendons that were tight from gripping his sword. 'No. He was trying to save me but it was not his right. It was not for him to deny me my place in that fight. I was shoulder to shoulder with him and Sigmund. I was killing men beside Slagfid and would have shared his saga.'

Sigurd looked round at the bench to the left of Harald's seat, beneath the yellowing bear's skull nailed to the wall which had been Slagfid's place but never would be again. Slagfid's father had killed that bear with nothing but an eating knife, men said, though there were one or two greybeards who chuckled when they heard the boys telling this tale.

'Any of Randver's men who saw me in the water being pulled into Sigurd's boat like a fucking fish will think that I jumped. Even now they are probably calling me a coward.'

'Ha!' Olaf exclaimed. 'You are arrogant enough to believe they discuss you at all! Or that they know your name? They will be far too busy counting Slagfid's arm rings and each of the swines claiming to be the one who gave him his death wound. As for men thinking you are a fish, you are the first one I have seen that breathes so well out of the water. You should be thanking your little brother for hooking you,' he said, nodding towards Sigurd. 'Between Sigurd and Thorvard they have given you something you could never buy.'

Sorli was drunk and tired and he dragged a hand across his mouth leaving a snarl of teeth in its wake. 'What are you talking about? Do not give me riddles, Uncle.'

'Thór's bollocks, boy, you got two portions of prettiness but they left plenty of room in your skull.' Sorli batted the insult away and mumbled some curse into his golden beard but Olaf waded on. 'You would have died in that red slaughter, as would I and Jarl Harald. We would have been hacked to bloody pieces and that maggot Randver would have pissed on our corpses and had his godi work some foul spells to keep us from ever seeing the Allfather's hall. At best you would have been given half a line in Slagfid's saga tale. Maybe a whole line in your father's if the skald was thirsty and your kin was within earshot.' Sorli did not like this but neither did he deny it, instead turning his gaze back to the dying fire and the secrets within it. 'This golden thing your brothers gave you is revenge, Sorli. Or the chance at it.' Olaf said this loud enough for other ears in the hall to hear and Sigurd sensed folk look up, never so wrecked by grief that they could not see the warming flicker of vengeance somewhere up ahead. Svein sat a little way off smouldering like a pyre. Beside him was one of his father's old shields, Styrbiorn's first helmet and a long-axe and no one thought it strange to see the young giant with his father's war gear.

'Who would get the blood price from Randver for all our dead brothers if not us? Even Harald knows this is the clot of honey in the sour drink of this thing, though he's still too pride-stung to admit it and give Sigurd here the arm ring he deserves.'

'Thorvard and Sigmund would want us to spill Randver's guts, brother,' Sigurd said. 'King Gorm's too for his treachery.'

Sorli looked up, his blue eyes boring into Sigurd's. 'Then there will be no more watching from the shore for you, brother. You will stand in the wall of shields and together we will feed the ravens.'

Sigurd nodded, feeling the weight of eyes on him and not just eyes but expectations too, for he had seen two of his brothers killed the day before and they demanded retribution.

'Good,' Olaf said, chewing his bread and nodding to himself. 'The fucking mist clears.'

But before any of them could say more a figure appeared at the hall's threshold, the light behind him painting his features black though Sigurd knew it was Solveig by his bronze cloak brooch, the ends of the broken ring representing a ship's prow and stern.

'Olaf! You in here, Olaf?' There was an edge to *Little-Elk's* skipper's voice that had Sigurd's hand on his spear.

'I'm here, man. What is it?' Olaf growled, then put the mug to his mouth and emptied it.

'You had better come and see for yourself,' Solveig replied and with that turned and disappeared back the way he had come.

Sigurd and the others followed Olaf out into the day and stood blinking in the golden morning light that flooded across the hill and the dwellings around it and made a glittering hoard of the sea to the south and east.

'Biflindi's men,' Svein spat and Sigurd felt his own hackles rise with the thought of violence.

'Come to calm the waters, I'd wager,' Olaf said as they walked towards the strangers who were already in conversation with Jarl Harald and Asgot. It was telling that Harald had not invited the men into his hall and this would have been taken as an insult to King Gorm. Though they were past such insults now.

'These men come with word from Avaldsnes, Olaf,' Jarl Harald said without turning to those approaching. 'They say our king is appalled by all that befell us in the strait yesterday.'

Olaf muttered something and one of Gorm's men turned and nodded respectfully to Olaf, for all men knew him. 'The king's heart is broken for the loss of his people in Skudeneshavn and for the deaths of Jarl Harald's sons Thorvard and Sigmund, though he was consoled to hear that their brother Sorli was able to save himself by jumping overboard.'

'Frigg's arse!' Sorli exclaimed, glancing at Olaf, but Harald cut off any further opinion with a raised hand. The jarl showed no signs of the wounds he had taken and neither would he reveal any weakness in front of Biflindi's men.

King Gorm's man might have come with words but he was dressed for battle in brynja and helmet, for all that the face beneath his fair beard was flushing red as the men and women and even the children of Skudeneshavn gathered around him and his uneasy-looking companion.

'The king was as surprised by events as you were, Jarl Harald,' the messenger reassured the jarl, turning from him to Olaf and back to Harald. 'Two of his captains had been bought by the rebel Randver and we did not know that they were attacking your ships until it was too late.'

'Too late?' Olaf blurted. 'We fought the dogs until our blades dulled and still the king did not send help!'

'We were trading arrows with Jarl Randver's other ships,' the man said, ignoring the insults that the spectators were flinging his way now like pebbles into the mire. Clearly his companion had no words to deliver, served no purpose other than to soak up some of the ill-will aimed their way lest the messenger swallow his own tongue through fear.

'The king thought it wise to deal with the threat to himself first for he would be no use to you if he were sprouting arrows,' this man managed. 'Indeed we were surprised when we saw you had been overrun. We thought you would hold them off longer. To give us a chance to send ships across.' The man was on thin ice now and must have known it, which meant he had a backbone beneath that mail and it likely saved his life.

'Bollocks,' Olaf said.

'My warriors sit in Óðin's hall while traitors live and breathe,' Harald said and Biflindi's man did not know whether the jarl was talking about the king or Jarl Randver, or the two captains who Biflindi claimed had sold their loyalty to Randver, and that was just as Harald intended. 'You say the king has not pissed on our oath of allegiance. And yet somehow that oath has lost me many men and two ships.'

Despite no doubt wondering if he would walk out of

Skudeneshavn alive, Biflindi's man was sharp enough to pierce the skin of that for he nodded sombrely. 'The king would pay you for your loyalty . . . your steadfastness out there,' he said, nodding towards the sea. 'You will receive a horn's worth of silver for each man lost and your ships will be replaced with two of the king's own.'

Harald pulled his beard between finger and thumb and eyed the man like a hawk appraising a mouse.

'Furthermore,' the man went on, 'he has sent silver to the traitor Jarl Randver to buy back the bodies of your men. The king invites you to Avaldsnes to receive your weregeld, to hear the pledge that you shall have the ships and to collect your dead so that you might bring them back to their kinfolk and pay them the respect they deserve.'

This was balm to many of the widows gathered, so that their tongues ceased their lashing and the messenger forged on. 'You will also renew your oaths each to the other so that the waters may be clear between you again,' he said. 'When this is done you will lay plans for Jarl Randver's defeat. The traitor must be killed before he can build on his success.'

'This has a stink to it,' a man named Asbjorn said. Asbjorn had not been in the fight the day before because he had some disease that had turned his right hand into a claw, and though he could fight well enough using his left he could not grip a shield, which made him no good for the shieldwall. 'I say we slit their throats and throw them into the sea.'

King Gorm's two men glanced at each other, their hands falling to their sword hilts, for though they were armed there were still men enough in Skudeneshavn to see the thing done without any trouble at all. And yet gone were the best men, those who had earned their jarl's silver with their death-work. Men such as Slagfid and Styrbiorn, Thorald and Haki were corpses now and the weight of this hung round Harald's neck like a quern stone.

'Kill them, Harald,' Asbjorn said.

'Hold your tongue, Asbjorn,' Jarl Harald barked, also shooting

Sorli a look that warned him to behave himself. For what choice did the jarl have but to accept the king's summons, for that was what it truly was.

'We will come for our dead,' Harald said. 'Tomorrow so that we might get them in the ground or the flame before they begin to stink. As for the horn used to measure each man's weregeld, I will bring my own drinking horn so your king had better have enough silver.' The man did not mention the *your king* in that and was wise not to. Instead he paid his respects again, turned and walked off, his silent companion wafting alongside like a bad smell.

When the men had mounted their ponies and were making their way through the gates in the low palisade Olaf looked at Harald and the jarl raised one brow.

'So we're going to walk up into Avaldsnes and jump into whatever pot of piss Randver has bubbling over his hearth?' Olaf said.

'What choice do we have?' Harald asked him. 'Come, Uncle, I am all ears if you can see another way out of this.'

Beneath the bush of his beard Olaf's face had the look of a skipper who sees grey rocks, a slack tide and a green crew. 'The dog's bollock was happy to watch us slaughtered while he sat on his arse out of harm's way. Likely as not he sent those two ships to help finish us off. And now we're to pull down our breeks and bend over for him?'

'Better to go there armed and half expecting a fight than to sleep with one eye open for the next five years half expecting to be burnt alive with Eik-hjálmr's beams crushing our wives and daughters. King Gorm or Randver, or both together, could bring their ships and enough spears to make short work of it even if we knew they were coming.' This got some *ayes*, for no man wants a bad death, the one that sneaks up from behind.

'I'll not get my throat cut in my own bed,' Asbjorn said.

'And no man is going to murder my wife and children and swive my bed slaves while I draw breath,' a man named Frothi said, his hand going to the Thór's hammer at his neck.

'Let us walk up to the king and look in his eyes, our backs straight and our sword arms ready,' Jarl Harald said. 'And we'll soon enough know where the thread of this thing ends.'

'In a pool of blood is where it ends, lord,' Asgot sneered from where he sat atop a nearby mound pawing through the innards of a cat. He was completely naked, his knotty body a mass of scars and strange shapes that were stained into his skin, and his hands were bright with the creature's blood.

Harald turned and looked up at the man, shielding his eyes against the sun's glare. 'Is this pool of blood in Avaldsnes?' he asked. Sigurd knew his father did not always like what his godi had to say but he always listened. Everyone else listened too, faces turned up to the small hill, the women's swollen, anguished eyes slitted now against a dawn that saw them widows.

Asgot held something purple and glistening between finger and thumb and put it to his lips then glared down at his jarl.

'No, lord. I see fire at Avaldsnes but no blood.'

'Funeral pyres for the dead perhaps,' Sorli suggested. 'We killed many of Jarl Randver's men but some of the king's too.'

Harald scratched his bearded chin, his brow furrowed like Skudeneshavn's bay with the first northerly beginning to blow across it. 'So you think we should go and hear what Biflindi has to say? Listen to him try to wriggle out of the carcass of this thing?'

'It is wiser to stand up to a bear than to turn your back on it,' Asgot said and even Olaf seemed to agree with this for he gave a curt nod.

'Then we need to prepare,' Olaf said. 'Who stays, who goes. The last thing we want is to come back and find the thralls gone and our silver with them.'

'Or Randver knocking on the gate,' Frothi said.

Olaf looked to his jarl but Harald was looking out across the harbour, his thoughts spear-flung somewhere far off. Perhaps he was hoping to see *Reinen* and *Sea-Eagle* coming in, oars beating like wings, Slagfid, Thorvard and Sigmund at *Reinen*'s prow, shouting the tale of their miraculous victory across the water to those on the shore. Sigurd had never seen his father look like that before and he did not like it.

'Come to the hall tonight,' Olaf announced. 'Jarl Harald will choose his war band.'

'What shall we do now?' Aud's widow Geirhild asked, grim-faced, all her crying done beneath her own roof.

'Fetch stones,' Harald said, still looking across the bay. 'And wood. My men will be buried in a stone ship. Together as they fell, so that they might enter the Allfather's hall as one fellow-ship.'

'And the wood?' Asbjorn asked, pulling a louse from his beard and crushing it between finger and thumbnail.

There was a silence as all looked to their jarl whose face had all the expression of a granite cliff.

'I will burn my sons,' he said, looking for ships that were never coming.

There was no singing in Eik-hjálmr, no fighting or boasting or fumbling in dark corners. There was drinking though. The mead flowed and horns and cups ran over but there was no joy and Sigurd was reminded of Hrothgar's hall Heorot burdened by grief from the havoc the monster Grendel had wrought.

But for those few men and boys at the beacon on the hill to the east and those at other lookout posts, it seemed that everyone in Skudeneshavn had crammed into Jarl Harald's hall. There was barely a nostril of clean air to be had and the benches along the walls creaked under the strain of so many folk standing on them to get a better view. Sigurd had managed to shoulder his way through the throng until he was standing before his father and Olaf, both of them standing on their benches adorned with warrior rings and wearing their finest tunics, cloaks and brooches. Harald even wore his jarl torc round his neck, the twisted rope of silver the final part of the display meant to put confidence in his people's bellies and remind them that they still had a great warrior watching over them.

And yet it was not lost on anyone that there were so many

faces missing from Eik-hjálmr, so many great warriors whose bluster would never again carry up to the smoke-blackened beams. In one day Skudeneshavn had been stripped of fifty-two of its men and now their womenfolk and sons filled their places in Harald's hall, looking to their jarl to salvage something from the wreck of it, to convince them that they would be kept safe.

And yet no matter how great a warrior Jarl Harald was he was now a wolf without a pack. He still had spears to call on, and good men too, but without his champion and his two eldest sons, his best warriors and his ships, his power was broken in Haugaland. No amount of silver lustre in that dark hall could paint its shine on that.

'How many is that?' Svein asked, all bristles and mead breath in Sigurd's ear.

'Fifteen,' Sigurd said, having gathered up every name that his father had so far announced and stored them in his mind like hacksilver in a chest. He could have repeated the muster perfectly, though it was as yet imperfect for the lack of his own name in it.

'Frothi. Agnar.' Harald went on above the hum of voices. Each man chosen raised his hand in the air so that his jarl could look him in the eye, and this was enough to let each know what was expected of him and also what an honour it was to be chosen, for all that Sorli had muttered that owning a spear and shield was enough to see you picked.

'Asbjorn. Where are you?' Harald nodded when he caught sight of the man in the thick of the gathering. 'You will also come.'

Sigurd saw the grin spread in Asbjorn's beard as the man ruffled his boy's hair. Saw the pride in the boy's eyes, too, and the fear in the boy's mother's.

'You would take a man with one good hand rather than me?' Sigurd said, hearing his own voice cut through the place like a keel through the dark water.

There was an intake of breath and some rumbles at this, for no one had yet interrupted the jarl. Besides which it was no small insult to Asbjorn. Harald's face, already dark as the mixing of two sea currents, now threatened a squall.

'Asbjorn stood in the shieldwall with me when you were nothing but an itch in my crotch, boy,' Harald said. Some chuckled at this but not many.

'And yet it was I who saved your life in the fight with Jarl Randver,' Sigurd announced. 'All of your other men were too busy being killed.'

'Hold your tongue, Sigurd,' Svein beside him growled as Eik-hjálmr thrummed with the ill-breeze of that shameful strike.

Harald's eyes were arrow points and Olaf beside him was shaking his head but Sigurd held his father's stare and braced himself.

'Leave, Sigurd, before you say something that cannot be un-said,' Olaf rumbled, nodding towards Eik-hjálmr's door. 'This is not the time.'

Then Sorli turned to his father and Olaf. 'If now is not the time then tell me when is?' he said, and Harald's eyes bulged with the audacity of this two-pronged attack in his own hall in front of his own people. 'Look around you, Father. What do you see? I see sheep waiting for the wolf. I see old men and boys where Sword-Norse stood but two days ago. The steel-storm thinned us and we would have joined our brothers in death if not for Sigurd.' He could not help but acknowledge Olaf with a nod then. 'Sigurd has given us the chance to see blood given for blood. But first we must show the king that we still have teeth. Let him see that you still have two strong sons at your back. We will walk into Avaldsnes like war gods and Biflindi will have no choice but to pay the weregeld he owes us or else face a hard fight of it.'

'Sigurd is only just a man,' Harald said.

'True. But he is a warrior,' Sorli said, holding Sigurd's eye then. 'It is all over him like a burnished brynja. If ever there was a man whose wyrd would make the gods sit up and take notice it is my brother. Even the birds speak to him.'

Sigurd glanced at Runa then and knew she had told Sorli about the raven whose warning Sigurd had heard as they watched the ship battle from the shore. Runa flushed and looked back to their father.

'He did put me on my arse,' Olaf admitted, a brow hitched and the twitch of a smile appearing in the bush of his beard. 'And only a man favoured by the gods would manage that.'

Harald glanced over at Grimhild and Sigurd saw his mother give an almost imperceptible shake of her head, then Harald turned to his godi who had up until now held his tongue. 'What do you say, Asgot?'

'Sorli is not famous for his wisdom but he has it right where Sigurd is concerned.' Asgot had some new bones tied in his hair, from the cat he had been up to the wrists in that morning perhaps. 'The lad is Óðin-favoured. It was the Allfather who sent that raven to warn Sigurd that you were doomed out there in the strait. And Sigurd has enough of the Æsir in him to have untangled the bird's voice and got sense out of it. I am not jarl and it is not my decision, but I would take him to Avaldsnes.'

The jarl grimaced but nodded and there was a murmur in Eik-hjálmr like that of the sea as folk discussed the rights and wrongs of it.

Eventually after much beard-scratching and lip-chewing Jarl Harald raised a hand to hush the gathering. 'Sigurd will go,' he said. 'And so will Finn Yngvarsson and Orn Beak-Nose.'

Svein slapped Sigurd's shoulder and Sigurd nodded to Sorli who shrugged as if to say it had only been sense that he'd been talking, for all that Sorli rarely talked sense.

Harald raised a hand to silence the hall again. 'Olaf will not come for he will go to the outlying farms to muster spears and spread word amongst the bóndi and lendermen of what has happened. He will see how things lie with Jarl Leiknir at Tysvær and Jarl Arnstein Twigbelly at Bokn. He has already chosen the men for that trip and they will know who they are soon enough.' Svein would be amongst those men though he did not know it yet.

'Those who stay here will have no lesser task,' Olaf said, 'for

while these men are off puffing up their feathers for King Gorm
you will keep your spears pointed east in case Jarl Randver
should grow the balls to attack us here. Keep your eyes peeled
and the timbers damp,' he added, slapping one of the thick oak
posts which supported the hall's roof. 'And you youngens put
the work in with spear and shield for we're raising a new war
band and there will be a place for any man who can prove he's
more useful in the shieldwall than he is in the pig pen.'

There was a buzz at this as young men, even those recently
made fatherless, saw greased and golden their chance to grow to
manhood and become one of Jarl Harald's húskarlar, his household warriors. Sigurd's own life blood was pulsing in his veins at
how things had turned out, though he tasted the sour in it, for
his own elevation all but stood on his brothers' burial mound,
not that they had one.

Even so, he would prove worthy of it. He would stand with
Sorli and their father and show King Gorm that the men of
Skudeneshavn were not beaten yet. They would avenge their
dead and skalds such as Hagal Crow-Song would weave their
tale for the ears of those yet in their cribs.

'If the lad's going with you he ought to look the part, Harald,'
Olaf said, scratching his cheek, lips pursed.

Harald almost smiled then. 'The boy *did* put you on your arse,
Uncle,' he said, thick fingers prising open the silver ring on his
arm which he had offered as a prize the night before the ship
battle. 'If you kick King Gorm in the bollocks too you can have
another one,' he said, pulling the ring off and flinging it at his
youngest son. Sigurd caught it, appraising its weight in his hand
for a moment before putting it on his own left arm.

And he was going to Avaldsnes.

CHAPTER FOUR

THE DAY BEGAN CLOUDY AND AS GREY AS THE SLEEPING SEA AROUND Karmøy. A thin rain that could barely be felt against the skin had nevertheless soaked cloaks and breeks and greased spear shafts by the time they had walked the seven rôsts to Snørteland. Another four rôsts would take them to the village of Kopervik and from there it was just five rôsts to King Gorm's stronghold at Avaldsnes, from whose vantage point on the hill kings had always sought to control trade and ships going north up the Karmsund Strait.

Sigurd was aware of a gentle trembling in his blood, like water passing the overlapping strakes on a ship's hull when the sail is up and the wind is good, yet the trembling was not from fear. It was because despite King Gorm's insistence that he was a loyal king and his promise to Jarl Harald of silver to pay for each of the jarl's warriors killed, the twenty men from Skudeneshavn had come dressed for war. Each had spear and shield and whatever head protection he could find, be it a leather skull cap or, in the case of a few, a steel helmet. Each wore his thickest woollen coat, normally only worn in winter, so that they were rain-soaked outside and sweat-soaked inside, but content that these would provide some protection against the blade's bite.

Some carried bows and quivers of wicked-bladed arrows.

Some had hand axes tucked in their belts, these weapons as useful for cleaving logs or breaking down a man's door as they were in the tight press of the shieldwall where they were often more effective than swords. A few carried the long-hafted, two-handed battle axes that could split shield, helm, limb or torso. It was with such axes that Harald's champion Slagfid and Svein's father Styrbiorn had woven their fame, killing men outright with a single blow and giving other men to foul themselves through fear. But there was no Slagfid or Styrbiorn amongst them today. Sigurd wished Svein was there too, but his friend had gone with Olaf and three others, taken the boat across to Tysvær.

Only two men had brynjur, their countless woven iron rings glistening with rain which was as much their enemy as the arrow, for the first would rot it and the second could pierce it. And yet to own a brynja was every warrior's ambition for it meant you were rich and powerful or that you had killed a rich and powerful man and taken his mail. It also meant you were a hard man to kill, for a good brynja will turn aside a sword or a hand axe, and Jarl Harald and Sorli looked like gods of war now with their iron coats and their polished helmets, the gold and silver metalwork on their sword pommels, belt buckles and brooches, and their arm rings of twisted silver.

They walked in single file so that to the Æsir in Asgard they must have looked like a vicious little serpent slithering north across Karmøy, Jarl Harald, Sorli and Sigurd at the head.

Sigurd felt like Týr, Lord of Battle, which was fitting, he thought, because Týr had placed his right hand in the jaws of the wolf Fenrir, just as they would now put themselves between the teeth of a king they no longer trusted. Týr had been tricked and earned himself a wolf-joint for his bravery, for ever after one-handed yet still associated with victory. What would they earn from King Gorm, Sigurd wondered.

Over his woollen tunic he had a leather coat which had belonged to Sigmund, his brother having worn it before earning his own brynja, and on his shins were his own greaves, the iron strips polished to a lustre against the dark leather onto which they were fixed. Like most of them he bore a scramasax, the single-edged knife that was so useful for finishing a felled opponent, but unlike most of them he wore a sword at his left hip. It was not an ornate weapon. It had no silver wire wound round the grip, no decoration in the pommel or cross guard, but it was straight, double-edged and had taken a moon's cycle to make. And though it was not a thing to turn heads it was certainly capable of taking them. The smith who had forged it had incised the name Troll-Tickler in runes on the blade where it met the guard, and Sigurd thought that such a name was worth more than gilt and silver wire.

The scabbard was a good wooden one covered with leather and with the mouth and tip protected by iron, and the inside was lined with sheep's wool whose lay was upwards to enable an easy draw. The grease in the wool prevented the blade from rusting and the curl in it held the sword firm in the scabbard, and the weight of it all at Sigurd's hip made him feel a foot taller.

'You are my second son now and must appear like a warrior who has done his share of killing for me,' his father had said that morning when he had given Sigurd the sword from his own great chest of war gear. 'But do not forget that you will be amongst better men today. Men who have stood their ground in the skjaldborg and traded blow for blow with our enemies. Many of them do not own such a sword even as this one and may begrudge you having something you have not earned.'

'Let anyone who does say it to my face,' Sigurd had replied, expecting his father's wrath at that. But Harald had half smiled and Sigurd had seen his eldest brother Thorvard in that smile.

'Let us show Biflindi that we still have teeth,' the jarl said, gripping Sigurd's shoulder as Sigurd drew the blade to fill his eyes with the strange pattern that swirled up its length like dragon's breath, markings as unique to that blade as Sigurd's dreams were to him.

'If the king betrays you, Father, I will kill him,' Sigurd said, thrusting the sword back into its scabbard.

Now it was a wolf's grin that broke the jarl's golden beard. 'If he betrays me he will already be dead,' Harald said.

'Ah, so there is a sun up there,' Orn Beak-Nose said now, looking up at the pale yolk of light that was trying to spill through the grey.

'It is warm enough already,' Frothi said, puffing out his cheeks and perhaps wishing he had brought only a spear instead of his long-axe with its huge crescent-shaped smiting blade and steel edge.

'At the least we are owed mead and women,' Finn Yngvarsson said, limping from an old wound. They were tramping up Sålefjell, the highest point on the island of Karmøy, which no one enjoyed doing in full war gear. But Harald would not risk the easier option of hugging the coast in *Little-Elk* and letting the wind do the work, for if Jarl Randver's ships caught them out in the strait they would be dead men in the time it takes to curse the Norns and the bad wyrd they had woven.

'After how he served us in the fight I would be afraid that any woman the king gave us was really a troll in disguise, her eating knife aimed at our bollocks,' Asbjorn said, which got some chuckles.

'I should think you'd be happy with a troll, Asbjorn, compared with what waits for you back home,' Orn Beak-Nose dared, which had the men laughing as Asbjorn thumped the butt of his spear against the shield slung on Orn's back.

'Mead will do for me,' Agnar said, getting some *ayes* all round, 'and the silver he owes us for our sword-brothers,' he added, which silenced them then as each man's mind filled with memories of friends they would never see alive again, like brackish water flooding a bilge.

Gulls shrieked overhead and the sun threatened to break through the cloud and Sigurd's hand kept falling to the hilt at his hip because after the years of training with the tools of death he was now one of a band of Sword-Norse. He had at last been given the chance to prove himself, to show his father and brother that he was worthy of the blood in his veins.

And then, as they entered the pine wood spilling from Sålefjell's heights like a dark green cloak off a giant's shoulder, a peal of thunder rumbled across the sky and with it came a seething, wind-making rain.

'Piss!' Frothi growled, he and the others holding their shields above their heads as the rain turned to hailstones that bounced off the limewood and the steel bosses.

'Just in time,' a thick-necked man called Ulfar said as they moved into the pines whose thick upper branches protected them from the deluge. Normally they would have taken the coastal path all the way to Avaldsnes, but no one questioned their jarl's decision to take this part of the journey through the trees. There was not a man there who wanted to see the Karmsund Strait at that point, to let their minds fashion again the image of their terrible defeat or let their ears hear again the shrieks of their butchered friends. The wound of that was still too raw and the sea there yet mixed with their brothers' blood.

Now Sigurd's mind wandered to his childhood and some ten summers ago when his father had brought him into these woods to hunt for elk at King Gorm's invitation. The two men, as close as sword-brothers in those days, had laughed and exchanged silver rings and fine blades. They had talked of building ships and of raiding to the north and west and Sigurd had all but burst with pride to see the esteem in which his father was held by the king. They had killed no elk that day but it had not mattered and at the end of it they had feasted in Biflindi's hall and Sigurd had watched his father swear an oath declaring before all that his sword belonged to the king. The jarl and his men would fight for Avaldsnes whenever King Gorm needed them. In return the king would safeguard Harald's lands and allow the jarl to keep any plunder he took from his own raids on their common enemies. He would also give Jarl Harald a ship and that ship was *Reinen*. The oath was sealed by a great silver torc which Shield-Shaker placed around Harald's neck though Harald rarely wore it these days.

'Ha, it is not the weight of the silver that your father has trouble with but the weight of its meaning,' Olaf had slurred in Sigurd's ear one night in Eik-hjálmr when the mead had greased his tongue. 'No man likes being under the foot of another, even if that other is a king.'

'Then why doesn't my father become a king?' Sigurd had said with a boy's unfogged view of the world.

Olaf had chuckled at that. 'Perhaps he will,' he said. 'And then he'll have some jarl wriggling under his foot, eh?'

And now they were heading to Avaldsnes to learn what had become of that oath sworn ten years ago and whether the king's hand was open in friendship or clenched round a sword's hilt.

The floor of the wood was covered in needles and dry underfoot and the pungent resinous smell of the trees filled Sigurd's nose just as the sudden silence of the place filled his ears. Most of the lower branches were stunted and bare, brown and brittle enough to snap if caught by a shield rim or spear shaft. But from those branches higher up green and silver lichens hung in the shapes of antlers and bones, sea wrack and old rags, and Sigurd felt the old magic of the place raise the hairs on his arms.

They followed an ancient path through the trees and soon the canopy above them defied the grey day utterly so that it was darker than the midsummer nights out amongst the pastures. The only sounds were of their own passing, feet stirring the forest litter and the occasional drip from rain that had seeped through the thick needled branches above.

'It is strange that there are no birds to be seen,' Sigurd said to his brother and this caused Sorli to frown as he glanced around to confirm Sigurd's observation.

'So, little brother, you see omens in the birds and now you see omens in the birds you do not see?' He smiled then. 'You are as bad as Asgot.'

'Still, there are no birds,' Sigurd said.

Sorli turned his head up to the heavy branches and after a few paces he lifted his spear and pointed its blade off into the distance. 'I see one,' he said. 'What is that, brother, if it is not a bird?'

Sigurd caught sight of a hooded crow up in the boughs, its breast the colour of cold hearth ash against the darker green of the pines.

Sigurd nodded, a weight suddenly lifting off his chest, though he could not resist telling his brother that perhaps only one bird was even worse than none at all. And the words were still in the air, like ripples from a stone dropped into water, when the first arrow whipped through the trees.

It *tonked* off Finn Yngvarsson's helmet and he yelped with the shock of it, no doubt blushing afterwards.

'Shields!' Jarl Harald roared and the column shuddered as each man unslung his shield and planted himself left foot forward, hefting his spear up by his right ear ready for the cast. Two more arrows streaked from the shadows, one of them thunking into a man's shield. 'Close up!' Harald yelled and the column drew in like a knotted rope until they made a square with five men in each of its walls, shields overlapping.

'Show yourself!' Jarl Harald demanded as men muttered behind their shields of treachery and what a piece of shit this king had turned out to be. 'I am Jarl Harald of Skudeneshavn and am bound for Avaldsnes at the king's invitation.'

There was a silence, then the cracking of twigs.

'I know who you are, Jarl Harald!' a voice boomed up ahead.

'Swiving goat's prick,' Sorli growled, for it had been a king's voice, one bloated with the arrogance of power.

'Show yourself, oath-breaker!' Jarl Harald shouted, lowering his shield and planting the butt of his spear on the ground. It was a defiant act and worthy of a jarl, though Sigurd and the rest kept their shields up and their spears ready. 'I would see with my own eyes the man who betrays me.'

Another arrow streaked from the trees and clunked off a shield boss.

'There he is!' Agnar called.

'I see him,' Asbjorn growled.

King Gorm did not answer and the forest was still, but for the heavy breathing of Harald's men and a few mumbled words to

Óðin or Thór. Sigurd felt a stream of sweat trickle between his shoulder blades, the thump of his heart against the shield of his breastbone. He thought of his dead brothers Thorvard and Sigmund and he willed King Gorm's men to come for them so that he might kill them.

Someone let out a great fart to split the silence and this got some chuckles.

'What are they waiting for?' Orn Beak-Nose said. 'The sooner they come the sooner we can kill them and get home. I am as thirsty as Styrbiorn used to get after a roll in the straw with that little dark-haired beauty he picked up in Førdesfjorden.'

'They are waiting for the men they had watching the coast road,' Jarl Harald said, and Sigurd realized the truth of that. King Gorm had split his force because he had not known which route Harald would take.

'Then we should run at them now,' Beak-Nose said, spitting into the forest litter.

'After you then, Orn,' Harald said, but Orn stayed as still as a rock.

'Fucking idiot,' someone growled at Orn who muttered a curse back in their direction.

Even if Shield-Shaker was waiting for the rest of his men he would still have more than enough to deal with the twenty Skudeneshavn men and all of them knew it. Nevertheless, Harald was reluctant to break up the defence of shields they had created, particularly as they could not yet see the men who had come to kill them.

'You have been raiding people who I am sworn to protect, Jarl Harald,' King Gorm accused, the words weaving through the forest, somehow filling it.

It was not true, or if it was then those people had made an alliance with the king which Gorm had failed to mention to Harald. But it did not matter. Biflindi needed the pretence, was simply looking to justify the breaking of their mutual oath.

'You lie!' Jarl Harald called, still tall, shoulders square as *Reinen*'s red sail, his chest inviting the arrow from any with the courage to loose it. 'You and Jarl Randver are snakes in the same nest. I am wondering, do you use him as a woman or does he use you?'

There was no sharper insult a man could hurl than this and it brought a silence down over everything as men waited to see what came next.

'I have come to an understanding with Randver,' the king said eventually. 'He has grown powerful. He has given me enough reason to weave an alliance with him.'

'You mean he has given you silver,' Harald said. 'And in return you mean to give him my land. My silver.'

There was the clatter of armed men to their right and voices calling to each other up ahead.

'Now we see the whoresons well enough,' Sorli growled, pointing his spear at a line of warriors coming through the trees towards them. They were coming in loose order, perhaps thirty warriors stalking through the trees like wolves.

'And there,' Sigurd said, pointing his own spear to their front left where another body of men and shields was appearing.

'Thór's bristling bollocks, this will be a hard fight,' Frothi said, scratching his nose with the rough inside of his shield.

'Well it's not my wyrd to die here,' a bull of a man named Orlyg muttered. 'I'll die at sea in a ship fight or not at all.'

'That old priest who came to Skudeneshavn last winter told him that,' Finn remarked, 'and you are a fool if you believe him, Orlyg, for he also said that I would be rich by the time the red hordes turned up, yet I have seen more curlew, sandpipers and red knots than any summer I can remember and I am still silver-light.'

'That old piss stain told me my toothache would be gone by the time he reached Kopervik and the folk there were pouring him his first ale,' Orn said. 'I have heard better foretelling in a dog's fart.'

'Well why do you think he wanders from village to village and is not kept by a jarl or a king? You fools,' Sorli said.

'Still, I won't die here. You can be sure of that,' Orlyg said.

'Here they come!' Sorli cried.

'Gorm!' Harald yelled as the king's men came on through the trees, no more than a spear-throw away now. 'You can hear me, oath-breaker! Let us settle this the old way. My champion against yours!'

There was a shout and the shieldwall coming from the front left halted, its men planting their spear butts on the ground. Then it parted and a huge warrior rode through the breach on a pony, his mail and helmet, belts and scabbard glinting with gold fittings. Sigurd could not help but be impressed by the king who had come to kill them.

'Your champion was Slagfid and he is lying on a bench in my hall so that my people can see him, though you would not recognize him now,' King Gorm said. 'My godi wanted to take his eyes so that he would never see the hall of the slain but I did not let him. He was a great warrior.' The king leant over and spat onto the forest floor. 'I afforded your sons no such respect.'

'You prickless nithing!' Sorli yelled, the fury coming off him like smoke from a pyre. Sigurd's belly soured at the thought of some godi prising out Thorvard's and Sigmund's eyes and the sudden craving to kill King Gorm engulfed him like a wave so that he could barely breathe.

But Jarl Harald was as a rock, unmoved and unwilling to give his enemy the satisfaction.

'My champion against yours, oath-breaker,' he said again.

King Gorm patted his pony's neck with ringed fingers as he considered this and Sigurd realized that he had some gold rings sewn amongst the grey ones of his brynja.

'Why not!' the king announced. 'My father always said it was a bad thing to rush a good feast. Send forward your champion and I will send mine.'

'Father,' Sorli said. 'I claim the right as your eldest son.'

Jarl Harald turned to Sorli and the smile in his beard reminded Sigurd of past times. 'No, my son. You are a great fighter but you can still learn a few things from your father, hey.' And with that Harald drew the pin from the great silver brooch at his right shoulder and took off his blue cloak, letting it fall to the ground. He gave the heavy brooch to Sigurd, winked at him then turned, hefting his spear and shield. He strode forward. 'Who am I to kill then?' he roared, and his men cheered their jarl and hurled curses at those facing them.

This was a good insult from Harald for every man in Skudeneshavn knew who King Gorm's champion was but the jarl had in those six words pissed on the man's reputation.

King Gorm's thegns began to thump their spears, swords and axes against their shields and chant 'Moldof! Moldof!' as their champion left the line and walked towards Jarl Harald, bending his neck from side to side to loosen it as he came.

'Frigg's tits, I wouldn't ask that ugly fuck to my house to share my night-meal,' Asbjorn said, and men muttered in agreement with that for the man was huge, as big as Svein's father Styrbiorn had been. It was one thing to know the man's reputation as a killer, even to have the memories of him smiting their common enemies. It was another thing to see him in the flesh now, knowing he was against you.

'Ah, he's only a head taller than Harald,' someone said. And only a touch broader, Sigurd thought.

'But he's much uglier,' Orn Beak-Nose said, which was something coming from him.

Harald pointed his great spear at Moldof. 'This ox of yours will low loud enough to wake our grandfathers when I gut him,' he said. 'And yet he is much smaller than I remember him. Have you not been feeding him, Gorm?'

Moldof grinned and it was a gruesome sight. No doubt in his time the man had heard every insult a man could come up with. That he was still alive to enjoy them meant that for plenty of men their insults had been their last words in this life.

'I pissed on your sons' corpses,' Moldof said to Harald, his face as straight as its ugliness would allow, and this statement was worse than any insult a tongue could weave.

'When Moldof has killed you, Jarl Harald,' King Gorm said, spitting the word *jarl*, 'my men will slaughter yours. And your sons.' He looked at Sigurd now and Sigurd felt as if his eyes were burning at the sight of the king, as if they had venom in them. 'You have grown, boy,' Gorm said. 'But I see you are not as pretty as your brother there.'

'I will kill you, worm,' Sigurd said.

King Gorm smiled at that. 'I always liked you, boy.' Then he turned his stare back to Harald. 'Your bloodline ends today, Harald.'

Sigurd did not need to see his father's face to know the wolf grin that parted his beard then. 'Perhaps,' he said. 'And we will wait for you in the Allfather's hall, oath-breaker.' Oath-breaker, a good play on the king's byname Shield-Shaker that, and it was not lost on any man there regardless of which side they were on. Such names stick to a man like shit to sheep, Sigurd thought.

'Do not disappoint me, Moldof,' the king said through a wall of teeth.

Moldof thrust his spear stave against the back of his shield and his sword-brothers roared encouragement and he came forward rolling his huge shoulders, the rings of his enormous brynja shifting like the grey sea.

'Open him up, Father!' Sorli was straining like a wolf on a rope but knew he had no choice but to stand his ground and watch. 'That ox will tire quickly,' Sorli told Sigurd, 'and he will not have the wits to match Father. Men as big as that don't hone their wits because they don't normally need them.'

'It's the same with pretty men,' Asbjorn put in, grinning at Sorli who called him a crab-clawed son of a mare.

'Gut him!' Frothi yelled.

'Go for his damned shins,' Orn Beak-Nose growled. 'I'd wager he can't bend down that far to do anything about it.'

'Aye, piss on his roots while he's not looking,' Finn said, for the king's champion stood there like an oak and despite the advice Jarl Harald's men gave him, it must have been hard for anyone to see how best to tackle the man.

Keeping his shield up Harald thrust his spear in an attack that would disembowel most men, but Moldof got his shield in the way and jabbed his own spear high and Harald dipped his head so that the blade went wide. Then the two warriors circled each other, eyes searching for weaknesses, muscle and sinew taut as a hauled halyard, both men set to strike.

Harald lifted his shield and thrust low but Moldof deflected with his own spear and then the two men's strength and skill bloomed for all to see as they used their heavy spears almost like swords, slashing and cutting, parrying and twirling them to hammer their opponent with the butt ends. Sigurd imagined the fire in their arms and shoulders from using the spears single-handed, yet neither man showed any sign of it.

Then Harald anticipated a thrust and brought his shield across and it struck Moldof's spear's shaft, knocking it aside, as Harald barrelled forward slamming his shield's rim into Moldof's face. The giant staggered backwards, spitting teeth and blood, and the men around Sigurd howled in pleasure as Moldof hawked and spat a gobbet of blood at Harald. The jarl strode forward then thrust for Moldof's face but as King Gorm's man got his shield up Harald dropped like a rock and thrust up from the crouch, his spear blade ripping into the rings of Moldof's brynja at his left hip and scattering them onto the forest floor. Moldof roared and Harald swung the spear in a throat-ripping arc but the giant got his shield up in time and Harald's swing had so much muscle behind it that the marrow in his arm bone must have trembled with the impact. Moldof brought his own spear round and it clunked against Harald's shaft which he forced down until the blade hit the ground. Then the bigger man brought his knee up and stamped down, snapping Harald's spear, but the jarl swung what was left in his hand, catching Moldof in the temple with a blow that would have dropped a bull.

Then Harald stepped back, hurling the broken stave which clattered off Moldof's shield, and the two men caught their breath and Sigurd hoped that Óðin Allfather was watching this fight.

'This is your champion, oath-breaker?' Harald called to King Gorm. Two or three of the king's men bellowed at their champion to have done with the thing and take the jarl's head from his neck, but most were silent, perhaps not used to seeing Moldof take so long to kill an opponent. The king himself had a face like a bucket full of thunder.

'I am insulted,' Harald said, drawing his great sword whose blade shone with its dragon breath pattern in the forest's strange half light like a mackerel's back ten feet down. 'Any one of my sons could beat this lump of cow shit.' The jarl was straight-faced but he must have been hoping his words would sting Moldof into foolishness, that in his rage the giant would present him with a killing opportunity. But Moldof was not so stupid as he looked and now he rolled those huge shoulders again and grinned, for he was the one with the spear whilst the jarl only had his sword and the scramasax.

In came the spear, striking like lightning, thundering off wooden shield and metal boss as Harald kept his feet moving, turning the giant round in slow circles to disorientate him, which was all he could do because of his disadvantage in reach. That spear blade glanced off his helmet, then off his left shoulder and then Moldof roared, bringing the spear over his head and striding forward to put his weight behind the thrust and the blade split the planks of Harald's shield and caught fast. Harald hauled the shield back, yanking the spear from Moldof's grasp, then slammed the whole lot into the ground so that the spear snapped, a foot of shaft jutting from the shield as Harald stood tall again.

To pierce a shield with a one-handed thrust was saga-worthy and every man knew it, which sent a shiver spidering up Sigurd's spine because he knew it was the kind of feat that the gods loved. And as if to drive this nail deeper Moldof took his shield in both hands and turned, then twisted back and launched the thing and it spun through the air, slamming into Finn Yngvarsson and knocking him to the ground. The king's thegns went wild at this, hooting and bellowing as Finn clambered to his feet and must have been glad for the beard hiding his red cheeks.

'Arse, Finn! But it would have been better if you had stayed on your feet,' Asbjorn growled, to which Finn asked Asbjorn what he would have done seeing as he had no shield.

'It would have cut you in half,' Finn answered for him, 'so shut your mouth, claw-hand!'

'Now now, girls,' Sorli said, as Moldof came at Harald with a huge sword, grunting with each strike, sending splinters flying from the jarl's shield which already had some spear shaft sticking from it.

Harald had no choice but to back off, then a downward strike cleaved into Harald's shield and stuck, which was the idea and Moldof hauled the shield towards him pulling Harald off balance, then leant in and hammered his right fist into the jarl's cheek and Sigurd heard the crack of bone. But somehow his father held on to the shield and staggered back with it still on his arm as Moldof strode forward and slashed his sword across, lopping off the bottom third of Harald's shield. His next blow took another chunk and when Harald tossed it aside Sigurd saw that Moldof's blade had bitten into the flesh of his father's arm too, for blood was blooming on the jarl's tunic where the brynja's sleeve ended.

'Bleed him, Father!' Sorli called. Sigurd saw the curl of their father's lip and knew he was in pain. Moldof sensed it too, like a wolf that knows its rival is wounded, and he came at Harald striking down onto the jarl's raised sword over and over like a blacksmith, clearly convinced that if either sword broke it would be Harald's. All the jarl could do was take shelter from the steel-storm under his own blade, his arm absorbing the impact and the ringing of it filling men's ears and maybe the gods' ears too.

Suddenly Moldof brought the blade down and in from the side and Harald was not quick enough, so that it struck him in the ribs and would have cut him in half if not for his mail coat, and the jarl roared with the pain of that.

Sorli cursed and every man there knew that such a blow must have broken ribs, though you would not know it to look at Harald, who straightened and drew his scramasax with his left hand, slashing it at Moldof's face if only to buy the time to get some air into his lungs.

Moldof thrust his sword and Harald deflected it with the shorter blade then stepped in smashing his sword's pommel into Moldof's face, but Moldof yelled and grabbed Harald's baldric and hauled him forward, ramming his helmet into Harald's face and when they stepped away from each other both men's faces were sheeted in blood, their beards dripping with it.

Harald threw his scramasax and Sigurd had seen him strike true with it before but perhaps there was blood in his eyes for the blade flew harmlessly past Moldof who came like a bull and slashed low, opening Harald's thigh, dropping him to one knee.

A groan went up around Sigurd and Harald's head dropped, his gory beard dripping blood onto his brynja as Moldof grinned through the mess of his own face and raised his sword to give the jarl his death blow.

Sigurd lowered his shield arm to touch his father's heavy silver brooch which he had fixed to his belt.

'He's going to cleave Harald like a log,' Agnar murmured. Moldof's sword came down and somehow Harald twisted out of its path so that it struck the ground beside him, then he bellowed in fury and brought his own sword up and over and onto Moldof's forearm, cutting it clean off.

The giant screamed and stepped backwards leaving his fore-arm and its hand still gripping the sword lying in the pine needle litter, waving the bloody stump before him.

'Kill them!' King Gorm yelled.

'Two shieldwalls!' Jarl Harald growled, up on his feet, back-ing away towards his men who formed two skjaldborgar in an arrow-head shape with the jarl at its tip and Sorli and Sigurd at each shoulder. 'Óðin!' Jarl Harald roared, full of the battle-fury. 'Óðin!'

But the gods were already watching. Sigurd could feel them in that place. And the Valkyries were there too, riding unseen amongst them all, already choosing the soon-to-be-slain.

The arrow-head shieldwall was a good tactic for stopping the enemy from outflanking you, but here Sigurd knew it mattered little either way. Even allowing that the king still had men watching the coast and others guarding Avaldsnes there were enough spears in his two shieldwalls here to see the day won and his old friend a corpse.

'Soon we drink with Sigmund and Thorvard, little brother,' Sorli said, giving Sigurd a smile. 'But not yet. Not before we've killed half of these traitorous whoresons, hey!'

An arrow thunked into Sigurd's shield and he saw the bowman off to his right grinning, enjoying himself.

'I'm proud of you, my boys,' their father gnarred through bloodied teeth, his broken jaw bones warping the words. 'No man had finer sons.'

Sorli nodded to Sigurd and Sigurd nodded back knowing that he would never look into his brother's eyes again in this life. 'Now then, men of Skudeneshavn,' their father said over his shoulder, 'make them think we've taken root, that we have growled an oath to the Allfather himself to hold this patch of ground until Ragnarök.'

'And then?' a sweat-sheened man named Hopp asked, quickly sweeping off his leather skull cap to swipe grease from his bald head with his forearm.

'And then wait for the jarl's word, you bone-head,' Sorli said.

'And then we kill the shits,' Asbjorn clarified.

Sigurd watched the two shieldwalls closing in, thirty men in each, and he felt as though his guts brimmed with ice water. Then here it is, he thought, glancing up at the dark boughs. This is where I make my name. Not the whale's road but the wound sea.

'I have told you all, I will not die here,' Orlyg said, hammering his spear shaft against his shield. 'So whoever wants to can drink himself stupid with me tonight once we have dealt with this crew of goat-fuckers.'

The others cheered this, no one disputing his foretelling now, and Orlyg stepped forward from the line, rolled his brawny shoulder in its socket, hauled his spear arm back and let the thing fly. It streaked through the trees and went straight through a man's shield, pinning his arm to his chest. Harald's men howled at this and it was worth losing a spear to see King Gorm's man fall out of his skjaldborg shrieking and clutching the whole assemblage without the first idea what to do about it.

'Heya, Shield-Shaker, meet Shield-Breaker!' Frothi yelled and someone began a shield beating that Harald's other hirðmen joined, rousing themselves to the coming slaughter.

Over his shield's rim Sigurd eyed those coming to kill them, could see the silver rings knotted into beards and hair, could read the thoughts in their minds the way some men could read the runes. They are afraid, he thought. Even with their numbers and for all their growling they are afraid of what a sword will do to a man's flesh. They are afraid of me. And so they should be, he thought, for I am spear-armed and have the blood of a jarl in my veins.

'Ready,' his father growled over his shoulder. 'Hold! Hold them, men of Skudeneshavn.'

Sigurd's muscles thrummed. His blood bubbled in his limbs and the rune-carved spear in his hand whispered to be un-leashed to the blood-fray.

Then King Gorm gave the command that Harald had known he would and his two long skjaldborgar stopped like a wave against a rocky shore. Each line would double up becoming two men deep, shields and swords or axes in the front line, spears behind to plunge over heads and through gaps. But, for a few heartbeats they would not be solid skjaldborgar with shields overlapping and feet planted. For those heartbeats they would be a snarl of men moving apart and coalescing and Jarl Harald knew it.

'Now!' he yelled, and his men roared and ran at their enemies, who had not even considered that they might be the ones attacked.

'Kill them!' Harald screamed, his sword cleaving a man's shield and the reverse stroke taking his head.

A man raised his shield to block Sigurd's spear thrust but

Sigurd dropped low to the man's left and thrust the spear in from the side, ripping into groin and genitals and releasing a scream from the man that was like that of a vixen. Sorli slammed his shield into an enemy shield with such force that the man behind it fell into his companions and Sorli gut-speared him before he could right himself, and it was bloody chaos.

'Hold! Hold!' someone was bellowing, perhaps the king himself, and though they did not run, the men from Avaldsnes were like a crew whose boat has struck a rock, and in those first moments of the fight they died in a hacking frenzy of blades.

A warrior swung his sword at Sigurd but it glanced off the leather and Sigurd repaid him by ramming his spear through the man's neck and hauling it free in a spray of glistening meat. Then he saw a spear blade burst from Agnar's chest and knew then that the king's men had rallied. The din filled the world and yet all Sigurd could hear was the blood in his ears as he caught blow after blow on his shield and jabbed or slashed with his spear. In his peripheral vision he saw Sorli plunge his sword into a man's mouth and twist the blade free in a mess of teeth and bone before turning to parry a sword blow that would have taken his arm off at the shoulder. Orn went down, his face cleaved off below his beaked nose, his eyes round with the shock of what had been done to him. Hopp took two spears in his back and another in his chest and bull-necked Orlyg bellowed defiance of his wyrd even as two swords hacked him to pieces and in that eye-blink Sigurd imagined Orlyg seeking out that old soothsayer in Valhöll and wringing his neck. All around Sigurd men of Skudeneshavn were dying and yet others had locked shields and fought in desperate knots, experience and fury braided together to keep them alive a little while longer.

'The jarl!' a man bellowed and Sigurd glanced round to see his father open a man's belly even as three more surrounded him, jabbing him repeatedly with their spears so that his fine brynja streamed with blood.

'You have to go, brother!' Sorli clattered into him, shoulder to shoulder, turning a blade away with his shield and scything a man down. 'You must run now.'

'No!' Sigurd had lost his spear now and Troll-Tickler was bloody yet thirsty still.

'Who will avenge us if not you?' his brother snarled. 'Go!'

'No, brother!' Sigurd's shield was battered and useless so he threw it down and caught a blade on his sword, turning it aside before hacking into a bearded face which spattered him with hot blood.

Beside them Frothi went down, a hand axe planted in his skull.

'Run, brother. Avenge us.' A spear streaked for Sigurd but Sorli hacked it out of the air a hand's breadth from Sigurd's chest. 'I will see you in Óðin's hall.' He grinned. *'Oath-Breaker!'* he roared, and through the chaos Sigurd saw King Gorm sitting his pony, his spear across his lap. Saw him look up and lock eyes with Sorli, and with that Sorli and Asbjorn ran towards the king and Finn ran with them. The Avaldsnes men drew towards their king like a fist around a sword hilt and Sorli took a sword blow to the neck and stumbled but ran on, screaming death to the traitor.

Sigurd turned and dropped to one knee and Troll-Tickler lopped off a man's leg at the thigh so that the man toppled over, screeching. Then Sigurd was up and with a two-handed swing he cut a man clean in half, bellowing with all the fury in the world. And then there were no more of Gorm's men before him but only trees and the gloom-filled pine forest.

And he ran.

CHAPTER FIVE

HE FLED SOUTH THROUGH THE TREES, HIS WOOL- AND LEATHER-CLAD bulk snapping brittle branches, his heart threatening to burst and the big muscles in his thighs burning though he would not stop to unburden himself. The leather coat had kept him alive and might do so still if any of King Gorm's men caught up with him. Besides which, they had taken enough from him already and he would give them nothing more.

He rejoined the old path and slowed a little then stopped, bent double and dragged the dry air into his scalding lungs, an ear turned back towards the scene of carnage. For five hammering heartbeats he held his breath and was sure he could hear the dim thunder of men striking their weapons against their shields and cheering. His mind wove the scene of the oath-breaker king standing over his father's torn and bloody body. Of Gorm's men stripping his brother Sorli of his mail and arms and dishonouring him in fouler ways.

They were all gone. All butchered.

Suddenly his stomach clenched and he was spewing hot sour fluid onto the ground and somewhere in the back of his mind he heard his brother Sorli laughing, saw the smile on his handsome face as he said: *They never told you about this part in the old saga stories, hey, brother!*

He straightened, dragging a hand across his mouth, then took his scabbard off his belt and thrust Troll-Tickler home still bloody. It would be easier to run holding the thing than having it catch against his leg. Then he thought of his mother and Runa and the blood in his heart froze as he turned and looked back the way he had come. There was no sign of the king's men yet but they would come. Gorm would know that Skudeneshavn was now spear-light and ripe for the taking and he would come.

So Sigurd ran. Even if his heart burst in his chest he would not stop until he had warned his people and seen them ready to fight, for what would be the point in them hiding now? We will all drown in the slaughter's dew, he thought, but not his mother and Runa. They would escape somehow. They would be safe.

But when he came within a mile of the village he knew he was already too late.

Smoke plumed against the heavy sky, the black of it darker than the cloud, so that Sigurd knew it was spewing from burning thatch or pitch-stained timbers even though the fire itself was obscured by the rising ground north of the village. A sudden *brrrrrruk* alerted him to a moorhen fleeing the tall grass in front of him, flying towards Sigurd rather than away from him, so that if he still had his spear he could have impaled its bluish black underbelly as it took to the sky. Then he saw what had put more fear into the bird than the breathless, blood-fouled man coming towards it had. An adder turned its face towards him, its forked tongue stabbing, head poised, sleek grey body coiled like a knot on a jetty. The creature's lidless, unblinking eyes looked as cold as bronze in the wedge of its face and Sigurd found himself impaled on the menace of it.

The snake is more dangerous than the warrior, he thought. The moorhen had known that and fled, just as Sigurd had run from the slithering oath-breaking king. And this thought filled Sigurd with shame as he ran past the adder towards his burning village.

*

What he found was more terrible in its way than what he had left behind and yet his eyes drank it in. They glutted themselves with it even as he retched but could bring up nothing, spitting only foul strings of saliva because he had already voided his stomach. The only buildings they had torched were the smithy, which had gone up like a hero's pyre igniting the dwelling beside it; Asgot's house, perhaps because they feared its seiðr; and Harald's hall, Eik-hjálmr, which was as yet merely scorched black for the most part because its timbers were damp. Though the western end had taken the flame and was burning feebly and the whole of the thatch was gushing steam and yellow-brown smoke.

The dead lay where they had been butchered, their faces frozen in aspects of surprise, as though even now they could not understand or would not accept that they were dead. Some of the men had fought by the looks, their corpses covered in wounds, and some of them must have fought well for there were patches of blood here and there, even puddles of it on the rain-slick earth, presumably spilled from the men who had brought death to Skudeneshavn.

The smoke from Asgot's house was fragrant with the dried herbs and spices and other nameless things that the godi used in his seiðr. As smoke will, it seemed to follow Sigurd, stinging his eyes and throat as it writhed between the houses of the slaughtered.

Women lay with their skirts hitched up and their white legs and private parts exposed and bloody. Their faces were the worst of all the dead because of what they had endured before the men had cut their throats and Sigurd dared not even think his sister's name as he saw them.

Then he saw a corpse move. The man was slumped on the ground, his chin on his chest and his white hair loose about his face and Sigurd knew it was Solveig. He called out and *Little-Elk*'s skipper slowly looked up and it was then that Sigurd saw the gash in the flesh across his chest like a fiend's grin.

'Sigurd. Boy.' The old man's voice was like the gush of air

leaving a fish as you slit its belly, but his eyes still had life in them. Sigurd crouched down beside him, glad to delay finding what else must be found.

'They came from the east,' Solveig said, his eyes flicking down to Harald's brooch on Sigurd's belt. 'Hopped like fucking fleas across from Bokn before we had a proper chance to see them coming. Whoresons must have been camped out there these last days.' He winced at the pain in his chest but did not seem to want to look at the wound now.

'Who?' Sigurd asked, though he did not need to.

'Randver, who else?' Solveig spat. 'Him and his spawn.' His eyes widened then but with hope, not pain. 'Your father? Is the jarl here?'

Sigurd thought about lying to him then but something told him Solveig had too much life in him yet to be worth the lie. Besides, the old man had seen the brooch on Sigurd's belt and that told the story of it. 'My father is dead,' he said. 'My brother too and all those who went to Avaldsnes. They were waiting for us, Biflindi and his húskarlar.'

'The king had no weregeld for us then,' Solveig managed through a bitter grin.

Sigurd shook his head. 'Just iron and steel,' he muttered, sweeping his sweat-matted hair back from his face.

'Looks like you let them know your feelings about that, lad,' Solveig said. Sigurd wiped a hand across his face, the sweat smearing his palm bloody. He realized that his face was caked in gore.

'I ran,' he said, the shame of it heavy as a rock in his belly.

'Your sister will be glad of it,' the old skipper said.

'My sister?'

'They took her. They took the youngens. The ones they hadn't murdered. Runa was among them. Others ran and might be running still, but they'll be back when they think it's safe. Runa didn't run.'

Sigurd's head spun with the whirlpool of that. Runa was alive!

'My mother?' he asked.

Solveig shook his head. 'I can't say, lad. I must have lost myself for a while when they cut me up. But the goat turd who cut me will be struggling with his mead horn about now.' He grinned then and for the first time Sigurd realized the old man was clutching something in one bony fist. The hand opened and inside it were three severed fingers the colour of bread before the baking. 'Took 'em with my scramasax before he opened me up. He'll be wiping his arse with his eating hand now.' The grin died on his face. 'Did the lads die well?'

Sigurd locked eyes with the old skipper then nodded down at the long wound in Solveig's chest. 'Are you going to meet them now?'

Solveig looked at the ripped flesh. Sigurd could see the gleam of bone deep in the cut. 'Not if you can stitch me up while I've still got some blood in me,' Solveig said.

Sigurd nodded. 'I'll fetch a needle.' He stood and saw an infant's crib upturned in the thoroughfare between two livestock pens. The pigs had gone, been carried off back to Hinderå. There was no sign of the infant, though Sigurd did not check amongst the filth of the pig pen for his mind had already spun the sorry tale of that. Then he approached the east end of his father's hall which was too damp still to burn and, with an arm that had never felt so weak in his life, he pushed open the door. Inside it was much darker than the summer's evening and he stood for a long while letting his eyes soak up the gloom. There were bodies in here too, those of his parents' thralls and even Harald's hounds Var and Vogg. The stink of death, of blood and piss and opened bowels thickened the fug of hearth smoke and the acrid reek of the smouldering thatch above. And beyond the hanging tapestries that separated his parents' chamber from the rest of the hall Sigurd found his mother.

Grimhild had not been raped, or if she had there was no tale of it in what Sigurd saw there by the dim, sooty light of the two oil lamps still burning as though it was just another evening. But she had fought. He knew this because the scramasax lodged in her chest, its reindeer antler crown handle as familiar to Sigurd as his mother's hand, had been a gift to her from his father. Sigurd knew his mother could handle the scramasax, knew that she would have fought like a she-wolf and he would not be surprised if one of Jarl Randver's men had gone home light between the legs, gelded like a beast and screaming. Or worse.

He knelt beside her and closed her staring eyes. With a shaking hand he pushed the spilled gold of her hair off her forehead and kissed her there, the skin as cold as a stone against his lips. Her left arm had almost been cleaved through just below the elbow from where she had raised it to defend herself from a sword or scramasax. He was ashamed to look at that, to see her severed flesh and the milky gleam of her bone; things no one should see, and so he tore some linen from her skirt and used it to bind the arm up, giving it the look of being whole again.

He put his mouth to her ear and told her that he was sorry, that he would give anything, do anything, to have the chance to fight for her. 'I should have protected you, Mother,' he said, as if those words poured in her ear might yet seep into her spirit somehow though her body was cold and dead.

Then, arming tears, snot and other men's blood from his face he took hold of the reindeer antler handle, murmured to Týr to give him courage, took a fjord-deep breath and hauled the blade from his mother's body. It drew easily enough, which was a small mercy at least, and when he saw the blood-glistened blade his breath caught in his chest like a hook catching in weed on the sea bed.

There were notches along the cutting edge that had not been there before, four of them and all as deep as a fingernail. These marks might as well have been runes carved in a rock telling of brave Grimhild's last stand and Sigurd's heart threatened to burst with bitter pride at the sight of them. Then he saw something else, a thing so small that it was only luck that he had caught sight of it at all in the gloom, but a thing more valuable to him then than a sea chest brimming with silver. A thread had snagged in the second cleft from the hilt. Sigurd took it between finger and thumb and spat on it, then wiped it across his tunic's sleeve and saw that beneath the blood the wool was the green of a full-grown holly leaf. His mother's under-dress was of undyed linen and her woollen apron-skirt was blue. The green thread had not come from her. Sigurd saw the fight in his mind, his mother's blade snagging on her attacker's green tunic as she pulled it from his sucking flesh, that fool who had underestimated a jarl's wife with a long knife in her hand.

'I will kill those who did this,' he said, and this was more for the gods' ears than for his mother's. 'May I never see Valhöll if I do not.' He thought of the Allfather and let the weight of those words sink in for a while and then he went over to Grimhild's chest and took out a fine bone needle and some thread, which were hairs from a horse's tail, and then he went outside, sucking in the air for all its tang of smoke, because it was sweet as mead after the stench of his father's hall.

He boiled some water and washed Solveig's wound clean and would have dulled the skipper's pain by getting him drunk on mead or ale, but Jarl Randver's men had drunk every drop they could find.

'Killing bairns is thirsty work,' Solveig had muttered, managing to spit in disgust and having to grin and bear it, growling curses and frothing at the mouth as Sigurd sewed the torn flesh back together. 'A blind woman with one hand and a grudge would have done a neater job than that,' the skipper complained when it was all done, looking down at Sigurd's handiwork, his face greasy with pain sweat, eyes sharp as rivet points.

'Next time you can do it yourself, old man,' Sigurd said and meant it.

'Ha! Next time? If I ever lay eyes on the horse-faced cunny who did this I'll blister him for his sloppy blade work then pay him to finish the job.' He grimaced. 'I've been alone since you were a boy, Sigurd,' he said. 'Now what have I got to live for? Without a tiller in my hand I'm not worth the hide on my own back.' For Jarl Randver had taken *Little-Elk*, which Solveig loved more than mead, silver or fame. 'Besides, your father will be waiting for me,' he said.

'He'll have to wait longer yet, old man,' Sigurd said. 'I'm going to need a man of your sea-craft.'

Solveig curled his lip into his white beard and closed his eyes and Sigurd left him to rest because he had work to do.

By the time he had carried most of the dead into Eik-hjálmr the first survivors were drifting back into the village. They came in twos and threes, stumbling like draugar, corpses which have dug their way out of their burial mounds to walk amongst the living. Their eyes bulged and the women clutched each other's arms and the children cried. Some found their kin amongst the slaughtered. Others found their loved ones vanished like smoke on the breeze and in some ways this was worse for they knew these were bound for the slave market. It can be better knowing a sister or son to be dead than knowing they are alive somewhere beneath another's yoke and cruelly used and you will never set eyes on them again.

Sigurd had been glad to see Ragnhild making her way over the rocks down into the village, her white-haired bairn cradled in her arms and her hair flying loose in the breeze. She had smiled through her tears to Sigurd but then before he could get the words out she had untangled the riddle of it for herself and knew that Jarl Harald and Sorli and all the rest of them were dead. At this horror she pulled little Eric so tight into her bosom that it was a miracle that the boy was not suffocated.

'My Olaf will know what to do,' she said with stone-cold certainty that her husband *would* be coming back, and Sigurd thumbed the little carving of one-eyed Óðin that hung against his chest, hoping for a measure of good luck where this was concerned.

It was as dark as it was going to get when the last of them returned clutching tools or jewellery or cloaks or their best furs; whatever possessions they had got their hands on before fleeing from Jarl Randver's men. There were some thirty-six in all, eight of them men, though these, three of them greybeards, would not look Sigurd in the eye, ashamed as they were to still draw breath when so many did not.

They gathered round, hands over mouths or cuffing at tears or fingering weapons, listening as Sigurd and Solveig gave them both edges of the heart-rending thing. It turned out that five young women and six young men had been carried off by the raiders. These would be bound for the slave markets if they could be broken, the scramasax if not.

'They will come back to kill us,' a woman said when Sigurd and Solveig had finished, which had others looking south down to the bay and the sea which was flecked with foam as the wind picked up.

Sigurd shook his head. 'They want this land and they have taken what they could carry. But when Randver comes again it will be to declare himself your new jarl. He will want you fishing again, planting crops and rearing pigs.' The dark thought of the infant's crib came to him then and he was glad he had thrown that thing into the fire of Asgot's house before the fugitives had returned. It was perhaps just as well that Unn, the child's mother, was dead.

'I saw Randver with his bollocks in a twist when his men tried to fire your father's hall,' Solveig said, his face as pale as his snowy hair as he nodded towards the hall. The flames had not taken at the western end though the thatch still smouldered, dirtying the dusk with yellow smoke. 'He wanted it for himself and why wouldn't he?' He looked back at the frightened faces around them and shook his head. 'His crew were blood-drunk. They weren't meant to kill so many. Randver was not happy about it.'

That was cold comfort to the survivors but it was probably the truth. Along with slaves, plunder and three ships Jarl Randver would get Skudeneshavn with its enviable position looking south across Boknafjorden. As for King Gorm, he now had in Randver a powerful ally instead of an enemy and an alliance that would bring him more silver than being oath-tied with Jarl Harald had.

When the anchor-heavy truth of this settled in their minds the survivors of the raid at least stopped looking over their shoulders long enough to take stock of their losses and look to their dead. Some boys without a whisker between them helped Sigurd bring the last of the bodies into Eik-hjálmr and when they had finished there were the corpses of thirteen men, women and weans and three hounds laid out around the central hearth. Aslak was not among them, which meant that they had likely taken him for the slave market along with Runa. Although Jarl Randver might have other plans for her if he had discovered that she was Harald's daughter.

What they had not discovered was the smallest of Jarl Harald's silver hoards. They had dug up the one buried beneath his and Grimhild's bed and they had taken the jarl's sea chest in which lay Harald's most precious possessions: scramasaxes with silver and bone handles, silver finger rings, Thór's hammers and arm rings taken from men he had killed in battle. And all this, though it was far from a Fáfnir's hoard, would have etched a grin in Jarl Randver's beard. But they had not found the nestbaggin, that leather haversack full of hacksilver which Jarl Harald hid out of sight up on one of the roof beams above where he slept off the mead or ale every night. Sigurd knocked it down with a well-aimed hand axe, his hand shaking as he undid the thong and reached inside, fingers touching the cool treasure that had belonged to his father. Tribute and plunder which Jarl Harald had won through trade, cunning and the sword. Even by the copper glow of the oil lamps Sigurd could see that the ingots and broken rings were dull, grey and black, tarnished and neglected and put away for lean times.

But silver was silver. And Sigurd was rich.

He had seasoned timbers and dry fuel brought in and piled around the dead and the whole lot smeared with cod liver oil from a stash which Randver's men had not found in one of the nausts, the boathouses down by the mooring.

'Any jarl would rather be food for the worms than see his folk spun this poor end,' a greybeard called Gylfi mumbled into his beard as he cast his eye over the scene by the light of a lamp hung from a chain.

Their wounds covered by linens now, Sigurd imagined they could have been sleeping off some great feast as they had all done so many times before, sharing this hearth, their jarl's meat and mead and each other's stories. But come the morning, when the summer sun warmed the air and scattered jewels across the fjord, these luckless few would still be cold and stiff. Sigurd's mother, whom he had laid separately in her own bed surrounded by the things she would need in the afterlife, would never see another day nor her son's face.

'We'll give it another day or two to dry,' he told Gylfi, for though Eik-hjálmr's resin-coated planks would burn like Völund's own forge once Sigurd's fire took, for now they were yet laced with rain and the sea water which Olaf had had folk bring up in pails and fling against the hall in case Randver came in the night to burn it.

'Aye, well this lot will still be here,' Gylfi agreed, kicking out at a rat that had wasted no time and was gnawing at a woman's stiff white finger. It scurried off into the floor reeds. 'When it burns it'll burn high enough to scorch the Allfather's feet.'

None had objected to Sigurd's plan of burning the hall with their dead inside it. 'Let Jarl Randver see the smoke from Hinderå and know he will never sit in your father's high seat,' a fierce-looking woman called Thorlaug had said. Sigurd had last seen her husband Asbjorn running with Sorli to kill King Gorm. To give Sigurd a chance of living. Asbjorn's claw hand had not stopped him surviving until the end and Sigurd would make sure the skalds knew it. For now, though, the news had made Thorlaug stand a little taller.

'We should wait till Randver is in there before we burn it,' a girl called Ingun said. She was pretty enough that Randver's thegns might have killed each other to be either the first to rape her or the one to carry her back to Hinderå to marry, regardless of whether the man already had a wife back there. But Ingun was as fast on her feet as she was beautiful and none had caught her.

'I'll not have that man share their flames,' Thorlaug said.

Sigurd knew the real reason they did not mind his burning Eik-hjálmr. It was not because they would never again find joy in that place, crammed to the roof beams with ghosts and gilded memories of happier times. It was because a roaring, leaping flame will carry the dead to the afterlife as fast as the smoke rises into the sky and almost as fast as a valkyrie riding to Asgard with a hero cradled in her arms.

And so when it was dry enough Eik-hjálmr would burn.

Sigurd was not their jarl. Yet it seemed that in their eyes he gripped the end of an invisible rope whose other end rested in Jarl Harald's hand, for all that Harald even now feasted with the gods in Valhöll. They looked to Sigurd to lead them and he felt the heaviness of it like a torc around his neck.

'You can't stay here, lad,' Solveig said as Sigurd held a tallow candle to the old man's face. Sigurd had been on his way to the high ground overlooking the bay when he had thought to make sure the skipper hadn't died in his bed. 'Randver won't bother about me or the rest of them but one sniff of you and he'll set his hounds loose. The oath-breaker king too, for he surely knows you gave him the slip.' He grinned then despite everything. 'He'll be scratching like a flea-bitten thrall to think of you out there somewhere when by rights you should be a corpse.'

That was a warm thought on the ice-sheathed serpent that sat coiled in Sigurd's gut, though in truth he doubted the king would lose any sleep over a boy barely into his first beard.

'Don't doubt old One-Eye,' Solveig said, warning Sigurd with a bloodstained finger. 'There's a reason you walked away from that steel-storm.'

'Ran away,' Sigurd muttered, but the skipper ignored this.

'And it wasn't so as you could do a shit-hole job of stitching me up, I know that much.' The old skipper's eyes searched Sigurd's. 'The gods love chaos. Don't they just.'

Sigurd knew that was true. He had learnt that in the pine forest when the battle-sweat had flowed and he had laid men low with spear and sword. He had known then that he had a talent for chaos himself. Which was just as well.

'When Olaf returns we will leave,' he said. 'You too, Solveig. Jarl Randver will come back to lay claim to Skudeneshavn in the name of King Gorm but we will not be here.'

'Where will we go?' the old skipper asked, pale as death, his chest wound only just drawn together like lips over a grimace, and yet he was as good as pledging himself to go wherever Sigurd's wind would blow them.

Which made Sigurd wish he had a better answer.

'I don't know,' he said.

There was no wind to speak of and the flames soared, tall as oaks, fierce and flapping and spewing bronze sparks that seemed alive, as though they had been set loose to search the world taking with them the news of what had befallen the folk of Skudeneshavn. The smoke billowed into the sky like a black sail from some god's longship and the old worm-riddled beams cracked and spat furiously. And Eik-hjálmr burnt.

Three days had passed since the raid, two of them dry, and Olaf, Svein and the others had returned to the bane of it all with no good news of their own to round the sharp edges.

'Our reception at Jarl Leiknir's hall was cold as a frost giant's tit,' Olaf said, 'but Leiknir made it ice clear that he wants nothing to do with this, him being sat between us and Jarl Randver. That should have been no surprise, I suppose, but then he said that with Randver being so silver-rich these days, if the people of Tysvær were going to come in on any side it would be his.' Olaf grimaced. 'I thought about putting my spear in his belly there and then to save us the trouble later.'

'And Twigbelly?' Sigurd asked, meaning Jarl Arnstein Arngrimsson at Bokn.

Svein rumbled a curse and Olaf shook his head. 'I've met rocks with more sense than that fool. He gave us meat full of gristle and ale that tasted like piss and told me that your father was a fool if he could not see that Biflindi and Randver were up to their necks in scheming.'

'They will not help us then,' Sigurd said.

Olaf scratched his bearded cheek. 'Not even were your father still alive. Now?' He shook his head again. 'They are happy on their island and will only rouse themselves from their beds if King Gorm needs spears for some raid. Goat-fuckers to a man. As for the bóndi and lendermen we visited, they said that their oath to Jarl Harald is worth nothing now that Jarl Harald has broken his oath to the king by raiding villages under Gorm's protection.'

Sigurd fumed at this, for they were the same lies King Gorm had levelled at his father in the pine wood.

Olaf raised a palm. 'They know it's got no truth in it but the fact that they all dribbled the same shit tells me that they've all been fed the same tripe.'

'The king's men have been busy then,' Sigurd said.

Olaf nodded. 'I should have saved my breath.' He glanced at Svein who was talking with Hendil, Loker and Gerth, those three being the others whom Olaf had taken with him. 'Five more spears would have been useful here. Things might have turned out differently.'

From what Solveig had said Sigurd doubted it and said so. He told Olaf and the others of the ambush in the pine wood and of his father's last stand, and Hendil said it was as honourable a death as any warrior could hope for.

'Given the damned treachery that wove it,' Loker said through gritted teeth.

Sigurd related what he had learnt from Solveig about Jarl Randver's raid and he even told Olaf what he had read in the warp and weft of his mother's own last stand, and Olaf had listened to this with tears streaming into his beard and not an ounce of shame for it.

'The gods are crueller than fang and claw and starvation put together,' Olaf said. 'Not that I need to tell you that, lad.'

He'd looked away then at a cormorant heading south towards Boknafjorden and Sigurd had been glad of it.

Now, everyone had gathered beneath the waxing moon to watch their jarl's hall become a pyre and their faces were sweat-sheened and tear-soaked as they raised hands before them to shield against the ferocious heat.

'Why did they burn Asgot's house?' Svein asked. He had bristled at Sigurd's telling of it and cursed himself for not having been there to fight the raiders. Solveig had called him an overgrown fool, telling Svein that had Olaf not taken him to visit the outlying jarls he would have been as dead as the others, but the words were like spit on flames to Svein.

'I'd wager he was working some spell on the whoresons and they didn't much care for it,' Olaf suggested. Sigurd could picture the godi foaming his beard with curses, damning Jarl Randver's men to the depths of Helheim. He imagined Randver's men's bluster as they set light to the godi's house, and the terrible shrieks of the birds and bats, polecats, rats and other small creatures Asgot had kept in boxes or tied to pegs stuck in the ground. For all their swagger in front of each other, the jarl's thegns would have felt fear squirming in their guts because it was no small thing to make an enemy of a godi.

'Randver didn't know what to do with him,' Solveig said. 'It was like they had caught hold of a wolf by the tail.'

'Aye, well I'd rather have hold of a wolf than Asgot,' Olaf said.

Jarl Randver's men had not killed the godi – that would be foolish by anyone's standards – but Sigurd wondered what they would do with him now, for neither would anyone in their right mind buy a godi for a slave.

Blackened timbers held dragon's eyes of glowing coals. Others collapsed sending waves of sparks rolling towards the onlookers to mottle tunics and breeks with little black scorch marks. The flames stretched up into the sky, the fire seeming to create its own wind that sounded like the whisper of a sad saga, and Sigurd watched the smoke ascend knowing that the gods would see it.

By now the heat inside Eik-hjálmr would have raised fat blisters on his mother's white skin. Her golden hair streaked with silver would have flared bright as a hero's helmet fresh from the forge and disappeared. Everyone gathered there knew that soon the smell of burning flesh would fill their nostrils but no one would raise an arm to their face or cringe at the stink. For they were all joined in this bitter thing from this day until the day of their own deaths, and they would imbibe every last drop of it out of respect for their dead.

And when it was done and only the main roof-supporting columns of oak stood flame-licked yet still strong, those who would go with Sigurd gathered what belongings they would need, said goodbye to kin if they had any, and prepared to leave.

Olaf told those staying in Skudeneshavn to give their new jarl no trouble and, more than this, to make Randver welcome as much as they could.

'Do what you can to make life easier for yourselves,' he said. 'Jarl Harald and the others are gone and you will never see their faces again in this life.' There were no tears in his eyes now. 'Swear an oath to Randver if he asks it of you, for there is nothing else to be done. And tell him that the hall burnt because of the fire his men put in the thatch,' he warned, 'for he'll be angry to see it gone.' He left his elder son Harek to look after his wife and little Eric and kissed each in turn, vowing to come back when he could. He did not draw the thing out for that was not his way. But more than this, Sigurd knew Olaf was conscious that Sigurd had no one to say his goodbyes to, had no kin but for Runa who was a prisoner at Hinderå, and Olaf wanted to spare him the sting of seeing others sheathed in loving arms.

There were seven of them who left Skudeneshavn next morning, turning their backs on the smoke that still rose lazily from the pyre that had been Jarl Harald's hall. Eik-hjálmr. Oak helmet. There had been humour in the naming of it but there was no mirth in its end and now its ashes were mixed with those of the dead. At the last there had been no protection to be found under Eik-hjálmr's great roof. Perhaps the gods found humour in this.

Well then, do not take your eyes from me, Allfather, Sigurd

thought as he climbed into the boat and turned his face to the sea, his eyes following a gull as it screeched down at them asking if they were going fishing. 'Not fishing, bird,' Sigurd muttered into his beard, placing Troll-Tickler on the bench beside him. 'Hunting.'

CHAPTER SIX

_____

THE BOAT WAS CALLED *OTTER*. IT WAS BUILT OF OAK IN THE SAME WAY as Jarl Harald's ships, but at just under thirty-two feet long and six feet wide it could have been *Reinen* or *Sea-Eagle's* offspring. It comprised six lengths of planking, the first two strakes curving sharply upwards, almost to the top of the stem and stern. It had five pairs of oars, oarlocks, floorboards, thwarts and rudder, and it was a handsome, well-built, reliable boat. But it was too small.

It wasn't so much the crew that was the problem – *Otter* could take seven men easily enough – but all the war gear: the shields, spears, axes and swords which they had brought because they were no better than outlaws now, men on the run from a jarl and a king. But whilst a man has a spear in one hand and a sword in the other he is free, Hendil said. He is alive.

Loker grumbled that Svein took up two men's space in the thwarts and Gerth cursed when he cut his shin on a spear blade, but for the most part no one complained about the discomfort. Only Olaf owned a brynja, which was now rolled and tied up in greased leather on the bench beside him, but each of the seven was weighed down with the cold truth that *Otter* and her little crew were all that was left of the power that Jarl Harald had wielded. Skudeneshavn had fought in the king's battles. It had sent men raiding every spring, north as far as Giske and south across the sea to the land of the Danemen, bringing back silver and metalwork, jewels, weapons, furs, bone and tall stories.

And slaves.

These slaves were taken in chains to the island of Rennisøy to the south-west of Bokn because in some distant time the strongest jarls of Haugalandet, Rogaland and Ryfylke had agreed that the island was accessible to all but not in the shadow of any chieftain's hall. Not even King Gorm had broken this tradition and so the sea around Rennisøy was to the trade in slaves as grease is to sledge runners, and for the first three days after every full moon men from a hundred different fjords would bring their prisoners to the block, drawing merchants like flies to flesh.

Which was why Sigurd was going to Rennisøy.

'They did not lay their hands on Runa so far as I saw,' Solveig had said, which probably meant that either Sigurd's sister had told them who she was, or else Jarl Randver had guessed it from looking at her, which would not have taken a völva's knack of divination.

'If the jarl knows Runa is Harald's daughter he is more likely to keep her for himself than sell her to some fat, balding farmer from Svartevatn,' Svein had said through a mouthful of horse-meat. Randver's men had killed the beast for the simple mischief of it and the first of the women to return to the village had set about butchering it while it was still warm.

Olaf nodded in agreement with this though his frown showed that he suspected Sigurd had another view of it.

'That would surely be true,' Sigurd said, 'had Jarl Randver thought that Harald and all his sons were dead, as he must have when he took her.' He'd stayed silent for a long moment then while the others took up the slack of it in their minds.

It was old Solveig whose eyes had lit first. 'But by now Biflindi will have sent word to him that young Sigurd here wriggled through the holes in his net,' the old skipper said. 'What with him and the king being in this as thick as a pail of pig shit.' One silver eyebrow lifted. 'And Randver knows Jarl Harald's reputation well enough to assume that any son of his would not hide under some rock while his sister sleeps under his enemy's roof.'

Sigurd nodded because Solveig had given words to his own thoughts.

'He's going to take Runa to Rennisøy,' Solveig went on, 'and he's going to dangle the girl like a silver chain and hope that Sigurd is fool enough to show himself.'

'Lucky for him then,' Svein said without even looking at Sigurd.

'You're going to Rennisøy?' Solveig asked, eyes flicking from Olaf to Sigurd.

'*We* are going to Rennisøy,' Sigurd said.

Now, they had rowed *Otter* across the mouth of the Karmsund Strait and were passing the skerries off the southern tip of Bokn. That was the easy part, for Njörd god of wind and tides had given them a sleeping sea for which they were thankful. But then they would have to cross Boknafjorden which would not be so easy, for even when there was only a mere breath of wind the open water there was more often than not flecked with spume. In *Reinen* and *Sea-Eagle* and even in *Little-Elk* the crossing would be a simple enough affair, but *Otter* was none of those. As it was, fully laden with men and gear she showed only a foot of freeboard above the brine and so they would have to be careful to avoid taking in water if the waves grew higher.

'I am not worried at all,' Hendil announced as Solveig pushed the tiller to turn *Otter* so that the dawn sun moved out of their eyes and onto their left cheeks. 'If old One-Eye wanted to drown us like a crew of ill-wyrded nithings why would he have helped Sigurd walk unscathed from that blood-fray?'

'I didn't walk, Hendil, I ran,' Sigurd said.

'Even so,' Hendil said undeterred. 'It can be no coincidence that an old goat like Solveig also survived when the others did not. The Allfather knew that we would need a skipper.'

'You hardly need a skipper for this,' Solveig said.

'Then you may row if you like and I will take the tiller,' Loker put in, at which Solveig called him a turd. The old man was still pale and wincing from his chest wound but Sigurd's stitches had held and there was no sign of the wound rot.

'Still, I am not worried,' Hendil said, 'and let that be an end to it.'

'I'll remind you of that if we see one of Jarl Randver's dragons ploughing the fjord,' Olaf said, at which some of them touched amulets or sword hilts because all men know that cold iron can turn away baleful spirits and ill luck.

In the event they saw no ships and *Otter* carried them safely so that they came sweating and red-faced to the island's uninhabited south-western shore and pulled the boat up into the tree line a mere stone's throw from the breakers. They had not wanted to risk mooring in the harbour on the north side of the island for fear that Jarl Randver's men would be watching.

'No shields,' Olaf said to Svein who had taken his from *Otter*'s thwarts and was strapping it onto his back. 'No spears. No helmets.'

'Your brynja?' Loker said.

'It stays here,' Olaf said, which must have been hard for a warrior like Loker to grasp, who would have set his own mother adrift for the chance of owning a brynja. 'Bring your favourite blade. Everything else stays here with Solveig and the boat.' The old skipper looked relieved then for he was still weak and had no great enthusiasm for whatever Sigurd and Olaf had in mind. 'We don't need the arsehole who cut Solveig open recognizing him.'

Solveig grinned. 'If you see the pig's penis tell him I have two of his fingers if he wants them back. The third I gave to my dog.'

'Keep your heads down and stay out of trouble,' Olaf said. 'If anybody asks, we are Lysefjorden men.'

'Unless the person asking is a Lysefjorden man,' Hendil said helpfully, 'then you are a Stavanger man.'

'And how will we know if the man asking is from Lysefjorden?' Svein asked.

'Because he will be the one trying to pay for slaves with mackerel and grunting that silver is silver,' Loker said, which got a few chuckles as they tucked hand axes into belts or strapped on swords.

'Stay buried in the crowds,' Olaf said, a brow hoisted as he glanced at Svein, who would have difficulty burying himself in an avalanche, 'and no matter who we see at the block, no one is to do anything about it.' He nailed each man with his stare then because he knew it would be no easy thing seeing Skudeneshavn folk chained and being bartered over. Harder still to stand there scratching their arses instead of putting their blades into the men who had put those chains on.

It was lucky that other than Sigurd only Gerth had kin taken by Jarl Randver's men and Sigurd looked at him now with eyes he had honed to an edge. 'If your cousin is there we will get her back if we can, Gerth,' he said, tying his hair at the nape of his neck, 'but we will do it cleverly.' Gerth nodded, but Sigurd had seen enough of the man to know that a nod was not exactly assurance of acceptance or even understanding. There were sheep cleverer than Gerth. Still, he was thought of as a good man to have with you in a fight and Sigurd would need fighters.

'Perhaps you should stay here with Solveig, Uncle,' Sigurd suggested, for Olaf did not look like a farmer or a merchant or a craftsman. He was broad-shouldered and barrel-chested and to look at him anyone would know that there was a man who earned his meat and mead with the sword. Even a blind man would know that Olaf was a warrior, just as a nose full of smoke would tell the man he was near a fire.

'You're drunk, lad, if you think I'm going to let you tangle with Jarl Randver's fart-catchers while I sit here arguing about the wetness of water with this old sea goat.' He thumbed at Solveig who muttered an insult in return. 'Your father will be waiting for me in the Allfather's hall and he'll take my head if I let anything happen to you.'

Sigurd did not argue as Olaf made some measure of compromise by fumbling at the stiffened braids in his beard and pulling from them the three silver rings and two small Thór's hammers. For all the difference it would make. But Sigurd was prepared to take the risk of Olaf drawing men's attention, or even being recognized, because having Olaf with you was the next best thing to having one of the Æsir at your shoulder.

He looked down at himself to make sure he had not left anything that might mark him as the son of a jarl and was satisfied with what he saw. He wore an old threadbare tunic and dirty breeks and even made sure his Óðin amulet was tucked away out of sight, for Óðin was a jarl's god. A young man who had yet to make his name was more likely to invoke Thór, Frey, Týr or Váli.

Troll-Tickler was scabbarded at his hip and though there were far more beautiful blades a sword was a sword and some folk might wonder how such a young man had come to own it. But that blade had killed men, made corpses of his enemies, and Sigurd would not be without it now.

'You had better not get yourselves killed,' Solveig warned as they turned their backs on him and *Otter* to make their way up through the trees. 'You hear me! I can't take this boat back by myself.'

'I can see why your father did not want him at *Reinen*'s helm,' Loker said, and though meant in humour that mention of his father's best ship, taken by that dung heap Jarl Randver, was another spark to the kindling of Sigurd's fury which smouldered and flickered deep in his chest. The only thing that could put out that fire was blood.

But first he must find Runa.

Once through the trees they scrambled up the cliff and across lichen-covered rocks until they reached the heights around which gulls screeched, tumbling through draughts scented with pine and the sea. Someone had built a cairn up there overlooking the fjord and Sigurd wondered after the person who had carried all those stones to this place and carefully set one upon the other up to the height of his shoulder. Perhaps it had been a woman who had raised it to remember a husband who had sailed west and never returned.

'I think I can see Ragnhild standing there with a face like thunder because you would not let her ride to Avaldsnes to cut off King Gorm's bollocks,' Svein said, arming sweat from his forehead and smiling. They stood in the tall grass looking out across the Boknafjord as thick grey cloud billowed westward across the sky towards Skudeneshavn. They could not see their own bay but knew well enough where it sat at the southern tip of the land mass beyond the island of Bokn.

'You may joke, lad, but you're close to the marrow with that one,' Olaf said through a wall of teeth. 'I'd sooner face Fenrir Wolf with an eating knife than Ragnhild when she's angry.' He shook his head. 'If she hadn't been seeing to the bairn she would have stayed to give Randver's lot the hospitality they deserved.' He looked at Sigurd then. 'They telling you anything we should know about?' he asked, nodding towards the gulls whose shrieks carried west with the breeze, and there was just enough weight in the question to show that Olaf cared about the answer.

Sigurd shook his head and Hendil said that was probably just as well for everyone knew that birds are famous liars anyway.

They saw a man and boy herding sheep and another farmer driving five pigs to the market, but most of the Rennisøy folk were along the coast and lived on fish, the interior being hard land to work on account of having having more ups and downs than a young man's arse, as Olaf put it a little later when they at last came, sweating, within sight of the Vik. At any other time it was nothing much to look at, just an inlet sheltered by an arm of pine-bristled rock reaching north and round to the east. But even a reindeer herder from the frozen northlands would see that this was a good sheltered place for men to bring their boats, and now on the second day after the full moon the Vik brimmed with craft. For Rennisøy's famous market had been making some men rich and others slaves since Valhöll's roof posts were still green and leaking sap, and it did not take long for Sigurd's eyes to pick out *Reinen* from those ships moored to the jetties criss-crossing the calm water.

'He's here then,' Olaf said, hackles rising at the sight of his jarl's ship in his enemy's hands. Men with shields and spears milled by the ship and others lazed aboard her and the sight burnt Sigurd too because he knew there was nothing he could do about it. But they had come for Runa, not *Reinen*.

They made their way down off the high ground and Sigurd looked up at the iron-grey clouds hoping it would rain, for men are less vigilant in the rain, more concerned with moaning about it and trying to keep dry. But the cloud kept rolling west, keeping its cargo to itself, and Sigurd touched the little carving inside his tunic, invoking Óðin who was known to be able to change his skin and his appearance into any fashion he chose.

'It seems there are more folk here this time than I have seen before,' Loker said as they passed the camp with its fires and tents and children running wild, and joined the throng amongst the traders' stalls hung with pelts and leather or laden with horn combs, glass beads, weavings, pottery, sword hilts, jewellery and food. The air thrummed with the din of vendors crying their wares, men and women greeting each other excitedly, merchants forging trades with the skill of swordsmiths making blades, dogs barking, ponies neighing and warriors laughing over cups of ale and horns of mead. Fish sizzled over braziers and fragrant steam rose from cauldrons hung over fires and Sigurd's mouth went slick with it all and he realized he hadn't eaten a meal for days.

They had split up now to better weave into the crowds, though Sigurd had little trouble tracking Svein's progress through the market, his friend's flaming red hair like a moving beacon above others' heads. But Svein had never stood in the shieldwall and nor had he been to Rennisøy before and so it was unlikely that anyone here would note him for any other reason than that he could have been related to the Thunder God himself. Sigurd, though, had fought in his father's war band and he had visited the slave market before and he was the son of a jarl, which all conspired to make it far from impossible that he would be recognized. So he kept his head down and avoided folk's eyes and was careful not to shoulder into any of the spear-armed growlers in the crowd because the last thing he needed was a fight over spilled drink.

He threaded his way north towards the harbour they had seen from the higher ground, the crowd becoming better armed and worse tempered the closer he got. For the slave trade was a serious business and few men who could afford to deal in it did not think it worth spending a proportion of their wealth on thugs and brawlers to watch their backs.

'Every arse wipe there thinks he's a jarl in the making,' Olaf had said earlier as they pulled *Otter* from the breakers up the shingle. 'And none of them minds spilling a little blood to prove it.'

Sigurd did not need to push all the way through the press of bodies near the blocks, for if Runa or Aslak or any of them were among the chained then he or one of his companions would catch a glimpse before long. Instead he held back, hoping he was all but invisible amongst all the merchants in their finely woven tunics whose necklines, cuffs and skirt hems were decorated with brightly coloured braid. At their waists hung fat purses bulging with silver and the belts they hung from dived through burnished buckles that were testament to their trading wits as much as an arm ring was proof of a warrior's bravery. Sigurd recognized some of them, too, those who had been guests in Jarl Harald's hall having come to Skudeneshavn to sell skins or ivory, whale oil or eiderdown. He hoped these men would not recognize him.

He caught Olaf's eye and Olaf nodded to a knot of grizzled, scarred spearmen near by who were clearly more interested in the crowd than in the lines of young men and women waiting their turn to be hauled up to the blocks. Sigurd nodded back, and even though there was a good chance that those warriors were Jarl Randver's, meaning the jarl had been expecting Sigurd to come to Rennisøy, he now shouldered through the throng to fix his eyes properly on the plunder that brought silver-rich men to the island like crows to carrion. For if Randver was here then so was Runa. Sigurd could feel that as surely as he could feel the weight of Troll-Tickler at his left hip.

'Piss off with those elbows, boy!' a fat man growled at Sigurd, licking sweat beads off his top lip though there was no sun to speak of. But then the man's pig eyes drank Sigurd in and he dropped his gaze and shuffled aside to let Sigurd through.

A merchant was tipping hacksilver out of his scales as a big, arm-ringed warrior led a flaxen-haired, tear-soaked girl from the block. The silver was barely in the man's purse before the warrior's hand was up the girl's skirts, but the girl was not Runa and Sigurd's eyes roved along the unfortunates as his heart hammered the anvil of his chest.

Then he saw Aslak. At first his eye had slid right over his friend because even Aslak's mother, were she alive, would have had trouble recognizing him. His face was a swollen, lumpy, green and yellow mess. His right eye was a black half moon and his bottom lip was split and his hair was a knotted snarl of dried blood and no one would buy him. Not because there were mountain trolls who would run shrieking from that face, but because a slave whose owner was prepared to beat him to a pulp before showing him at the block was clearly more trouble than he was worth. But Sigurd would buy him.

Sigurd noticed Hendil slowly working his way towards him, instinct perhaps impelling him to group at the sight of one of their own in such a poor state, and Sigurd gestured for him to come closer still. When Hendil was beside him Sigurd breathed his plan into his ear and when he had finished Hendil counted ten heartbeats then threaded his way back through the crowd. Sigurd turned to the fat man beside him who had his eyes on a small dark-haired girl standing naked on the block. She had a smile etched on her face in the hope it would give her a better chance of being bought, which did not say much for the man holding the other end of the rope around her neck.

'You see that slave who looks like he's had a face full of Mjöllnir?' Sigurd asked the fat man, who narrowed his eyes at Sigurd and nodded. 'I want you to buy him,' Sigurd said.

The fat man palmed sweat from his face. 'I would not buy that ugly runt even for two farts. Not even to dig my turf and empty my cesspit,' he said.

'You will buy him,' Sigurd said, 'but it will not even cost you one fart. I will give you his price and twice as much again for your trouble.'

'You?' the fat man scoffed, then straightened his slick face. 'Why?'

'Because I want him,' Sigurd said. 'And because if you do this you will have the silver to buy the black-haired girl off that man who just got her for next to nothing.' The fat man's pig eyes bulged then and his tongue licked his lips again. 'She will be in your bed tonight and I will have the ugly slave to empty my cesspit.' Sigurd forced a smile onto his own lips and the fat man turned his gaze back to the black-haired girl.

'Show me the silver,' he said.

When it was Aslak's turn to be pushed up onto the block Sigurd lowered his own head because he did not want his friend to see him. Jarl Randver's thegns would be watching like hawks and as Sigurd had predicted, Aslak did not have many men reaching for their purses, which meant that the few who did were more conspicuous for it. Randver himself was there somewhere. Watching. He had come to Rennisøy in Jarl Harald's ship and he was dangling the bait in the hope that Sigurd would bite. How disappointed he must have been then to see a fat man from Mekjarvik come forward and put his silver in the scales. Jarl Randver's man at the block took the iron collar off Aslak's neck and replaced it with a rope that was thrown in to the trade at no extra cost, placing the other end in Aslak's new owner's greasy palm. Even as he led Aslak off away from the block the fat man's eyes were glued to the little black-haired girl, which Sigurd thought was unwise. For Aslak was likely to cut the man's throat at the first sniff of a chance, though hopefully not before Sigurd had met up with them after the auction.

Sigurd watched Aslak being hauled off back through the crowds towards the camp where Sigurd had arranged for his friend's new owner to deliver him to Hendil. Then the fat man will be rooting after that girl like a boar after acorns, Sigurd thought, as a murmur like that of the sea rose around him, turning his head back to the heckle and barter of it all. It was no mystery what had got the crowd excited, what had got men hooming in the back of their throat and wondering what they had with them that they might sell. One or two might have even wished they could put their wives in that pot, for the girl who had stepped onto the block now was a beauty. Her face was clear and smooth as cream and her eyes were bright blue beads the colour of the fjord on a warm summer's afternoon. Her hair was pale gold and hung straight as an anchor rope in a sleeping sea, and her back was straight, so that even a fool would know she had not been a slave long.

Nor would she be, Sigurd's mind growled as he fought every instinct in his body that clamoured to rush to his sister and strike the iron collar from her neck. Runa. Standing proud as a goddess even after all that had befallen her, for she was a jarl's daughter and that iron ring around her neck might as well have been a silver torc for the way she wore it.

Sigurd felt Olaf's eyes on him and looked up to see him shake his head, warning him against any action. Sigurd's limbs were trembling now, as though the blood in his veins were coming to the boil. Troll-Tickler was whispering to him, begging Sigurd to haul it out into the day and let it feed on the blood of their enemies. Not yet, Sigurd's mind warned. Not yet. Still, perhaps he could let Runa see him at least, let her know that she was not alone in the world and that she yet had a brother and so hope. Olaf shook his head again, reading the warp and weft of Sigurd's thoughts, but Sigurd looked back at Runa, willing her to see him amongst the crowd as Jarl Randver's man opened the bidding and the first offers flew in like starlings.

Randver's man spun some tall story about the girl having been taken in a raid on the Swedes to the east.

'She was a princess among her people,' the man spouted. 'Look at her. She is as beautiful as Freyja herself and will give

some lucky man many strong sons. The man who . . . found her
. . . swears she was not touched. No man in his crew so much
as breathed on this pretty neck,' he said, almost touching Runa.
'Of course, the man who buys her today will be able to verify
the truth of this for himself.'

This got some laughs and no few bawdy remarks. One man
offered to test the goods in advance of anyone handing over
their silver. Another said it was a wise man who bought the
girl now for he could sell her on for even more once her tits
had finished sprouting. Runa stood there as though the whole
noise was nothing but the chatter of rooks in a tree and Sigurd
filled with pride. And yet his jaw ached with the clench of his
teeth and the muscles knotted around his bones. What would
Thorvard or Sigmund or Sorli do? He could not picture his
brothers standing there like a rock as he did now while their
sister was brandished and bartered over like some karl's best
cow. Gods, what would Harald do! That picture was clear as
fjord water in Sigurd's mind. There would be blades and blood
and chaos.

Men were offering good silver for Runa now but they might
as well have been pissing into the wind. The merchant steering
the trade was on the end of Jarl Randver's chain no less than
Runa was, and made a show of shaking his head and wafting
men's offers away and sometimes not even letting them put
their ingots in the dish of his scales, as though by eye alone he
knew the balance would not be met. And yet Sigurd saw that
other merchants, men he knew to be rich because they had
boasted as much before in his father's hall, did not go forward
or let their hands fall to their purses. They could taste the taint
in this, he thought. Perhaps they recognize Runa, or perhaps
they have heard about Jarl Randver's raid on Skudeneshavn
and they would rather keep clear of the mire of it all. For it was
not the normal way of it for prisoners of a raid to be sold in the
shadow of their former homes. Normally a trader would take
them to a market far away to lessen the risk of runaways and
reprisals.

Not that Randver was going to actually sell Runa it seemed, for the jarl's man put up his hands now appealing for hush.

'Enough of this! Do you take me for a fool? I would not sell a pig even for the best offer I have received for this girl! No more insults, please.' He gestured for Runa to step down off the block and she did it without looking at him. 'If anyone wants to be serious about this then you can find me when we have finished here, but I will not waste any more time. I know the man who owns this girl and he will not even give an ear to any offers of less than fifteen aurar.' There was a hum from the crowd at that because a good male slave would cost around twelve aurar of silver and would be arguably more useful around the farm. But the hum died away soon enough. Because Runa was golden and straight and young and beautiful.

'Now then, here is another young honey pot to wrap your ogles around,' he said, pulling a girl up to the block. But the girl wriggled out of his grasp and a warrior showing a beard full of teeth took her roughly by the arm and hauled her back to the block, handing her neck rope back to the slave dealer. He yanked on it and the girl lurched awkwardly then spat in his face and Sigurd cursed under his breath as the dealer back-handed her across the face.

Movement caught Sigurd's eye and he looked across to see Gerth shoulder through the crowd, sword in hand. The trader looked up, eyes bulging like boiled eggs as Gerth scythed his blade at him, opening him up from left shoulder to his right hip. The crowd roared and Sigurd, already moving, hauled Troll-Tickler from its scabbard.

'No, lad. Hold fast. Hold fast!' It was Olaf, his arms clamped round Sigurd like roots on a rock, and Sigurd could not move. 'We can do nothing,' Olaf growled, his beard bristles filling Sigurd's ear as Sigurd watched a man plunge a spear into Gerth's back and Gerth's cousin Svanild screamed. Suddenly warriors schooled like fish, blades glinting everywhere like scales, and two more spears were sunk into Gerth who was on his knees now, staring helplessly at his shrieking cousin. 'Put the blade

away, Sigurd,' Olaf said. 'We can't help Runa if we're dead.'
The crowd was thinning like smoke, though there were enough
there still who had been persuaded by the sight of blood to stay
and watch how it played out. Sigurd saw Loker turn his back
on Gerth and move off with the rest. He glimpsed Hendil then,
walking off laughing with another man, as Olaf with the tide's
persuasion turned him away from the slaughter. 'We're leaving,
lad, which is easier without a foot of spear in you.'

Sigurd sheathed Troll-Tickler and walked away, risking a
glance over his shoulder as they moved off with the crowd back
up to the market. Warriors had made a shieldwall before the
slaving block so that he could not see Runa now, nor the bloody
ruin of the dealer or Gerth who had shown no fear as they killed
him. But he saw Randver clearly enough, the jarl craning his
silver-torced neck, his eyes hopping across the crowd like fleas
over a fur, looking for those he had known would come. And as
Sigurd walked away he let his own mind weave the tapestry of
Jarl Randver standing there, so that it would hang in his memory
as a reminder of a face he would see dead. If his own wyrd was
not poisoned by the same blight that had struck his kin's.

Away from the sea they went, the merchants and traders full
of the chatter of what had happened, filling the air with jokes
about the slave dealer being paid in steel instead of silver, and
mutterings that that is what is ever likely to happen when pretty
girls are involved.

And Sigurd hoped that neither the gods nor his brothers and
father were watching from Valhöll.

CHAPTER SEVEN

'STILL, IT WAS A GOOD DEATH,' ASLAK SAID, THE WORDS ESCAPING FROM somewhere in the purple lumpen mess of his face.

'Ha! You think that was a good death?' Olaf challenged him. 'Gods, but it is going to be tiring work burying all of you young fools.'

'Well I am ashamed for standing there while our brother got himself filled with spears,' Svein muttered into his beard.

Sigurd said nothing but he did not need to for the others to know what he thought about it. He felt the shame of it hot on his face and did not want to draw more attention to it with words.

'We are being tested,' Olaf said, biting into a hunk of smoked boar's meat that he had bought from the market on their way back to meet Solveig and *Otter* across the other side of the island. 'I'll grant you it is a sore fucking test but they often are.' His eyes were on Svein and Aslak but Sigurd knew that the words were for him. 'You saw how many blood-worms rasped up scabbards when Gerth chose his moment to show everybody what a short-wit he was. I stopped counting after twenty.'

They had rowed to a little island off Rennisøy, pulled *Otter* up onto the shingle and now sat on a large flat rock looking north over the calm water they had crossed.

124

'That arsehole Jarl Randver appeared out of nowhere,' Loker said. 'Did you see him, Sigurd?'

'Sigurd saw him,' Olaf confirmed. 'The lad's hackles grew hackles.' Sigurd looked up at him then, their eyes locking for a moment. 'Your father was just the same as a young man and would not have lived long enough to become jarl if I had not held on to his tail when he was frothing at the mouth.'

Sigurd would have taken offence at this had he not heard his father say the same thing enough times over his mead horn.

'It is a test,' Olaf went on. 'Old One-Eye is laying this thing out for us like waves before the bow. Any fool can get his sword red only to get himself hacked to pieces a heartbeat later. You think that will buy you a saga tale? Pah! That won't even get you a skald's fart. Not a decent skald anyway.'

'And not a decent fart,' Solveig put in.

'It is like tafl then,' Svein suggested, which might have been the cleverest thing he had ever said for all eyes turned to him and his face flushed as red as his beard.

'Exactly like tafl,' Olaf agreed through a mouth full of meat. 'You move your pieces around the board and you use your wits doing it. And when you are in a stronger position than your opponent you finish him.' He grimaced, fluttering greasy fingers at them all. 'In case it has escaped your notice, we are not in this stronger position. We have barely one piece left on the board and must be clever with it.' He almost smiled then, but Gerth's death had been a blow even to Olaf who thought the man a fool. 'But we are still in the game,' he said. 'And Óðin still has one eye to watch it with.'

'You think Jarl Randver knew you were there?' Aslak asked, turning the mess of his face first to Sigurd then Olaf.

'He couldn't know it,' Olaf replied. 'I didn't see Gerth say much while he cut that mouthy trader in half nor when Randver's men sheathed their spears in him.'

'He knew, Uncle,' Sigurd said.

Olaf shrugged as if to say maybe he did, maybe he didn't.

A silence fell over them then as each man turned over in his mind all that had happened in the last days. They had lost Gerth but gained Aslak, meaning that they were seven again, and only five with any experience of the blood-fray. Seven against not only the most powerful jarl in Rogaland, but against Gorm Biflindi, Shield-Shaker, to whom a dozen other jarls owed fealty. Somewhere the gods were laughing. Sigurd could almost hear it amongst the whisper of the sea and the shriek of gulls. The gods were laughing.

But at least that meant they were watching.

'Tell me more about Asgot,' Sigurd said, turning to Aslak.

'Aye, so they're too squeamish to cut his throat, are they?' Olaf asked.

Aslak dabbed at the split in his bottom lip which had opened again with eating. 'Two days after they took us some of the king's men came to Jarl Randver's hall. They wanted to know how the raid had gone, wanted to know how many thegns Randver had lost in it.' He grinned fresh blood onto his lip. 'But really they wanted to know how much plunder Randver had got his hands on.'

'A king must make sure his jarls do not grow richer than him or else he will not sleep well at all,' Loker said as though it were the wisest counsel a man could hear.

'So they brought us into the hall along with half of the plunder,' Aslak said.

'As much as half?' Olaf remarked wryly, one eyebrow arching.

'They did not show Gorm's men Runa,' Aslak went on, glancing at Sigurd. Sigurd nodded. That was no surprise, for King Gorm was a famous tickler of women's ears. He had more bed slaves than hunting hounds and was even said to have three wives. But Jarl Randver wanted to keep hold of Runa.

'Aye, well there was more chance of Yggdrasil pulling up its roots and walking off than there was of Randver selling your sister at the block,' Solveig said, which got a murmur of agreement all round.

'The king's men looked us over and the one who spoke for

them, a dangerous-looking cunny called Bok, told the jarl he was welcome to sell us for whatever profit he could make. Bok also told the jarl he could keep the rest of the plunder he had taken from Skudeneshavn, that of Jarl Harald's silver which Randver must have forgotten to show him. So long as Jarl Randver gave the king *Reinen.*'

'It doesn't do for a jarl to have better ships than a king,' Olaf said.

'Randver was not happy about that,' Aslak said, 'but he held the grin in his beard and had his men bring a gift out for Bok to take back to the king.'

'Asgot,' Hendil said, untangling the knot of it.

'Some gift, hey,' Svein said.

Aslak grinned, licking the blood from his lip. 'They had hooded him like a damned hawk for fear of his spells. No one was very keen on touching him and even when they hauled him into the hall everyone reached for their mjöllnirar and sword hilts and the air was thick with whispers as men sought the gods' protection from Jarl Harald's priest.'

Even now Svein touched the iron Thór's hammer that hung at his throat because just the thought of earning Asgot's hate was enough to set men's teeth on edge. Sigurd nodded for Aslak to go on with the tale.

'Jarl Randver told Bok that Asgot was his gift to the king, and now it was Bok's turn to etch a smile onto the granite of his face,' he said.

'Doesn't do to turn down a gift freely given,' Olaf said.

Aslak grinned. 'Of course, every man, woman and dog in that hall knew that the real reason Randver was giving the king Asgot was because he didn't dare to kill him himself.'

'When I was a boy I heard about a jarl from Hardangervidda who killed his godi,' Solveig put in. 'By the next full moon the jarl's cock had turned black and by the moon after that it had fallen off.' This put grimaces in beards.

'They handed Asgot over,' Aslak said. 'You could hear him spitting curses inside that sack they'd tied over his head, and to give Bok his due he took hold of Asgot firmly enough, as though to show that curses meant nothing to him. That was when I heard Bok say he'd like to hear Asgot curse the tide.'

'Curse the tide?' Svein said, taking the ale skin which Hendil offered him and rinsing his insides with the stuff.

'Aye, well there's no mystery in that,' Olaf said, drawing all eyes to him. 'King Gorm's hall sits on the hill overlooking the strait where it's snarled up with islands and skerries. He has boats moored up in the wider channel and they're so close you could jump from one to another.'

This was probably Olaf exaggerating but it might as well have been true given the stranglehold King Gorm had over any skippers who wanted to go north. This was after all how he had become a king in the first place, by filling his sea chests with tolls.

'Nearest Gorm's shore is a narrower channel threading between Karmøy and Bukkøy island and here the water is too shallow for anything deeper than *Little-Elk*, unless you know the channel and its rocks like you know your wife's face,' he said for Svein, Aslak and Hendil who had never been to Avaldsnes. 'There is a place of flat rock bigger than this,' he said, slapping the rock upon which they sat, 'though when the tide comes in you can see no sign of it at all. But it takes a long time to sink and that is the point of it.' His full lips twisted in his beard now as though the words he was about to say tasted foul. He looked at Sigurd. 'Not long after Gorm started calling himself a king and squeezing oaths and silver out of every man with a boat bigger than *Otter*, he invited your father and me up there for a feast. Though in the event the feast had little to do with it. He wanted us to see what he had planned for his unfaithful wife. The whisper was that she had been flattening the straw with Gorm's prow man. Not Moldof then, some troll called Gunthiof. Gorm put his own sword in Gunthiof—' Olaf raised a thick finger '—Gorm can fight. For all that he is, the treacherous whoremonger can fight and don't ever doubt it. But he came up with another scheme for his wife, whose name I do not recall.

They chained her to that flat rock at low tide and we sat down to meat and mead in Biflindi's hall and that night we stumbled down to the shore to see the moon shining on the poor woman's head.' Olaf stretched his neck so that you saw his neck below the beard – a rare sight. 'Her head was the only part of her you could see, mind. Two or three horns later we were blind drunk and she was gone.' He fluttered a hand at Loker who passed him the ale skin. 'They might have fished her out next day or they might have left her for the crabs.' He shrugged. 'We left at dawn and so did the others who had been invited up to Avaldsnes to see it.'

'The woman should have kept her legs crossed,' Solveig muttered, 'for you have to be tired of living to cheat Shield-Shaker.'

And Sigurd wondered what that said about him.

Because he was going to Avaldsnes.

Hendil went first. Not as far as Avaldsnes because of the risk in it, but near enough, to three villages south of King Gorm's long hall, dressed like a nobody and pushing a cart full of goose and duck feathers. Using Sigurd's silver, they had bought most of the down from a merchant on Bokn. The rest they had gathered themselves from nests recently abandoned and in all there were twelve sacks of the stuff piled up on the cart which Hendil had pushed north smiling from ear to ear.

'This is some low cunning,' he had said, lifting the handles to begin his journey, proud to have been chosen for the ruse.

'Hardly,' Olaf had said. 'Peddling feathers and duck shit suits you, Hendil. I doubt Loki is brimmed with envy and wishing he had the shrewd in him to have come up with it.'

Hendil had shrugged, steadied the cart and been on his way, and despite what Olaf said, it had been clever enough to choose Hendil for the task, because he was easy to like, which meant people talked to him. In the event, though, he discovered nothing about Asgot in any of the villages. But that had not mattered, for he had met one of the king's thralls and the woman had told Hendil that the royal arse was crying out for new pillows.

Thinking the king would thank her for it, she had invited Hendil up to Shield-Shaker's farm at Avaldsnes and there Hendil had learnt all he needed to know.

'It turns out the king is going to drown Asgot,' Hendil had reported on his return, as pleased to have sold all of his feathers – and at a profit too – as he was to have come back laden with information.

'I thought we knew that bit,' Svein had said, to which Solveig had reminded them that nothing is certain where kings are involved. 'But he has no desire to make a big thing of it,' Hendil went on. 'Everyone up there is itching at the very thought of killing a godi, though most agree if you have to do it then this is the best way.'

'I didn't kill the man,' Olaf growled, mimicking Shield-Shaker, 'my sword slept in its scabbard the whole while and yet he is dead. It must have been Njörd's doing so don't look at me.' He spat. 'Serpent-tongued son of a flea-ridden goat.'

'Huglausi shit,' Loker said, though Sigurd doubted Loker would call King Gorm a coward to his face. *Or* put his sword in a godi come to that.

'So when will it be done?' Sigurd asked.

'When this moon has waned enough that only the fish and the crabs know that your father's godi is chained to a rock with the tide coming in,' Olaf put in before Hendil could reply.

'Or if there is cloud across the moon,' Sigurd said, glancing up at the sky, which drew a curse from Olaf because of course this was the truth of it.

And so now they were rowing *Otter* up the Karmsund Strait as rain dimpled the water and the summer night got as dark as it would at that time of the year. Which was not very dark at all really. Furthermore, what darkness there was would not last long and they knew that if they were still anywhere near Avaldsnes when the sun came up they were dead men.

They were sweat-drenched and puffing and Sigurd's arms had grown impossibly heavy though he said nothing about it and nor would he even were those aching, rock-heavy limbs to drop through *Otter*'s hull and sink them all. They had set off early because they had far to go. Too far without a sail to help them, Hendil had griped, but Solveig had reminded them all that it was not so long ago that no ships had sails and all were moved with muscle alone.

'Give me a sail and I'll get us there with my arse wind alone,' Svein had said, taking one hand off his oar to wave at a knörr sailing south. Two of the knörr's crew waved back which was a good sign for it meant that neither *Otter* nor her crew had any whiff of violence about them. Nor was *Otter* big enough to tempt other ships into attacking her for plunder, her thwarts being clearly full of flesh and bone and not silver or ivory or furs. Though this time they came armed, for all that none of it was on show. Olaf had even brought his brynja because he thought the scheme had such a poor chance of working and said that if it came to a fight, which it probably would, then he would fight in his brynja and kill as many men as he could.

Where they could they stayed within a stone's throw of the shore as this way they were at least some of the time concealed by bluffs and skerries. Often, though, they were right out in the channel and at these times Sigurd's heart hammered in his chest and his palms grew slick on the oar stave. They barely spoke, for all knew how well a man's voice will carry across water, and yet only Svein seemed as calm as the fjord, a half grin nestled in his beard like a cat in straw, as though it was all a fine adventure. As for the others, their eyes shone in the gloom and Sigurd supposed he would have heard their hearts pounding too if not for the rhythmic *splosh* of the oar blades. Solveig worked the tiller and Loker, who claimed his eyesight was so good that he had once seen Rán, mother of the waves, casting her nets in the dark depths, hung over *Otter*'s bow, peering below the surface for rocks that might be their undoing.

Sigurd had brought sword, axe and shield, but they were safely stowed in the thwarts, as were Svein's. In the leather nestbaggin at his feet were the things he would need, the items they had managed to lay hands on at such short notice. Lying across the thwarts behind him was just over five feet of new pine trunk and this was perhaps the most important thing they had brought, despite Olaf still having no confidence in the whole idea. Not least since they had passed the vik just south of Kopervik and so now had a foot firmly inside the bear's cave.

Every now and then a fish jumped somewhere out there in the murk, each *plunk* yanking on taut nerves and turning heads, though it was not likely that any skipper would be sailing at night, which each of them knew, if only he stopped to think about it.

'The last thing Biflindi or any of his arse welts will be expecting is for Harald's last breathing son to come within sight of Karmsundet let alone within sniffing distance of the royal shit bucket,' Olaf had said, 'but it won't matter who we are if we get up to the skerries where he collects his tolls. They'll think we're a crew of halfwits trying to slip through the net without paying and they'll kill us just the same. Dead is dead, as my father used to say.'

So now Solveig was looking for the skerries that sat in the middle of that stretch of water which was the entrance to the fairway men called the north road, for these rocky islands were as far as *Otter* would go. Men on the sniff for taxes have noses like hounds, as Hendil had put it, which meant they dared not go beyond that point. And it was Loker's eyes, as the only other pair looking the way they were going, that saw the skerries first. Which in the event came as a great relief after a day's rowing, not least to Olaf's backside which, he moaned, had died somewhere back near Blikshavn.

When they came to the rocks Solveig guided *Otter* into a sheltered inlet that was as dark as the inside of a sealskin purse and there the others pulled in their oars, rolling tired shoulders and shaking the pain from their arms while Loker tied them up to a tooth of rock jutting from the dark water. Somewhere close by a bird took off squawking from its nest, a flash of white in the murk, and something else plopped off a rock into the water.

Inland, towards the king's hall up on the hill, a fire burning out of sight hazed the dark sky with burnished bronze, the tang of smoke brought to Sigurd's nose on the westerly breeze that had wanted to push *Otter* out into the channel. It was a warm breeze, as sweet as Freyja's breath, and Sigurd wondered if the goddess had come down from Asgard to watch them cheat the king.

'Asgot will have the Allfather's ears ringing with curses and spells aimed at Gorm and Randver,' Svein had said when they'd learnt of the godi's fate, and Sigurd had not doubted it. Saving the godi because he had been his father's friend and a Skudeneshavn man was one thing, but perhaps not worth dying for. Saving the man from a drowning death because he was a priest and therefore the gods were ever likely to be watching him? That was worth any risk, because Sigurd had lost everything, including the gods' favour, and perhaps some act of courage and daring would turn back that ill-lucked tide. And these thoughts hung like loom weights in his mind now as he looked at the distant shoreline which gleamed as though the stones upon it yet held an ember of the day's light.

'It may not be tonight,' Olaf said, threading his arms through his brynja's sleeves, then throwing them up above his head so that the weight of those iron rings pulled the whole thing down and over his head and torso like water from a pail. 'Or they may have done it already and there are crabs down there puking their guts up,' he said, shrugging his shoulders to help the rings settle and find their place. He strapped on his sword belt and tucked an axe into it but left his helmet and shield in the boat.

'It is tonight, Uncle,' Sigurd said, taking off his tunic and leaving it with his weapons by the row bench. He did not know how he knew that but he did. Hendil and Loker lifted the pine trunk from *Otter*'s thwarts and passed it to Svein who laid it across his muscled shoulders and waited for Sigurd who was tying the haversack of essentials over his own shoulder so that it hung across his back.

Hendil stepped ashore to join them, buckling his own sword belt and gripping an ash spear in his left hand.

'Wait for us as long as you can,' Sigurd said to Solveig and Loker whose eyes he could just see, by the glow coming off the water. 'But don't be here when it starts getting light.'

'With just the two of us rowing we'd need to set off yesterday,' Solveig grumbled, which was not far off the truth, but Sigurd could not concern himself with that now.

'Are you ready, Svein?' he asked, making sure the scramasax at his waist was secure in its sheath. Other than that blade he was unarmed and Olaf grimaced to see it, though he knew why it had to be so. Svein's answer was a flash of white amongst his beard and with that they turned, Sigurd, Svein, Olaf and Hendil, and set off across the rock like shadows chasing after bodies which had cast them off.

They splashed through shallow pools, slipping now and then on slick weed thrown up by the last high tide, then came up onto higher ground and pushed north over the skerry's spine, Olaf leading the way, a dark, looming, upright shape against the barren rockscape. Sigurd came next with Hendil behind him and Svein at the rear lumbering like some mountain troll with the pine log across his shoulders. The air was cool against Sigurd's skin. The whisper of the sea against the skerry's sinking edge seeped into his ears beneath his own hot breath and his beating pulse, and he felt like a boy again, up to mischief on a summer's night. He hoped that the tide had not already risen high enough to seep into Asgot's mouth and lungs, choking his curses and drowning him. And he hoped that the gods were watching.

Soon Olaf threw a hand back and hissed, crouching, and the others bent low or went down onto their haunches as Sigurd saw the glow from a fire up ahead beyond a swell of rock. A man's voice drifted over the skerry followed by laughter as flat as a stone skimmed across the bay and Sigurd licked dry lips and clutched the Óðin amulet hanging round his neck. His stomach felt like it was full of startled moths as he watched Olaf signal to Hendil to take off his sword belt and move up to get a better look. For Olaf's mail would scrape noisily on the rock, whereas

Hendil, in nothing more than leather and wool, could crawl as quietly as a fox to a hen coop.

Even so, Sigurd held his breath as Hendil, his spear left behind, skulked past him and bellied up the swell until the top of his head stuck out against the iron grey and darker charcoal sky. Another voice carried over to them, the sense of the words shredded by the breeze, but loud enough so that Sigurd wondered how they had not heard them before, how they had almost blundered into a camp and burnt their feet on their fire.

In the time it takes to put an edge back on a sharp knife Hendil returned, the white of his palm bright as he spread the fingers wide. Sigurd and Olaf nodded. Five men and no doubt well armed was not something to be taken lightly. But then from the slur of their voices it seemed the sentries were making the best of being stuck out there on that barren rock while their friends flattened the straw with women or slept off the mead in their lord's hall.

Svein laid the pine log down and hauled his big scramasax out of its scabbard. Hendil gave Sigurd his spear and drew his sword and Olaf gripped his sword in one hand and his short axe in the other. No one said a word but each man knew they would have to be fast. They would have to hit the men together, like a wave against the strand, and kill fast before any of the sentries had a chance to run or signal to the far shore.

They will not be expecting us, Sigurd told himself, the blood-thrill announcing itself in his trembling hands. That strange feeling was in the big muscles of his thighs too and he did not try to fight it but rather let the sensation course through his body, filling bone and flesh, warming him from the inside out like spiced mead.

Olaf gestured for Svein to work his way round the left of the mound before them and Sigurd nodded at the low cunning in this, for any boat the king's men had would be down at the water's edge and so that was the way they would flee.

Svein moved off and for twenty heartbeats Sigurd and the others watched him go. Then Olaf was up and Sigurd and Hendil rose beside him and together they ran up the swell, tight-lipped as the dead, and as they came over to fall upon King Gorm's men Olaf threw his axe which thunked into a man's chest before the man could have known what was coming. Another hauled at his sword's hilt but drew not a foot of it before Sigurd's spear struck him in the chest and he dropped to his knees clutching at the shaft. Another warrior raised his spear, growling, and thrust it at Olaf who twisted his torso and scythed down with strength and edge enough to sever the shaft. Then he swung the blade back up, lopping off the man's left arm and taking him under the chin to cleave his face in two before he could scream.

Another man fled. Straight into Svein. Not fancying his chances against Svein's scramasax, even armed with a good spear as he was, the sentry turned and got a belly full of Hendil's sword. Hendil clutched the man's beard braid and hauled him further onto his blade which he rammed home up to the cross guard, spitting curses into the man's face.

The last of them knew better than to waste his breath begging for his life. He threw down his spear in disgust, turned towards Olaf and dropped to his knees. For a moment he looked up at Sigurd, a spark of recognition perhaps flashing in his eyes, then he nodded at Olaf, trusting the sharpness of the mailed warrior's sword, and tilted his head forward.

'Give him your blade, Hendil,' Olaf growled, and so Hendil did. The warrior wrapped his fingers around the hilt and smiled. Then Olaf's sword flashed in the gloom and took off his head.

They were on the island's edge and Olaf pointed his gore-slick blade out across the water to another rock a good arrow-shot away. 'If he's not drowned yet he'll be somewhere out there,' he said.

But Sigurd could see no sign of Asgot. Taking off his shoes he turned to look at the far shore which sat below the king's hall, his eyes searching for movement there, his ears sifting the breeze for any commotion that would tell him that someone had seen the fight on the island, which was not impossible due to the glow from the fire crackling beside them.

All quiet it seemed.

'We'll tie rocks to them and sink them,' Olaf said, gesturing at the nearest of King Gorm's dead men. 'It will look as though they vanished like sea mist.' Sigurd nodded as Svein came back over the swell with the pine log across his shoulders and a few moments later he and Sigurd eased themselves down into the water, their breath catching in their chests with the coldness of it. There were little lights in the water, fishes' eyes glowing in the dark, and Sigurd could feel slimy weed beneath his feet and sharper things, mussels and limpets stuck to the rocks.

'Don't you go and bloody drown,' Olaf said over his shoulder, retrieving his axe from a dead man's chest. 'I don't want to be coming down there to pull you from Rán's cold embrace. That would rot this brynja and you don't have the silver to buy me another.'

Sigurd did not reply. He and Svein had their arms over the pine trunk and their chins all but resting on the rough, scaly bark whilst their bodies found their own buoyancy. Without a word they kicked their legs beneath the water to push themselves off, keeping their bellies full of air and trying not to break the surface with their feet. Then out into deeper water, legs stirring the cold depths, the sound of the sea against the rocks fading with the fire's copper behind them as they kicked into the darkness, pushing the pine log before them.

It was dark and cold and the breeze was pushing low waves against the left side of Sigurd's face, but before they had slipped into the water he had fixed the moon's place in the sky, the cloud-veiled glow of it anyway, and by glancing up now and then, or turning to see where they were in relation to the fire on the island behind them, he was able to keep them on the right course. At least, the course which Olaf had shown them.

They swam and they shivered and in the darkness it was hard to know how far they had gone. Sigurd was about to say as much to Svein when he heard oars in the water.

They stopped kicking and held their breath, ears straining to weigh up the sound, Svein's eyes glowing in the murk. But within no time they were drifting on the current like sea wrack and so they kicked again lest they undo the hard work they had put in so far. But the dipping of oars was getting louder. They stopped again, holding their position as best they could by flailing their legs directly below them and gripping the log as though their lives depended on it. Which more than likely they did.

Then Svein hissed and Sigurd followed his line of sight and saw the boat they had known was out there somewhere. Saw the black shape of it and knew it was smaller than *Otter* by a foot, perhaps two, not that that was any comfort as it came straight for them, four pairs of oars pulling it against the current.

'They'll see us,' Svein hissed, and they would too, because Sigurd and Svein's pale arms would show against the darker bark as they clung on. They could not grip the log any other way because Svein had lopped off the little stumps and knobs where branches had been, and to take their arms off the log risked being carried off with the current.

The boat was getting closer now, so that they could hear the voices of those rowing.

'Your belt,' Sigurd hissed, fumbling with one hand to undo the buckle beside the hilt of his scramasax. Svein did the same as Sigurd pulled the belt off and threw one end over the trunk then reached underneath to gather it up. When Svein had done likewise they turned the log to shield them from the view of those in the boat and held on to their belts with two hands, their heads all but submerged so that the waves washed over their faces, the salt stinging Sigurd's eyes as he shivered and stayed corpse-still, waiting for the shout to go up from the little boat's crew.

At one point the king's men were no more than four spear-lengths away and Sigurd had thought they would hear his teeth chattering for he was getting very cold now. And it seemed as if the boat was taking an age to pass, so that Sigurd was glad that his ears were waterlogged for he could not hear the gods laughing at him half drowning to avoid a spearing. But the eight oars dipped and rose, dipped and rose, and the boat headed back to the king's shore leaving Sigurd and Svein freezing but alive. Better still, they knew it must have come from the rock upon which Asgot had been left to drown and so they turned their tree trunk north-east and kicked some warmth into their freezing flesh.

Ahead of them Sigurd saw a flash of white and for a moment he could not say what it was but then his eyes made sense of it. Two swans were gliding side by side across the water, their feathers raised like sails to catch the breeze, and Sigurd wondered if Asgot had sent the birds to show him the way. They followed the swans and after what seemed a long time they began to feel weed-slick rock beneath their feet. Then they clambered up, bringing the pine log with them, stumbling and falling now and then because the water was up to their thighs and they could not see where they were putting their feet. Sigurd turned to look for the swans but the creatures had vanished. Yet, this was the place. Surely.

They waded on, numb-legged, the pine log back on Svein's shoulders, scramasaxes belted at their waists and the wet skin of their arms raised into bumps by the breeze. And they did not need the swans to tell them that the pale, knotty figure a stone's throw off to their left was Asgot.

The godi was on his knees, the water up to his gnarly collar bones and soaking his beard which had been stripped of any silver, though the little white bones were knotted there still. He twisted at their approach and with his neck stretched above the brine seemed to be sniffing the air like some beast, lips hitched back from his teeth.

'Rán will not have you tonight, Asgot,' Sigurd said, the words slurred through frozen, trembling lips.

'That greedy bitch was never going to have me,' Asgot gnarred, lifting his chained right arm out of the water and spitting into the waves, which had Svein touching the iron hammer at his neck – and Sigurd did not blame him for they would still have to swim all the way back and Rán was not the kind of goddess you wanted for an enemy.

Sigurd took the nestbaggin off his back and with a shaking hand reached inside, pulling from it a hammer and chisel. Svein squatted in the water beside Asgot holding the pine trunk so that Sigurd could use it as a work bench.

'Harald's whelp and Styrbiorn's troll,' Asgot said through the twist of his white lips. 'King Gorm will be pissing in his boots.' And yet for all that the godi seemed unimpressed, he nevertheless put his iron-ringed wrist on Svein's log so that Sigurd could place the chisel on the join and take his hammer to it.

'We can leave you here, godi,' Sigurd offered before striking the first blow.

But Asgot chuckled at that. 'I think I'll come with you, young Sigurd,' he said, 'for all that I'd like to see Biflindi's face when he sees this ring empty in the morning.' Svein winced at the sharp *chink* of steel against steel but after five strikes the iron split and Asgot took his arm away, rubbing his wrist with the other hand.

'Not empty,' Sigurd said, opening the haversack again. This time he fetched out a fox's leg, the dark fur soaked and slick and the flesh of the severed end white and bloodless after being in the water so long. He grabbed hold of the dark paw, squeezing it to bring the claws together, then pushed it through the iron manacle as far as it would go before the leg became too thick near the thigh. Hopefully the leg would remain wedged in there even at high tide with the currents playing with it.

Svein was grinning like a fiend and Asgot, who understood the trick of it, muttered to the Allfather and Loki the Mischief God that he hoped they were watching this.

For next day, when the tide went out, King Gorm and his people would return expecting to see a crab-picked, wave-licked corpse lying on that flat rock. Instead they would find a fox's leg and perhaps none would even dare go near enough to see that the iron ring was broken. The story would jump around Avaldsnes like fleas that Jarl Harald's godi had shape-shifted into a creature with teeth sharp enough to gnaw through its own leg and escape the tide-death coming for it.

'That is some powerful seiðr,' Asgot said.

But for now there was a blush of dawn light in the east and they needed to be gone. Asgot was corpse-white and bone-stiff, the strange swirls and patterns all over his body seeming alive with his shivering. But he was alive.

And the gods were watching.

Runa could still feel the trembling deep in her bones, though she told herself that no one else would notice it. Not by the light of the cod-oil lamps chain-hung from the great beams of the jarl's mead hall.

She would never have imagined that the slave trader's blood could fly so far as to slap her face when Gerth had cleaved the man apart, but she thought she could still taste the iron tang of it in her mouth. She could still hear her friend Svanild's scream deep in her ears, as though it had burrowed in there like a maggot and could not find its way out. When she closed her eyes she could still see Gerth's face, like a stain behind her eyelids, as Randver's men plunged their spears into his back and sides. Gerth's expression had been one of fury and shame because he knew he had failed to save his cousin. Or was the fury for his sword-brothers, who had not burst from the crowd to fight beside him?

For Runa had seen Olaf and Svein and Hendil, despite their attempts to blend in with the merchants, craftsmen and farmers. She had seen Sigurd too, and the sight of him had stopped her breath like a bung in a flask. Randver's thegns had told her that her father and brothers were dead, killed in a fight up near King Gorm's hall at Avaldsnes, and when she had heard this Runa had wanted to die too, for it meant all was lost.

But seeing Sigurd alive at the slave market on Rennisøy, close enough that she could have called out to him, had hauled her spirits out of that dark mire and set her heart pounding in her chest like a hammer on an anvil.

And Runa suspected that the trembling in her bones now was not because she had been as close to blood and death that day as a warrior in the third row of the shieldwall, or even because of the horror of seeing her friend sold to some greasy-bearded karl – for that had been Svanild's wyrd when the chaos had passed and Randver's men had dragged the gory bodies away. No, Runa was shaking because Sigurd was somehow alive! He had escaped the death that had taken the rest of their family, even their mother, whom Runa had last seen being cut down by one of Randver's warriors though not before she had opened another man's belly with her scramasax.

Her brother, who men whispered was Óðin-favoured, was alive. And she knew he would come for her.

'What's the matter, girl? Not hungry?'

She glared at Jarl Randver, letting the hate in her eyes wrap around him like an ill-weather cloak, but the jarl simply shrugged and turned back to the man with whom he was talking and drinking.

She had been so desperate to lock eyes with Sigurd, to let him know that she had seen him, if only to stop him doing something stupid, for perhaps he did not know that Jarl Randver had seeded the crowd with his warriors. Yet though it had taken every ounce of will she possessed, she had avoided her brother's eye, for she knew Amleth, Randver's second son, was watching her. She could feel his eyes in her flesh like a hawk's talons, and was sure Amleth would know the moment she looked at Sigurd.

Then Gerth had stormed from the crowd and the slave dealer had died by Gerth's sword before Svanild's kinsman had been slaughtered in his turn and Runa had willed Sigurd to stay hidden and not let his pride get him killed too. Perhaps the Allfather had guided her brother then which was why Sigurd had not drawn his sword and waded into the fray, though Runa doubted it. Did not Óðin's very name mean 'frenzy' and if anything the Spear-God would have urged Sigurd on and laughed as the blood flew.

More likely was that her father's sword-brother Olaf had guided Sigurd's blade back into its scabbard. With Harald's bloodline all but snuffed out by oath-breakers and ambitious men, Olaf would surely not let Sigurd throw his life away so cheaply. He had treated all of Harald and Grimhild's children as his own and

Runa knew he would protect Sigurd now, which was a comfort to her.

And yet, as she sat in their enemy's hall eating his meat and drinking his mead, Runa could not salve the disappointment which smarted like a burn that her brother had not tried to rescue her. She was ashamed of herself for it but there it was. For she had seen the way Amleth and the jarl's eldest son Hrani looked at her, like men wondering how they might steal a man's sword from under his nose. Even their little half-brother Aki, who could not have been older than eleven, stared at her with undisguised hunger, which gave Runa the feeling of ants crawling up her arms and the back of her neck. But of the sons only Hrani had come with the jarl to Skudeneshavn that day, bringing death and despair, and she hated him for it.

'Your mother was not to be harmed,' Jarl Randver had told Runa when his ship had moored at the wharf at Hinderå and his blood-lust had receded like the tide. 'But she opened Andvett's guts and his friend did not stop to see if she would do the same to him.'

Runa had watched Andvett writhing in the thwarts of Randver's ship, his glistening purple gut rope bulging from a hideous wound, the green wool of his tunic having wicked so much blood it looked black.

The other men had gathered round him grim-faced, assuring him of his place in Valhöll and giving him messages for their friends and fathers who were already there. Not that Andvett cared for all that, gnashing his teeth and mewling as he was.

He had died before Randver's thegns had taken down *Fjord-Wolf*'s snarling prow, when the jarl's hall was still but a dark imposing shape on the gull-wreathed heights, and Runa had seen Randver's face pale when another man brought him the news. But for all her fear, Runa had brimmed with pride in her mother, in her courage and refusal to yield. And she had thought that Harald, if he still lived, would be proud of Grimhild too.

But now she knew that her father was dead. Her brother Sorli too. Murdered up in Avaldsnes by Biflindi, the traitor king.

'Well she is pretty but for all we know she might have no teeth in that cat's arse of a mouth of hers,' the man beside Randver said now, leaning round the jarl to get a good look at her. 'Perhaps she does not think much of your mead, Jarl Randver.' Runa did not know who Randver's guest was but she knew she would like to put a blade in his eye.

Randver wafted a hand in her direction. 'Ah, she is brooding because her brother did not think her worth fighting for,' he said. Then he held her eye, his lips curling in his fair beard. 'But he *was* there, your brother, wasn't he, girl? That fool whom my men skewered, he had gone there with young Sigurd, I'd wager an eyrir on it.' Runa kept her face as changeless as a sleeping sea, giving nothing away. Randver shrugged. 'Clearly your brother did not think much of his witless friend either, to stand there and watch him speared like an animal.'

'King Gorm could not kill my brother and neither could you,' Runa said, unable to hold her tongue any longer and letting her eyes sharpen themselves on the jarl's face. A hush swept across Jarl Randver's hall, warriors and women hungry to hear what Jarl Harald's girl had to say to their lord. The weight of it was like an anchor on Runa's chest but she held her chin high and kept her eyes on Randver's. Was she not a jarl's daughter? Only Randver's hounds could see her legs trembling under the table. 'My brother is Óðin-favoured,' she said, loud enough for all to hear. 'As anyone who knows him will attest. You—' she turned, raking them all with her glare '—all of you will regret making an enemy of him.'

Jarl Randver's eyes narrowed. Was that respect she saw in their flame-played depths? Or murder? 'Your brother has barely grown into his beard,' he said. 'He is alone in this world and his future is not now what it once was. He is nothing.'

'Then why are your men looking for him?' Runa asked. There was some murmuring amongst the drinkers then.

'Slap the insolent bitch!' a man barked.

'Give her to Skarth to play with,' a woman called, Skarth being Jarl Randver's new champion and prow man, and Runa's courage wavered at that, for up until now no man there, or anywhere come to that, had touched her in that way. And in her gut she knew it was only a matter of time before one of them did.

'My men are looking for your brother because I am a generous man and I have decided that I am willing to accept his oath of fealty, along with that of any who are foolish enough to follow him like hounds after scraps.' The jarl smiled then. 'And for all that your own value has . . . well . . . sunk, your dowry not now what it once might have been, still my second son Amleth has it on his mind to marry you.'

Amleth at least had the decency to flush red beneath his beard at that, putting his horn to his mouth and drinking deeply, avoiding Runa's eye.

She had heard whispers of this but hearing it now, and from the jarl himself, was another thing. She felt as though the bench was a skiff adrift, the reed-strewn floor an undulating storm-stirred fjord.

She felt sea sick.

'For what it is worth, your brother's blessing on the marriage would smooth the waters around here,' Randver went on. 'My men tell me that the folk of Skudeneshavn have not taken well to the changing tide. More importantly, some of the wealthier karls and more powerful men are watching to see how things unfurl.'

This at least was no surprise. Other jarls would be uneasy about the king's betrayal of his oathman Jarl Harald, wary too of the newly forged alliance between Gorm and Randver. Calming the waters with Jarl Harald's people, moreover with his son and daughter, would be no bad thing from where Jarl Randver was sitting at Hinderå.

Like a snail before a crow, Runa retreated back into her shell, wishing she had her mother's courage. She yearned to stand up and defy them all, as Grimhild had defied some of the very men before her now, her scramasax lashing out like a bear's claw. But even as she wished it the men and the few women drinking at the other benches turned back to their own conversations and the hall was soon humming once again.

'Is it true they burnt Jarl Harald's hall?' the man beside Randver asked. 'Eik-hjálmr. That was its name, wasn't it?' Runa listened.

Jarl Randver nodded though clearly did not wish to talk about it.

'A shame,' his guest said, shaking his head. 'It was a fine mead hall. Bigger than this one, hey?' The jarl did not like that, not one bit. Yet he held his tongue, which told Runa that the other man must be someone important. From what she had seen of her captor he was not normally a man to keep his tongue sheathed on a matter that meant something to him. 'Men said it was a hall to rival Hrothgar's hall Heorot,' the guest went on. He made a ring of his arms, fingers laced. 'Roof posts a man couldn't get his arms around.' He looked up at his host's soot-blackened, smoke-slung roof. 'Beams you could hollow out and sail across the open sea.'

'The girl's people will build me a new one,' Jarl Randver said. 'Once they accept that I am their jarl now. Perhaps Amleth and Runa will remain here and I will go there.' He shrugged as though it meant little, then gestured at a serving girl to fill his guest's horn and then his own. 'These things take time.'

The other man nodded. 'Well when you dig this young Sigurd out of whatever troll hole he's hiding in, send someone to fetch me for I would like to meet him.' Randver nodded. 'What about Jarl Harald's godi?' the man went on. 'Is it true what folk are saying about him? That he escaped a drowning death at Avaldsnes by shape-shifting?'

Jarl Randver was clearly tiring of his guest. He sat back in his chair, his handsome brow furrowed. 'Do you believe it, Broddi?' he asked. It was as though the scales were out and he would be judging the man on the answer he gave.

'A fox's leg? That's what they found chained on Biflindi's flat rock. That is what I have heard,' Broddi said.

The jarl nodded. 'So they say.'

'I suppose foxes can swim, though I have never seen it,' Broddi said. Then he leant forward. 'Why don't we ask the girl? She must know if her father's priest was capable of such a thing.' Jarl Randver shrugged and tipped his mead horn towards Runa, inviting Broddi to do what he must. 'Well, Haraldsdóttir? Could your father's godi have turned himself into a fox and chewed off his own leg to escape the king's chains?'

Runa felt a smile nestle on her lips then, the first one since before that day when she had watched her father's warriors and two of her own brothers slaughtered out in the Karmsund Strait, which seemed so long ago now.

'I am just surprised he did not change himself into an otter and swim away when the tide came in,' she said.

CHAPTER EIGHT

THE SWIM BACK TO THE ISLAND WHERE OLAF AND THE OTHERS WERE waiting had seemed to take half the time of the one out to Asgot's rock. That had less to do with the godi's thin legs adding to the kick and more to do with the renewed strength that flooded Sigurd and Svein's limbs at seeing the rope of their scheme play out so neatly.

'Low cunning can be a better weapon than any sword,' Sigurd's father had told him once, and having the godi back now was proof of that. But when they were drying by a fire Asgot confirmed that King Gorm was looking for Sigurd.

'He will not rest until you are dead,' he said, picking flesh from the bones of a fish he had cooked over the fire. 'He was beyond fury that his men let you escape that day in the woods.'

'It was Sorli who let me escape,' Sigurd said, 'and Asbjorn and Finn.' His mind weaved those last moments when his sword-brothers had run at King Gorm and how Biflindi's men had closed around the king like a fist, giving Sigurd the chance he needed. Sorli and those other two brave men had bought Sigurd's life with their own.

Asgot blew on the steaming white meat between his fingers then popped the flakes into his mouth. 'Gorm's champion Moldof is not the man he was.'

'He lives?' Sigurd had watched his father cut the huge warrior's sword arm off at the elbow. Usually a man bled to death from such a wound, unless he could burn the flesh to seal it and even that could kill him. But Moldof was granite-hard, for all that he would no longer be his king's prow man.

'He lives but he broods like a troll-wife in the dark corner of Gorm's hall because the king is ashamed of him for losing that fight against your father.'

'We would do well to put a knife in Moldof's heart at the first opportunity,' Olaf said, 'for a one-armed man out to prove himself can be more dangerous than a two-armed man who is happy with a mead horn in one hand and a wench in the other.' This got some murmurs of agreement.

Asgot fixed his eyes on Sigurd's. 'To the king, leaving you alive is like leaving a flame unattended in his hall in high summer. Better to snuff you out, boy.' He half grinned, licking his fingers. 'He has men all over Karmøy looking for you, Sigurd Haraldarson, and Jarl Randver will have his hounds sniffing for you from Bokn to Tysvær.' He glanced at Olaf. 'You were fools to think Twigbelly or Jarl Leiknir would help you keep your head down. Now that Randver is Gorm's chained wolf there is not a jarl or any man of note within twenty days' sailing who will put themselves on the wrong side of those two.' He picked up his cup and drained it. 'Not for the runt of a worm-riddled jarl.'

Sigurd looked at Olaf but he simply stared into the fire, having nothing to say that would add any shine to the grim tale Asgot told. Not that Sigurd saw the situation in a better light. They were just eight men and all that remained of his father's once fearsome war band. The fortunes of the folk of Skudeneshavn had sunk quicker than a quern stone rolled off a jetty and that was the hard truth of it. His sister was Jarl Randver's prisoner and he was being hunted. This was not the golden wyrd he had always imagined the Norns had spun for him.

'So we have no ship, no men and no safe hall to shelter in,' Olaf said glumly. 'What *do* we have?'

'Nothing but a cart full of ill-luck,' Loker said, pulling a louse from his beard and flicking it into the fire.

'It is true that we do not have men,' Asgot said then, 'and neither are we likely to get any, for what fool would tie himself to the mast of a sinking ship?' He looked from Sigurd to Olaf and back to Sigurd, pointing his cup at him accusingly. 'But a thousand spears would be no good to us now because we lack that which we need most of all. It is a prize which your father once had but let slip through his fingers.'

'Silver?' Hendil guessed.

Sigurd shook his head. 'The gods' favour,' he said.

Asgot nodded. 'Most men believe their wyrds are spun long before they are born. That if the Norns have woven him a drowning death then there is nothing to be done about it. Or that a bairn who will not take his mother's breast was wyrded to starve before it ever had the strength to crawl.' He pursed his lips. 'And that is true in most cases,' he said. 'But there are some men in whom the Æsir and the Vanir take a close interest. These men can unpick the threads of their wyrd for good or ill . . .' he held up a finger, 'though more often than not the gods will cut a thread here or tie one there for they cannot help themselves.' All eyes turned to Sigurd now and he felt the weight of them like a brynja. 'It may be that you have it in you to be such a man, Sigurd.' A snarl of teeth showed in the godi's grey beard. 'Or it may be that you will starve before you have crawled.'

'It can be a fool's ambition seeking the attention of the gods,' Olaf grumbled.

'The Allfather must have heard your sword song enough times over the years, Uncle,' Sigurd said. 'He must have watched you and my father cut men and heroes down in the red war. You have hardly lived the life of a farmer.'

Olaf arched a brow. 'That is true, but once you start playing tafl with the gods you run the risk of them tipping up the board for the sulk or mischief of it. They are capricious.' He fluttered meaty fingers. 'Flighty as the fucking wind.'

Asgot nodded. 'Still, the gods like the game and we must play it.'

'Well if you're looking for some poor bastard to stick your knife in for some offering, don't look at me, old man,' Olaf said. 'And as you can see we are running low on thralls these days.' He scratched his beard. 'Besides which, you slit that unlucky lad's throat the day we sailed out to fight Jarl Randver and that did not do us much good as I recall.'

'There are other ways,' Asgot said.

'You know how I can draw old One-Eye's gaze?' Sigurd asked, for as capricious as the Æsir were, he would rather earn their scorn and die trying something than do nothing and be ignored.

'I do, Haraldarson,' Asgot said, but from the twist of his sharp face it looked as if even the thought in his head was painful, which did not bode well.

Asgot seemed to roll the words around his mouth for a while. Or else he was communing with the gods perhaps.

'Well you might as well stop chewing it and spit it out, priest,' Olaf said, 'so that we can all agree it's a goatshit idea and move on from there.'

Sigurd raised a hand to silence Olaf and to his surprise the man fastened his lips, though he gave a shake of his head to show what he thought of where this conversation was leading.

'Tell me, Asgot,' Sigurd said.

'I will tell you soon enough,' he said, 'but first we need to find a place that puts us out of reach of Gorm and Randver's spears.'

Solveig looked up at them, stroking his beard between finger and thumb. 'I know a place,' he said.

They took *Otter* east to Rennisøy, where six of them stayed within reach of the oars while Solveig and Hendil went to buy food and mead with Sigurd's silver. Then they rowed to Mekjarvik and hopped from island to island, rowing the sheltered waters until they could see a headland due east which men called Tau. Not that many men visited that place. The name itself came from the word *taufr*, meaning witchcraft, for it was said that there was a fen there into which the ancient folk offered sacrifices of blood and silver, food, mead and clear water. And when Solveig had suggested the place Asgot's eyes had lit up like wicks in cod oil and later Olaf had growled to Sigurd that he would not be surprised to learn that the godi had put old Solveig up to that suggestion, the two of them going back together as far as the time when Yggdrasil was but a seedling.

Still, a place where few men went was a good place to go and even Olaf could not deny that, as they found a suitable mooring and made their way towards a farmstead up on a hill which was the only dwelling within sight. For it was better to square things with whoever lived there first than have them running off scared into the fen or telling others that outlanders had come to Tau.

The farmer's name was Roldar and he did not care for people much, which was probably why he lived out there in a place where men feared to go. Roldar had a wife called Sigyn, two surly sons named Aleif and Alvi, and a big-boned daughter called Hetha, who Svein made great efforts not to look at, which was a sure sign that he liked the look of her very much. For her part Hetha filled Svein's ale cup to the very brim so that he had to slurp at it or spill it. Then, before the night meal, she made a show of removing the knotted kerchief from her head to rebraid her straw-coloured hair and all for Svein's benefit, until her mother hissed at her to come and help her serve up the broth to their guests.

'So have you seen any ghosts out there?' Loker asked Roldar before he had even put his lips to the fish broth. They were eating outside because there was not the room for them all by Sigyn's hearth. It was plenty warm enough and though midsummer had passed the days were still pleasant and long. 'Any haugbui climbing from his grave or draugr wandering the marsh?'

Olaf glowered because they had hardly begun to talk with Roldar yet and this was not how he had planned to start it.

Roldar matched Olaf with a frown of his own but it was Alvi who nodded, thumbing behind him to the sheep pens and the marshland beyond. 'I've seen one,' the lad said, 'three winters ago when I was mending fences out there. Blue as death it was, and swollen to the size of an ox, its eyes glowing in the moonlight.' His brother scoffed but Alvi took no notice. 'It was sniffing round the sheep and would have carried two of them off, one under each arm, had I not challenged it and thrown my axe.'

'We are lucky to have such a warrior to protect us,' Aleif said through tight lips, earning a black look from their mother who had it all over her that she preferred Alvi to his elder brother.

'And a skald too,' Olaf muttered under his breath, which got a grin from Aleif.

'There are old burial mounds close by?' Asgot asked.

Aslak touched the intricate black soot swirls of Thór's hammer Mjöllnir, which he had etched into his left forearm just up from the wrist, for he was uncomfortable with all this talk of ghosts and spirits.

'It would not surprise me,' Svein rumbled under his breath to Sigurd, 'for now and then I keep getting a nose full of something foul.'

Though they all knew this had less to do with mound dwellers and more to do with the cesspit that had been dug too close to the house. Why it was so close was anybody's guess, for it was not as if Roldar had neighbours or a shortage of land. But then if there *were* draugar nearabouts, who would want to meet one in the black of night while emptying buckets or bowels?

'Seeing as you seem so keen to talk of such things,' Roldar said, frowning, 'there was a man two days' walk from here who was killed by such a creature.' This lifted eyebrows, Sigurd noticed. 'His kin found him with all his bones crushed and his animals dead on the ground around him. Folk said the beasts had been ridden to death.'

Asgot nodded as though he had heard such tales many times. 'The dead long for the things of life. They envy the living.'

'I don't see why they would envy us,' Sigyn told him, 'for as you can see we do not have much.' Sigurd heard an edge of bitterness in that aimed at her husband, but mostly the words were for her guests. For though the couple had given them what hospitality they could, a barn and clean straw, food and ale, they would have been wary of eight strangers even had those men not been carrying more sharp steel than you would find in a dozen smithies. Especially with them having a daughter in the house.

'We will pay you for your hospitality,' Sigurd reassured her, glancing at Roldar, 'and pay well too. But you will tell no one that we are here.'

'It would be bad if you did,' Olaf put in, his eyes adding the *bad for you* part that might have put a cloud over the meal if he'd said it aloud.

'Who would we tell?' Roldar asked with a shrug. 'The only time I leave this place is to sell my wool at the market over there at Rennisøy and sometimes to the folk of Finnøy. I've been known to go to Jørpeland too, but they have their own wool and I rarely get a price that's worth the trip.' He looked from Olaf to Sigurd. 'Besides which, I don't know who you are and neither do I need to know.' The first sign of a smile appeared in his brown beard then. 'Although I am asking myself if you have got yourselves on the wrong side of King Gorm.'

'Never mind which side of what bloody ring-giver we're on,' Olaf growled, and the farmer paled, showing his palms.

'We do not want to know any of it, my lords,' Sigyn said, which showed that she was not short of sense for all that she might as well have been penned in with the sheep and gained as much worldly experience. 'But we would hope to see some of the silver you mentioned before we slaughter one of our beasts for your meat,' she said.

Solveig shot Hendil a look that said *She's got bigger balls than you* as Sigurd took a thumb-sized piece of hacksilver from his purse and tossed it to Roldar who was lucky not to choke on the thing, his mouth being agape at the sight of it.

'We'll want to be well fed,' Sigurd said, which got a nod of agreement from Svein although he had one eye on Hetha who was taking Olaf's and Loker's bowls back inside to fill them again.

154

'And I want you to take us into the fen,' Asgot said, eyes like rivets on Roldar. Sigurd was surprised the godi had sat on the thing this long. For a long moment Roldar looked as though his thoughts were pulling in opposite directions, even with that hacksilver cold against his palm, then he looked again to his wife for guidance.

Before Sigyn could speak, her younger son did.

'I'll take you,' Alvi said, glancing at his father, who clearly wanted to ask why they wanted to go into the fen but didn't dare now.

'And why are we going into the fen, Asgot?' Olaf asked instead, frowning and licking his spoon while he waited for Hetha to return with more broth.

'The boy knows why,' Asgot replied, nodding towards Sigurd, his own thin lips drawing together tighter than Sigurd had sewn Solveig's chest wound. All eyes turned Sigurd's way, including both of Svein's which was the first time since they had got there.

'Does he now?' Olaf said, his right eyebrow curving like Bifröst as Hetha returned with his food, looking at them all in turn as if she had walked into the middle of a hólmgang.

Asgot said no more about it and neither would Sigurd. Not yet. Olaf and the others would have to wait despite their fish-hook stares trying to haul it out of him.

And the next day after the morning meal they went into the fen.

It was still more dark than light when they set off east past the animal enclosures and across the close-cropped pasture, dew soaking their shoes. Then on through longer grass thronging with yellow flowers and flecked with cuckoo spit that streaked their breeks, and glistening spider webs that shimmered in the breeze. They passed the burial mounds which Roldar and his kin had spoken of the previous night, making sure to give them a wide berth so as not to risk disturbing the corpses who dwelt in them. Then on into the salt marsh, the air streaked blue and green with dragonflies and thick with clouds of biting insects.

Here and there the reed beds were beginning to bustle with wading birds, but where there were no birds the tall plants stood still and silent as time itself.

'I steer your father's ships for years, loading and unloading *Little-Elk*'s ballast with these very hands more times than I can recall and up to my arse in the bilge,' Solveig moaned at Sigurd, 'and yet on my second trip out with you I ruin my damn shoes.' He shook his head, the two grey ropes of his hair swishing. 'Survive a bloody chest gash and the worst stitching I've ever seen, only to die of foot rot in this hole.'

'It was your idea to come here, old man,' Olaf reminded him, wincing as his own foot sank in the brackish water. He had not brought his brynja, for it was not men they were expecting to find, though they had all brought spears, which were useful as staffs if nothing else.

'Aye, so it was,' Solveig said, shooting Asgot a glower.

The farmer's boy Alvi led and Asgot, who had a rope looped over his shoulder in case anyone got stuck in the fen, walked behind him. The godi carried a drum too, strung from the belt over his left shoulder so that it hung in the small of his back beside his nestbaggin. He had made the thing in Rennisøy when Solveig and Hendil had gone to buy food for their journey and it was no bigger than the first shield Sigurd's father had made him when he was yet learning his words. A thing of reindeer hide and birchwood, Asgot had painted on its face the tree Yggdrasil with the Nine Worlds, and from its sides he had hung various tokens and charms including animal bones and rune stones. On the back, inside the frame, he had hung a strand of seed casings and a raven's foot, and Asgot said this drum would be useful to appease the fen spirit, which no one thought was a bad thing.

Sigurd, Olaf and the rest followed, trudging their way beside the snake-coils of a stream, one of hundreds that fed sea water deep into the marsh and beyond like the countless roots of some great tree. 'From here if you keep your eyes open you might see a corpse candle,' Alvi said, by which he meant the lanterns that guard the barrows of the ancient folk. 'But I have something even better to show you,' he said, grinning. 'Not far now.'

And though their eyes were never still, their tongues for the most part were, as the shallow weed-bristled water deepened, becoming home to woody trees and mosses thick as Olaf's beard. For men were not generally welcome in fens and not even Olaf would say that he did not believe in the malevolent spirits that lived there. They were places that were neither fully earth nor water and this made them passages between worlds, so that the times you went into such places you did so respectfully and only to leave offerings before leaving just as respectfully. All men knew this and Sigurd, who could not think of such a place without thinking of the tale of Beowulf, could feel the foreboding seiðr as heavy as wet clothes on his back.

'Fens have ways of guarding themselves from humans,' his mother had told him as a child. 'But we can appease the spirits that dwell in them with offerings. Gifts which the marsh will suck into its muddy depths.'

With the rising sun came rising mist, thickening the air that smelt of death and decay, so that Hendil asked Asgot if he thought it could be dragon's breath that hung around them, tainted by the rotting flesh of the men it had eaten. But Loker pointed out that this could not be so for there were no men hereabouts for any dragon to eat and that the smell was more likely to be coming from Svein's backside.

The chuckles this stirred were welcome to Sigurd's ears, for a moment lifting the heavy shroud which seemed to stifle the land here. But soon enough teeth were clamped shut once more and they were simply nine men intruding into a place of silence, stillness and death.

'Here,' Alvi hissed eventually, 'here it is.' The rasp of his voice was cut with awe and he leant in to Asgot and Sigurd, close enough that Sigurd smelt his ale- and cheese-soured breath. 'I found him when I came here to dig the peat.'

'Him?' Svein said loud enough to earn black looks from Asgot and Alvi both. Alvi had stopped by a gnarled old alder tree and now pointed down into the water a spit away, his eyes as round as a fish's mouth on a hook. At first Sigurd saw nothing and was about to say as much when suddenly he saw it all.

'Frigg's arse,' Aslak gasped, recoiling as though snake-bitten.

There was a man below the surface, pale as the barkless alder, white lips tight as ship's caulking to keep out the water, eyes closed so that Sigurd guessed that Alvi had whispered because he feared those eyes might snap open, that the man was merely asleep and might wake any moment.

'If you look closely you will see there is a rope around his neck,' Alvi said.

Sigurd could see the rope and he guessed that someone had hauled the man into the fen by it then used it to hang him from the alder. Or perhaps there was a hidden wound beneath his still-bearded chin and they had slit his throat.

'Is he a kinsman of yours, Svein?' Hendil murmured through a grin, for the man's beard and hair, floating around his corpse-white face, was as red as Svein's.

'You can ask him when I throw you in there with him,' Svein said under his breath.

'Hold your tongues, fools!' Asgot rasped like a sword from a scabbard. 'This offering was likely made long before your grandfathers' grandfathers were hanging from their mother's tit.' He pointed a finger at them upon which he wore rings made from human hair. 'I'd wager the spirits here would welcome two fresh corpses.'

'There are weapons hereabouts too,' Alvi said, never taking his eyes from the man beneath the surface, 'though my mother said I must never touch them. Not even were the blades of hammered silver and the hilts solid gold.'

'Your mother is a wise woman,' Olaf said, slapping his neck to squash an insect that was biting him. 'We're done here, let's move on.' He pulled his foot from the sucking mire with a squelch and pop that released a foul stench. 'Before this place thinks we're offering ourselves up.'

Sigurd glanced at Asgot who raised a grey eyebrow before

turning to follow Alvi. And Sigurd took one last look at the bog corpse and the braided leather noose around his neck, then touched the Óðin amulet hanging from his own neck for luck and turned east towards the veiled sun to follow the others.

In some places there were ancient planks laid on stakes, walkways through the weed-snarled water and stunted trees, but mostly these had long rotted away and you trusted your weight on one at your peril. But Alvi seemed to know where he was going, which earned him Sigurd's respect for the young man must have had stones for balls to come into this place alone. Perhaps he really *had* seen a draugr off with his axe three winters ago. Perhaps it was the lad's bravery and not his story-telling which his brother was jealous of.

By the time Sigurd's breeks had wicked water right up to the crotch and Svein had offered to carry old Solveig if it would put an end to his mumbled curses which ground on like a quern stone before a feast, they had come further than Alvi had dared come before. Even with the mist and the gloom that seemed to cling to the fen as thick as the stench raised with every sucking step, they could tell by the hazed sun that it was well past midday.

'Well that's it then,' Alvi said with a shrug, turning back to face the others. Clearly he had never gone further because of the time it would take to get safely home again and only a fool would risk being caught out there when night fell, as Loker reminded them now.

'What does that make us then?' Olaf said, wiping sweat from his brow and glaring at Asgot. 'Is this spot not good enough for whatever spells you've got bubbling in that thought pot of yours, godi?'

Asgot glanced around then closed his eyes for a long moment before opening them on Sigurd. 'This would be a good place to make a modest offering,' he said. Near by, some creature plopped into the water. Somewhere far above an eagle cried but when Sigurd looked up he could see nothing in the wan sky. He nodded, reached into the purse on his belt and took out a half of a twisted arm ring, the rest of it having been spent by someone long ago.

Asgot's brow furrowed. 'Perhaps not quite so modest,' he said, and Sigurd did not need to look at Olaf to know the look that was on his face. He would be thinking this was silver they could use to buy food and weapons or even spearmen if it came to that. Nevertheless, Sigurd had not come here to show the gods and the spirits what a careful and thrifty man he was. He found another piece of silver, as long as his hand, curved slightly but thinner than his finger. He guessed it had been part of a beautiful stirrup once and he wondered after the man rich enough to own such a thing even as he handed it to Asgot.

'Better,' the godi said, weighing both pieces in his hands that were the scales by which he did his business with the gods. 'Normally we would woo this fen like a chieftain's favourite daughter,' he said.

'With mead then!' Svein put in.

'And a good saga tale,' Aslak suggested.

But Asgot ignored them. 'We would make several offerings and ask for nothing in return. Over time we would gain the spirit's favour. We would not rush it.' He put the silver to his nose as though smelling it, then tossed both pieces into a sinkhole and they vanished without so much as a glint into the blackness. Into the world beyond.

'If I'm owed silver I prefer not to wait for it,' Olaf said and no one could argue with that. Though perhaps they were too busy peering into the sinkhole, especially Alvi who had likely never seen so much silver, let alone so much silver thrown into a hole. Sigurd wondered if the young man might find the courage to come back to this place and jump in the hole himself to fish the plunder back out.

'Now what?' Solveig asked, clapping his hands before his face and wiping the squashed insect down the front of his breeks.

'I've known Asgot long enough to wager my beard that we did not come all the way out here rotting our bollocks off to appease some fen spirit,' Olaf said. All eyes turned not to Asgot but to

Sigurd. 'For one thing, that much silver can only mean that we're staying out here tonight,' Olaf went on, 'which if you ask me is not even good enough to be a bad idea.'

Neither Sigurd nor Asgot denied this.

'We are going to stay out here tonight?' Loker said, wide-eyed.

'Aye, and for that much silver this fen spirit ought to lay on meat, mead and women,' Olaf said, then turned back to Asgot and Sigurd, planting his spear's butt into the swamp. 'So now you two have got us out here, far enough from food, ale and comfort to know that we'd likely sink up to our necks if we tried to go back alone, why don't you put us out of our misery, hey? Poor Solveig here has never been so far from the sea.' He cupped a hand to his ear. 'Listen. You will hear Rán sobbing because she misses the old dog.'

'When I find what I am looking for, Olaf, then you will know why we are here,' Asgot said.

'We should have left you chained to Gorm's rock,' Olaf growled.

Asgot grinned sourly. 'Did you really think my wyrd was to drown out there in the dark, swept out of sight by some *ormstunga* king?' *Serpent tongue*, a good name for King Gorm that, Sigurd thought.

'Well you would have if not for us,' Olaf said.

'You see, Olaf, the gods have uses even for you,' Asgot said, which had Olaf muttering into his beard as the godi turned his back on them all and trudged on. Perhaps it was because no one wanted to turn and go back alone or be the first to say they wanted to, or maybe they were too far on the hook of what-ever Asgot and Sigurd had in mind not to see it through now, but they all followed the godi, squelching through the sucking plunge, sweating with the effort of it and getting bitten out of their minds by unseen creatures.

And then, after the time it would take eight men to unload the ballast from *Little-Elk*, Asgot found what he was looking for. At first it had just been a dark shape in the hanging fog, but

Sigurd had felt the dread rising in him as they drew nearer, so that even before the shape revealed itself he knew this would be the place.

'It is no Yggdrasil,' Asgot said, 'but it must have deep roots to find clean water in this reeking place.' They had stopped before another alder, this one still living, though stunted, standing alone on a peat mound, proud of the sedge and twig rush, the bog arrow grass and the stinking water. And when Sigurd saw it a shiver ran from his arse up to the back of his head, like a rat escaping the mud.

'We've come all this way for a tree?' Svein said.

'Ygg's horse,' Asgot murmured. 'Óðin's steed.'

'Not from where I am standing,' Olaf said. 'It's a gnarly old tree in a reeking fen.' He looked at Solveig. 'Albeit a fen that is richer than I am,' he said.

Asgot looked at Sigurd and Sigurd took a breath, planted his spear in the sucking earth and turned to the others.

'You had better make it quick, lad, for it doesn't do to stand still too long. Not when you're a short-arse like me,' Solveig said. This got some *ayes* from the others who were already beginning to sink into the mire and were continually pulling their feet free as though they feared the fen was trying to claim them for the silver rings on fingers and tied in beards, the scramasaxes and knives on their belts, and the iron or silver amulets at their necks.

'You have all seen that the gods have turned their backs on my family,' Sigurd said, and some of them would not meet his eye at that. 'It is no secret. My father, who was beloved of the Æsir, was betrayed by an oath-breaker. My brothers were butchered. My mother, who ever respected Freyja the Giver and was favoured by the goddess, was murdered by her own hearth.' Every word was like a loom weight caught in his throat and yet every one needed to be said. 'My sister Runa was taken from her home and is even now that worm Jarl Randver's prisoner.'

They looked at the mud or at their shoes, or anywhere but at him and at first Sigurd thought it was because they were embarrassed for him because the gods had deserted his family. But then he realized that was not it. He was certain it was shame that they felt, shame because they had let all this happen. That they had not protected their jarl and their people.

'Look at me, Svein,' he said. His friend looked up, fixing his blue eyes on Sigurd's and Sigurd nodded. 'Like a fish that is small enough to slip through the holes in a net I alone of my father and brothers escaped this treachery. Perhaps this was good luck. Or perhaps the Allfather spared me for some reason he alone knows.'

'Who cares, lad?' Olaf blurted. 'You're alive and at your age that's better than being dead.'

'No, Uncle,' Sigurd said. 'It is not so simple.'

'Never bloody is,' Olaf muttered.

'You all knew my father. If he were alive what would he do?' Sigurd watched them look to each other and then to Olaf, expecting him to answer.

But it was Solveig who spoke. 'Even had he been a damned pig farmer instead of a jarl, Harald would take his revenge on those who had betrayed him. That is what any man worthy of his ancestors would do.'

Sigurd looked at Olaf. 'Then would you expect me to do less? Should I hide under rocks for the rest of my life, happy just to have survived?'

Svein turned his head and spat into the mire. That was his answer to that.

'We wouldn't be here with you if we thought you were a coward, Sigurd,' Olaf said. 'We could pledge ourselves to another jarl. Maybe Randver himself or even Biflindi would have use for us if we kissed their steel and muttered the right oaths.'

'And yet instead of drinking another lord's mead you are standing up to your knees in fen mud waiting for me to win back my family's honour,' Sigurd said and no one denied it. 'But I do not know how to do that. I am no jarl. I have neither thegns to command nor the silver to buy good fighters.'

'And neither will you if he keeps chucking it into the mire,' Olaf said, thumbing towards Asgot.

'Tell me that tonight, Olaf,' Asgot sneered, 'when you feel the fetid breath of spirits on your neck and see corpse candles flickering out there in the dark.'

That was enough to still Olaf's tongue for a while and have Loker looking over his shoulder.

Sigurd turned back to the alder. 'This is why we are here. I have come seeking answers.' He glanced at Asgot. 'I have come to show the gods that regardless of them turning their backs on my father I am Harald's son and I will not skulk off and find a fire to sit by. Let the Lord of the Spear torment me with betrayal like he did my father. Let him throw me into the wolf pit if that is his wish. But he *will* notice me. And if he is true to his name, that all men know means *frenzy*, then let him guide me while I hang from this tree. Afterwards I will know what to do. The Allfather will show me.'

Hendil looked at Loker who looked at Olaf, whose face was all protruding eyes, flaring nostrils and teeth.

'You think I came out here to watch you hang yourself from this tree?' Olaf said.

'You don't have to watch, Uncle,' Sigurd said.

'For nine full nights Óðin hung on the windswept tree Yggdrasil,' Asgot said. 'You all know the story well enough. He hung there without food, without water, slashed with a spear. He sacrificed himself to himself until, screaming, he was able to reach down and take up the runes. The mysteries of death were borne up to him from the depths below the World Tree's roots and the Níðhögg's den.'

'You'll die, you damned fool,' Olaf blurted to Sigurd, ignoring Asgot entirely.

Sigurd nodded. 'I might,' he said.

'Well you'll get old One-Eye's attention, I'd wager my arm ring on that,' Solveig said.

'Aye, we'll hear him laughing at the lad's bone-headed stupidity,' Olaf bawled, waving his spear and spraying his beard with spittle. 'Alvi, take us back, lad, before we bloody sink.'

'I'm staying, Uncle,' Sigurd said.

'If Sigurd's staying I'm staying,' Svein said, making a show of it by standing still and letting his feet sink. His point made, he pulled one free and then the other with two great farting squelches that halfway ruined his heroic gesture.

'Well I haven't got it in me to walk all the way back now anyway,' Solveig said, 'and neither do I much feel like getting lost in the dark.' He gestured to the peat mound on which the alder stood. 'To my eyes that's the only dry bit of ground within an arrow's flight. What do you say, Olaf? Might as well try to make ourselves comfortable, hey? While the lad does what he needs to do.'

Olaf shook his head, bewildered, then glared at Sigurd. 'Tell me you're not going to let him cut you while you're at it,' he said, gesturing at Asgot.

Sigurd looked at Asgot.

'Just a small cut,' the godi said, taking the rope off his shoulders and rubbing the flesh where its weight had sat all day.

Olaf huffed and growled a curse. 'This bog stink has addled the whole lot of you up here,' he said, looking round them all and tapping a finger against his skull.

And maybe it had, Sigurd thought. For they stood there staring at him, all of them but for Olaf, as though they half expected him to take his knife and prise out his own eye to use as payment for a drink from Mímir's Well of Wisdom.

So I have my war band, Sigurd thought to himself, feeling a smile tug at the corner of his lip, even if they are only here because there is nowhere else to go. But he would need more than that and he knew it.

And so he would take Asgot's rope and they would tie him to that tree. And after nine days, if he was still alive, he would know what to do.

And the gods would know his name.

CHAPTER NINE

GODS, BUT LOKER AND HENDIL HAD DONE A GOOD JOB WITH THE TYING. He had a rope around his hips and his chest, lashing him to the alder's trunk so that he suspected he would hang there even without the branch below his feet which he could just reach. But he was glad of that branch for it meant he could share the burden between the ropes and his legs. Either side of him his arms were tied to smaller boughs with reeds which they had braided because they had not enough rope.

He was cut, too. Asgot had taken his wicked sharp knife to Sigurd's right side, to the soft flesh beneath the twelfth rib. He had not cut deeply, the wound no longer than Sigurd's thumb, but the sting of it felt twice as long and Olaf had cursed and smouldered like a day-old pyre when it was done because even a small cut like that can get the wound rot and kill a man as surely as an axe to the head, if only more slowly.

'I don't even want to think about what your father and brothers would say if they could see you now, lad,' Olaf had growled at Sigurd as Hendil, who claimed to be a champion tree climber, had straddled the boughs checking the knots.

'The boy's father and brothers are dead because Jarl Harald let the Spear-God's favour slip through his fingers like ale from a cracked horn,' Asgot had said and they were hard words but perhaps not untrue.

'I will win that favour back,' Sigurd had said, wincing as Hendil yanked one of the reed ropes.

'And a lot of good it'll do you half dead on that tree in the middle of this shit hole,' Olaf said, then batted a hand up at him. 'If you think I'm going to sit on my arse and watch you kill yourself . . .' He shook his head, scratching his sweat-beaded beard. 'Thór's bollocks, Sigurd, but you're just doing King Gorm's job for him. He'd be raising his mead horn to the sky for this piece of good luck.'

'I'm not going to die, Uncle,' Sigurd had said.

And neither was he.

But that first night was hard. The flesh in his arms prickled and numbed and all he could do was clench his fists over and over to try to keep some life in them. The rope over his chest made breathing difficult and knowing that he couldn't move made him desperate to. But the worst thing that first night was the insects that fed on him wherever his skin was exposed and especially on his wrists and neck. The canopy around him seemed alive with tiny creatures who must have thought some god had laid on a feast for them, if they thought at all.

The others slept on the peat mound around him albeit fitfully because any sound at all out there in the fen had them touching spears or sword hilts or Thór's hammer amulets and mumbling invocations to the gods to guard them from fen spirits or some bloody-minded draugr venturing from his grave. Though none of them, other than Sigurd himself, slept less than Alvi. If the lad's eyes were not scouring the gloom they were riveted on Sigurd and wide as oar ports, so that Sigurd thought that maybe he had never heard the story of Óðin hanging on the great ash where the Æsir hold their daily courts. Perhaps the young man thought the men he had led into the fen were moon mad. Or perhaps Alvi knew the story well enough and was waiting for the Allfather himself to appear spear in hand, his one eye blazing beneath his broad-brimmed hat.

Despite his discomfort Sigurd felt a grim smile on his lips at that thought. What would Olaf say then, he wondered.

In the morning Alvi led the others back to the farmstead, but for Asgot who said he would stay until the end. Svein had wanted to stay too but Sigurd told him there was nothing he could do and that he would be better off making himself useful to Roldar and Sigyn around the farm.

Olaf had needed no such encouragement to leave, though he muttered something about his time being better spent keeping an eye on Alvi's kin to make sure none of them went off anywhere running their mouths about the men who had come to Tau. Sigurd had rarely seen the man in such a black mood, not even when he had returned from a hunting trip to find that Svein's father Styrbiorn, Slagfid and Harald had drunk Eik-hjálmr dry of mead and Styrbiorn had even used Olaf's horn doing it.

'I'll bring you some ale tomorrow, Sigurd,' Aslak promised, rubbing his ear, barely able to meet Sigurd's eye because he felt guilty leaving his friend there.

'No ale,' Asgot said. 'Nothing must pass his lips but that which I give him.'

'Then he really is a dead man,' Olaf had barked, already trudging off, for the godi was not known as a good man to have in charge of the cook pot.

Sigurd watched them until they had disappeared from view and then began to feel more uneasy than he had since setting off from Roldar's farm the previous dawn.

'Do you fear me, Sigurd?' Asgot asked. The godi had been collecting plants from the fen before sunrise and now he sat on the mound below Sigurd, sniffing them, crushing and rolling leaves between finger and thumb or slicing them into small pieces with his eating knife.

'Why would I fear you?' Sigurd managed, his tongue feeling like a sliver of dried cracked leather in his mouth. But the truth was he did fear Asgot. The godi was like the sinkholes out there in the fen, part of neither this world nor the next. Asgot was a doorway between men and the gods and though he had always been loyal to Sigurd's father, how could you fully trust a man you believed would slit his own mother's throat – if he had a mother – if some capricious god had laid out the runes telling him to.

'Your father had feared hirðmen around him. Men like Slagfid and Olaf and even your brother Thorvard who had the makings of a great champion. But they could not save him in the end.'

Sigurd felt himself bristle at this, or perhaps it was the needles pricking his flesh because he could barely move his limbs. 'You did not save him either,' he said, fixing his eyes on the godi which sometimes was like looking at any man but sometimes like staring into the heart of a flame. Now it was the latter.

'No, I did not save him,' Asgot admitted. 'Though I had warned him not to take his ships out to fight Jarl Randver. For I had dreamt that Karmsundet was a sea of blood and I told Harald of it. He would not listen.'

'He was oath-tied to King Gorm and would not stay at home because of a dream,' Sigurd said. 'Besides, you always talk of blood.'

'Still, Sigurd, he is a fool who does not try to untangle the knot of his dreams.' He sniffed at a leaf which he had rolled into a ball and stretched out his other hand as though grabbing at the air. 'Dreams are nothing. And everything.' Then he glared back at Sigurd. 'I could not save your father but I will see that he has his revenge. You, Sigurd, will be Harald's sword from beyond the grave. You will be the fire that consumes our enemies.' He grinned then and it was a grim sight on his wolf-thin face. 'If you do not die up there on that tree,' he said.

Sigurd did not give that a reply. His mouth was so dry that he would not waste the spit. And he did not speak to Asgot again until the long dusk began to stretch out before them and the biting flies came out in hateful clouds again. And then he only spoke because he needed the godi to climb up with the shit bowl.

The next day Alvi, Svein and Aslak returned. He did not see them arrive but by now he was slipping in and out of consciousness and his vision was as blurry as if he had his eyes open underwater, so that it had taken him a long while to work out who was there and who wasn't.

He heard one of them telling Asgot that he thought Sigurd had died for his face had turned the colour of a dead man's, but Asgot had told whoever it was that it was none of their concern now. There had been more conversation but to Sigurd it was like the murmur of the sea and his ears could not fish the words out of it. Perhaps Svein and Aslak slept on the peat mound with Asgot that night, but perhaps not. At one point Sigurd thought he saw tongues of flame out there among the sedges and spike rushes and his guts twisted like Jörmungand because he thought it must be King Gorm's men or even Jarl Randver's. That somehow they had found him and now he would die without lifting a finger because he was a fool, weak and starving and lashed to a tree as helpless as a hen strung up by its legs. But no blades pierced his flesh and the flames came no closer, so that in his stupor Sigurd realized they must be corpse candles held by unseen spirits.

He tried to ask Asgot about these flames but the words left his mouth in a slew of sound, like snow sliding off a roof, and nor could he be sure which bleary shape below him was the godi and so he closed his eyes again. He did not fear the fen spirits, because they must surely have thought he was dead, if they saw him at all. For Sigurd felt as though he were becoming part of the tree now, as though the alder's limbs were folding him into its embrace.

Besides which, what could the dead do to him that was worse than what he was doing to himself? He felt himself laugh at that thought. Then pain flooded back in and for a heartbeat he knew one of the hateful draugar had put a flame to his side to punish him. Until he remembered the cut in his side, felt the sting of it and knew it was done by steel not fire, and with that thought panic rose in him again. How could he have been so stupid? Had he not seen Asgot's knife at work a thousand times before? Had he not watched that blood-hungry blade reap lives for the gods ever since he could walk on his own legs?

Asgot has tricked me, his mind screamed. I am his sacrifice. I am the price they are paying to lift the gods' curse. He struggled and screamed and yet there was no movement and no sound. It was as if the fen were swallowing him and this horrifying truth churned a pool of despair deep in Sigurd's soul.

And then he knew he was drowning, thought he must have fallen into the fen and that rotten water was pouring into his throat and killing him and he could do nothing about it.

'Drink, Sigurd.' The voice was close. 'Drink, boy. It will help.'

And so Sigurd drank.

The beat of the drum was slow at first, like the ebb and flow of the tide. Sigurd noticed his own heart aligning with its beat and then it got faster, sounding like the hooves of a running reindeer striking the earth and Sigurd was riding that beast, being borne across worlds. The rhythm was hoof-beats and the beating of a bird's wings. It was sunrise and sunset, rain and wind, sleeping and waking. Life and death. It was the in and out of the act between a man and a woman.

It was the Norns, Urd, Verdandi and Skuld weaving the wyrds of men's lives, and Sigurd began to see the warp of the threads as what is, what was, and what will be, and the weft as what he would choose to do. But then he saw that the great loom was strung with intestines and weighted with skulls. The three Spinners were weaving with the blood and guts of men's lives and he felt the horror of this shiver through his own tortured flesh.

Then he saw the yellow eyes set like polished amber in a great head. He heard the deep guttural growl coming from the creature's throat and saw the hackles raised on its thickly muscled neck.

The fool's drumming has brought wolves, Sigurd thought. Or else they smelt the cut in my side.

He waited for the beast's teeth to puncture his flesh. And yet wasn't Asgot still beating his drum? Surely the godi would not stand by and watch the wolf devour him.

Darkness swallowed him again like a cold ocean wave.

Then he was in an oak forest, crouching behind a thicket because there was a creature near by snuffling and snorting and coming closer. He held his breath and the boar emerged from the undergrowth, a mass of stiff bristling black fur and muscle, those great gut-ripping upper tusks having been ground to sharp edges against the bottom ones.

Moving through the undergrowth, its hide too thick for the biting insects to penetrate, the boar searches for its treats. Even those which are undergound are not safe and will be rooted up. All the world is to be plundered and feasted upon and now the beast sniffed the air and turned its massive head towards Sigurd. Its eyes flamed and it charged, snapping branches, flying across the earth, fearless and fast, and Sigurd knew that nothing could turn it aside. That bristling fury would hit him like a forge hammer, those tusks ripping into the big muscles of his legs. But the boar blurred past him, the wind from it stinging his side below the ribs, and the creature flew into the scrub beside him and was gone.

He let out his breath and looked up and saw through a gap in the canopy a shape soaring against the blue, its barn-door wings from tip to tip longer than a spear, its tail feathers white as snow. He felt the bird's shadow pass across his face like a cold sea breeze and heard its plaintive call of *kli kli kli* piercing the sky. Then it too was gone, but Sigurd knew it had been a great sea-eagle, whose talons could snatch fish from the fjord or even a goat or a deer from the hillside.

And then he sank into oblivion again.

He was woken by rain. Cold, fresh, fat drops falling from the leaves and branches above and splashing on his upturned face and into his open mouth. In the distance, far to the east, thunder cracked and rumbled across the sky and seemed to be coming his way.

'What did you see, Haraldarson?'

Sigurd's neck was as stiff as a fire iron and he did not try to look down at Asgot. Nor could his mouth form a reply or any shape but the ring which caught the rain that tasted of iron as it mixed with the blood from his cracked lips. For he was bound more by the dreams now than the ropes. They were all over him still, heavy as a brynja and as real as the living tree to which he was lashed. But neither did he want to shrug them off.

'What did you see, boy?'

He did not want the dreams or visions or whatever they were to dissipate now that he was back with the living again. He wanted them to seep into his bones and marrow, like hearth smoke staining the grain of Eik-hjálmr's roof beams, because he knew they were important. That they were god-given.

Then the boughs and leaves and the fen were disappearing again, like a boat drifting off into the mist, and Sigurd tried to shout, tried to raise an arm as though he could grasp on to consciousness itself, but his limbs might as well have belonged to the alder for all the mastery he had of them.

His heart was beating fast now. He could feel that well enough. And then there were fingers in his mouth and he thought he was choking but he swallowed what he could and fought for breath. Then came that bitter draught again, scalding his throat, making him retch.

I am going to die, he thought. I will never meet with my father and my brothers and my ancestors in Valhöll. They had good deaths. In the steel-storm. They would have been chosen. I will die here like a fox in a trap and my name will be less than a shadow. To my enemies I will be less than a starling flying through the door of their hall and out through the smoke hole.

The drum again. Beating slowly. It was the stroking of a lover's hand. It was the pulsing of Sigurd's blood in his ears. It was his mother stroking his hair when he was a boy and the lullaby she would sing him to sleep.

Mother.

He dreamt of the king of the beasts then, the bear, who the elder folk believed was their older brother because it could stand upright and walk short distances on two legs like a man. Gods but this bear was a proud beast! It had ranged far from its cave on the hunt for honey but when at last it came to the place, the bear saw that the hive was protected by a swarm of raging bees. The noise from them filled the world, the beating of ten thousand little wings making the blood in his veins tremble.

'Will you endure the swarm for that sweet plunder?' Sigurd asked the bear. 'You know that they will sting you terribly. Perhaps they will kill you.'

The bear turned to Sigurd and laughed like a man and it was the sound of thunder.

A breeze against his temple, running between his braids and through his beard to cool his scalp and face. The wind from a great raven beating the air with its wings so close to Sigurd's head that his eyes were full of its purple, green and black gloss and its thick beak.

I am not dead, corpse-eater, his mind told the bird. If you have come to feast on me you will be disappointed.

But then Óðin Draugadróttin, Lord of the Dead, had two ravens. The raven god would send Hugin and Munin out at daybreak and in the evening they would return to perch on his shoulders and speak into his ears all that they had seen. Perhaps this bird was one of them. It had come not to peck out his eyes but to see for itself this son of a jarl hanging from a tree.

Tell your master what you have seen here then, bird. The All-father loves chaos. Then let him follow me.

Like the tide, awareness came and receded. Sometimes he was in terrible, unbearable pain, his body trembling as though his bones had turned to ice. At other times he felt nothing at all, and now and then he was entirely free, soaring like a bird, flying fast as an arrow, turning on an updraught and seeing the tops of single oaks and deep green pine forests, the thatch of houses blurred by hearth smoke and the glittering fjords specked with fishing boats.

Perhaps he believed he was soaring like a hawk when Olaf climbed the tree and untied the ropes, leaving one round Sigurd's chest and beneath his arms so that he could slowly lower him to the others waiting below.

'We have not finished!' Sigurd heard as though the voice were far away.

'Yes we bloody have!' someone roared. And when Sigurd came round again he was lying in Roldar's barn on a fur upon a bed of straw.

'How you're still alive, lad, I'll never know.'

Sigurd's vision was blurred but even then he knew it was Olaf who was sitting on the stool beside him. Olaf put the cup to Sigurd's lips and he drank deeply, the sweet honey of the mead recalling his vision of the bear. 'Sigurd the Lucky.' Olaf shook his head.

Sigurd shifted to get a look at the cut in his side but he could not see it for they had wound linen around his stomach.

'There's no rot,' Olaf said. 'But we didn't sew it. It had stopped bleeding and Asgot kept it clean. Least he could bloody do,' he said, shooting Asgot a dark look as the godi walked into the barn with another man, the two of them dark shapes against the golden light flooding into the place.

'Crow-Song?' Sigurd said, sitting up as Hagal the skald came to stand by the oil lamp hanging from the wall beside Sigurd's head.

Hagal nodded. 'Sigurd Haraldarson. I am relieved to see you well after your ordeal.'

'I am as well as I have ever been,' Sigurd lied. His head was swimming and he thought he would vomit. 'What are you doing here?'

'I had Hendil and Loker and Roldar's other boy Aleif out looking for him the day after we strung you up,' Olaf said. 'It seemed to me that if you were going to do something that only a god would be mad enough to do, we ought to have a skald around to weave the tale of it.' He thumbed towards Hagal. 'Unfortunately I don't know of any decent skalds so we had to make do with Crow-Song.'

Hagal ignored the insult. He had earned his byname Crow-Song on account of his stories which men said were told bluntly and without polish or eloquence, though Hagal himself insisted the name referred to his knack of finding trinkets and treasures in the world around him and turning them into shining tales.

'I would not have believed it if I had not seen it with my own eyes,' the skald said, those eyes bulging like boiled gulls' eggs.

'They found him in some hole up in Tysvær, up to his beard in ale and notch and no doubt taking some nithing's silver in return for weaving him into a saga tale he had nothing to do with.'

'Would you have me starve, Olaf?' Crow-Song asked. 'There are fewer jarls and halls around these days and I make a living where I can.'

'Watch your tongue, skald,' Olaf growled and Hagal at least had the decency to flush beneath his beard at that.

'How long?' Sigurd asked, looking from Olaf to Asgot.

'Six days,' Olaf said. 'Asgot would have let you hang there for nine but I was thinking that when I meet your father again in the Spear-Lord's hall I would have no decent explanation for letting you die tied to a tree in some stinking bog.'

'Is six days long enough?' Sigurd asked Asgot. He took the cup from Olaf and drank some more, hoping to wash down the bile that was rising like fire in his throat. But his arm was shaking and the ale spilled onto the straw, so Olaf helped guide the cup to his lips.

'It had better be,' Olaf said.

'The Alder Man came on the third night,' Asgot said, his wolf eyes sparking like steel and flint. 'He was thin as a switch, dressed in furs with birch-pale skin stretched over the bones of his face.'

'Sounds to me like you saw your own reflection in the mire,' Olaf put in. But Hagal was lapping this up like a cat tonguing milk.

Asgot curled his lip. 'His eyes were red and his face was etched with the valknuter which is old One-Eye's own sign. He carried a bow and a knife on his back and in his hands a bowl of red paint.' He nodded at Sigurd, raising a hair-ringed finger towards Sigurd's face. 'He marked you.'

Sigurd raised a hand to his own cheek and felt, above the beard line, a gritty coating on the skin. He scratched at it and saw red ochre beneath his fingernails.

'The Alder Man has three powers, Sigurd,' Crow-Song took up in his best saga voice. Olaf and Asgot both looked at him and he shrugged. 'When I am not talking I am listening,' he said by way of explanation.

'Crow-Song is right,' Asgot said to Sigurd. 'The Alder Man can help you connect with animal spirits, as his red side offers. This is his gift to hunters and trackers. He can help you connect with the spirits of a place, as his green side offers. This is useful if you want to appease the dead.'

'That could have saved us some silver then,' Olaf murmured.

'And he can help you remain hidden. Invisible to your enemies,' Asgot said, 'as his brown side offers.' He held up his finger again. 'But he will only give you one of these gifts, and then only if he likes you.'

Sigurd's mind flooded with the visions he had received and he glared at Asgot.

'That was some boar, hey, Sigurd?' the godi said, his eyes on Sigurd's like one ship strake upon another.

'You saw it too?' Sigurd asked. How could it be that Asgot had shared the visions? Or some of them at least. But then who knew what was possible where the godi was concerned.

'When the Alder Man put his mark on you he told you something,' Asgot said. 'Do you remember what it was?'

Sigurd shook his head. Then three words dropped into his mind like stones into a pool. 'Blood and fire,' he said, as surprised to say them as Olaf looked to hear them.

Asgot's lips pulled back from his teeth and he laughed. It was a sound to chill the blood and have Hagal touching the iron pommel of his sword. 'Then the Hangaguð is watching you, Sigurd,' the godi said, and any other time Óðin's byname of the Hanged God would have washed over him, but now it made him shiver.

'Does that mean we can leave this spirit-ridden place and go and break some heads?' Olaf asked, standing and tucking his thumbs into his belt.

Svein appeared at the door, teeth flashing in his beard at seeing Sigurd alive and sitting up. 'Are we leaving?' the giant asked.

'Aye, the moment your bone-headed friend can stand on his own two feet,' Olaf replied, half smiling.

'Let us leave today and I'll carry him!' Svein said.

And Sigurd tasted blood on his tongue as his own cracked lips spread in a wide grin. Because the time for hiding was over.

And the gods were watching.

CHAPTER TEN

THE WOMAN CRADLED IN HER ARMS WEIGHED LESS THAN A CHILD, less even than the brynja Valgerd wore, and this was the last nail driven into Valgerd's heart, for she knew it meant that the woman did not have long left. Days at most. Probably less.

'Are you still with me?' she asked and saw a flicker beneath the closed eyelids that told her that Sygrutha had not given in to death yet, for all that it was over her like a scent. As a völva Sygrutha had the gift of foretelling, could summon spirits to show her the future, and yet she had not foreseen her own death. Or perhaps she had but had chosen not to share that with Valgerd, which was a sharp stick poked into the beehive of Valgerd's anger then. But the face of the bundle in her arms dissipated the ire. Even now. Like it always did.

'We are nearly there,' she said. She had walked this path a thousand times and often in the dark, but now she placed every foot with exquisite care, not because she thought she might fall, but because she feared every little jolt must hurt the völva who was nothing now but skin and bones.

But Sygrutha had been beautiful. She had been dark-haired, dark-eyed and had a quickness for which Valgerd had given her the name Sygrutha 'Ikorni', meaning 'squirrel', though she never called her that in range of others' ears for such things were not to be shared. Besides which, Sygrutha had protested at the name, saying that she hoped Valgerd thought her more beautiful than a squirrel. But she had not minded really, Valgerd knew, for there was more in the name than that. It was a squirrel named Ratatosk that ran up and down the World Tree carrying messages between the eagle in the upper branches and the serpent, Níðhögg, which gnaws away at Yggdrasil's roots.

'You are a messenger between worlds,' Valgerd would soothe as Sygrutha feigned umbrage. 'You can move from ice to fire and everywhere in between. My Ikorni.'

And Sygrutha could not help but smile or gnash her teeth or ask if Valgerd had any acorns for her to eat.

'Not far now,' Valgerd said and this time there was no stirring beneath the eyelids and Valgerd stopped, feeling the blood drain from her own face and vital organs, and stood there on the well-worn track hardly daring to look at Sygrutha's face for fear of seeing death there at last. But in that moment of stillness she felt the völva's heartbeat travel through the withered flesh of her thigh. A tremor in the blood no stronger than the beat of a moth's wing, yet more precious than anything in the world.

'You cannot have her yet,' Valgerd murmured, as though Freyja the seiðr mistress stood beside them, as if the goddess held her arms out ready to take Sygrutha from her. 'Not yet,' she said, an edge of threat in the words this time. And yet it was too late for all that. Valgerd's whole life had been given to the protection of the völva, as her mother's had before her to Svanhvita the last spae-wife of the spring. And the gods knew she had done her best, fought spear warriors and outlaws, and even a bear once, the crazed beast having answered a birthing woman's cries with tooth and claw. But she had failed to protect Sygrutha from death. Her sword and spear-craft and her hard-won skill had been useless in the end.

She walked on. Faster as the roar of the waterfall, which Sygrutha had taught her was the voices of the forskarlar, the fall spirits, singing and shouting their mirth and fury, grew stronger and the path became slick from where the breeze had carried the mist from the torrent back up over the ridge. They passed between a stand of birch whose leaves flickered silver and green, and then down through the long grass and boggy ground which tried to claim Valgerd with every plunging step. The air this close to the waterfall was cold and crisp like the air after a heavy rainstorm, but scented with earth and moss too, and Valgerd drank it in now because she knew they would never share that draught again.

In the past they had clambered down the slick rock to slide behind the waterfall and stand against the wet stone, the sheeting water less than a foot from their faces, their world full of its roar.

'The forskarlar are givers of joy and courage,' Sygrutha told her once. 'They are both beautiful and aggressive. Only a fool would anger them.' Only in time had Valgerd come to realize that Sygrutha had been talking about her as much as the forskarlar, and the next time they had climbed down to meet the spirits Valgerd had taken an arm ring from a defeated enemy and pushed it deep into a crevice in the rock. A gift to the spirits amongst whom she felt so at home.

Now they came to the rock pools and the streams that converged at the cliff's edge to hurl themselves in a seething white fury down its craggy face.

Disturbed from its catch, an otter loped away across the rocks and poured itself into a stream, gone from sight in a breath. 'Here we are,' Valgerd said, going down onto her knees and laying Sygrutha on a flat rock beside another pool. Their pool. Then she began to undress Sygrutha, as she had done many times before. She unfastened the brass brooch that was in the shape of the goddess and took the cloak from Sygrutha's shoulders, rolling it up and placing it beneath the völva's head. Then, with more care than she had ever done anything, she took off the over-dress which Sygrutha had made with her own hands from the skins of the big forest cats that were sacred to Freyja and pulled the goddess's chariot.

Sygrutha moaned when Valgerd pulled the woollen under-dress over her head, but then it was done and the dying woman lay pale and naked on the rock and Valgerd felt tears welling in her eyes because Sygrutha looked like a child. Her collar bones strained against taut skin and her breasts, though never the sort that inspire men's songs, were now no more than sagging skin.

That skin over the cage of her ribs was tight as a spirit drum and now Valgerd could see it beating. Not shallow, as she had felt it before in Sygrutha's thigh, but vigorously, like a sword pommel against the inside of a shield. But Valgerd would not let herself dare to hope that Sygrutha was somehow fighting back the dark tide that was coming for her. Valgerd had seen enough of death to know better than that.

She stood and undressed herself now, taking the belt with its scabbarded sword and her bone-handled scramasax and laying them on the rock beside the dying woman. Normally she would never be unarmed in the völva's presence, just in case, for it was up to her to protect Sygrutha. But what did it matter now?

She bent and shrugged off her brynja and then removed her boots, breeks and tunic, placing them neatly as she always did. Then she bent and took Sygrutha into her arms again and walked barefoot across the damp rock and for once the cold water did not steal her breath. She went deeper, feeling the familiar smoothness beneath her feet, taking Sygrutha into the water so that its darkness cradled her, though Valgerd would not let her go. Would never let her go, and a smile, faint as a whisper, touched the lips upon which Valgerd put her own with the softness of a snowflake touching the sea.

'Don't leave me,' Valgerd said, but then wished she could take back the words because it was not an honourable thing, to ask for that which can never be given. She did not want Sygrutha to fight. Not for her. Not now.

Together they turned slow circles in the water, Sygrutha's black hair floating out like sea wrack, and it seemed to Valgerd that she was giving the völva back to the earth.

Sygrutha's lips were turning blue though she was not shivering

yet and if anything there was a stillness in her face that Valgerd
had not seen for a long time. And so she began to wash the
fragile body, cleansing it of the sweat and the soot and the pain
that had ingrained itself over the last weeks. And because she
did not know what else to say she began to sing. She sang the
Varðlokur, which she had never done before because the chant
belonged to völvur like Sygrutha and not to warriors like her.
But surely the gods would not begrudge her doing it, and if they
did then damn them for she would sing it anyway.

When Sygrutha had sung the Varðlokur it had wrapped
Valgerd like a warm cloak. It had soothed her and lifted her
spirit from her body like smoke from a hearth and though she
had never received the visions that some talked of, she knew a
part of her had travelled far away. Valgerd never sang and now
the sound of it was like a stranger to her ears and if her tongue
around the words had been the warp and weft of wool on a
loom, the dress would be a poorly made thing of rough cloth
and loose threads. But it was all she had. She poured the melody
into Sygrutha's ears as their bodies sought each other in the cold
water.

Skin against skin.

It was dusk now. Iron-grey clouds were rolling into Lysefjorden
and Valgerd did not wish to carry Sygrutha back in the dark
across rocks that were slick with rain. So she lifted her out of the
pool, laid her on the flat rock and dried her with her own cloak.
And when she had dressed the völva again she cradled her in
her arms and carried her home.

Despite Svein's offer to carry him, they had waited another two
days until Sigurd was strong enough to walk, albeit he still felt
weak on his legs and his skin was stretched like the Alder Man's
over his cheekbones and ribs. Roldar and Sigyn had been glad
to see them go. That had been clear as mountain water and who
could blame them? For Sigurd's self-sacrifice in the name of the
Frenzy God was a business they wanted nothing to do with and
they had looked at him with suspicious, fear-filled eyes since

the day Olaf had carried him back from the fen. But they had made good silver and Svein and Aslak had helped around the farm and so they had nothing to complain about. Alvi had asked Sigurd if he could go with them and Sigurd would have said yes if there had been the room in *Otter*.

'I will have a ship soon enough,' he told the young man, 'and I will come and fetch you. Your brother too if he wants to join us.' And Sigurd had meant it too, for a man who chases off a walking corpse with his axe is likely to be a good man in the shieldwall.

First, though, they needed to build bridges with powerful men, any minor chieftains or jarls who had an axe to grind against Jarl Randver. If there were any such men.

'I want to know everything that you know,' Sigurd had told Hagal the day after he had woken up in Roldar's barn, for Hagal's skald-craft took him to every rich man's hall from Rogaland to Haugalandet, and further north beyond Hardangerfjorden, and Crow-Song's ears held gabble and rumour like a horn holds mead.

'I want to know who is scheming and who is moaning about paying the king's tribute,' Sigurd said. 'I want to know which karls have ambition and I want the names of any bóndi who would rather go raiding than break their back working another man's land.'

'But Sigurd, I am a skald not some peddler of other men's secrets,' Hagal said without conviction.

Sigurd had given him a steel-edged look then. 'Where were you the day my father took his ships into Karmsundet to fight Jarl Randver?' Hagal paled at that like a man with his throat cut. 'We went to watch from the shore and I was surprised I did not see you there,' Sigurd went on. 'Surely such a sight was worthy of one of your blood-drenched tales?' Sigurd tilted his head then like a hawk inspecting its prey. 'Or perhaps you were too busy drinking the king's mead at Avaldsnes?'

'No, lord!' Hagal blurted, glancing round to see if there was a blade coming for his back. But Sigurd had not told the others of his suspicions where the skald was concerned. Such things were better stored to be used as currency at times like this. 'You knew Jarl Randver and King Gorm would betray my father, didn't you, Crow-Song?' He all but spat the skald's byname.

'I knew nothing of it, lord,' he said, finger and thumb working in his beard, twisting strands into a thin rope. Then under Sigurd's glare he raised that hand. 'There had been a rumour when I was last in Hinderå under Jarl Randver's roof. But there are always rumours. Randver's cousin was to marry and he wanted me to come up with a new tale for the wedding night and I—'

'Shut up, Hagal,' Sigurd said. 'You are mine now, skald. You will share with me the worms you dig up and in return I will not cut open your back and pull out your lungs and nail them to the side of Roldar's barn.'

No one ever said that Hagal was a coward. He wore a sword and had been known to use it, but he was all sweating terror then, unblinking eyes round as finger rings, one thumb burrowing deep in the palm of his other hand. Perhaps he was afraid because he had known of the scheme to cast Jarl Harald out of his high seat and knew Sigurd had the right to kill him for holding his tongue on the matter. Or perhaps he was afraid because he had watched Sigurd survive being lashed to a tree, sacrificed to the Allfather himself. And a man who will do that would not blink at ripping out the lungs of a skald he believed had betrayed him.

Crow-Song hoisted one eyebrow. 'Sometimes I hear things,' he admitted. 'When the ale flows and tongues flap like fish in a net. I keep to myself and I earn my silver but sometimes I wish I had stuffed my ears with wool rather than have them filled with men's schemes and secrets.' He almost smiled then. 'Women's secrets too,' he said. 'Gods, but you would be amazed at what they tell me about their husbands.' He frowned under the weight of Sigurd's glare. 'Not that you care about any of that of course.'

'Svein!' Sigurd called. 'Bring an axe. And nails!'

Crow-Song raised his hands. 'Wait, Haraldarson! There is no need for that. I am just coming to it. Like all stories there is always a little smoke before the flame, hey.' He forced a smile then and it was that very smile, Sigurd thought, that had women filling Hagal's ears with their mead-sweet breath. 'I did hear something up near Hjelmeland that might interest you. There is a rich man up there called Guthorm . . .'

And so they had rowed *Otter* north up the ragged coast past Finnøy, Årdal and Randøy and that evening they had seen one of Jarl Randver's longships belly-sailed out there in the Boknafjord. But Randver's crew had not seen them, or more likely they had but knew that there was little point turning their prow eastward to investigate the little boat because she was in the shallows and her crew could make landfall and vanish long before Randver's crew had trimmed and tightened their sail again.

So they had come safely to a village near a place which Hagal called Moldfall and there Olaf had offered two boys they had found fishing from the rocks a small bone-handled knife if they looked after *Otter*.

'If I find a mark on her that wasn't there before I'll use this to skin you both,' Olaf threatened, giving them a good look at the blade.

The boys seemed happy enough with that arrangement even though Olaf could not tell them how many days they would be gone, and despite there being only one knife between two. But that was their issue and Sigurd had all but forgotten about *Otter* now as they sat in Guthorm's small smoky longhouse drinking sour ale but eating a pig which their host had had slaughtered on their arrival – which would have been a generous thing for a jarl to do, but said much about a karl like Guthorm, even if the meat was tough because it had not been hung.

The farmer sat at the end of the table with his wife Fastvi beside him wearing a glass bead and amber necklace and a smile that could do nothing for her looks. As for her husband, the brooch at his shoulder was a modest thing of bronze though handsome enough, but more interesting were the two warrior rings on his right arm, one silver the other brass by the looks. The man was keen for folk to see he had earned some honour in the storm of swords. His house could have fitted into Eik-hjálmr four times over but it looked well made and the hangings along the wall were thick enough to keep out the worst of the winter, so that to Sigurd's eyes Guthorm was a man who had done well for himself.

'It is not often that anyone comes to visit us here,' Guthorm said, raising his horn to the newcomers sitting across the long table from him. His own men sat opposite their guests, backs against the wall, smiles in their beards but eyes itchy with suspicion. 'Apart from King Gorm's fart-catchers who come now and again in the spring to take our young men off to some pointless fight.' His brows knitted together then as he eyed Olaf, who was wearing his brynja and with his hair and beard braided looked as though he was ready for a battle. 'But you assure me you are not king's men, Olaf . . .'

'Just Olaf will do,' Olaf said, not being drawn into saying who his father was or giving away anything more about them than they had already offered. For Sigurd had done up his cloak with his father's great silver brooch and so Guthorm knew his guests had some story behind them, even if he did not know yet what that story was.

'Well if you have not come to take my young men away to fight the king's wars then you are welcome here, friends.' Guthorm was perhaps ten years older than Olaf and whatever muscle he had was kept warm under a generous layer of fat. 'Let us drink to new friends and perhaps some future trade, yes?' He swept his horn towards those on the other side of the table, his eyes lingering a moment on Asgot who, with the bones tied in his grey hair and the menace coming off him like a stink, often had men touching anything iron within reach, even if they did not know he was rune-caster and priest.

Men and women sat drinking on the benches around the walls, talking amongst themselves, though with an eye or ear turned towards Guthorm's table and the strangers around it.

'We have the best bear skins you will find in all Rogaland,' Guthorm went on. 'Wolf pelts too and some fine reindeer antler for which I recently paid good silver.' He smiled. 'But you will see that it was worth much more.' He thought he was a cunning trader, this one.

'And slaves?' Solveig said, pointing towards the dark corner of the house over their left shoulders.

Sigurd looked round and saw something on the floor that he had not noticed before, something dark-haired and brooding like a kicked hound, and he was surprised that Solveig's old salt-crusted eyes had beaten him to it. It was a young man, his wolf-like, beardless face obscured by twists of grimy black hair hanging to his chest.

'Slaves, eh?' Guthorm repeated, eyes narrowed, chewing his fleshy lip in thought. 'None that are for sale,' he said after a long moment, picking a meaty bone from his plate and gnawing at the gristle around the joint. Sigurd saw the whites of the slave's eyes flash in the dark and heard the rattle of the chains which bound him there. Guthorm tossed the bone into the dark corner and there was a flurry of movement as the offering was snatched up.

'Must be a spirited dog that you need to keep it on a short leash,' Olaf observed lightly, though there was a barb on that line and everyone knew it. He might as well have asked Guthorm if he were afraid of the half-starved slave.

Guthorm's brows arched and he was about to reply when his wife raised a hand to silence him.

'Only a fool lets his silver out of his sight, yes?' Fastvi said, running her own plump fingers across the beads at her neck. 'We keep our precious things close, Olaf son of no one. That way they remain ours.'

Olaf made a deep *hoom* in the back of his throat, for none of them could see why the young thrall was so precious that he needed chaining. 'If a man takes something of mine then he needs to have either the speed of a hare or the power of a king,' he said, 'and even then he's a good chance of ending up dead.'

Fastvi picked the warning out of that. 'Your weapons will be safe. No one around here would dare lay a hand on them,' she said, for as custom had demanded they had left their own precious things – their swords and their axes – outside Guthorm's longhouse and none of them was happy about it.

Sigurd nodded, appreciating her assurances, then looked at her husband. 'This is a fine house, Guthorm,' he said, which was not quite a lie but generous all the same.

'But your ale tastes like horse piss,' Olaf said.

Fastvi's mouth fell open. A shadow fell across Guthorm's face and his men began to rumble. But then the karl burst into a deep belly laugh and flung the contents of his horn across the floor rushes.

'I can see you are men who appreciate good drink and straight talk,' he said, 'and that is good for I am such a man myself. Geirny! Bring the good ale for our guests!' This had the men around Guthorm's table cheering and all of them upending their horns or cups, either into their mouths to be done with it or onto the floor which must have pleased Guthorm's hounds who took to licking it up. 'They can stay on the horse piss though,' he added cheerfully, thumbing towards those folk around the longhouse's edges. 'Bleed me drier than a corpse's fart they do.'

Sigurd shot a look at Olaf, who shrugged. 'What? We're getting the good ale now and you can thank me for it.' Which was true enough, Sigurd had to admit, though if Guthorm had intentionally served them his worst ale it seemed unlikely he would have butchered a pig just for them. More likely was that the animal had died a straw death that morning, from old age perhaps, which was why the eating of it was like chewing a shoe.

'You are here for the Weeping Stone then,' Guthorm said.

Sigurd had never heard of the Weeping Stone. 'What is that?' he asked. He glanced at Asgot and Olaf. The first shook his head, the second shrugged his mail-clad shoulders.

'Ah, that is not the reason for your coming to my hall?' the karl said, frowning for a heartbeat. Then he flapped a hand through the smoke. 'No matter, there must be another even more fortuitous reason. Trade perhaps.'

'So what have you brought?' a man named Eid called. Guthorm had introduced each man round the table when Sigurd's party had taken their benches. 'There is nothing in that little boat you came in. So my boys tell me.' He was a big man and had that look in his eye that was meant to prick Olaf's pride like a needle in the thumb. But it was a look that Sigurd had seen get men killed, and only a man who did not know Olaf would get it out for him.

Asgot turned to Eid, the bones in his braids rattling. 'Do we look like traders?' he sneered, which had some of Guthorm's men touching the blades of their eating knives to ward off evil.

'We have not come to trade,' Sigurd said, holding out his cup so that Guthorm's thrall could fill it from a jug. He took a drink and took his time, wiping his beard with the back of his hand as their hosts murmured amongst themselves, brows wrinkled and eyes narrowed.

'You come here armed like Týr himself but with nothing to sell and in a turd of a boat,' Eid said. 'Then you must be outlawed.' Teeth split his beard.

'Perhaps they are all skalds like Crow-Song here,' a bald, sweating man suggested.

'Then I will tie a rock to my leg and jump into the fjord,' another man said and this got some laughter, even from Hendil, Aslak and Svein.

'Which one of you pissed up Biflindi's leg, then?' Eid asked. His dark eyes nailed themselves to Olaf who simply raised his brows and scratched his bird's nest beard.

'Shut your ale hole, Eid. This is no way to speak to our guests,' Guthorm said, though even he must have been wondering by now who he was wasting his meat and ale on. His teeth pulled some greying bristles onto his fat bottom lip. 'Still, if I was to lay a wager on it I'd say it was young Harek here who had fallen out with the king. Only, your name is not Harek. Is it?' He was looking right at Sigurd, a half smile on his face, and Sigurd mused that his plan of using Olaf's son's name had unravelled sooner than he had expected.

'My name is Sigurd,' he said.

'Sigurd,' Fastvi repeated under her breath, dredging her mind for a memory. 'Haraldarson?'

Guthorm nodded before Sigurd could reply. 'The same Sigurd who rowed out to the ship battle in Karmsundet and saved Jarl Harald, the great warrior having jumped from his dragon to avoid a steel-death.'

Sigurd glared at Hagal, who blanched. 'That is not how it goes in my telling of it!' the skald exclaimed.

Sigurd turned back to Guthorm and poured an icy look on him. 'My father did not jump,' he said.

'I meant no offence,' Guthorm said with a flash of palm. 'We have all heard the tale of it. And of how your father led a war band to attack the king at Avaldsnes. That was bravely . . . if unwisely done.'

Sigurd would not waste the breath putting him right on it. 'That is all water off the stern now,' he said. 'I have heard it said that you are an ambitious man, Guthorm.'

'You must not believe everything Crow-Song tells you,' Guthorm replied, then he pursed his lips. 'Though I do not deny that when I see a stripling barely grown into his beard wearing such a cloak pin as that—' he gestured at Sigurd's right shoulder, '—the silver lust stirs in my breast and I wonder if I should put a crew together. I wonder if I should pack my old sea chest and go raiding again.'

This was why Sigurd had worn the rich brooch and why Olaf sat there straight-backed like an iron-barked tree in his brynja. These were things to make any man envious, to give him that pulling feeling in his gut.

'What kind of a crew could you put together, Guthorm?' Olaf asked, just enough scorn in the words to draw out a reply that might otherwise never get past the teeth without greater acquaintance.

'I can bring forty spears to an argument,' Guthorm said.

Which meant thirty if he were lucky. He looked at Eid and the scar-faced man beside him whose name was Alver. 'Though I would perhaps only need one,' he said, which got chuckles, nods and some *ayes* from his men. Then he looked back at his guests. 'I may not be a jarl, but then being a jarl can be a tricky thing if you are the kind of man who enjoys being alive.' Sigurd felt Olaf beside him bristle at that but he said nothing and Sigurd was glad of it, for this whole thing was in the scales and needed careful handling.

There were shields hanging from the walls and spears standing in the corners, but all of these had the look of things that were as much part of the furniture as Guthorm's fur-clad seat and his great table. That war gear was a home for spiders who knew they would not be bothered often. Guthorm loved his own hearth too much.

'Are you on good terms with Jarl Randver?' Sigurd asked.

'Subtle as a dog's balls,' Olaf muttered under his breath, which Sigurd thought was a fine thing coming from Olaf.

Guthorm tilted his head to one side. 'I have the honour of being invited to his son's wedding,' he said, letting the weight of those words uncoil and watching Sigurd like a hawk.

The revelation struck Sigurd's gut like an anchor clumping onto the sea bed, though he tried not to show it.

'Ah, I see that you have not been invited?' Guthorm said. 'And yet is it not your sister who will marry Jarl Randver's boy?'

Sigurd did not need to look at Olaf to know what he was thinking. He would be as shocked and sickened as Sigurd was himself to learn what the jarl had in store for Runa. And yet at least she was safe.

'When is this marriage to take place?' Sigurd asked, the word 'marriage' like a foul taste in his mouth.

'At the Haust Blót feast,' Guthorm said, belching into a fist. 'Which tells me that Randver is not so eager for the match as I am sure his boy is.'

This was almost an insult but Sigurd let it go. Besides which, there was probably some truth in it, for though the in-gathering, as the last harvest of the year and a time to prepare for the long winter months, was a time of some celebration, it was a pale shadow compared with the Midwinter feast, when folk drank enough ale and mead to float a longship.

'Perhaps the eldest lad, Rathi—' Guthorm frowned. 'Or is it Hrani?' He looked at Eid who shrugged as though he could not give a fart either way and Guthorm fluttered fat fingers as though it were unimportant anyway. 'Whatever the young man is called, I'd wager he will have *his* wedding celebration at the Jól feast and I will take my own horn to that.' He glanced at the horn in his hand and turned it slightly, making sure Sigurd could see the silver-gilt rim and the pattern etched in it. 'I have one much bigger than this for such occasions,' he said.

Two young thralls, a boy and a girl, were clearing the food scraps from the table and Alver was eyeing the girl as though he were still hungry. Guthorm belched again and gestured for the boy to take some ale to the young man chained in the darkness.

'It is a dark thing, what has happened to you and your kin, Sigurd Haraldarson,' Guthorm said, 'and a young man like you must be cursing the Norns for the wyrd they have spun you.' For a heartbeat or two there seemed to be pity in the karl's eyes but it did not last and Sigurd was glad for that. 'But I can see that you are all proud men and have not come for my sympathy.'

'What have they come for, is what I am asking myself,' Eid put in.

The hoods of Guthorm's eyelids rolled slowly over the eyes, which then fixed on Sigurd's own. 'You wanted to hear me say that Jarl Randver and I are enemies, hey? That I hope the jarl falls off his ship and drowns under the weight of all his silver, yes? But the truth is I bear him little ill-will. He did not promise me anything for turning a blind eye to his scheming with King Gorm where your father was concerned. I swear to you I knew nothing of all that until after.'

Which told Sigurd that other powerful men *had* profited by his father's death.

'But neither did Jarl Randver ask me for spears to help put his arse in your father's chair, for which I am grateful for it would have been a hard thing to refuse, us being but pissing distance from Hinderå.' He shook his head and pinched his bulbous nose. 'If you have come here seeking an alliance against your enemies you will be disappointed, young Sigurd.' He smiled, though it did not reach his eyes. 'I mean no offence, but no one would side with a new beard against a jarl and a king, not even a new beard with the steel in his eyes that I see in yours.' He gave Hagal a cold look. 'If Crow-Song here led you to believe I would help you get your father's jarl torc back then you should sink him in the fjord for wasting your time.'

'And wasting our ale,' Eid said.

'Now now, Eid, we can still be good hosts here. Hey? I will not have this young man and his friends sail off saying different.'

'I can make you rich, Guthorm,' Sigurd said. Short. Simple.

'You can make me dead, boy!' Guthorm growled, the veil slipping off his good humour now.

'You can fuck off back the way you came,' Eid said and suddenly Olaf and Svein had pushed their end of the bench back and stood with their hackles raised up to the roof beams. Eid and Alver and several others stood too and the men and women around the room's edges fell silent as they anticipated violence. But the only men in Guthorm's longhouse with edged blades – killing blades – were Guthorm's men, and Solveig, still seated, swore because he thought they were all about to become dead men and for what?

'May I have words with you, Guthorm?' It was Crow-Song and he had his hands raised and open to show that he did not have an eating knife in them.

'That's it, Crow-Song, you flap your wings out of this,' Loker said, shooing him off with a hand. But one of Guthorm's men was standing between Hagal and Guthorm, his hand on the sword hilt at his hip.

'It's all right, Ingel,' Guthorm said to the man with the sword. 'Just because he has never put you in one of his stories there's no need to look for an excuse to gut him. Crow-Song has always been welcome here.'

Hagal nodded in thanks as Ingel stepped aside, and Guthorm stood and beckoned the skald to join him behind the tapestry partition at the back of the longhouse. 'The rest of you put your pricks away before someone is hurt. I will not have blood spilled in my hall.'

'Hall? Ha,' old Solveig muttered into his ale.

Sigurd gestured at his friends to sit and they did, albeit Olaf was unable to resist pointing a finger at Eid that spoke of business yet to be settled.

Alver barked at the serving girl to fill their guests' cups, which was as good a peace offering as any, and Sigurd raised his own cup to Alver to show his appreciation, whilst around them those on the outer benches resumed their blathering as if nothing had happened.

When Guthorm and Hagal came back to their seats Sigurd knew straight away that the skald had told the karl about what had happened in the fen at Tau. It was all over Guthorm's face and in his eyes which were now on Asgot as much as they were on Sigurd. It was not every day a man like Guthorm had a godi, a man who communed with the gods, in his longhouse, and from the look of him he did not much care for it.

Still, at least he would know now that Sigurd had thought as deeply as any man could about this idea of taking revenge on those who had betrayed his father. Furthermore, his having hung himself on that tree and survived showed that he was either Óðin-favoured or had an iron will, which were both good things to know about a man. It would make Guthorm at least wonder if the Allfather really was turning his one eye towards Sigurd and his blood feud.

'Our friend Crow-Song vouches for you, Sigurd. He has told me of your sacrifice, though it is a hard thing for a man to swallow. Yet I can see now that you have recently suffered.'

Sigurd knew that his eyes were sunken pools. That his face was lean as a wolf's. At least Guthorm now knew there was a reason for it, that he was not sickly or beset by some illness.

'It is a wonder you survived,' Guthorm said. 'Nine days hanging in a tree? It is the stuff of fireside tales. I am sure Hagal has already begun the weave of it.'

Sigurd struggled not to glare at Hagal then for adding his own lustre to it. Nine days? Was six days not enough then, skald? Mind you, Crow-Song had once boasted of reciting an old story for two days and nights straight and remembering every piece of it. Hagal felt the same way about stretching the truth of a thing as a woman felt about stretching the dough to make more bread.

'The gods are with me, Guthorm, and I will have my reckoning,' Sigurd said. 'Those who help me will find me generous.' Truly he did not know if the gods were with him, though he was sure they were watching, which was not quite the same thing. But neither Guthorm, nor anybody else, needed to see the inside of his thought chest. Let them just know what would be.

'I admire your spirit, Sigurd,' Guthorm said. 'If I were a younger man I might be tempted to get involved with all this, just for the fun of it.' By fun he meant silver, for there would be much of that if Sigurd won. 'But you may as well try to change the tides, lad.'

'There is more to all this than that, husband,' Fastvi said, keeping her eyes on Sigurd. 'You being here in my husband's hall will count as a black mark against us when Jarl Randver and King Gorm come to hear of it.' She curled her lip. 'We would have been better off turning you away.'

'Aye, your wife has the right of it, Guthorm,' Eid said. 'Knowing who they are, outlaws and enemies of the two richest men for as far as a bloody crow can fly, I am asking why they are still drinking our ale?' This stirred some murmurs of agreement from the men on his side of the table.

A grin wormed onto Alver's scarred face and Sigurd wondered who had done that to Alver. The scar not the smile. 'I know why they are still here,' he said. Had he earned those scars in the shieldwall, Sigurd wondered, or were they gifts from some fury of a woman who did not welcome his attentions? 'They're still here,' Alver went on, 'because Guthorm thinks they might enjoy the festivities tomorrow.' He turned his grin on Guthorm, who arched a greying brow to show that Alver had hit the rivet square.

'If you are the sort of men who enjoy a wager in between scheming your revenge and chasing your blood feuds, then you are welcome to join us at the Weeping Stone tomorrow,' the karl said with a nod. Alver and some of the others grinned at this idea and not even Eid spoke out against it. 'Seeing as that is why we thought you had come. Before we learnt the unfortunate story of it.'

'What is the Weeping Stone?' Sigurd asked, recalling Guthorm's earlier mention of it.

'Just bring your silver,' Alver said before Guthorm could answer, nudging the man beside him who was all teeth and rubbing his hands together like a wool merchant who has just sold three bales for the price of five.

Olaf leant in close to Sigurd. 'If there're wagers to be made there's silver to be won,' he said in Sigurd's ear. 'Frigg knows we could do with some. The way this is all going we'll need it to buy a ship and a crew of Danes to help us deal with Randver.'

'I'd take two Danes over every man in this place,' Solveig muttered under his breath and if any of Guthorm's friends heard this they pretended not to.

'More silver in the pot, more to be won, hey!' a sallow-skinned, mostly toothless old man named Hrethric exclaimed, hoisting his cup into the smoky air.

So this was why they were still sitting in Guthorm's long-house, Sigurd mused. The farmer never had any intention of helping him throw Jarl Randver out of his high seat, but he would happily take their silver in whatever contests had been arranged for the following day.

'Will there be fighting?' Olaf asked. 'Tell me it's not some bloody foot race.'

'I cannot swear to you that there will be fighting, but I can assure you there will be killing,' Guthorm said, clearly thinking he was very clever.

Svein looked at Olaf and Olaf looked at Sigurd and in that moment Sigurd knew that they would be sleeping on the ale-soaked rushes of Guthorm's longhouse that night.

'You will meet some of my friends, young Sigurd,' Guthorm said, 'Æskil In-Halti and Ofeig Grettir being the richest of them.'

Lame-Leg and Scowler. 'They sound like great company,' Hendil said with a wink at Aslak.

'You will also meet Grima Big Mouth and if you take some silver off him I will be happy about it,' Guthorm added. 'Perhaps you will persuade some of them to join your adventure, hey.'

'The lad will need a bigger boat first,' Eid said, which was true enough, Sigurd thought, as the young serving girl filled his cup.

And as he drank, he thought about Runa marrying the son of his enemy.

'I know it is nothing to be happy about,' Olaf said, and Sigurd did not need to ask what he was talking about. 'But at least it means he must be treating her well. If she is going to marry his boy.'

'She is not going to marry Amleth,' Sigurd said, 'or any other man of Randver's choosing. There will be no marriage.'

Olaf dipped his head and raised a placating hand. 'It means they have not touched her,' Olaf went on, daring to say it because it was an important thing.

And by 'touched' Sigurd knew all too well what his friend had meant. He was right though. That was something to be glad about.

Still, Runa marrying that treacherous turd's son?

'I don't want to talk about it, Uncle,' Sigurd said.

'Fine by me,' Olaf replied.

Sigurd thought someone must have crept up to him in the night and sheathed an axe in his skull. The sun had been climbing above the snow-capped mountains in the east when they had eventually laid their heads on the floor rushes and closed their eyes. They had soon finished every drop of Guthorm's good ale and had made do with the sour stuff then and Guthorm could not be faulted for his generosity, for all that it was clear he believed he would make it back again with a profit from Sigurd and his crew the next day.

They had drunk until their beards and tunics were soaked and none of them could walk along a spear shaft without falling off, which had been Olaf's idea of an amusing game, and a cock had started crowing somewhere outside, which had Svein growling that he would go and eat it there and then if only his legs would obey him.

And then they had listened to Hagal telling the blood-drenched, revenge-brimmed tale of the hero Sigurd the dragon-slayer, who looted the dragon Fáfnir's hoard. Sigurd still had just about enough sense left in him to be embarrassed at the skald's choice of tale, especially when it came to the part about the hero being greater than any man in strength and talents and vigour and bravery. Still, it was no bad thing to let them all hear about how rich the hero Sigurd became through his daring and prowess, and at least Crow-Song stopped short of the doom-laden events of later in the tale. Or else Sigurd had passed out by then.

And now they were making their way, along with every living soul from the village it seemed, up an old flinty drover's path to the high ground, everyone thrumming with the excitement of it, except for Sigurd's lot who were squinty-eyed, sweaty-browed and foul-tempered.

'I feel like some troll peeled off the top of my skull and did a shit inside it,' Loker said, wiping grease from his forehead. They carried spears and wore all their war gear except for their shields which they had left at Guthorm's hall.

'That is nothing, Loker,' Aslak said. 'I am seeing two of you.'

'A curse if ever there was,' Hendil said.

'Pah! You bairns cannot hold your ale!' Olaf said, though in truth he did not look any less miserable than the others. 'When I was your age the Boknafjord was not salty water, but sweet golden mead. I used to swim from Skudeneshavn to Kvitsøy every morning with my mouth open all the way.'

This got a laugh despite the sore heads. Asgot wafted Olaf's boast away with his long fingers. 'I remember you spewing your guts over Slagfid's shoes the day Harald took the jarl torc from Ansgar Iron Beard,' he said.

'I was there,' Solveig said. 'Slagfid threw those shoes in the pit for he said he would rather go barefoot than live with the stink.'

'Aye, well the fish we had was rotten! That was the cause of it,' Olaf said, which got some crowing before they fell silent again, perhaps retreating back inside their ale-soaked misery. But more likely, Sigurd thought, because each of them was remembering old times, when friends and kin were full of life and Harald's hall shook with feasting and drinking and boasting. All that was gone now.

'Look, there's Guthorm and his hound,' Svein said, pointing further up the path.

'Thrall or no, it's a poor thing to see a man kept on a chain like that,' Olaf said.

Guthorm and his friends were trudging up the hill, the karl leading the young dark-haired man on the end of his iron leash which attached to a neck ring. Eid was cradling an assortment of axes and swords and Alver behind him carried a stack of spears across his shoulders. Fastvi was there too, walking amongst a knot of women who were all laughs and smiles as though they were on the way to the market.

'I am put in mind of Fenrir Wolf,' Sigurd said, watching Guthorm's thrall and noting how the other villagers were pointing at him and chattering like finches though keeping their distance by the looks.

'Better to slit a troublesome thrall's throat and offer him to Loki Mischief-Maker than have to sleep with one eye open,' Asgot said. No one could disagree with that.

'Maybe that's what Guthorm is doing,' Aslak suggested. 'Why bring a thrall out here on the end of a chain otherwise?'

'Maybe Guthorm likes the black-haired whoreson enough to

give him a good walk on a fresh morning,' Olaf said, filling his nose with a breeze that carried the scent of moss and dew-laced grass off the hills.

But Sigurd doubted that was it at all. Guthorm's people were afraid of that young man with the crow-black hair and wolf eyes. The karl had said there was going to be killing done today and Sigurd would wager every last piece of silver in his purse that Guthorm's thrall was going to play his part in it one way or another.

'There it is then,' Svein said as they came over a rocky brow to the Weeping Stone and the crowd that was already gathered around it. Standing as tall as Svein the stone was carved with Jörmungand the Midgard Serpent, its rune-filled body snaking over the rock's surface in burnt ochre red, yellow from orpiment or saffron, green from copper salts and black from charcoal.

'Hey, boy! Come here!' Olaf called to an urchin racing up the hill with his friends and a barking mutt. The boy ran over to them, his eyes wide and ready to glut themselves on whatever lay in store up there on the crown. Olaf pointed his spear up to the standing stone. 'Why is it called the Weeping Stone?' he asked.

The boy had a wooden sword tucked into his belt and a comb hanging round his neck that he had forgotten was there by the looks of his straw-tufted head. 'Some woman called Aesa put it up,' he piped. 'Her husband and their son went raiding to the west and never came back. The runes speak of it.' He wrinkled his stubby nose. 'To those who can read them,' he said.

'Well there is Lame-Leg,' Loker said, pointing at Guthorm's friend who was limping up to the gathering with an expression that could have been a smile or a grimace.

'Aren't you a clever one, hey?' Solveig said, earning himself a growled insult from Loker.

In-Halti was richly dressed in a fine blue kyrtill, the hem of it lifted and tucked into his belt, as many of the other folk had done too because the day was getting warmer. There were others with him including two bristling warriors, one a bear of a man who lumbered under the weight of an enormous brynja and a long-axe over each shoulder, and the other a smaller man in leather armour hefting a shield and spear and with a sword scabbarded at his hip.

They came up to the stone and Sigurd watched Guthorm greeting the visitors in turn, some with smiles, others with a clasp of wrists and still others with little more than a nod. Ofeig, bynamed Scowler, was likewise easy enough to pick out of the throng for he had a face like a pail of thunder, though it said nothing of his mood. The expression was the result of a thick and gnarly scar that ran across his forehead and down through his right brow to below the eye, though the eye itself looked usable still. The flesh knitting together had twisted the skin giving the man the look of someone who had just found some young swaggerer in the hay with his daughter. And he had brought fighters too, four of them and all armed to the teeth and mean-looking. Three wore mail, short-sleeved brynjur that left their arms bare but for the patterns carved in them. The fourth man wore leather armour and carried a boar spear whose haft was as thick as his arm, but he had brawn enough to handle it, and Solveig observed that this one had the look of a farm thrall about him.

These were not the only fighters there. There were perhaps a dozen more, all come to this deserted place to stand amongst the wind-rippled grass to win silver.

'I am looking forward to this but I wish I had brought some ale,' Svein said, apparently ready to begin drinking again though that idea turned even Sigurd's stomach.

'We won't know who to put our silver on,' Hendil said, eyeing the fighting men among the gathering.

'*Our* silver?' Olaf said, cocking an eyebrow at Hendil who scratched his beard and looked at the floor. 'You can get the feel of it just by looking at them,' Olaf said. 'I wouldn't wager much against that lump of meat,' he said with a nod towards the giant with the two great axes. 'That's a fine brynja from the looks and with those arms and a long-axe he'll knock men into the next life before they're even close enough to smell him.'

Silver was already changing hands and it was Guthorm's wife Fastvi, a spear-armed bóndi at each shoulder, who was dealing with all that. Her land, her scales, Guthorm's rules. Which as it turned out were not exactly unfathomable.

The men would fight until they were either killed or too injured to continue. Or until their masters – or lords in some cases by the looks, for not all were thralls – cast a spear into the ground to say that their man yielded, which was the same as being killed so far as the silver was concerned.

Olaf and Solveig and the others were just arguing about who they thought would or should be matched against who in the first bout, when Guthorm led his young thrall to the Weeping Stone and began to fasten the end of the chain to a ring that had been put into the rock where the serpent's open mouth was. The black-haired young man went along with it and simply stood there eyeballing the crowd while tying his hair in two braids either side of his wolf's face. Guthorm raised a hand to silence the assembly and as a hush fell across the place the thrall and Sigurd locked eyes for a long moment until Svein tugged on Sigurd's sleeve, drawing his attention to the axe-wielding giant who was coming grinning into the circle of men, women, children and dogs.

'I see that after what happened here last time you have re-turned with worthier opponents,' Guthorm told the gathering, as Sigurd watched Aslak wander off. 'Well, they look worthier at least. We shall soon see the truth of it.' Some among the assem-bly hurled insults at one another or barked curses in Guthorm's direction, but the karl could barely keep the smile off his face. 'May bravery be rewarded and slowness punished. Make sure you have placed your wagers with my wife. The first fight will begin soon.'

And that was all the talking there was, for it seemed they had all done this before and there was no mystery in any of it.

The chained man walked to the extremity of his little world

which was roughly seven paces in a crescent around the Weeping Stone's face, then with his foot scored lines in the earth. He did the same thing halfway between those marks and the stone, which spoke of experience, for you would not want to outrun the length of a chain when it is fastened to your neck. In some places you could see old marks but he gouged fresh scars here and seemed unconcerned whilst doing it.

'Frigg knows what sort of useless sods this lot brought to the last fight,' Olaf said, noting how calm the chained man was, 'but this lad will be dead in a sparrow's fart. Not that he seems to have the wits to know it, which is probably just as well for him.'

'Put some silver on the giant,' Svein said, leaning on his own hafted axe, his great arms folded upon the iron head.

'Aye, but we won't win much for everyone is doing that,' Solveig observed.

'Have you placed your wager, Harek?' Guthorm called across, to their relief using the name Sigurd had arrived at his farm with.

Sigurd nodded, giving Guthorm a half smile.

'When did you do that?' Olaf asked, then saw Aslak emerge from the knot of folk around Fastvi and her scales. 'You fox,' he muttered. 'You put it on the lad, didn't you?'

All eyes were on Sigurd. Solveig was muttering that he might as well have tossed the silver into the sea for at least that way you might get Njörd's favour.

'Sigurd put the silver on the big man,' Svein said, 'for anyone can see that he is a warrior and will cut the thrall in half.' Sigurd looked at the giant with the long-axes and his guts knotted because Svein was right, the man looked like a champion, his hair braided for battle, his arms criss-crossed with scars and adorned with silver rings. He was a man to put at your prow and turn your enemy's bowels to sour water and Sigurd suddenly thought he should have used that silver – enough to buy a good sword – to buy the giant's loyalty.

Instead of putting it on Guthorm's thrall, who had yet to grow a man's beard.

'Wait,' Olaf said, 'what is that I see in Sigurd's face?' He frowned and turned to Aslak. 'Have we put our silver on the boy?'

'Our silver?' Hendil said with raised brows, and got a cold look for it from Olaf.

Aslak glanced at Sigurd, who nodded. 'And we were not the only ones,' Aslak said, 'though most went for the giant.'

'You are very quiet about all of this, godi,' Olaf said. 'What do you have to say of it?'

Asgot tilted his head to one side as he studied the young man with the crow-black hair. 'There is a reason he is kept on a chain,' he said.

'It is because otherwise he would run east as fast as those young legs could carry him,' Solveig said, 'for who would want to be lashed to a stone and made to fight a troll like that?'

'Bad enough that he has no mail or helmet, but they are not even giving him a shield,' Loker said. Eid handed the thrall a hand axe and he seemed happy enough with it, testing its weight and balance as he strode back to the Weeping Stone.

'Well what good would a shield be against him?' Hendil said, nodding towards Lame-Leg's man who was grinning at his opponent now, and Hendil's point was not one you could argue with. That much muscle behind a long-axe could see the blade slice straight through a shield and the arm holding it.

'Well I am looking forward to this,' Svein said. He was not the only one. Those who had come up to the Weeping Stone had made a half circle around it, the hum of their excitement like that of bees near a hive.

Sigurd saw Guthorm nod at Lame-Leg who stood shoulders back, chest out, chin high like a man who knows he is about to be proved right. He swept a hand out before him in a gesture that told Guthorm to begin the fight and this gave rise to shouts of encouragement from the crowd, most for Lame-Leg's man but some for the black-haired youth.

Who spun the axe butt over blade, the haft slapping into his palm.

The giant hawked and spat a gobbet of something nasty into the tall grass. 'Tell your nithing ancestors you are coming,' he said, 'that you will join them in Niflheim soon.' This put shivers into some because Niflheim was the dark world, a place of freezing mists and rivers of ice where those who died a poor death were bound. 'I am Waltheof, son of Asgaut. I would boast of deeds and of the men I have killed, but there does not seem much point.' With that he held the long-axes out wide, twirled them once in great cart-wheel circles, and strode forward.

And the chained man threw his axe.

It spun end over end twice and embedded itself in the giant's forehead with a crack that echoed off the Weeping Stone. There was a collective gasp from the crowd as the big man stood for a long moment, the axe sticking from his head the way you might leave it in a block after chopping wood, blood leaking from his skull to drip from his nose. Then, still gripping the long-axes by their hafts, the giant pitched forward and slammed onto the earth as dead as any standing stone put up in memory of a lost husband and son.

'Óðin's arse,' Olaf rumbled. 'That hardly seems fair.' He looked at Sigurd. 'That's the sort of thing you'd do,' he rumbled, perhaps recalling the fight in Eik-hjálmr when Sigurd had laid him low with a well-placed foot.

'Still it was a brave thing, throwing the axe,' Aslak said. 'What if he had missed?'

Sigurd shrugged. 'He didn't miss,' he said.

'Well I for one am happy about it,' Loker said, 'for the silver will come in useful.'

But most of those gathered around the Weeping Stone were not happy and they were letting Guthorm know about it to the extent that Guthorm's spearmen guarding Fastvi and the silver were beginning to sweat. Neither was Guthorm happy about it by the thunderous look of him. He snarled something foul at his thrall and hid it with a smile.

'Seems our host did not want it over so fast,' Hagal said, which was true, for such a thing was not good for business.

Lame-Leg was so furious that he had yet to summon the words, as two of his friends took hold of his dead champion, one foot each, and dragged him away, the axe's haft scoring the earth as he went.

'That thing will take some getting out,' Solveig observed.

The chained man went back to the rune stone and sat down against it, digging dirt from his fingernails and waiting for the storm to pass through the gathering.

'You cannot call that a fight, Guthorm!' Lame-Leg managed, spraying his own beard with white flecks.

Guthorm held his arms out wide. 'Maybe you will have better luck next time, In-Halti.' Lame-Leg looked around for support but the others were over the thing now, many of them off crowding round Fastvi to be the first to make their wagers on the next contest. Sigurd gave Aslak some more silver and his friend nodded and ran to join the throng.

'The lad again?' Olaf asked.

'Would you bet against him?' Sigurd asked, which had Olaf scratching his bush of a beard.

'Just because the boy can throw an axe straight doesn't make him a fighter,' Loker said, 'and whoever fights him next will be ready for that trick.'

This was true enough, Sigurd admitted.

'You have missed your chance, In-Halti,' Ofeig Grettir said, wafting ringed fingers in Lame-Leg's direction. 'Now it is my turn to feed the worms with this troll shit of a thrall.' He gestured at one of his four men to step forward and so the warrior did, though he did not look quite as cocky as the giant had, and who could blame him after what he had just seen?

But then Fastvi sent a boy running over to her husband and after listening to what he had to say Guthorm raised a hand for silence. 'This will not do.' He shook his head. 'No one is putting their silver on Ofeig Grettir's man.'

'Grettir is,' Solveig murmured, 'and he'll be jarl-rich if his man wins.'

But Guthorm would not let it continue this way. 'In order to balance the scales I will allow all four of Grettir's men to fight him,' he said, pointing at his thrall who still sat at the base of the Weeping Stone, his back to the carved rune serpent. This got the crowd humming and Fastvi's weights clanking in the scales as folk parted with their ingots, bars and ring silver.

'Guthorm is a greedy fool,' Olaf said, thinking the farmer had gone too far now just to make sure enough people bet against his man. 'One man can't fight four. Not when he is chained to a damn rock and without mail or helmet or even a bloody beard on his chin.'

Sigurd cursed under his breath because he agreed with that, but it was too late to fetch Aslak back now without losing face and so he touched the iron pommel of the sword at his hip and invoked Óðin Hrafnáss, the raven god, because only his intervention now could save the young thrall from an end soaked in slaughter's dew, and save Sigurd from being silver-light.

The young man with the crow-black hair was interested now. He had climbed to his feet and stood studying the four men arrayed before him, three in mail, one in tough leather armour, all with spears.

'This could be one for your tales, skald,' Solveig said to Hagal.

'It'll be too short for one of Crow-Song's tales,' Olaf said, to which Hagal replied that folk did not mind short tales as long as they were even more bloody than the long ones. This was well said and no one disagreed with him.

'I'll wager he won't throw the axe this time,' Svein said.

But Eid did not give the thrall an axe. This time he would fight with a spear, though Sigurd did not see how it could be much of a fight against four, whatever weapon they gave him. To sink his spear point into one of them would be to invite three more blades to gore him. And yet clearly some people had wagered their silver on the strange young man, which suggested they had seen more in him than the skill of throwing an axe well enough to sink it in another's head.

Ofeig Scowler's men had seen more too, for they did not simply stride in and gut him and neither would any of them risk losing their weapon by throwing it. Instead they spread out in an arc and came slowly, like men closing in on a boar.

Or a wolf.

The young man gripped his spear with two hands, the shaft under his left arm just below chest height, its blade favouring each of his opponents in turn as they edged closer.

'What are you waiting for? Frigg's tits, there are four of you!' Loker barked.

'Keep your oggles peeled, lad,' Olaf growled. 'One of those whoresons will scratch his itch soon enough, won't be able to help himself. He'll want the glory of it, even against a chained thrall.'

And then it happened: one of the spearmen to the young man's right came in fast with a double-handed mid-level thrust, but the thrall had known it was coming and brought his stave across to block, then he thrust with his left hand, slamming his spear's butt into the man's temple. The man staggered but the thrall stepped with him, keeping close, and scythed the spear blade up to rip open the man's groin in a spray of the bright red blood that signals a man's doom.

Another spearman roared and thrust high and the thrall snapped his head out of the way and brought the butt end up to parry, so knocking the other's blade skyward. Then almost too fast to see he twirled the spear a half circle and thrust the blade overarm into his enemy's mouth, hauling it out again before the steel could catch on the jaw bones.

'Their mail is not doing them much good,' Hendil observed, as another of Scowler's men slashed his spear at the thrall's legs and the thrall jumped the blade neatly, spun the spear and thrust it back under his right arm to impale the man through his neck. But the man clutched at the blood-soaked shaft and with impressive strength pulled himself further onto the spear so that his dead weight ripped the weapon from the thrall's backwards grip. And this was the chance his companion needed as he struck with a slash and cut that would have ripped the thrall's chest open had the young man not stepped towards him and caught the stave on his forearm. The young man stepped further in and rammed his forehead into the spearman's face, bursting his nose with a crack, then he turned his back on the stunned man and slowly walked back to the Weeping Stone.

Only one of the other three was still breathing but he was corpse-pale, as the last of his blood welled up through the hands he had pressed to his groin.

'We should use your silver to buy this thrall,' Olaf said to Sigurd.

'Would you sell him if you were Guthorm?' Sigurd said.

Olaf did not need to answer that, as the last of Scowler's men roared his defiance through a mouth full of blood, levelled his spear and charged.

The thrall stood still as the standing stone. Then at the last moment he twisted like smoke, grabbed the chain that hung behind him and brought it up and round the man's neck. He hauled on the chain, teeth clenched with the strain of it, and Scowler's man's face filled with blood, his eyes bulging so they looked as though they would burst. Desperate hands clawed at the chain but the thrall held on and the folk gathered there watched as the doomed man's tongue swelled and poked from blue lips and a dark piss stain bloomed in his breeks.

'Never seen the like of it,' Solveig murmured, which was saying something when you'd lived as long as he.

'How did a wet behind the ears lad learn to fight like that?' Loker said.

'A wolf knows it is a wolf,' Asgot said.

'You don't learn spear-craft like that.' Olaf had his spear across his shoulders and his brawny arms draped over it. 'You're born with it.'

'Well I would like to know how Guthorm got his hands on the lad in the first place,' Hendil said, which was a good question given that Guthorm was no longer a raiding man, if he had ever been much of one.

'Well seeing as Guthorm is not missing an arm or a head I would say that he likely won the lad from some axe-swinger,' Olaf said.

Which was probably why Guthorm stayed in his longhouse these days rather than taking a crew out on the hunt for plunder. He likely made more silver at the Weeping Stone than he did from his fields and his pigs and sheep.

But the other karls who had brought fighters to the Weeping Stone backed out of the thing now, any confidence they had come with as broken as the bodies which lay in the grass drawing flies. Folk were muttering that Guthorm's man was Óðin-favoured and that no one could be expected to fight against a god as well as a man. As for Guthorm, his fleshy face was sweat-sheened now and the smile on it had all the substance of steam from a cauldron. He was worried and so he might be, for the way things were going no one would bring their fighters and their silver here again just to see the former slaughtered and the latter go into Guthorm's purse. And if they did not come, Guthorm would have to get up off his arse and do some proper work.

Svein gripped his long-axe beneath the head and lifted it in the thrall's direction. 'I'll fight him, Sigurd,' he said. 'Put all your money on me and we will empty every purse here.'

'Have you been rinsing your guts with some stash we don't know about, lad?' Olaf asked him. 'That son of a she-wolf would put a dozen holes in you before you knew you were worm food.'

Svein looked offended. 'I'd only need to hit him once,' he said, slapping the axe's cheek.

'No, Svein,' Sigurd said. 'We have done well enough here today. You carving up Guthorm's thrall will have our hosts in a poor mood this evening and I am thinking we should stay another night if Guthorm will have us.'

Svein nodded, happy enough with that.

'Well this is turning sour faster than milk left in the sun,' Solveig said, watching Ofeig Scowler jabbing his finger into the chest of another karl who had brought a fighter but now refused to let the man get anywhere near Guthorm's thrall. Sensing that the festivities were over and having doled out what she owed, Fastvi was on her knees behind her husband's two spearmen squirrelling their shiny winnings and her scales into a nestbaggin as discord spread around her, crackling like fire in dry grass.

'Maybe we'll have some more excitement to wash down the bad taste of it all,' Olaf suggested, nodding at two of Guthorm's friends who had squared their shoulders to one another, hands on the grips of the scramasaxes sheathed above their crotches. And perhaps they would, Sigurd thought, for Guthorm was losing his grip on the day, much to the black-haired young man's amusement if the curl of his lip was anything to go by.

But it was Lame-Leg who got everyone's attention, banging the hilt of his sword against the back of a shield, for he had sniffed out an opportunity to make up for his losses. 'We have come all this way, myself I have come from Lysebotn,' he shouted, 'and it does not seem right that we will not get a fair chance to go home with a little more than we came with.'

'My man will fight anyone who dares to face him at the stone,' Guthorm insisted, arms out wide. 'It is not my fault that there are some pale livers here today.'

That last was not clever but Guthorm could not resist it.

'You might as well cut your own belly open as fight him!' a man yelled, pointing at Guthorm's thrall.

'There's some seiðr about the lad,' another man called. 'It's not natural.'

'So we leave him out of it,' Lame-Leg said. 'I have brought another man, as you can all see. Will someone offer to fight him?' There was a murmur among the crowd as all eyes turned to this warrior, who puffed up his chest and tried to put some granite in his face. 'I am feeling generous and would let him fight despite my losses here today.'

Lame-Leg's man seemed to have grown half a foot since Sigurd last looked, his confidence blooming now he knew he would not have to fight the chained thrall. 'That is what we have come for,' In-Halti said. 'My man will fight anyone here, so long as that man does not have a god at his shoulder.'

'Who here has seen this man fight before?' Guthorm asked, throwing his sword arm out wide.

Folk shook their heads or answered that they had never laid eyes on the man.

'Good,' Guthorm went on. 'Then we just need another man whom no one has seen with a sword in his hand and we will have a fair contest with no one whining about it afterwards.'

'What about you, Olaf?' Eid called. 'You look like a man whose ears have rung with the sword song. That is a fine brynja you have been showing off since you came here. Will you fight Lame-Leg's man?'

Guthorm dismissed Eid's invitation with a flourish of his arm. 'Are you mad, Eid?' he said. 'Olaf is our guest. Why would he wish to risk his life here today?'

'Because his young friend from Skudeneshavn there needs silver and Olaf can win some if he is as good a fighter as his war gear would suggest.'

The folk at the Weeping Stone were all murmurs and eyeballs then as they stared at Sigurd.

'Big-mouthed goat-swiver,' Solveig muttered, for most of the folk there must have heard of what had befallen Jarl Harald of Skudeneshavn and his people. Furthermore, many would have heard on the wind that the jarl's youngest son Sigurd had escaped the king's net and perhaps it might have reached their ears that Harald's godi had changed himself into a fox and chewed off his own leg to escape a drowning death on the skerry below Avaldsnes.

'I'll fight anyone you like,' Olaf called, stepping forward to draw their eyes to him instead of Sigurd.

'No, Uncle,' Sigurd said, gripping his shoulder. 'Eid has laid us bare here. Look at them wondering what kind of man I am. I will fight Lame-Leg's man.'

Beneath the beard Olaf's face was all scowl. 'Listen to me, lad, I am with you to the end of all this, whatever that may be. But you are not my jarl. Not yet.'

'I'm sorry, Uncle,' Svein said, coming to stand in front of Olaf, holding his long-axe across his body. Olaf was a big man but Svein was a mountain even then.

'You had better either swing that thing or move out of my way before I rip your arms off and ram them down your damn throat,' Olaf snarled. Svein did not move but Sigurd did and he walked towards the standing stone and the dark-haired thrall sitting at its base.

Then he turned to face the crowd. 'I am Sigurd son of Jarl Harald of Skudeneshavn who was betrayed by the oath-breaker King Gorm. I will fight In-Halti's man.' He saw their eyes light up, none more than Guthorm's, because the karl knew that his reputation was saved. Whatever happened now his guests would go away with a story worth telling and that was almost as good as a purse full of silver.

'We are honoured, Sigurd Haraldarson, and we accept your offer,' Guthorm said. Sigurd nodded and turned to glance at his friends to make sure there was no blood being spilled there, but Olaf and Svein were side by side watching him. Even Olaf knew he must stay out of it now, for this was an issue of pride and Sigurd had no choice but to swim with the current of it.

Not that Sigurd wasn't cursing himself for a fool. He was still weak from the ordeal of the hanging tree and the thought of a hard fight now greased his palms and loosened his bowels. But the only way he would ever be strong enough to fight Jarl Randver and King Gorm would be if he drew men to him, if Sword-Norse were prepared to follow him into the blood-fray. Which they would never do if he was the kind of man who hides behind others when a challenge is hurled.

He looked at Lame-Leg's fighter to get his measure. He was not a big man but he had an arrogance about him, a fire in the eyes that made Sigurd wonder why he had not noticed him before. But then, the man had quite literally stepped out of the shadow of In-Halti's other fighter, the giant who lay all but forgotten out there in the long grass, though at least they had yanked the axe from his head.

'Sigurd, what weapons will you use?' Eid asked him. Clearly the man had wanted Olaf to fight but he seemed happy enough now that Sigurd stood in Olaf's place and that was because he expected Sigurd to lose and he knew that would hurt Olaf more than a blade between the ribs.

'My sword is all I need,' Sigurd said. He shrugged. 'I could use an axe or a spear or even a forge hammer and the end would be the same. I am favoured by the Frenzy God and cannot lose.'

This was some boast but it did the trick, for Lame-Leg's man forced a grin into his lips even as the colour drained from his face. Those at the Weeping Stone this day had already seen enough to make them suspect that the gods were amongst them. There was a thrall with crow-black hair and not a scratch on him to prove it. Not a scratch, and five fresh corpses buzzing with flies.

I did not hang from that tree in that stinking, wretched place for nothing, Sigurd's mind growled, his eyes glancing up at the blue sky which was wisped with cloud as thin as bramble-caught wool. Fastvi was busy with her scales again and Guthorm sent a boy running over to her with his purse. Sigurd could not say who the karl was putting his silver on to win. He knew though that Aslak would put at least half of Sigurd's own wealth on him. Probably more.

'Do you want a shield, Sigurd?' Eid asked. Sigurd shrugged as though he did not care either way, though he took the shield which Eid offered and in truth was glad to have it. Without the shield he would have to be as light on his feet as a cat in order to avoid his opponent's blade, and he was not strong enough for that. Even walking up the hill that morning had made his head spin and his chest tight as the skin of Asgot's spirit drum. But with the shield he could stand his ground and take some hits. It would give him some time to work out how he was going to beat the man.

Guthorm came over to Sigurd and for a moment he just stood there, the eyes beneath those heavy lids on Sigurd like fingers amongst a knotted rope. 'If you are alive at the end of this you will be my guest again this evening. It may be that we have things to talk about after all.'

Sigurd nodded and walked past him to where his opponent, whose name was Hagberth, waited, spear and shield gripped and ready. Sigurd did not blame him for having a spear as well as a sword, but Sigurd had claimed the Allfather's favour and so what need had he of a spear? That would have to go for his armour too, seeing as he wore none apart from the greaves on his shins whose iron strips were dark now against the leather they were fixed to.

A helmet would have been good, he thought.

Folk were cheering now, rousing themselves for what they hoped would be a proper fight.

'Cut him a new arsehole, Sigurd!' Svein bellowed.

Sigurd turned and saw Asgot sitting on the ground casting his runes as though he could tell more from them than he could from watching the fight itself. And perhaps he could. Olaf nodded and Aslak pointed to the ground meaning that Sigurd should put his opponent down as quickly as possible. Hendil stood twisting his finger ring, Loker was chewing his thumbnail and Solveig was holding his belly as though he needed to empty his bowels. The muscles in Svein's jaws were pulsing beneath his red beard and his hands were great white knots on his long-axe's haft and Sigurd knew his friend would swap places with him in a sparrow's fart if he could.

And then Hagberth was coming for him, his leather skull cap and eyes the only things Sigurd could see above the iron-rimmed shield.

Hagberth struck first, his spear blade streaking for Sigurd's face, but Sigurd knocked it away with his shield at the same time as swinging his sword which would have opened Hagberth's throat had he not been quick to yank his head back. The spear came again and this time Sigurd blocked with his sword but then Hagberth crouched and the blade would have cut open Sigurd's right shin had it not turned off his greave. Sigurd hacked down into the stave, cutting it clean in half, and Hagberth leapt back then hurled what was left at Sigurd to buy the time to draw his sword.

He came again. Hacking at Sigurd's shield, three great blows to test his enemy's strength and the quality of the limewood.

216

Sigurd's shield held and he loosened his shoulders as they circled each other. Then Hagberth struck again and this time Sigurd aligned his shield so that the blow glanced off downward and towards his opponent's left and might have allowed Sigurd an opportunity for a counter strike had Hagberth not been as experienced a fighter as he clearly was. Hagberth had his shield across in time to catch the blow and they parted again already sweating and breathing hard.

'I thought you would be better,' Sigurd said. 'But now I can see why Lame-Leg kept you at the back. Like the runt of the litter.' He went in with a downward strike to Hagberth's shoulder but the man got his shield in the way and then they traded blows and slivers of limewood flew.

When they parted again Sigurd's vision was blurring. There were dark spots moving through his sight like the shadows of birds across the surface of a wind-rippled pool, and he knew he did not have the strength yet for this fight. And yet he could not let anyone see that and so he went in with a low-level strike to Hagberth's leg which missed and Hagberth stepped in and slammed his sword's hilt against Sigurd's head, filling his skull with lightning.

He heard the crowd roar and felt his legs moving beneath him.

'Stay on your feet, Haraldarson!' someone roared. Olaf.

Sigurd staggered out of Hagberth's reach and did not fall but neither had he time to gather his wits as the man was on him again, the thunder of his sword against Sigurd's shield pulling Sigurd back to the present, like a drowning man hauled from beneath the fjord's surface.

Sigurd put his shoulder into his shield and drove it into his opponent, who stumbled backwards and fell on his backside, which brought more cheers and a wave of laughter that had his face flushing crimson as he climbed to his feet. Sigurd armed the sweat from his eyes and tried to blink away the dark motes that were storming his vision.

'What is the matter, Hagberth?' he called. 'Are you tired? You must be older than you look.' He shot the man a grin and held his sword and shield out wide inviting Hagberth to come at him again.

In-Halti's man needed no invitation. He strode forward and the steel-song of their swords rang out, echoing off the Weeping Stone. It was what these folk had come to this place for and they lapped it up like cats at the cream, shrieking and squawking at every blow. Blades thundered against limewood and *clunked* off shield bosses and then Sigurd leapt, thrusting his sword into Hagberth's right shoulder, but the man's leather armour stopped the blade and he roared in pain, slamming his shield into Sigurd's and forcing him back.

'You are a dead man, Hagberth,' Sigurd said, then nodded at the Weeping Stone beneath which the black-haired thrall sat watching him, his face still spattered with dead men's blood. 'Do you think your wife will raise a stone in your honour?' Sigurd grinned at him. 'I do not think so, Hagberth. I think she will get over your death by getting under the first man she sees.'

'Hold your tongue, whelp!' Hagberth snarled but Sigurd laughed. He had practised with sword, shield and spear since the first day he had been strong enough to lift them, but he also knew that words could be weapons too. They could rob a man of his self-possession. A well-placed insult could pierce an enemy's battle-craft like a spear through a shield. It could make a warrior do something reckless.

But not Hagberth. With a man like that it did the opposite, because he had fought too many battles to fall for such tricks. If anything such a tongue-lashing only made a man like Hagberth more careful.

Which was precisely what Sigurd was counting on. No thundering charge from Hagberth now. In-Halti's man would not fall for this pup's wiles. He came slow. His shield across his body, eyes sharp as rivets, sword arm not too far from his body and the shield before it as if to offer it as a target.

And Sigurd let him come.

He waited, his heart pummelling his breastbone, the muscles in his arms and legs bunched tight as ships' knots. He would get one chance. No more than that. The crowd and his own friends were shouting but to Sigurd it was the sound of waves hurling themselves against rocks, or the murmur of blood pulsing in his ears.

Come on then. Let us end this.

There was little more than a stride's worth of ground between them now. Suddenly Sigurd swung his left leg, smashing his greave-guarded shin into the lower rim of Hagberth's shield and driving the shield up into the man's jaw and throwing his head back with a loud crack of bone.

Hagberth stumbled back, desperate to put distance between them, his mouth welling with blood that spilled into his beard and poured down the hard leather sheathing his chest.

'Do you yield, Hagberth?' Sigurd asked, not that he expected to hear an answer for Hagberth's jaw had shattered like an ill-forged blade and he would never speak again. And yet his answer could not be mistaken by anyone there as he shook his head, slopping blood left and right, then struck his sword's hilt against his shield, and Sigurd admired him for it. 'I told you you were a dead man,' he said, striding forward, then he swung Troll-Tickler with all the strength he could muster and it chopped Hagberth's shield in half, taking off his arm. Gasps and groans rose on the breeze as Lame-Leg's man dropped his sword and fell to his knees, clutching the gory stump, his eyes impossibly wide, his beard frothed with blood.

Sigurd bent and picked up the man's sword, then yanked Hagberth's right hand from the messy stump where the left had been, wrapping the blood-slick hand around the weapon's grip, keeping his own hand tight on Hagberth's so that the man could not let go.

'When you see my father Jarl Harald sitting with the Æsir in Óðin's hall, tell him I will not join him and my brothers until my sister is safe and I have avenged him.' Hagberth was dying now. Sigurd could see the light fading in his eyes like a guttering lamp flame. 'Did you hear me, Hagberth?' he yelled. 'Tell my father I will avenge him.'

Hagberth managed to nod, the gesture loud in the silence which now reigned at the Weeping Stone. Still gripping the man's hand around his sword, Sigurd placed the point of Troll-Tickler against the inside of Hagberth's collar bone and brought his weight down, driving the blade deep into the man's body to rip open his heart. Hagberth gasped and shuddered and died, and Sigurd stood, hauling his sword out and noting the dark gobbets hooked on the blade's notches. Then he turned to Guthorm and those gathered around the rune stone.

'Does anyone else want to fight me?' he roared, struggling to see their faces for the black spots marring his vision. But no one did, which was just as well for he thought he might fall flat on his face. Then he felt an arm round his shoulder and Olaf was there, the bulk of him like a tree for Sigurd to lean against and together they walked away from the Weeping Stone. And the wolf-eyed young man who watched them go.

CHAPTER ELEVEN

'WELL I DON'T THINK WE HAVE MADE MANY FRIENDS HERE,' SOLVEIG said, looking around Guthorm's dark, smoke-filled longhouse. Æskil Lame-Leg and Ofeig Scowler were there salving their wounded pride with Guthorm's ale and so were many others who had brought silver to the Weeping Stone – and lost it in most cases – who had accepted the karl's invitation to spend the night in his hall before setting off for their homes in the morning.

'If anything I'd say you've got another enemy in Lame-Leg,' Solveig went on, turning Sigurd's eye towards Æskil who had his beard half stuffed in Guthorm's ear and a scowl on his face worse than Ofeig Grettir's.

'That may be so, Solveig, but they know Sigurd now,' Olaf said, 'and that is worth something.' He downed a great wash of the bad ale and dragged a hand across his mouth, frowning. 'Still, I don't think we will find many arms for our oars here as it turns out.'

'Arms for our oars?' Solveig's grin was sour as the ale. 'We don't even have a ship.'

'Yes, well that is another thing,' Olaf said, drowning the words in his cup. 'But these are not real fighting men anyway. They like their quiet lives and now and then watching the blood

fly up at Guthorm's rune stone, but they are no good to us.' The
mood in the hall was sombre. Men and women talked in low
voices and drank steadily, and by the hearth, where Hagal said
he had told many a saga over the years, an old man sat on a stool
playing a bone whistle while his ancient friend sang in a voice
as worn as an old shoe. The song was the one about a fisherman
who swam down to Rán's kingdom under the sea to steal an
arm ring for his wife. But the man fell in love with the Mother
of the Waves and drowned in her embrace, which, according
to Olaf, was his own fault. And neither was this sort of song
likely to lift the mood, he told the old man, who showed what
he cared by launching into a song about a boy whose bad luck
brought him to outlawry and a bad death.

'A reputation is like a good sword,' Hagal said, 'or a good saga
tale come to that. You cannot make it overnight. It takes time.
Word of Sigurd's time on the ash tree—'

'Ash tree? It was an alder,' Loker said.

Hagal shook his head. 'Now it is a great ash, Loker, like the
one from which Óðin One-Eye hung for nine days in his search
for wisdom. That is the way of it in my stories and word of it,
and of Sigurd's fight against the giant at the Weeping Stone—'

'Giant?' Olaf said.

Hagal raised a hand to still any objections before they could
come. 'I think it sounds better that Sigurd beat the giant than
that other little man,' he said, which the others conceded with
grunts and nods. 'These tales will hop from ear to ear like fleas
across a bed fur and like the roots of Yggdrasil itself Sigurd's
reputation will spread.' A broad smile filled his beard then. 'It
has already begun.'

Sigurd did not doubt it, for he had watched the skald wreathe
amongst Guthorm's guests like smoke from the hearth, sharing
their ale and pouring the spiced mead of Sigurd's tale in their
ears.

'We have made no friends here but we have made plenty of
silver,' Svein said, not seeing, or perhaps not caring, that those
two things were linked as surely as the chain at the neck of the

young killer who was back in the corner of Guthorm's hall.

'Aye, and you earned that silver, lad,' Olaf said, raising his cup to Sigurd who nodded and raised his own, glad for the rough-hewn bench beneath his arse and the pea and goat-meat broth that was putting strength back in his bones. 'But next time kick the shield into the whoreson's face at the beginning rather than waiting till you look like you're about to drown in your own sweat.'

'It was all part of my scheme, Uncle,' Sigurd said.

'I'm sure it was,' Olaf said, one eyebrow hoisted.

'Sigurd was drawing it out to give all those folk a reason not to string Guthorm up by the bollocks,' Hendil said, banging his cup against Sigurd's.

'And while Guthorm must be grateful for it, for he is sharing his food and ale with us, all the same I do not trust him,' Aslak said. 'What is to say he has not sent a man off to Hinderå to tell Jarl Randver that we are here? Or even sent to the king at Avaldsnes?' He gestured at the steaming bowls and hunks of bread on the table before them. 'Perhaps he has put this on just to keep us here until our enemies arrive.'

'We could be the flies in the web,' Loker conceded. 'There is no doubt Guthorm has a nose for easy silver and he would make himself jarl-rich by giving us up to either Randver or King Gorm.'

'Perhaps that is what they are talking about,' Asgot said, nodding towards Guthorm and Lame-Leg and slurping broth from his spoon, 'for they seem to be friends again now.'

'We will leave in the morning,' Sigurd said.

Olaf nodded, saying that skulking off now would not look very good, besides which you didn't throw a man's hospitality back in his face even if you did not entirely trust him and the only ale he had left tasted like horse piss. 'I would speak to Guthorm to see if he knows of any other karls in Rogaland or Ryfylke, or even east in Nedenes Amt, who might have a reason to prefer a dead Jarl Randver to a living, breathing one.' He looked at his friends, trying not to wince at the taste of Guthorm's ale and wishing they had saved some of the better stuff the night before. 'It would be good if you all did the same instead of huddling together like women around the loom.' There were some murmurs at that but they could not disagree that their time would be better spent finding out what they could than sitting there like boys too shy or too arrogant to join in with the rest.

'There is a girl over there who looks the kind to know all the important things,' Hendil said, smiling at a pretty girl with long wavy uncovered hair. To the others' surprise she smiled back.

'And if she doesn't then perhaps her friend does,' Loker added, slapping his friend on the back as they emptied their cups and got up from the bench.

And in a few moments Sigurd and Asgot were alone but for Solveig who had fallen asleep, his head against the old tapestry behind them, his mouth catching smoke and flies.

'What do you think, Asgot?' Sigurd asked.

The godi lifted his bowl, eyeing the room over the rim as he drained the last of the broth. 'I think if I were to sit down next to any of these sheep they would piss themselves.' It was true, for since they had learnt that Asgot was the priest who had shapeshifted to escape a drowning death at Avaldsnes they had looked at him the way livestock will look at a prowling wolf, wide eyes fixed on him but greasing off the moment he looked their way.

But that had not been what Sigurd meant and the godi knew it. Still, Asgot held his tongue until the sharpness of Sigurd's glare hooked the words out of him.

'I think it is not about Guthorm at all. Or Lame-Leg or his handsome friend,' he said, nodding towards Ofeig Scowler, 'but then you know that better than I.' He turned and looked into Sigurd's eyes, their glares squared up like opponents at the Weeping Stone. 'Or do I have to mix up one of my draughts again and pour it down your throat?'

'Can't be worse than this,' Sigurd said, lifting the cup to his lips though their eyes were still locked. 'I remember,' he said.

'I know you do,' Asgot said, turning his gaze towards Guthorm who had his mouth against his wife's ear now that Lame-Leg was limping off through the throng to empty his bladder.

'But I don't know what it means,' Sigurd said. Fastvi looked up at Sigurd then and gave him a smile that did not venture north of her lips. Sigurd smiled and nodded at her then turned back to Asgot. 'It is like trying to make sense of one of Hagal's stories after too much mead.' Sigurd's body ached and he was so exhausted that his very blood seemed to want to stop flowing and rest. His skull hurt so much that he wondered if Hagberth had cracked it with that blow from his sword's pommel, and the last thing he wanted to do was to try to untangle the knot of the visions that still stalked his mind to the shadow beat of Asgot's spirit drum.

'You are tired, Sigurd,' Asgot said half smiling, fingering a silver ring he had knotted into his beard. Sigurd could not say where he had got it. 'Perhaps this will all be clearer in the morning.'

Sigurd closed his eyes and for a moment he was back in Eik-hjálmr his father's hall, the hum of his people in his ears like the sea breaking on the rocks down in the bay, the sweet smoke of the hearth in his nose, his eyelids burnished by the golden flicker of lamp flames. But all that was gone now and only existed in the thought chest of his mind where he would keep it for as long as he could. He opened his eyes and the truth hit him like a pail of cold water. This was no jarl's mead hall but the low-roofed, ill-made longhouse of a karl who thought more of himself than he had the right to. A farmer who grew fat on the scraps but lacked the courage to run the boar through himself.

I do not need such men as these, Sigurd thought, shaking his head. Not men but sheep, and sheep are no good to me.

The ale was beginning to dull the edge of his thoughts and he welcomed it because it also numbed the aches and pains in his muscles and bones.

'It tastes better the more you drink,' he said to Asgot. 'That is something at least.'

'It tastes less the more you drink,' Solveig beside them said, his eyes still closed, head still back against the planks. 'There's a difference.'

'Bollocks,' someone growled and Sigurd turned round to see Ofeig Grettir standing behind him, a lump of cheese in one hand, his ale cup in the other. He gestured with the cheese towards Solveig. 'I had put a wager on the old man being dead,' he said and Sigurd waited for Solveig to bite but it seemed he had fallen asleep again. 'Mind if I sit?' Scowler asked.

Sigurd gestured to the empty bench across from him and Ofeig Scowler nodded and went to take his seat, slamming the cup down on Guthorm's rough-hewn table.

'What do you want, Ofeig Grettir?' Sigurd said.

'I wanted to thank you for winning today,' Scowler said. 'I had already lost four men to that Hel-spawn boy,' he said, nodding to the thrall chained in the dark corner, 'and things were as bad as they could be. But at least I won some silver on you.' The scar that gouged across his forehead and down over his right eye was even more terrible close up but the man seemed quite used to it. 'Though if I am to tell the truth, for a moment out there I thought Lame-Leg's man had the better of you.' He grinned. Or at least it was what passed for a grin on that face. 'That was a Loki trick with the shield, hey. I must get myself some greaves like yours. You'd have cracked a shin otherwise.'

'Do you find yourself in many fights then?' Sigurd asked.

'Look at me,' Scowler said.

Sigurd nodded and could not help but smile.

'But I choose my fights carefully,' Ofeig went on. There was a glint in his right eye then, telling Sigurd that he still saw out of it despite the gash. 'Unlike you, Sigurd Haraldarson. And I'm not talking about your little brawl up at the Weeping Stone today. Kings and jarls is a different thing. A heavy thing, lad.'

'I did not choose this fight,' Sigurd said. 'It lies before me like the sea before a ship's bow. Those who betrayed my father and slaughtered my mother, my brothers and my friends, they wove their own deaths when they did not kill me.'

'That's as may be,' Scowler said, 'but you might as well fight a troll with a toothpick. Still, I can see you are a young man of purpose, Sigurd, and from the looks of it you have some good spear arms to call on, friends who will follow where you lead, and that's to your credit. Though you will need many more than this,' he said, gesturing towards Olaf and Svein where they sat talking to a knot of local folk.

'Will you join me then, Ofeig Grettir?' Sigurd asked.

'Me? Ha! No,' he said, biting off a hunk of cheese. 'The only decent fighters I could bring to a disagreement lie dead in Guthorm's barn. As for me, I have little affection for Jarl Randver or King Gorm, but neither do I have any great desire to get a spear in my belly for helping you.'

'There will be plunder in it,' Sigurd said. 'Even Jarl Randver is as rich as Fáfnir these days.'

'Silver is little good to a dead man,' Scowler pointed out. 'But I do know of two men who would walk through dragon's fire to join a crew that had the balls to take on Jarl Randver of Hinderå. And not for the silver either but just for the blood of it.' He washed the cheese down with ale and wiped his mouth with his hand. 'These two are brothers who were stupid enough to get themselves outlawed for killing a man and refusing to pay the weregeld to the dead man's kin.' He wafted a hand through the smoke. 'Some fight over a woman, I heard, and what with brothers being brothers once one was in the mire the other soon followed. Jarl Randver had their father thrown from a cliff.'

'Why did Randver care so much about it?' Sigurd asked.

Scowler pursed his lips, scratching the thick bristles of his beard. 'Something to do with the man whom the brothers skewered being married to Randver's sister. These boys did not concern themselves with the details of the thing,' he said, sharing a look with Asgot that said *You know what young men are like these days.* Then he shrugged. 'But they were very fond of their father from what I could see.'

'And why would I want two trouble-makers in my crew?' Sigurd asked, though the truth was he already liked these two brothers from the sound of them.

'Because when Jarl Randver sent six men to their stead to bring them to trial those men came back dead. Stiff-limbed and corpse-pale as my fighters in Guthorm's barn.' He shook his head. 'Óðin's arse but you took your time killing that proud fool today.' Then his eyes lit. 'Bjarni and Bjorn. Yes, that's the lads, if memory serves.' He barked at Guthorm's serving girl to bring more ale. 'The brothers have gone to ground now of course, like a couple of foxes, what with the jarl's men sniffing all over for them.' The man tapped his nose with a thick finger, looking from Asgot to Sigurd. 'But I know where they can be found.'

'I am listening,' Sigurd said.

Scowler held out his cup and the girl filled it to the brim. 'First let me have another look at those greaves of yours, lad,' he said.

The last thing Sigurd remembered before he fell asleep amongst the reeds of Guthorm's floor was a sad tune worming from the bone flute into his ear and wondering if he had just been a fool to give Ofeig Grettir his greaves in exchange for the whereabouts of two brothers who hated Jarl Randver. A greave per brother. He hoped they would be worth it. If they could be found.

The first thing he *heard* when he woke in the heart of the night was the shrieks of the dying.

'Get up, Sigurd,' Asgot rasped, his face much too close, 'the wolf is in the sheep pen.' Sigurd blinked his eyes, trying to make sense of the shapes whirling in the gloom around them. Women were screaming and men were roaring to each other to arm themselves and get more lamps lit. The door was flung open onto the night and folk were spilling out of Guthorm's long-house.

'Here,' Svein said, offering Sigurd a spear which he had got from somewhere. Sigurd took it, standing and kicking off the furs he'd slept in.

'What's happening?' It was Olaf beside them in the murk, long knife in one hand, the other rubbing the sleep from the bags of his eyes. 'Who is attacking us?' Somewhere a man was dying, the life gurgling from his throat as a blade ripped up into the precious meat behind his ribs.

'Jarl Randver?' Loker suggested, handing a shield to Hendil who was only just climbing to his feet. Aslak and Hagal were there too, meaning they were all accounted for which was a relief, for the stench of open bowels had hit Sigurd's nose now and death was tainting the thick fug.

'Doubt it,' Solveig said, coming up behind them. 'We'd be halfway to Valhöll on a plume of smoke if it were Randver. Jarls like a good hall-burning.'

And suddenly Sigurd knew who this death in the darkness was.

He muscled his way through the chaos to Guthorm's hearth, Svein at his shoulder, and there threw two handfuls of kindling into the glowing, flame-licked ashes. After a moment light bloomed and they looked across the hall and saw the thrall with the crow-black hair cut a man's throat with a scramasax. The scream died on the man's lips and Guthorm's thrall leapt back from a sword swing that would have cut him in half at the waist. It was Æskil In-Halti and he all but tripped over his lame leg as he tried to regain his balance, but the thrall stepped in and clasped Æskil round the throat then drove him back against the wall, punching the scramasax up into his belly.

The thrall turned, snarling in the flamelight that chased the shadows from the place, as Lame-Leg slid down the wall behind him, hands pressed to his death wound.

'I'll put a spear through him,' Svein said.

'No, Svein.' Sigurd clutched his friend's shoulder. 'Not yet.'

Fastvi was wailing and Sigurd saw that she cradled her husband in her arms, the two of them down in the ale-soaked rushes. Guthorm had been skewered through the stomach with his own sword, so that over a foot of bloody blade stuck from his back. That had taken muscle, to get through so much fat.

'We'll get no more horse piss ale from Guthorm then,' Svein said.

Most of those who had been sleeping in that place had vanished into the night by now, though a knot of armed men were closing in on Guthorm's thrall, Eid, Alver and Ingel amongst them.

'How did the lad get free?' Olaf asked but no one could answer that and then the thrall's blade streaked out, cutting the arm that was scything an axe towards his face and he caught the axe before it hit the ground, sweeping it up to hack into the man's groin. The man shrieked and fell away, scrambling off and leaving a wake of blood in the rushes. Then the thrall caught Ingel's blade between the axe's beard and haft, twisted the sword out of Ingel's hand and slashed open his neck with the scramasax and turned to face the last two.

Alver backed away, his own hand axe raised, then turned and fled leaving his friend Eid to his inevitable death.

'Well, Sigurd,' Eid called over his shoulder. 'Are you going to help me send this Hel-spawn back into the freezing fog?' His eyes were locked on the thrall's and he seemed reluctant to make the first move for he might have known it would also be his last, and it seemed the young man was content to spin the thing out a little longer. 'There are nine of you standing there. Do you not owe it to your host Guthorm to kill this animal?' There was an edge of fear in his voice but his sword arm was steady enough.

Sigurd lifted his spear in an overarm grip.

'Kill him, Sigurd!' Eid called. 'I will pay you with Guthorm's silver. Kill him now!'

Sigurd looked at Asgot and noticed that there was a small key hanging from a thong around his neck. It was the kind of key that fit a set of slave irons. Asgot's lip curled and Sigurd pulled back his arm. The spear cut through the smoke of Guthorm's hall and plunged into Eid's back between his shoulder blades and he staggered forward with the impact of it, right into the thrall who sank the scramasax up into his gut then shoved him off.

'I never liked him,' Olaf muttered.

'He's more dangerous than winter that one,' Solveig said as they stood staring at the thrall, who stood with his own eyes riveted to Sigurd. There were shouts outside in the night and you didn't need too much clever in you to know that whoever came in now might think that Sigurd and his Skudeneshavn men had had some hand in this slaughter. Eight men lay dead or dying amongst the floor rushes and the only other living person was Fastvi, who was insensible now anyhow, rocking over Guthorm's body like some moon-mad crone.

'What now then?' Sigurd said to the thrall.

The beardless lad grinned. 'Now we leave,' he said.

'It talks,' Hagal muttered.

'How do we know you're not going to put that axe in our heads the first chance you get?' Sigurd asked him.

'There'll be no chance of that if we gut the lad here and now,' Olaf suggested. 'Wouldn't want him on the row bench behind me.'

'This young man is good for your saga, Sigurd,' Hagal said.

'It's all gone!' Aslak said, having gone outside to fetch their own weapons from the racks outside the hall. 'Someone's pilfered it all.'

'This is turning into a strange night,' Olaf said.

'You can blame that horse piss ale we've been rinsing our guts with,' Solveig said, 'for nothing good comes of drinking bad ale.'

'Why would they take our gear?' Olaf growled.

'Because they were going to murder you for all that silver you won up at the Weeping Stone,' Guthorm's thrall said, 'and for whatever else they might find on you.' He shrugged. 'They are not used to good swords but they like the idea of them.' He gestured to Olaf with the hand axe. 'Mail too.'

'Guthorm was going to murder us in our sleep?' Olaf asked. 'Pah! He didn't have the balls, that one.'

'How do you know this?' Sigurd asked the blood-spattered, black-haired thrall.

'I saw him spinning it with Æskil In-Halti,' he said, then turned those wolf eyes on Olaf. 'They chained me. They did not poke out my eyes or cut off my ears.'

231

'Aye, well I'm thinking they wish they had now,' Olaf said, still bristling with the promise of violence, which was hardly surprising given what they had just seen. They had gone from sleep to slaughter in the blink of an ale-blurred eye and were all sharp with the shock of it.

'But this is not our mess,' Solveig said.

Loker nodded. 'We should be gone before daybreak for they are bound to fetch some loudmouth and his crew to deal with it.'

'Aye, this place is one of Jarl Randver's piss posts,' Olaf said, 'and he's sure to send men to find out how Guthorm and all these nithings got themselves cut up.' He turned to Sigurd and gestured to Guthorm's thrall. 'If it's true about them planning to kill us in our sleep then this lad has done us a favour.' He scratched his bearded cheek. 'Maybe it would be ungrateful to spear him.'

'Don't let that stop you trying, Olaf,' the thrall said, throwing out his arms as an invitation to them all to go and kill him. Or to try at least.

But Sigurd remembered seeing Guthorm and Lame-Leg in each other's ear holes earlier like maggots in old flesh. Recalled the look of Fastvi's face too, when their eyes had met through the smoke. And given what kind of man her husband was, Sigurd was beginning to get a grip on it all. He considered walking over to Fastvi, who still sat in the reeds with her skewered husband, and putting a knife to her throat to make her spill the truth. But what difference would it make? He was not going to kill this thrall now. Not even if the lad's story about Guthorm and Lame-Leg's intended treachery had all the truth of one of Hagal Crow-Song's taller tales.

'I'd like to know how he slipped out of those irons,' Svein said, nodding towards the dark corner in which the young man had been chained. Sigurd glanced at Asgot but the godi seemed to have his lips sewn on that matter and so Sigurd did not mention the key around his neck.

'It seems to me you could have killed Guthorm and his friends

232

any time you wanted,' he said to the thrall, who was no longer a thrall really. 'Why did you wait until now?'

The young man tucked the axe into his belt then bent and pulled his scramasax's blade through a fistful of Æskil In-Halti's tunic. As for Lame-Leg he was as dead as a man could be though his eyes and mouth were open. 'It seemed like a good night to do it, Sigurd son of Harald,' he said. 'Besides, if Guthorm had cut your throat I would have nothing better to do than stay under this roof eating his food and killing the fools who come to the Weeping Stone.' He sheathed the knife and swept the black hair back from his face to reveal hollow cheeks and bones as sharp as the scramasax. His eyes bored into Sigurd's. 'You knew I would leave this farm with you one way or another,' he said. 'We both knew it up at the stone.'

Sigurd could have tried to deny this but there was no point and so he just nodded.

'Well if he's coming with us then we'll chain him again,' Olaf said, 'at least until we know he is not mad.'

'No,' Sigurd said. 'This man will not be chained again.' He walked over to the former thrall and stood square to him, his spear's butt planted in the reeds. 'What is your name?'

'Floki,' the young man said.

'Well then, Black Floki, will you help me avenge my kin and swear an oath to be my man if I balance that oath with food and silver and the favour you would expect from a good jarl?' Sigurd felt the eyes on his back then for he had yet to ask any of them to swear an oath to him though he had always had it in his mind to.

'Take me with you and I will kill whoever needs killing,' the young man said, which was good enough for now, until Sigurd came up with the warp and weft of whatever oath by which he would bind them to him and him to them. Better not to get into it now seeing as it was the first any of them had heard of it and it was not as though Sigurd were a jarl. Not yet.

'We should leave now,' Asgot said, his first words since waking Sigurd during the killing. The night beyond the pine walls was quiet now, which was to be expected with many of the able-bodied men lying dead and the women and children and old ones having fled the place.

'Was Ofeig Grettir in on it?' Sigurd asked Floki, pointing his spear at Scowler who lay throat-cut on the floor. Unlike some of the others he was not armed other than with the longsax which lay by the claw of his white hand.

'I did not ask him,' Floki said. 'But neither did he ever ask if I wanted to be chained to that rune stone up there and set upon by his turd-stinking boasters.'

That was fair enough, Sigurd thought, for all that he had liked Scowler. Still, he would have his greaves back now and that was something to be happy about.

He turned to Aslak, Solveig, Loker and Hendil. 'You four arm yourselves with what you can find and go down to the sea. Judging by how many folk came with Ofeig Scowler he must have come in a good-sized boat.'

'He won't be needing it now,' Olaf put in.

'No, but his folk might be climbing into it now,' Hagal suggested.

'Perhaps,' Solveig said, 'but they won't dare take it into the fjord now. They'll wait till morning.'

The four of them nodded to Sigurd and began to gather up what weapons they could find amongst the corpses, which was too many for men who had not had murder on their minds, as Solveig pointed out.

Meanwhile, Sigurd and Floki and the others left Fastvi with the dead and went out into the night and filled their lungs with the clean, spruce-scented air, and in the barn beside Guthorm's longhouse they found their war gear. Svein also found a brynja worth a small hoard. It was still on the giant whom Black Floki had killed with an axe to the skull up at the Weeping Stone but it did not take Svein and Hagal long to pull it off the stiffening body, and it had to be Svein's for it would have drowned any of the others but for Olaf and he had a fine brynja already.

And when he was in it Svein looked like the Thunder God

himself. Olaf nodded and growled deep in his throat which they all took as a sign that he thought Svein looked as fine as a man could look in a brynja. Though Sigurd knew there was more to it than that and that Olaf was seeing in Svein the young man's father, his old friend Styrbiorn, who was dead and gone now like so many of Olaf's sword-brothers.

No brynja for Sigurd yet. That war gear which had belonged to his father and brothers and should have come to Sigurd in turn had gone as spoils to King Gorm in the pine wood near Avaldsnes. War Song, his father's great sword, now sat silent in its scabbard in the oath-breaker's hall, along with Harald's helmet with its panels of polished silver plate and its high crest of bronze that came down to a raven's face between the brows. Such things alone were worth facing death for and they would be Sigurd's in time. Or he would be a corpse himself.

'I have left something,' Black Floki said, stalking off back towards Guthorm's hall. Sigurd glanced at Olaf who shrugged and said there was nothing else for them to do but get down to the shore.

But Svein suggested they might as well see what food there was for the taking, seeing as Guthorm would no longer be getting fat on it. 'And all his guests have gone,' Svein added, sweeping an arm across the rolling moonlit pasture across which folk had fled in terror like shadows at sunrise, back to their own farms and steads.

'I'd have said the same thing had I not still been half asleep,' Olaf said through a yawn.

'What about Guthorm's woman? There would be no honour in taking all her food,' Hagal said. 'She has always been kind to me.' The words were barely off his tongue before a shriek like that of a vixen in heat tore the night. They looked across the yard towards the longhouse.

'Well that is that then,' Olaf said.

Some moments later the door creaked open and Black Floki came out holding Fastvi's bead and amber necklace in one hand and the two brass brooches which had fastened her dress in the other. On his right arm he wore Guthorm's warrior rings, one silver, one brass, which Sigurd thought might have caused some muttering being on the arm of a man not yet into his first beard. But had they not all just watched Floki beat five men?

'No one can say he has not earned them,' Sigurd said. 'Who knows how many others he's made corpses of up at that rune stone since Guthorm put that chain around his neck.'

'True enough,' Olaf admitted, 'but if we're going to let him pilfer from the dead, and he's with us now, we might as well see if any of the others have got anything worth having.'

'What's done is done,' Svein agreed.

So they went back into the longhouse and they took brooches, knives, belts and buckles, rings and bone combs, and Asgot found a dozen pieces of hacksilver which Ofeig Grettir had sewn into the hem of his tunic.

'Keep it,' Sigurd said when the godi offered him the silver. 'Use it to buy the gods' favour when we need it.'

'Or mead,' Svein suggested, shrugging at Sigurd when Asgot hissed something nasty at him.

And when they had plundered as thoroughly as any raiding party they left Guthorm's farm to the dead and their ghosts and made their way down to the sea upon which the moon spilled its glow like molten silver from a die.

Where Solveig and the others were waiting aboard a fine-looking knörr, their beards split by smiles almost as broad as the boat they stood in.

Bjarni's foot caught the big man square between his legs and the big man doubled over and probably would have roared in agony had Bjarni not brought the two-foot length of smooth ash down onto the back of his head, breaking the stick in two and doing who knew what to the man's skull.

The crowd bellowed and cheered, gasped and winced and Bjorn swore at his brother who shrugged as if to ask what the matter was. Not that Bjorn had the time to explain. He caught a blow on his own stick and forced his opponent's length of ash wide and stepped in to hammer a fist into the man's bearded chin. The man staggered backwards, raising his shield as he fell to one knee, but Bjorn was on him and grabbed the shield's rim with his left hand, pushed its bottom edge into the ground and leant over the thing to smash his stick down onto the shield arm just above the elbow joint. On both knees now, his shield dropped, the man looked wide-eyed at the two brothers coming for him.

'Yield! I yield!' he screamed, as the crowd hurled insults at him and waved their arms in disgust and disappointment. And Bjarni stepped up, lashing him across the temple with what was left of his stick. He sprawled onto the ground and lay still as a corpse.

The crowd roared even louder now, their fury carving a smile on Bjarni's face, like a moulding iron cutting a handsome groove on a ship's prow.

'He had yielded,' Bjorn snarled, hoisting a hand to placate the crowd. 'He was screeching it like a fucking cat.'

Bjarni looked down at the man whose head was leaking blood onto the flattened grass, and shrugged. 'I did not hear him,' he said, all beard and teeth.

His brother shook his head, bewildered. 'If we kill them we cannot beat them again next time, you half-wit,' he said, then cursed under his breath and went to collect their winnings.

CHAPTER TWELVE

THE KNÖRR WAS A GOOD VESSEL, FORTY-FIVE FEET LONG, ELEVEN FEET wide and with a draught of a little under three feet. She had half decks both fore and aft, each with a few oar-holes for manoeuvring in harbour, and between these decks an open cargo hold lined with brushwood mats to protect the hull strakes. She could easily be run right up onto a beach for unloading and when she was in the sea she was as watertight as you could hope for, though still needed one man bailing on and off in a rough sea.

'Ofeig Scowler was a lucky man to own such a vessel,' Solveig said a little after dawn when they had the sail up to catch a fresh wind that blew them south along the pine-bristled coast.

'He was not so lucky to get himself killed by being friends with that worm Guthorm,' Sigurd said, and this got some *ayes*. For they were sure now that Guthorm and Æskil In-Halti had intended to murder them in their sleep for their silver and perhaps for whatever reward they would get from the oath-breaker King Gorm or Jarl Randver. For why else had Guthorm's other guests had their weapons to hand in the dead of the night when the previous evening they had left them in the racks outside with those of the Skudeneshavn men?

In all likelihood Scowler had woken when the killing began,

saw his host being attacked by the thrall and drew his own knife as any man would do, for all the good it did him.

'I would sooner believe he was in on it too,' Hagal said, 'seeing as we have robbed him and made off with his ship, when he likely has kin somewhere looking out to sea for his return.'

'You can believe whatever you like, for all the difference it makes now, Crow-Song,' Olaf said, standing at the bow, eyes closed, enjoying the warmth of the sun on his left cheek.

And now and again Sigurd saw one or other of them staring at their new crew member as though there was some seiðr about him as dark as his long crow-black braids, or as if they were waiting for him to talk about that slaughter-filled night. Not that Black Floki had much to say about it, or about anything come to that. Solveig observed that clearly the lad did his talking with sharp edges, which was fine by him seeing as with Loker and Hendil aboard there was already too much talking for his ears.

'What shall we call her then?' Olaf asked, glancing from Sigurd to Solveig who stood at the stern like a king because he had a tiller in his hand again and that was all Solveig wanted from his life.

'She's wide, Olaf, so how about *Ragnhild*?' Solveig said.

Olaf grinned at that, stroking his hand along the knörr's sheer strake. 'She's too easy to handle to be named after my wife,' he said, which got some laughter. A good sound on an unfamiliar ship.

'How about *Sea-Sow*?' Aslak suggested.

'Frigg's white arse, Aslak,' Hagal blurted, 'that is not a name that fits well in any saga tale I can think of. Can you imagine Jarl Randver trembling with fear at mention of the *Sea-Sow*?'

'Well I like it,' Sigurd said, for the knörr's hull was round and deep like a sow's belly, and so unlike his father's dragon ships *Reinen* and *Sea-Eagle* that to give her a saga-worthy name might cause her offence. At least *Sea-Sow* was an honest name, as Olaf observed, and as soon as Solveig nodded his assent it was done.

'We will name her properly when we find some good mead to throw across her bow,' Sigurd said.

She was no fighting ship, and if a crew of raiding men, or even worse one of Jarl Randver's crews, saw the knörr as prey and came after her, *Sea-Sow* would have no chance of outrunning them. So Solveig would keep them snugged up to the coast, giving them the option to make landfall rather than being caught at sea. But with her high sides she was as seaworthy as you could want and certainly more comfortable for living on than *Otter*, which they had left up on the beach below Guthorm's longhouse and which was likely being rowed off somewhere even now as the wind played across *Sea-Sow*'s woollen sail. For there had been folk around *Sea-Sow* – or whatever she had been called while she had belonged to Ofeig Grettir – readying to push her back into the sea, when Aslak, Solveig, Loker and Hendil had come onto the shingle, swords and spear blades glinting in the moonlight. But at the sight of them those wide-eyed folk had scarpered like mice before an owl.

'Did you see the lads who were looking after her?' Olaf had asked Loker, nodding towards *Otter* as they put their shoulders into the knörr, shoving her back into the surf.

'Not a hair of them,' Loker had said, which was hardly surprising given that it was the third day now since the Skudeneshavn men had arrived at that place. Still, Olaf seemed disappointed about it for as far as he was concerned an agreement was an agreement.

'Lads today have no honour,' he grumbled into his beard, but was soon cheered when he and Sigurd had raised *Sea-Sow*'s sail and the day broke into that golden sort of morning on which you feel as though you could happily sail off the edge of the world and never look back.

'Just think how much booty we could pile in there,' Svein said now, looking down into the great hold which was empty but for the ballast, for Ofeig Scowler had not gone to Guthorm's farm to trade. 'Silver and bronze, furs, ivory and good drinking horns. And women.' Teeth flashed in his red bristles.

'Aye, we could carry a king's hoard, lad, and wallow about out here until someone comes along to relieve us of it,' Olaf replied, 'which they likely wouldn't break out in a sweat doing, seeing as we are only ten. And that's including old Solveig whose best fighting days are behind him.'

'Tell that to the seven-fingered goat-fucker who cut me!' Solveig called from the stern, proving that for all his years his ears yet worked.

Olaf batted his objection away with a big hand, looking back to Svein. 'Then of course there's the how of us getting our hands on so much plunder in the first place.'

'Well I am a big man and so have big thoughts,' Svein said, tapping two thick fingers against his temple. 'I cannot help it if you do not have the space in your thought box for such ambitions.'

And though the mood aboard *Sea-Sow* was as light as the white spume which the wind whipped off the choppy water, Olaf's words sat in Sigurd's skull like stone net sinkers. For ten men in a broad-beamed knörr was not something to trouble a man like Jarl Randver who could put nine ships into the fjord and at least six of them bristling with Spear-Norse. It seemed to Sigurd that his revenge sat far ahead of him, beyond his reach. A thing as unclenchable as Bifröst, the shimmering path connecting the worlds of gods and men. And even if he had got the Allfather's attention on the hanging tree or up at the Weeping Stone, it would not last if he did not continue to earn it.

He put this to Asgot who unlike Sigurd seemed untroubled as the wind flicked his bone-tied braids around his face and *Sea-Sow* followed the jagged coastline east between Jørpeland and the hammer-shaped island a Thór's throw from the shore.

'The gods *are* capricious, Sigurd, as your father would attest if he could,' the godi said. 'But now that they have taken an interest in you, which I am certain they have for we have called them as though with the Gjallarhorn itself, they will not turn their backs again in a matter of days. For them the lag between two full moons is like the time it takes for a sparrow to fly into a longhouse and out through the smoke hole.' His mouth warped like a bad oar. 'It is more likely they will treat our ambitious undertaking as they would a game of tafl.' He moved an imaginary gaming piece through the air. 'Placing obstacles in our way to see how we measure against them.'

A cheer went up from the bow where Aslak was pointing at a shoal of flying fish that splashed into the waves like a handful of thrown pebbles. The men were happy to be at sea again and in a proper boat. And not rowing.

'Gather your strength, Sigurd.' Asgot pressed a gnarly finger against his own temple beside a greying braid. 'And hone your purpose to a keen edge. Every step you take, every wave against the bow brings you closer to the spoils.'

But not the spoils of a raiding man, Sigurd thought. Not silver and slaves and weapons, though those things might be his too. But rather the blood plunder he would take with the blade, from those who had earned his hate. Those who had killed his parents and his brothers and taken Runa.

These thoughts raised the hairs on Sigurd's neck. They fanned the glowing coals in his gut, making them red hot.

The godi saw it and nodded. 'Feed the fire of it, Haraldarson,' he said. 'Keep that fire burning and the gods will stay close.' He grinned. 'Even the Æsir love a good fire. More now than ever with Fimbulvetr approaching. For that bone-cracking winter marks the beginning of their doom. They search the world for the worthiest of men to stand beside them at Ragnarök.'

'I need men too,' Sigurd said, watching a gull dive to snatch something up from the waves.

Asgot nodded towards Black Floki who stood amidships on the port side with his face to the sea spray that was soaking his crow-black hair. 'We have found our wolf, yes?'

Sigurd looked at the strange young man who was death with a blade, a warrior who might even have made his father's great champion Slagfid bleed if the two had ever faced each other in a fight. Perhaps Asgot was right and Floki *was* the spirit wolf of Sigurd's hanging vision. And perhaps they *were* playing some sort of game in which the gods had a hand. And so Sigurd would take *Sea-Sow* up the Lysefjord to search for the brothers Bjarni

242

and Bjorn, for men foolish enough to murder a man who was Jarl Randver's kin by marriage were just the sort of men he needed. If he found them he would persuade them to oath-tie themselves to him and then there would be two more swords aimed at Randver's throat.

But in Valhöll the gods were moving their pieces across the board and their laughter must have been shaking the great roof beams and spilling the mead from their horns.

'I feel like I'm sailing up Frigg's cunny and might never get out again,' Olaf said, mouth open, head tipped so far back that from behind you could not see his neck at all.

'Then Gungnir should be the least famous of Óðin's two spears,' Hagal said, also looking up at the towering rock around them, 'if he has to fill this.'

It was Sigurd's second time down the Lysefjord but he had been an infant the first time and now he was as awe-brimmed as the others, for the place stole a man's breath from his lungs. Green water against brutal, majestic mountain walls which rose some three thousand feet up into the cloud fog to give a man neck ache.

'You are right, Olaf,' Solveig said, filling his lungs, 'you can almost smell the gods. There is as much magic here as there was in that fen.'

No one disagreed with that, their eyes round and glutted yet still unable to drink it all in. Protected from the day's northerly breeze the water was calm enough that ducks bobbed in lines in the shadows of the cliffs and every jumping fish made great moving rings that your eyes could follow for fifty feet or more. Hendil observed that you didn't need to crane your neck if you were clever about it, for rock and sky were reflected upon the still water in such perfection that a drunken man might think he could step over the knörr's side and not get his shoes wet.

And though there was only a breath of wind, barely enough to push them along at more than a walking pace, no one complained. For that breath was like a god's whisper and every man felt it on the back of his neck.

'It is the kind of fjord you think of when men tell their stories of the old times,' Svein said, 'when heroes fought trolls and Thór came down from Valhöll to brain great serpents with his hammer.'

'Ah,' Hendil said, grinning, 'I am sure Solveig remembers it well.'

'Watch your tongue, youngen!' Solveig barked. 'I may be old, but my belt still knows its way around an arse.'

They lined *Sea-Sow*'s sides, staring up at the great jagged walls and mist-wreathed heights, some of them touching iron amulets or knife blades for luck, or muttering invocations under their breath. They were deep into the fjord now and if *Sea-Sow* sprang a leak, or if a storm whipped up from somewhere, they would die. There was nowhere along those steep cliffs to make landfall, no beach or cove, no man-made wharves or jetties. There was just rock and water as deep, Solveig said, as the distance between Yggdrasil's leafy canopy and its Níðhögg-gnawed roots.

'Well it is easy to see why the brothers came up here,' Loker said, which was true enough, Sigurd thought. For if the water was calm and you *did* take your boat up against the rock wall, and if you *could* find a suitable place to put your feet and hands, you could scramble up like a goat and vanish into the trees and who would ever find you? The ancient rocks cried fresh water into the sea and there must be more fish in those dark depths than stars in the night sky, which made the Lysefjord a good place to hide from a jarl who had dragon ships and spear-warriors and a thirst for your death.

'Which makes me wonder how we will ever find them,' Sigurd said.

Much of the towering granite either side that was not obscured by dark green pine and scrub was bone-white, which was how the place had got the name Light Fjord. At least that was what Crow-Song told them, though with a skald you could never be sure. Still, it was as good an explanation as anyone could think of.

'This Bjarni and Bjorn,' Solveig said, 'either they were carried here by a bloody great sea-eagle, or else they came by boat. Let's assume they would want to keep hold of that boat but would not want anyone coming up the fjord to see it.'

'So they've pulled it up somewhere and hidden it,' Olaf said.

Solveig nodded. 'We keep our eyes skinned and we think like them. Maybe we see smoke. Maybe we hear something.' He shrugged. 'If they were brought by a sea-eagle I do not know what to say.'

'Well I am busy, as you can see, so do not ask me to find these brothers you are after,' Svein said, standing at the port-side stern with a weighted line and hook in the water. They had found four such nettle-hemp lines wound round blocks of pine and stowed in a chest by the tiller, along with two good whetstones, an old set of scales, a fur hat, an iron cauldron and Ofeig Grettir's drinking horn.

'You cannot be so busy seeing as you haven't caught anything yet but for a tangle of slime,' Aslak said.

'That is because you all talk so much and the fish can hear you,' Svein grumbled.

Hendil glanced at Loker, a smile in his beard. 'I have never seen a fish with ears,' he said, then let out a long rumbling fart. 'I wonder if they are afraid of thunder.'

'I am afraid of thunder when it comes out of your arse, Hendil,' Olaf growled.

'See there,' Asgot said, pointing to a stand of flickering birch set back from the shore across the other side of the fjord.

At first Sigurd saw nothing but then he made out a thin curl of smoke rising from amongst the trees. 'It is a landing place at least,' he said.

'And it took Asgot's old eyes to see it,' Olaf said. 'It would be on the other damned side though. Chances are they'll see us coming and have plenty of time to disappear into some troll hole.'

'Still, it was not so difficult after all,' Hendil said, which was the way with Hendil, he always saw the sun through the clouds and thought things would turn out well.

But when they had moored *Sea-Sow* and found the log house among the trees it turned out not to be the two renegade brothers but an old man and his wife. They had seen the knörr coming across the fjord, yet rather than hide they had stood waiting patiently on the shore and even when Sigurd and the others had jumped onto the rocks with spears in their hands the old couple had seemed unworried.

'We don't get many visitors,' the old man said, 'much less raiders.' He turned his gummy smile on each of them in turn. 'But then we've got nothing worth stealing. Well, there's Vebiorg here,' he said, waving at his wife. 'You can take her. But I warn you she can't cook like she used to.'

'You are a braver man than I,' Olaf said.

The old man shook his head. 'She's deaf as a rock,' he said, 'and if you take her away you'll be wishing you were too before long.'

Vebiorg narrowed her eyes at her husband, telling Sigurd that she might be old and deaf but she was no fool.

'So why do you live out here with only fish and goats for company, old man?' Sigurd asked. For a moment the old man seemed to be considering whether or not to answer this, but then he pointed west back towards the fjord's mouth. 'I upset a powerful man,' he said, then shrugged his narrow shoulders as though to say it was a thing easily done.

'Not Jarl Randver of Hinderå?' Olaf said.

The old man frowned. 'Randver? Don't know him. This was a long time ago.' He glanced back to Sigurd. 'Before you were born, youngen.' He clawed his wispy beard. 'Gunnlæif, who men call Grunter, was jarl at Hinderå when I was last there.'

'Then you *have* been hiding a long time,' Olaf said, 'for they burnt Grunter in a handsome karvi some twenty summers ago or more.'

'Ah, I would like to have seen that, for you do not get so many proper send-offs like that any more.' His white brows arched above his rheumy eyes then. 'Or maybe you do, but what would we know of it?'

'We are looking for two brothers. Bjarni and Bjorn.' Sigurd smiled at Vebiorg to include her in the conversation even though she could not have known what they were saying. 'We mean them no harm.'

'You come well armed for men who mean no harm,' the old man observed.

'I cannot deny it,' Sigurd said. 'We find blades serve us better than trust these days.' Now it was his turn to point west back down the fjord. 'Out there the wolves are stalking each other and it will get worse by the time we are through.'

'Aye, you are better off out of it, old man,' Solveig said, enjoying calling another *old* for a change.

'So you're not raiders, eh?' The old man took the sweat-stained skull cap off his head and dabbed his watery left eye with it. 'But you're not traders either, even though you've got a good ship for it.'

'How does he know we are not traders?' Svein asked, his red brows knitting together.

'Because she is sitting high in the water,' Solveig said, thumbing back to *Sea-Sow* moored up behind them, 'which tells him there is nothing in her but rocks. Nothing to trade.'

The old man nodded, giving Svein his gummy smile.

'There are quicker ways to get the truth from him,' Black Floki said, his first words that day. He stood there with two short axes in his belt, a scramasax above his groin, a sword scabbarded at his left hip and a spear in his right hand.

But the old man was too old to be afraid even of Floki.

'I couldn't run now, not even if I was going to get my guts spilled by a beardless meyla like that,' he said, raising a few eyebrows, for calling Floki a little girl was not a clever idea to anyone's mind. But Floki simply grinned and the old man stared at him for a moment before returning his gaze to Sigurd and Olaf. 'But I do not know of these brothers,' he said. 'How do you know that they came up the Lysefjord?'

'A man named Ofeig Grettir told me,' Sigurd said. By the old man's face he did not know of Ofeig Grettir either and why should he? 'Are there many people living up here?'

'Not many. But some.' The old man took his wife's hand in his own then and nodded as if to tell her there was nothing to worry about. 'And not all of them are as good as us at keeping to themselves.' He nodded towards *Sea-Sow*. 'So you really have nothing in that good-looking boat of yours?'

He dangled that like a hook and had more luck than Svein had enjoyed all morning, for Sigurd told Aslak to fetch Ofeig Scowler's drinking horn from the chest by the tiller while they asked the old man more questions about the folk living up at the arse end of the Lysefjord.

When Aslak came back with the drinking horn he gave it to Sigurd who gave it to the old man. It was not the finest thing any of them had ever seen but it was well polished and mounted with silver at the rim. The terminal fitting had perhaps been silver once too but now it was pewter, and the old man made a show of noticing the replacement.

'I'm up to my eyeballs in goat horns,' he said.

'You can get more mead in that than in a goat horn,' Svein pointed out.

'And which jarl might you be?' the old man asked him. 'We do not get to drink much mead here.' But he tucked the horn into his belt anyway and told them where they might find other folk to ask about the brothers Bjarni and Bjorn. 'I'd wager they won't be as welcoming as us,' he warned, to which Olaf said if this had been a warm welcome then he must have closed his eyes for a while as the ale was passed round. The old man ignored this. 'The folk up there do not like outsiders,' he said, turning his watery eyes east along the fjord. Then he touched the woollen skull cap on his head. 'If you've got something to put on your thought box then I would keep it to hand when you get to the hole.'

'The hole?' Sigurd said.

The old man grinned. 'You'll know it when you see it.'

With that they bid the old man and his wife farewell and cast off once again into the calm water and the cold shadow of the rock walls, each of them with their eyes looking up the Lysefjord towards the cloud-shrouded granite looming before them like a gateway to Valhöll itself.

Except for Svein, who was fishing.

They spent the night moored in a sheltered place where the cliff sloped down into the water. Finding somewhere shallow enough to drop the anchor had not been easy but they had done it at last, dropping the great iron hook over the steerboard side and tying *Sea-Sow* bow and stern to stop her being pushed against the cliff face. As luck would have it they were moored less than a spear-throw from several streams which cascaded down the rock into the sea, and in the morning they used the stern rope to haul the knörr close enough to fill three barrels and their own leather flasks with fresh water. Though they needn't have taken the time or risked *Sea-Sow*'s hull against the rock, for by midday it was raining so hard that the bilge would have filled had Svein and Aslak not soaked their shoes and breeks bailing.

The rain was still seething into the fjord at dusk when they came to the hole. They had seen no fishing boats. No houses. No smoke. No people. But that meant nothing for as Olaf put it *Sea-Sow* would have stood out like the balls on a dog coming up that fjord to anyone on the water or the cliffs. 'Whoever lives here will have their rocks which they crawl under at the first snap of sail or slap of oars,' he said. Which was why Sigurd had made them stow their war gear, but for their spears, out of sight in the hold.

'She is a trader not a fighting ship,' Sigurd had said, running a hand along the knörr's sheer strake. 'So let us look like traders, hey.' He had grinned at them, amused by their reluctance to hide the axes and helmets and swords of which warriors are so proud. 'With any luck they will come to see what we have to trade, for it must be a rare thing for them to get a ship full of furs and antler, silver and leather this far up the fjord. For that is what they will think when they see us.'

'Aye, they might come to see what we have to trade, but they might come to see what they can steal,' Solveig grumbled.

Sigurd nodded. 'Either way they come,' he said.

'Which is all well and good so long as there is not a bloody great horde of them,' Olaf put in, 'for it does not make sense to lose three or four of us whilst looking for just two brothers.'

'Two brothers who may not want to join us anyway,' Loker reminded them.

'They will want to join us,' Sigurd said, throwing an arm out towards the ancient sleeping rock, 'for who can make their fame in a place like this?'

'Men do not hide like mice in little holes,' Svein said. 'And if this Bjorn and Bjarni would rather stay tucked up here in Frigg's cunny then we do not want them anyway for they must be white-livered nithings.'

No one could disagree with that and so now they came into a small cove that would have been shadow-shrouded even on a sunny day, but on a day like this, with the rain hammering down, was a gloom-filled hole.

'Only a troll would live in a place like this,' Aslak moaned, wrapping his cloak around him for it was suddenly cold as *Sea-Sow* slipped between two towering cliffs into the sheltered hollow where the water looked black.

Neither was there any breeze to be found in the cove and so they had to get the oars out at bow and stern and give *Sea-Sow* enough encouragement to beach up on the shingle, which was only twice as wide as the knörr was long.

The sound of her keel crunching the stones was made unnaturally loud by the cavernous rock all around and Solveig could not resist singing some words of an old sailing song, his voice as loud as a god's in that dark little bay. The song was about a skipper who unknowingly sailed his ship into a giant's mead horn thinking it was a cove such as this one, and ended up being drunk by the giant but sailing out of his cock the next day to return to a hero's welcome.

'Well if they didn't know we were here before, they know

now,' Olaf told Sigurd, who did not begrudge Solveig his nerves, because no skipper likes to beach his ship in an unknown place. 'What now?' Olaf asked, and his were not the only eyes on Sigurd, so that in that moment Sigurd was struck by the thought that they really did look to him to lead them. And yet what if some idea of his got them all killed? Some idea such as coming more or less unarmed into a cove where brigands and renegades, men who had offended jarls and kings, were said to dwell.

'Now we wait,' Sigurd said, his eyes searching the rain-lashed heights and the dark crevices and the cave high up in the rocks before them which the old man the day before had called the hole.

They did not have to wait long.

Aslak speared the first one, gashing open his face the very moment it appeared above *Sea-Sow*'s sheer strake, and the man shrieked as he fell away.

'Here they come!' Olaf roared, as his crewmates jumped up from their skins and furs in the thwarts, spears ready, and lined the knörr's sides. But for Solveig and Hagal who were pulling up the planks that covered the hold and laying their hands on the war gear stowed there.

Black Floki slashed a man's neck and Sigurd felt a slap of hot blood across his face as he turned to take the shield which Hagal offered him. An arrow thumped into the deck behind him closely followed by another.

'Archers!' he called, the salty iron tang of another man's blood on his lips. 'Shields!'

'Sigurd!' someone yelled and he spun to see a wild-eyed man with an axe coming for his head but got his shield across just in time, the axe head splitting the limewood just above his arm. Sigurd threw the shield arm wide and rammed his spear into the man's gut even as Svein roared and swung his long-hafted axe, whose blade scythed straight through the man's back, all but cutting him in half before embedding in *Sea-Sow*'s deck planks.

251

'It's good to make sure, eh?' Hendil said, slapping Svein's shoulder, as another outlaw turned tail and jumped back over the ship's side to join his companions who were fleeing for their lives up the shingle.

'You don't like our hospitality?' Olaf called after them from *Sea-Sow*'s bow, not even flinching as an arrow thunked into the stem post beside him. But Svein, Black Floki and Aslak leapt over the side and gave chase, and Olaf glanced at Sigurd, who shrugged and jumped after them.

Sigurd heard Olaf yell at the others to stay with the ship as he ran up the strand after the fleeing shapes, slipping and stumbling on the slick weed and loose stones as men's shouts echoed off the high rock walls around him. And his blood simmered with the thrill of it as his eyes sought an enemy into whom to plunge his spear.

'They've gone!' Svein said as Sigurd caught up with him and the others at the end of the beach, the four of them panting for breath, heads turning this way and that. 'No sign of the slippery eels.'

Before them was a tower of jagged, night-cloaked granite, and whilst they could not see any crevices into which the out-laws might have disappeared like surf amongst the shingle, they surely existed.

'Up there. In that nest,' Black Floki said, pointing his spear at the cave high up in the rock. 'That's where they are. And all around,' he added, gesturing at the surrounding cliffs. Olaf came up, his face like thunder by the thin silvery light that seeped into that cove.

'Well I'm not climbing—' A rock thunked off Svein's helmet and he stumbled, cursing, as Sigurd raised his already split shield above his head. The next rock sheared off the top half of his shield leaving only four planks of it on his arm, and suddenly missiles were striking the stones around them in a deadly hail that would smash skulls and break bones.

'Back to the ship,' Sigurd called, though they did not need telling, and in a heartbeat they were the ones fleeing, Sigurd hauling Svein along by his tunic sleeve because the big man was dazed and lurching on unsteady legs.

'Well that was about as clever as swimming in a brynja,' Solveig said to them as they climbed back into the knörr.

'Don't look at me,' Olaf said, his chest heaving. 'I only went after them to tell them not to be so bloody witless.' He nodded at Svein. 'Svein Half-Troll there nearly got his brains spewed across the beach. Not that that would be much of a loss.'

Svein managed a grimace but no more and slumped down against the ship's side while the others stood looking out into the damp night, shields above *Sea-Sow*'s sheer strake like a rampart.

'They won't come again,' Asgot said, prodding a body with his spear to make sure the man was dead. The only reason the godi wasn't on his knees was because it was clear that the only thing the man had worth taking had been his life.

'Aye, not now they know we're stupid enough to run off into the murk after them,' Olaf said. Still, Olaf was shrugging himself into his brynja anyway and the others would have done the same had they owned one.

'Maybe they will want their friends back,' Hagal suggested. 'Perhaps there will be a negotiation worth having.' They had killed five outlaws that they knew of and no doubt there were others out there somewhere regretting their decision to attack the strangers who had come to their cove.

'How are you enjoying this raiding life, Crow-Song?' Solveig asked the skald. For all he was a man more used to weaving words than wielding a spear no one could say Hagal was a man to shirk the blood-fray.

'I am just hoping to live long enough to put you all in my saga tales,' he said, which was some low cunning, Sigurd thought, for knowing the men around him they would be more likely to try to keep Hagal alive if they thought they might make an appearance in one of his fireside tales. Not that he had done much skalding in these last weeks.

'It is all going in here,' Crow-Song had said, tapping his head when Sigurd had said as much some days before. 'A mail coat is not made in a day, Sigurd. Each ring must be forged and riveted to the others and then the whole thing must be polished. Perhaps I will let you hear it when you are sitting in Jarl Randver's high seat.' And Sigurd had felt a smile on his lips then.

'Let us see what dawn brings,' Sigurd said now, for what else was there to do? They could not launch *Sea-Sow* in the dark for fear of ripping her hull on a rock. Besides which they had not yet got what they came for. So they set a three-man watch, bow, amidships, and steerboard, while the others tried to sleep, though this time with their blades to hand and their shields wedged to protect their faces in case arrows streaked down from the cliffs again.

No more arrows rained down that night and when the first grey light touched the world beyond the narrow entrance of the cove, showing rainclouds as smudges against the lightening sky, they woke to find the place as quiet as the inside of a burial mound. But for the sounds of the waves lapping at the shingle. And the farting. And men hawking up phlegm, and yawning and pissing over the side.

The first thing Svein did when he opened his eyes was throw his guts up over the shingle, which Olaf said was often the way of it when a man takes a good blow to his thought box. There was an egg-sized dent on his father's old helmet and a matching swelling on Svein's head judging by how gingerly he ran his fingers through his thick red hair.

'If I ever find the man who dropped that rock on me I will take him far out to sea and drop him over the edge of the world,' he said.

'I'll wager it was a child,' Hendil teased, 'maybe a little girl.' He grinned. 'Yes, I like the idea that it was a snot-nosed brat that brought the giant Svein the Red to his knees.'

'You should put that in your tale,' Loker said to Hagal. 'No one will see it coming.' And Hagal's brows arched as though he was considering it.

'My knees did not touch the shingle,' Svein grumbled, suddenly grabbing the sheer strake and leaning out to spew another steaming load.

'It is getting rough out there,' Solveig said. He was standing on the mast fish looking out to sea through the gap between the great cliffs either side of them. 'I won't be happy taking her out of here until it smooths over a bit. Not when I'm still getting to know her ways,' he added, running a hand up the knörr's pine-wood mast as though it were a lover's thigh.

Sigurd nodded. From the shelter of that cove it was hard to tell which way the wind was blowing out there in the fjord, for the white-haired waves seemed to be racing one way and the grey clouds another. Not that it mattered anyway, for he was not leaving this place. Not yet.

'Who is coming with me up there?' he asked as they broke their fast on Guthorm's salted pork, smoked mutton and cheese, washed down with the fresh water they had collected from the rocks.

'Did you get hit on the head too?' Olaf asked him, waving a flap of meat in Svein's direction before pushing it into his mouth.

'I did not come here to sit on my arse, Uncle,' Sigurd said. 'Bad enough that we showed them our backs yesterday and skulked off.'

'You mean bad enough because the gods might have been watching,' Olaf said.

Sigurd did not deny it. 'Did you enjoy running away from them then?' he asked, turning his eyes on the others too. 'From brigands and goat-fuckers who hide here like fleas in a giant's arse crack.'

'Running is for rats and dogs,' Svein grumbled.

'And rivers,' Hagal said cleverly.

'Well then,' Sigurd said, flaying them with his glare.

'The gods love courage,' Asgot said.

'Are you volunteering then?' Olaf asked the godi.

Asgot grimaced and flicked a bony hand towards the cliffs. 'Do I look like a mountain goat, Uncle?'

'You smell like one,' Solveig said and Asgot hissed at him.

'Listen to me,' Sigurd said. 'We came to Lysefjorden to find these brothers who think nothing of making an enemy of Jarl Randver.'

'Aye and maybe they're lying on the shingle out there being picked at by the crabs because they thought nothing of making an enemy of us either,' Solveig said through a mouth full of cheese.

'It is possible,' Sigurd admitted. 'But from what I have seen of the corpses none of them look like they could be brothers.' He had seen nothing much at all of the dead outlaws lying bloodless on the beach, but the others did not need to know this. 'I am going up there to see if I can find these men.' He scratched his beard, noting that it felt thicker now. The salty sea air perhaps. 'Now that they have seen us fight they will be less likely to attack us.'

'Or more likely,' Olaf muttered.

Sigurd ignored this. 'Furthermore, they will be more likely to want to join us, because they have seen that we are men who know our spear-craft and who fear nothing.'

'Nothing except falling rocks,' Solveig said.

'I will go,' Loker said.

'And me,' Aslak put in.

'Well I am going of course,' Svein said, still sitting against one of *Sea-Sow*'s ribs, eyes closed and ashen-faced.

'You are hardly made for climbing,' Black Floki told him.

'And what do you know of it, little man?' Svein said, turning groggy eyes on Black Floki.

'No, Svein. You stay here and rest,' Sigurd said. 'Floki is right. You are more likely to pull the mountain down on top of us.' This put the curl of a smile amongst the red bristles.

'Don't worry, Svein, if I find a piece of your brain out there I'll make sure to bring it back for you,' Aslak said with a grin, which got him a stinging insult in return.

'I could climb to the top of Yggdrasil itself,' Black Floki said, 'and you have already seen that no man can kill me.'

This got some grim looks from the others, for in truth no one quite knew what to make of the young man who had yet to grow a beard but could make a slaughter to turn Týr the Battle God green with envy.

'We cannot all go. We must guard the ship or risk being stranded in this gloomy hole until Ragnarök,' Hagal said, which was true enough even if it was just his way of wriggling out of it.

'Well I'm not going, if that helps,' Solveig put in.

'Whatever I think of the scheme, you're not going without me, lad,' Olaf said.

And so it was decided.

CHAPTER THIRTEEN

THE CLIMB WAS TREACHEROUS, NOT LEAST BECAUSE A FINE RAIN FILLED the air and made the rock slippery as snail snot, as Loker put it, cursing as his shoe slid from a foothold and his knee crunched against the stone. It would have been easier without having shields strapped to their backs, but they knew the outlaws had bows.

'I'll not get myself killed by an arrow shot by some cave-dwelling, dwarf-swiving nithing,' Olaf had said, and now he had the hardest job of them all, with his brynja and his years. Not that he would have admitted to being less able to climb that rock than any other man.

'This way,' Sigurd said, pointing at a boulder- and scrub-strewn crevice leading up the cliff face. He led, followed by Olaf, Aslak, Loker and then Black Floki last, the young man seeming as undaunted by a perilous climb as he was by sharp steel aimed at his flesh.

Sigurd nodded at a pile of glistening dung pebbles. 'If goats come this way it must be possible,' he said.

'And see that gull there,' Olaf said, pointing at the shrieking bird wheeling above the cove and the knörr beached on it. 'He is flying, so how hard can it be?' Sigurd's reply to this was to climb.

Rather than take the more direct route up to the cave's mouth they had waded across the shallows back in the direction of the open fjord and there found another way up. After what had happened to Svein no one thought it a good idea to climb up to the cave from the beach below it.

'These brothers had better be worth it,' Olaf said, grunting as he took hold of the tufted grass and hauled himself over an outcrop. They had left their spears behind, bringing swords, scramasaxes and axes tucked in their belts because they had known they would need two hands to climb.

'Ofeig Scowler told me that they were two of the best fighters he had ever seen,' Sigurd said. 'They killed six of Jarl Randver's thegns who turned up at their farm.'

'Pah! I have killed six men with a fart,' Olaf said.

'And it was only six because four others had left the hall,' Aslak behind him put in, slipping on the scree and falling to his hands and knees.

'Need some help there, youngen?' Olaf asked him, enjoying seeing the younger man struggle.

Sigurd watched from a ledge two or three spear-lengths higher up. 'That is like a snake offering a fish advice on walking,' he said.

'Watch your tongue, lad,' Olaf growled up at him. 'I was climbing rocks like this when you were still sitting on a hill of your own shit.'

Sigurd looked down at *Sea-Sow* and Solveig waved to show that all was quiet down there. Then they scrambled left and edged along a rain-slick lip until Sigurd found another route leading up towards the tree line, which was itself higher than the cave entrance. But he would rather come to its mouth from above than below and so it was worth the time it would take, even if his heart was forging a nightmare on the anvil of his chest. For to slip or miss a footing now was to fall one hundred feet to the rock or the black water, neither of which likely ends would make it into the kind of tale they hoped Hagal was weaving.

When they got to the trees they sat for a while, getting their breath back and replenishing their nerve, then they made their way back round into the cove and down towards the black yawn of the cave's mouth. But when they crept into that dark, dank place, shields raised before them, swords or axes in their hands, they found it empty.

Black Floki toed a pile of charred sticks and ash. Here and there were animal bones and crab claws, some gourds and a pail of water.

'Well would you sit here waiting for us?' Sigurd said.

'I would probably go that way,' Aslak said, pointing to a well-trodden path that led back out of the cave and round to the left of it and up into the trees.

Sigurd looked at Olaf, who nodded, so they took the path, which the spindly pine and wind-bent birch hid from sight of anyone on the beach or in the bay below, and followed it up to the cliff top.

Where armed men were waiting.

'They don't look like much.' Olaf loosened off his neck and shoulders and hefted his shield and sword.

Black Floki's grin was like a wolf's as he took the short axe from his belt and swept it once through the rain-hazed air.

'We're not here to fight them,' Sigurd said.

'Try telling them that,' Olaf said.

There were eleven men and seven women and all armed with spears but for three of the women who had bows, arrows nocked and pointing their way. Sigurd spotted movement amongst the trees off to the side and for a moment thought the outlaws planned to ambush them.

'Just children,' Olaf murmured, nodding towards the trees. Children who were meant to be long gone but were staying to watch how things unfurled.

'We do not want to fight you,' Sigurd called to the armed folk, who were formed up in a shieldwall, albeit only ten of them had shields.

In their centre was a bald-headed, broad-shouldered man whose black beard stuck from his chin in three stiff braids, and

he said something at which the three bow women stepped forward, drew back their strings and loosed. But the distance was
too great to do any damage and Sigurd stepped forward and
swept his shield through the air, knocking one of the arrows
out of its flight. Of the other shafts one fell short and the last
flew wide.

'The folk around here really don't care much for visitors, do
they?' Olaf said.

'We are looking for two brothers,' Sigurd called, 'but we mean
them no harm.'

'No harm?' Three Braids yelled. 'You come here in your
fat-bellied ship, looking like trading men, then ambush and
slaughter our brothers. You deceived us!'

'You attacked us,' Sigurd countered. 'What would you have
done in our place?'

'I would have stayed away from here,' Three Braids said. 'Now
our friends are killing those you left on the beach. You will all
die.'

'He's bluffing,' Olaf growled. Sigurd nodded. If Solveig and the
others were in a fight now Hagal would have blown his horn,
but there was no horn nor any battle din that they could hear
coming from the cove.

'You are lying,' Sigurd accused. 'Do you know the brothers
Bjarni and Bjorn? I have an offer for them.'

Now another man, ruddy-cheeked and fair-bearded, raised
his spear and pointed it at Sigurd. 'The last men that said the
same thing ended up eaten by dogs and crows,' he called.

'So he is one of them,' Loker said under his breath.

'And that one with the curls and the spear is his brother,'
Sigurd said, glancing at the man who had just growled at the
other for all but introducing himself as one of the sought-after
pair.

'At least we did not kill them last night,' Loker said.

'There is still time for that,' Olaf put in, as the bow women
nocked arrows and strode forward, aiming higher this time.
'Shields,' Olaf said matter-of-factly.

261

This time Black Floki stepped forward and to the side, scything his sword at an arrow and cutting it in two, which was quite a thing to see, as Olaf admitted, after letting another shaft embed itself in his shield. 'Ha. I was young and stupid once,' he said to Floki.

'We are enemies of Jarl Randver of Hinderå,' Sigurd shouted along the stony path. He heard the rain hitting the leaves and branches around them and a moment later it was striking his own head and shoulders. 'I have an offer for Bjarni and Bjorn.'

'And here's my offer to you,' the man with the ruddy cheeks yelled, then ran towards them and hurled his spear, which streaked in a blur of bladed death and struck Sigurd's shield like a hammer blow. Sigurd staggered back under the impact and now looked down at the blade which had punched right through the wood and might have planted itself in his ribs had he not held the shield away from his body.

'Thór's arse, that does it!' Olaf gnarred.

The spear had not cut Sigurd and yet it might as well have, for the fury flowed out of him like hot blood from a gash. He hurled the useless, spear-pierced shield aside, pulled the scramasax from its sheath and, this in his left hand, Troll-Tickler in his right, charged.

'Hit them hard!' Olaf coming after him roared, and Sigurd knew that he was pissing away all that they had come for but he did not care. He was in the beast's maw now and the beast wanted blood.

The outlaws did not. Like leaves before the wind they scattered, vanishing into the pines either side of the track. But for two of them, who stood there for a moment, one with a shield and an axe and the other with just a scramasax now. Then these two, who looked too similar not to be brothers, glanced at each other, turned and ran.

And Sigurd ran after them.

The outlaws ran uphill, which was clever of them seeing as they were not cumbered by war gear like their pursuers, then they left the path and tore off through the trees like a pair of boars. An arrow streaked past Sigurd's right shoulder, whipping through leaves and branches, but he was not interested in the others now. He jumped deadfall and splashed through puddles, slipped on greasy roots and squelched through blankets of thick damp moss. He could hear his companions behind him, the snap and crack of the brittle branches they broke, the bellows hiss of their hard breathing as they wove between the rough pine trunks.

He saw Aslak leap a fallen trunk and pull ahead off to the left, a fleeting shape in the gloom.

'Leave one for me!' Olaf called, falling behind in his brynja and helmet, his voice almost lost in the rain's seething.

Up they went, leaping brooks where they could, splashing through the shallow water where it was too wide, being drawn deeper into a land that they did not know. A crow clattered from its roost, croaking bitterly, and Sigurd caught a glimpse of a fox slinking off into the ferns, and he did not slow because Black Floki was off his right shoulder and Sigurd wanted to kill the brothers himself.

The brother with the shield cast it aside now and the two of them scrambled up a steep bank, hauling themselves up using roots and rocks and brambles, and so Sigurd sheathed his own blades and climbed after them. And when he got to the top he stood dragging breath into his scalding lungs, his face running with rain, blinking it away as he watched the brothers charging off towards another rocky mound. And like an arrow to the gut Sigurd was struck by the senselessness of what he was doing, chasing two men in the arse end of Lysefjorden when he should have been avenging his murdered kin. The muscles in his thighs felt as though they were on fire and his forearms were scored bloody from raising them to shield his face from bare branches and scourging fronds.

Then he cursed and took off after them.

'What now?' Loker asked, arming rain and sweat from his face, his chest heaving. He and Sigurd stood on the bank of a stream, eyes scouring the forest into which the outlaws had vanished. Sigurd did not know where Black Floki, Aslak or Olaf were. They had taken different routes through the trees and had become separated.

'They cannot run for ever,' Sigurd said.

'And we can?' Loker asked, spitting a wad of thick saliva into the singing stream. 'Who knows if these brothers can fight, but I would vouch for their running. If Jarl Randver has not managed to get hold of them then maybe we should give it up.'

Sigurd eye-riveted him. 'You will learn that I am not a man who gives up so easily, Loker,' he said, sweeping his long wet hair from his face, and just then they heard a shout, the voice cut off in half a heartbeat.

Loker pointed north and Sigurd nodded. 'Listen,' he said. Loker stilled his heaving chest and they both held their breath, ears turned towards the direction from which the shout had come, sifting the low roar of the falls from the higher pitched hiss of the rain and the drips finding their way through the forest canopy. 'A waterfall,' Sigurd said.

Then he was running north, loping like a wolf because he knew they were close to whoever had called out and he did not want to blunder onto the edge of a blade. Loker ran with him, matching him stride for stride, a short axe in his right hand.

And neither of them could have foreseen what they would find.

They climbed a steep narrow track up onto a ridge and followed a grassy trail which snaked between several rocky mounds and led them to an ancient maiden ash, whose vast canopy spread far and wide above them and whose roots had somehow found purchase enough in this rocky place to support it. As he passed the ash Sigurd reached out and placed a hand on the trunk, whose old bark was grey as iron and etched like a rune stone that only the gods could read.

'Over here, Sigurd,' Loker barked, raising his axe and striding towards a hole in the ground partially covered by sticks and leaves. It looked to Sigurd like a trapping pit for wolves or boar, or even elk perhaps. But when they peered into the pit, which was a crevice in the rock rather than a hole dug in soil, the eyes looking back at them belonged to a man. 'Óðin's eye!' Loker said.

'Óðin had nothing to do with it,' the man growled back at them, cradling his left arm which he had clearly hurt in the fall. His cheek was cut too and blood was working its way through his fair beard. Lucky for him he had not broken his neck for the pit was near twelve feet deep, its rock bottom and walls criss-crossed with the giant ash's roots.

'Where is your brother?' Sigurd asked the man, whom he recognized as the one who had thrown the spear at him.

The outlaw winced with pain and took up the scramasax he had dropped amongst the old roots and the debris which had fallen with him into the pit. Then he looked up at Sigurd, smearing blood across his cheek with the back of the hand gripping the long knife's bone handle. 'It is not my brother who you should be worried about,' he said.

And then Sigurd looked up and saw her, a spear-throw ahead of him amongst a stand of white-skinned birches. A woman in a brynja of polished rings, hefting shield and spear, a sword scabbarded at her left hip and the hilt of a longsax sticking out behind her, nestled in the small of her back in easy reach of her right hand. She wore a helmet almost as fine as his father's, with eye guards and at its crown a spike from which hung a crest of white horsehair. Her own hair lay on either shoulder in two thick golden braids.

And Sigurd could have stared at her until Ragnarök, had she not come at him shrieking like a hawk. He got his sword up in time to turn the spear blade wide, then slashed with the scramasax, but the shieldmaiden blocked with the spear shaft and hammered her shield into Sigurd's face, sending him reeling. Then Loker was there and his axe blow gouged a sliver of limewood from her shield but she swept her spear low and Loker had to leap back or get his shins ripped open.

But Loker was a good fighter and knew that if he got past the spear blade his axe would make short work of the woman, even in her brynja. He leant back and that blade cut the air a finger's length from his face, then he threw himself forward but the shieldmaiden got her shield up and Loker's axe smashed into it, the head sticking in the wood, then she hauled the shield back, ripping the axe from Loker's grip, and cast the ill-weighted thing aside.

And Sigurd saw his chance.

'Move and I'll gut you,' a voice snarled in his ear, and he felt an axe blade pressing against the small of his back and he cursed because he had found the other brother. Or rather the brother had found him.

The shieldmaiden shrieked again and jabbed with the spear but Loker turned side on and grabbed hold of it, wrenching it from her hands, yet even as he turned it over to bring the blade to bear she whipped the longsax from its sheath behind her back and brought it down with a grunt, hacking off Loker's leading hand.

Loker bellowed in shock and pain and Sigurd twisted, knocking the axe head wide, then ran at the shieldmaiden and put everything he had behind a sword swing that would have cleaved her in half had she not got her own sword and longsax up to meet the blow, though it drove her to her knees.

'Sigurd!' Aslak yelled, rushing from the trees to stand between him and the outlaw. Then Black Floki was there and he threw an arm round the shieldmaiden's neck, putting the edge of his long knife against her pale throat.

'Hold,' Sigurd called out, 'don't kill her!'

'Fuck! Kill her!' Loker screamed, spittle flying or hanging in his beard. He was on his knees, right hand gripping the spurting stump of his severed wrist, blood welling through his fingers and running down both arms.

'No, Floki!' Sigurd roared, turning back to face the outlaw who seemed unsure what to do now that he could hear his brother calling to him from the trapping pit. 'Drop the axe,' Sigurd said, as Aslak edged round to the outlaw's left, giving the man something to think about.

'Better do what he says, lad, unless you want me to spit your brother here and turn him over a good fire.' Sigurd glanced round to see Olaf bent double and panting like a hound over the pit, the shieldmaiden's spear in his hands.

The outlaw growled a curse, turned and hurled the hand axe and it turned end over end before thunking into a birch tree some twenty paces away. Sigurd nodded, as much at the skill in that throw as with the relief of not having to kill either brother. 'If he does anything other than sit on his arse, kill him,' he told Aslak, who nodded and moved in with his sword.

'I need fire,' Olaf said, going over to Loker whose face was bone-white now and clenched in agony.

'Asgot will know what to do,' Aslak called.

'Loker will be dead long before we get him back to the ship,' Olaf said. 'Gods, it's wetter than a fish's fart, but I need fire and quickly.'

Sigurd went over to the birch trees to see if he could find some dry bark to use as kindling. Even the litter beneath the maiden ash's huge canopy was slick with rain. 'Everything is wet,' he said.

'Who are you? Why are you here?' the shieldmaiden asked.

'Hold your tongue or I'll cut it out,' Black Floki hissed at her, hauling off her helmet and throwing it aside.

Sigurd went over to her while Olaf tied Loker's belt off around the bloody stump. 'We came to find these men,' he told her, pointing to the pit and back towards the man on his arse by Aslak. 'I have a blood-debt to settle with Jarl Randver of Hinderå and heard that these brothers might like to help me collect it.'

'You are not here for the spring?' she said, her blue eyes sharp as arrow heads and shining like the rings of her brynja, which looked more like silver than iron or steel, Sigurd thought.

'We know of no spring,' Sigurd said. 'We came only for these men. They ran. We followed them.'

The shieldmaiden held his gaze for a while then, during which Olaf was muttering that Loker did not have long and they should at least put a sword in his other hand. 'I have fire,' she said. 'I will take you.'

Sigurd turned and strode over to the brother Aslak was guarding and took his tunic in one hand, putting the scramasax in the other to the man's neck. Then he hauled him to his feet and dragged him through the clearing to the pit in which his brother stood looking up, helpless as a trapped beast. Then Sigurd threw the man into the pit and he fell to all fours, spitting a foul insult up at Sigurd, who turned back to the shieldmaiden, gesturing at Floki to get her on her feet.

'Show us the way,' he said.

Smoke had billowed out of the dwelling when the shieldmaiden opened the door, wreathing them and making them cough, splutter and curse. But it had been Black Floki who said there was more to it than the dried herbs smouldering on the hearth stone and the scent of the birchwood cracking and popping in the flames beside them.

'There is seiðr here,' he had muttered, 'thick as a bear fur.' Sigurd had known he was right and the others had touched iron hilts or axe heads as they ducked under the rune-carved lintel and entered the flame-licked dark.

They had not waited for their eyes to adjust to the gloom but had carried Loker straight in despite their own misgivings, for the man was already more than halfway to Valhöll, as Olaf had pointed out when he had put a scramasax in Loker's hand, clutching both with his own as he and Sigurd had lugged him through the forest. They had left Aslak guarding the pit trap with orders to spear the brothers if they tried to get out of it, and Aslak had taken up the woman's shield in case they hurled a blade at him, for they had refused to give up their weapons.

Now Sigurd had one eye on Loker and the other on the woman who had cut off his hand, because it was not impossible that she had brought them to that place to murder them with steel or with seiðr. Though if so she would have to be quick about it,

quicker than Floki's long knife, which never strayed far from
that pale throat of hers.

'Ale?' Olaf asked the woman. She shook her head and Olaf
spat a curse because ale would have numbed Loker's pain at
least a little. 'Get it hot,' he told her, nodding at the fire. 'Very
hot.' She was feeding it the driest logs she had found in the pile
under the eaves outside and when the last of them was in place
she took a pair of bellows and pumped them so that the flames
roared angrily, lying flat with each gust but leaping hot and ever
more furious after. Then the woman pulled another bunch of
herbs down from amongst those hanging from the rafters and
threw it into the fire, where the dry leaves crackled and flared.
The pungent smoke stung Sigurd's eyes and got inside his skull,
and Olaf growled that he knew now how the mackerel felt when
they were strung up through the gills in the smoke house and
left to dry.

'It will help with the pain,' she said, nodding towards Loker.

'Aye, by choking him to death,' Olaf murmured, looking
around the pine-log cabin for the tools he would need.

'Maybe that's what happened to her,' Black Floki said,
pointing to the bed against the far wall. A chain-hung oil
lamp flickered near the head end and by its sooty light Sigurd
saw a braid of black hair against pale skin. Then he made out
the face, white as an owl's egg, the eyes closed and still as a
waveless sea, which told him the woman was dead. Even in
the smoke and the dark Sigurd was surprised they had not
seen her before now. But then, there was not much to see. The
silver and brown pelts lay neatly over the figure as they would
over nothing more than a bolster or two. Or over a corpse from
which the flesh had wasted, leaving skin taut as a spirit drum
over bone.

'Frigg's arse!' Loker suddenly roared, spitting saliva and fury,
the torment of that terrible wound bringing him back from
death's darkness for a moment and drawing all eyes to him
again. Squirming, his eyes sharpened with pain, he tried to
look at the belt-tied stump, but Olaf told him there was nothing

much to see and he was better off thinking about some pretty girl. Not that he would ever hold one properly again.

'Hold him still,' Olaf growled at Sigurd, who was slathered in Loker's blood now as he tried to force the man's shoulders back against the cabin's wall whilst holding out the ruined arm for Olaf to work on.

Without a word the shieldmaiden went over to a dark corner and when she turned around she was holding a hafted axe. Black Floki's sword whispered out of its scabbard and Sigurd's hand fell to his scramasax, but the woman paid them no heed as she went over to the fire and burrowed the head of the axe into the fire's heart where the birch was burning fast and hot.

'Aye, that will do,' Olaf said. 'And if it kills him then it's better he dies by axe than by griddle.' Sigurd's eye went to the two pans sitting on the hearth stones, thinking that their flat bottoms would have been better but knowing that if it was him dribbling blood from a handless stump he would prefer men said it was an axe, rather than a griddle, that finished him off.

Olaf turned back to Loker. 'Here, lad, get your teeth round this.' He put the sheath of his eating knife between Loker's teeth and Loker bit down on the leather so that he looked like a snarling dog, his eyes wide with terror and pain.

'We don't have mead, Loker,' Sigurd told him.

Not that Loker needed warning about the horrendous agony that was coming. He garbled and growled around the sheath something about there being mead in the Allfather's hall, which was where he thought he would be soon enough. Sigurd nodded. In Valhöll someone was already filling a horn for Loker, he thought.

'Is it ready?' Olaf asked the shieldmaiden, pushing Loker's tunic sleeve out of the way, revealing old scars and the soot-stained lines engraved in the skin, all blood-slathered.

She lifted the axe head from the fire. The iron was beginning to glow and the wood inside the eye, along with the haft's heel and shoulder, was smouldering from the heat.

'It'll have to do,' Olaf said. It was not yet red hot but if they waited any longer Loker would be as dead as the woman in the bed. 'Give it here.'

The woman shook her head and gestured for Olaf to hold the stump out, and with this Sigurd put his weight into Loker, making sure the other arm was pinned by his side, and then it came: that scalding axe head onto the raw flesh. Foul smoke bloomed. Blood bubbled and seethed. And Loker screamed.

His eyes bulged in his head and he bucked against the wall and against Sigurd who held him the way a man would hold a boar he knew would turn and gore him if he let it go. The scream was a strangled, throat-clenched thing that raised the hairs on Sigurd's arms and the back of his neck and Black Floki suggested hitting Loker hard on the head so that it might knock him unconscious but Olaf would not risk it because he had seen someone kill a wounded man trying that.

'Enough!' Olaf said and the woman pulled the axe with its new sheath of charred flesh from the wound, and Loker's eyes rolled back in his head and his body went still.

'Tell my father and brothers I will join them when I have avenged us,' Sigurd said, grimacing against the stench that filled the place like poison in a boil.

But Loker did not take that message to Sigurd's kin in Valhöll. Because he was still alive.

They knew this because when he next opened his eyes he looked at his shortened left arm, the blackened end of which they had smeared with a poultice of mashed leeks and honey and bound tight, and cursed the gods in a foul-mouthed torrent. The sight of the woman who had cleaved off his hand almost gave him the strength to stand, but Olaf pressed him back down, Loker bawling about how he was going to open her from cunny to neck. Then he fell back against the wall and passed out again.

'Who are you?' Sigurd asked the woman, who had so far said more with her weapons, one way or another, than she had with her tongue. But Sigurd had never seen a woman in such a fine brynja – in any brynja – nor had he ever known a woman so skilled with sharp steel.

'She's a corpse goddess,' Olaf said. 'A valkyrie. What else can she be?' He was half serious.

'My name is Valgerd,' the woman said. 'I am sworn to protect the völva of the spring. As was my mother sworn to protect the last völva.'

'She's the völva?' Sigurd asked, nodding to the bed in the flame-played shadows and its dead cargo.

Valgerd did not need to answer that.

'I failed,' she said, those two words like stone anchors dropped into still water. She looked back at the bed and her next words were for the dead woman in it, not the men standing by her hearth. 'I could not hold to my oath. It is broken.' When she turned back to Sigurd he saw in her piercing eyes not sorrow but anger. 'The gods are cruel,' she said, a flash of teeth in the gloom. 'Their greatest pleasure is to torment us.'

'Aye, I'll not argue with that,' Olaf agreed. 'They'll show you a sleeping sea and watch you cast off, laughing into their ale as a storm comes out of nowhere and you're bailing for your life.'

'You live up here alone, Valgerd?' Sigurd said. There was only one bed in the cabin and Sigurd wondered if Valgerd had been sleeping next to the dead völva these last days or whether the woman had died in the last night. His nose might have told him the answer to that if not for the pungent herb and hearth smoke filling the place.

'For five years now,' she said.

They had seen no other dwellings in the forest. Valgerd and the völva had been lovers, Sigurd knew then, living alone by the sacred spring, each bound to the other in their way. You are alone now, he thought but did not say. Instead he asked why she had attacked them, wondering if he was doing a better job of hiding his thoughts than Olaf was. Because, gods but this woman was beautiful! She was Freyja herself. The gold ropes of her hair hung beside a face that was fiercely proud, eyes the blue of glacial ice and sharp as rivets. Hunter's eyes. Hawk's eyes. That thought struck Sigurd like a forge hammer to his chest, as the mist from his hanging visions swirled in his mind.

She shrugged. 'Men come sometimes. They come and I kill them.'

'Why?' Sigurd asked, tearing himself from the spell of her face and wondering where she had got such a brynja, its many hundreds of interlinked rings swathing her like iron skin and worth a decent hoard. He supposed a smith – and a skilled one at that – must have made it specially for her.

'Why do I kill them?'

'Why do they come?' Sigurd asked.

She hesitated then. With Loker unconscious on the floor, all attention had turned to her now and she looked at those standing around her, at Floki, Olaf and Sigurd, who got the impression Valgerd was wondering if she could kill them all there and then.

'Some come demanding that the völva tell them their future,' she said. 'Some come for the spring and the silver which folk have offered it since the beginning of the world.' She sharpened those eyes on Sigurd now. 'They come to take and so I kill them.'

'Do you know the men in your pit?' Olaf asked her.

'I might have seen one of them before, if he is one of those who live on the shore. They don't bother us and we don't bother them.' She flinched slightly at the *we* of that. 'I have no quarrel with them if they stay down there.'

'Well our friend here has a quarrel with you,' Olaf said, thumbing at Loker who was slumped and milk-white where the skin was not bloody. 'You owe him. Tell me you have the silver to pay for the hand you took and the soreness of it.'

Soreness. That fell a little short, but Olaf was being proud on Loker's behalf.

Valgerd stared but said nothing.

'What about that brynja?' Black Floki suggested. 'Some jarl with more booty than brains would buy that off him for his wife, I'd wager.'

'You will have to kill me to take it,' she said.

Now it was Olaf's turn to shrug. 'Your life for his hand. That should cover it,' he said.

'What about the silver in the spring?' Floki said, but there was little weight in it and no one answered. Not that Floki could have expected much from that suggestion, for none of them was of a mind to steal from a sacred spring. You might as well poke a spear in Óðin's one eye.

'You could come with us.' Sigurd heard the words before he knew he had said them. Olaf laughed and Black Floki swore.

'This smoke's withered your wits, lad!' Olaf said, but Sigurd did not take his eyes from those hawk's eyes before him.

'It seems to me that you have no reason to stay here now.'

'Fuck, but I must need to clean my ears out for I could have sworn you just offered this valkyrie a sea chest and a nest in the thwarts.'

'She is a good fighter,' Sigurd said. 'Loker would attest to that.'

For a while Olaf just stood there wide-eyed, mouth gaping, then he gave a short bark of a laugh. 'Loker will want to put a spear in her! And I won't blame him!'

That was like water off a gull's wing to Valgerd. 'Where are you going?' she asked Sigurd.

'I am going to kill Jarl Randver of Hinderå,' he replied, as though it were no more of a thing than taking a plunge in a river.

'Why?' Valgerd asked.

'Because he has taken from me,' Sigurd said, knowing that after what Valgerd had told them about men coming to steal from the spring she would understand. 'If you join us I will treat you as I would any of those who follow me. There will be silver. And there will be blood.'

'I have no need of silver,' she said distastefully, though Sigurd knew the hook was in her mouth all the same. 'There will be sword fame too,' he added, 'for we are few and Jarl Randver is a powerful man. When we beat him word of it will spread quickly.'

'Like fire in dry thatch,' Black Floki said through a grin.

The four of them stood looking at each other in the flame-played gloom which they shared with a dead seeress and a wolf-jointed warrior who looked dead but wasn't.

'Well *you* can tell Loker,' Olaf said, shaking his head and scratching his great bird's nest beard.

And Sigurd nodded.

Because Valgerd, his hawk, was joining the crew.

CHAPTER FOURTEEN

THE BROTHERS BJARNI AND BJORN WERE PRICKLY AND PRIDE-STUNG when Sigurd and Aslak pulled them out of Valgerd's pit trap, but they had enough sense to be glad that Sigurd and his men were not oath-tied to their enemy Jarl Randver.

'You came all the way up Lysefjorden to find us?' Bjorn said, not quite able to get the suspicion out of his eyes. They were walking back through the woods now towards the beach, though the brothers had said they wanted to speak to their friends – the ones who had run off and left them – before they set sail with Sigurd.

'A man called Ofeig Grettir told me you were good men in a fight,' Sigurd said, 'and that you were no friends of Jarl Randver.'

Bjarni spat. 'That festering weasel's turd demanded weregeld for a man who wasn't worth three drips from a giant's cock,' he said.

'We wouldn't pay it,' his brother put in, 'and so Randver murdered our father.'

'Threw him off a cliff, eh?' Olaf said, which got two scowls as the brothers recalled the sour thing.

'He declared us outlaws and after that it seemed there were more men that wanted to kill us than there are bristles on a boar's back,' Bjorn said then shrugged. 'We had no choice but to lie low.'

'Not that low,' Olaf said. 'As I recall you couldn't resist trying to steal from us while we slept last night. Though that did not go so well for you.' He had not been able to hold back, and Sigurd gave him a hard look.

Not that the brothers seemed worried. 'We are outlaws,' Bjarni said, as though that were explanation enough, as though Olaf had accused a dog of barking.

'But we are good fighters,' he added.

'Hmm, I hope you are better at fighting than you are at avoiding holes in the ground,' Olaf said.

Bjarni turned and glared at Valgerd who was walking a dozen paces behind them, more interested, it seemed, in the trees and rocks around her than in the men's conversation. She was saying goodbye to the place, Sigurd knew.

'You will not lack for opportunity to show us your courage and your blade-craft when we fight Jarl Randver,' Sigurd said, steering the conversation back towards the common enemy.

'Just put us within a spear-throw of that snot worm and you will see what kind of men have joined your crew,' Bjorn said.

'Aye, well Loker lost his hand finding you,' Olaf said, still sore-headed about the whole thing and doubting the gain was worth the loss. Loker was awake but did not have the strength to walk so Aslak and Black Floki had him slung between them, his shoes' toe-ends scuffing through the leaf mould and his chin more often on his chest than off it.

'*She* gave him that wolf-joint not us,' Bjorn said, thumbing over his shoulder towards the shieldmaiden, who was mailed and armed like a champion and had a nestbaggin containing her worldly possessions slung over her back beneath the shield.

A gust blew from the west bringing the scent of smoke to their noses, for Valgerd had refused to leave her dwelling until they had hacked apart enough of its driest timbers to make a pyre and doused the wood with fish oil. Upon this platform she had laid the völva and set the whole lot ablaze, and now, unseen because of the trees, a massive pillar of smoke sped the seeress to the afterlife. As the fire roared and the seeress's skeletal body, bound in her blue cloak, charred and burnt, her spirit drum, feathered cushion and other belongings relating to her seiðr-craft burning around her, Valgerd had prepared to set off. Sigurd had told her that they would wait if she wished to stay until the flames had devoured it all, but she had shaken her head. 'I am ready to leave this place,' she said.

'Will you not cast the ashes into the sea?' Sigurd had asked.

'The wind will do that well enough,' she had replied, hefting her shield and slinging it across her back.

Sigurd had wanted to ask her what would happen to the sacred spring now. Did Valgerd not have a duty to find and protect a new völva? But he said nothing. She was more useful to him aboard *Sea-Sow* than she would be stuck at the arse end of the Lysefjord tending to a witch and her water. Besides, it seemed to him that the shieldmaiden believed the gods had betrayed her, as they had betrayed Sigurd's own kin. The woman owed them nothing now. Let men pillage silver from the spring if they dared, and let the Æsir deal with that.

The brothers showed them an easier way down to the cove in which *Sea-Sow* was beached and after Sigurd had introduced them and Valgerd to the others – their eyes barely lighting on Bjarni and Bjorn or even Loker with his new stump once they saw the warrior woman – Bjorn set about calling up to the cave and the high ground to get the attention of those he knew would be watching.

Eventually, as Solveig was muttering about the bad luck having a woman aboard would bring them and Hagal was arguing that she would make a wonderful addition to the saga tale, and Svein was murmuring to Hendil that she was the most beautiful – if also the most dangerous-looking – woman he had ever seen, a knot of folk appeared at the cave's entrance, peering down, armed with bows and spears. They seemed confused by the sight of the brothers unhurt and, furthermore, armed still, amongst the knörr's crew, and it was the bald-headed, broad-shouldered man with the three-braid beard who called down to them.

'Are they friends of yours then?' he asked the brothers.

'This man is the son of Jarl Harald of Skudeneshavn who was betrayed by King Gorm and Jarl Randver,' Bjorn shouted back.

'Then he has more enemies than we do,' Three Braids called.

Bjorn was about to answer when Sigurd stopped him with a raised hand.

'While that is true, I also have a ship, silver and good weapons,' he shouted. He gestured to the brothers. 'These men tell me you are a good fighter, that you have fed the crows with plenty of enemies.' He gave a shrug that was big enough to be seen from the bluff above. 'All I have seen is how well you can run.'

Three Braids did not like this and nor should he for it was a sharp insult. Sigurd knew it demanded a response and he hoped that a man who had been forced to hide like a runaway thrall might still have enough pride in him to want to prove himself.

'Are you a jarl then?' the bald man asked.

'Not yet,' Sigurd called.

'So I would not have to swear an oath to you?'

Sigurd half smiled. 'Not yet,' he said again and this had the man scratching his chin.

'Sigurd has promised us an equal share in the booty we take,' Bjarni yelled up, which was, Sigurd thought after, what brought Three Braids and two other men down from the heights onto the beach like wolves to a carcass. Three Braids' name was Ubba and the other two, one as thin as an iron rod, the other broad and deep-chested, introduced themselves as Agnar Bjarnason whom men called the Hunter and Karsten, bynamed Ríkr – according to himself – which had lifted a few eyebrows. Whether Karsten, who it turned out was a Dane, was indeed as mighty as he thought he was would perhaps be known in time, but what Ubba would say was that he was a great helmsman who had more sea-craft than a whale. Which did not go down well with Solveig of course.

'I wouldn't put a Dane at the tiller,' he rumbled to anyone in earshot, 'not unless you want a closer look at the rocks.'

But Sigurd was glad to have them aboard. The new crew-men waved farewell to the other men and women, who had not dared to come down from the rocks, and they set to work tacking *Sea-Sow* into the wind back up Lysefjorden. Valgerd sat by herself at the bow and not once did Sigurd see her turn to look back at the smoke from her lover's pyre which still stained the sky a darker grey above the woods atop the sheer rock walls. And it seemed that the others were content for the shieldmaiden to keep to herself, for as Olaf had said as they cast off, it was one thing to have a woman aboard, quite another to have a corpse maiden in the crew.

'A jarl should have a hawk,' Asgot had said, glancing at Sigurd to judge his reaction to that, for the godi knew all too well of the vision Sigurd had had as he'd hung from the alder, caught in a maelstrom of pain and strange, potion-induced dreams.

But Sigurd did not give the godi the satisfaction, instead keeping his thoughts about that to himself.

'Look around you, Uncle,' he said to Olaf who was watching Solveig drive the tiller hard over, turning the knörr into the wind so that the wind against the face of the sail halted her progress and soon began to blow *Sea-Sow* backwards. Olaf ran his eyes over the crew, over Black Floki, Bjarni and Bjorn, Asgot, Hagal Crow-Song and the red-haired giant Svein, men who had been thralls and outlaws and retainers of a dead jarl.

'Aye, we are a strange crew,' Olaf admitted, as he and Hendil released one corner of the sail while others released lines on the bow, beside the mast in midship and in the stern. Aslak and Svein pulled hard on the yard ropes, drawing the sail to the other side of the boat and catching the wind well enough to move the knörr forward again. Those at the bow worked with the bietas, that great heavy pole, and other men secured a rope to the opposite corner of the sail before the bow men pulled hard and strong, and Solveig waited for them to do their work so that he could turn on to course, at which point Olaf and Hendil would pull in to trim and tighten the sail. 'I suppose having a valkyrie with us can only add feathers to our fame's flight,' Olaf said, spitting onto his palms and rubbing them together. 'For we are going to need more of a crew than this.'

And Sigurd looked over at Hagal, who had not got his byname from hunting for outlaws or hauling on ropes sticky with resin. Because Olaf had given him an idea.

Sigurd knew he was not the only man aboard who felt as though there were loom weights tied to his guts and needles piercing his heart when they rounded the southern tip of Karmøy. And yet like him, Olaf and Solveig, Aslak, Svein, Hendil and Loker Wolf-Joint let their eyes drink in the sight of Skudeneshavn, their home, like a bitter draught. For each of them knew he could never go back there. That thread of their lives had been cut, though no one spoke of it, each chasing fleeting memories amidst a dizzying swirl of them, like trying to keep your eye on one fish amongst a shoal of darting silver.

Some of them had, like Olaf, family still living there and Sigurd thought that in some ways that must be worse than having just ghosts, as he did. For those men knew they could never hold their wives and comfort their children, not without putting those loved ones' lives at risk. Perhaps, when this was all over and if they lived through what was coming, they could take their families and start new lives somewhere, on some island that was out of reach of kings and jarls or beyond their care. But first there would be blood and so Sigurd stood silently at the stern as they passed the familiar skerries and the wave-lashed shore and even glimpsed, through the sheltered inlet, the wharf against which Jarl Harald's great ships *Reinen*, *Sea-Eagle* and *Little-Elk* had once berthed.

Let it burn them like a hot stone in the hand, Sigurd thought, looking from his crew to the shore and thinking how strange it was that Eik-hjálmr his father's hall stood no more beyond the moss-dappled rocks, the birch and pine and the sheep-flecked mounds. Let them feast on what they have lost, like crows picking scraps from bones. Let them know what they are fighting for.

As for those new to the crew, some like the brothers Bjorn and Bjarni were here for revenge, which Sigurd understood better than any man. Others, men like Ubba, Agnar Hunter and Karsten Ríkr, would wade into the blood-fray for silver and Sigurd would make sure they got it. He glanced at Valgerd then who sat on the stern deck, running a whetstone along her sword's edge, her legs hanging over the edge into *Sea-Sow*'s open hold. He could not say why she had joined him, but he knew the shieldmaiden was the hawk from his hanging vision and he believed that their wyrds had always been spun into one another's. And even if that was just a weaving of his own mind, she was a great fighter, as skilled with a blade as any man aboard perhaps, and that made it worth having her along in spite of how Loker and some of the others creaked like loose boards about it.

And then there was Crow-Song. It was true that Sigurd had threatened to blood-eagle the skald unless he went with them, but there was more to it than that. Hagal was in the mire of this thing for the story. He was a man who fed on the gasps and cheers, on the round eyes, the horror-stricken eager faces, the beard-nestled smirks and the raised eyebrows of those who gathered to hear his tales. He had no home, was a man not oath-tied to any other, and spent his life going from hearth to hearth and cup to cup.

And they had put him ashore at Rennisøy that dawn as the sun had spilled red light across Boknafjorden like blood from a wound. There he would visit the market and learn what he could about Jarl Randver's pursuit of Sigurd and what folk were thinking about their king up at Avaldsnes. He would sidle up to important men, perhaps winning himself an invitation to some jarl's hall, and ask them what they thought of the oath-breaker King Gorm's treachery. Weighing these men and their ambitions carefully Hagal would, if the moment arose – or if he could fashion it himself – bring up Sigurd, the wrong done to him and his intent to repay the offence in kind. From Rennisøy Hagal would go to Mekjarvik, Jæren or Sandnes, or even further south or east into Rogaland, calling on old friends and those who had shared their halls and hearths with him. And though Sigurd knew it was unlikely that any jarl or rich man would be prepared to risk all that he had by siding with some revenge-hungry son of a dead jarl with no reputation to speak of, there was more to it than that. For many of these men would be invited to Hinderå for the Haust Blót feast and celebration of the jarl's son's marriage, and when they first laid eyes on Sigurd he wanted them to know who he was and what he had come for. Such men might then have to make a choice.

'So what do you know of the man?' Bjorn asked him then, gripping a mast shroud and swinging around it into Sigurd's line of sight. It took Sigurd a moment to emerge from the fog of his thoughts but then he realized Bjorn was asking about Jarl Hakon Brandingi, which means burner, who was the reason why they were sailing north.

'All I can tell you is that he got that byname because in his time he burnt more halls than any other jarl,' Sigurd said, wondering just how many halls that was. 'But it is Olaf who has met him,' he added with a nod towards the big man.

'Aye, though I was a wean at the time,' Olaf said from the stern where he stood gripping the tiller, taking a turn there to give old Solveig's eyes a rest. They were lucky to have Karsten now too. But with sixteen crew and all their war gear *Sea-Sow* had become cramped, even with some of the big hold decked over to give more sleeping room, and Sigurd knew they would soon need another ship.

'Sigurd has it right about the man's fire-fame though,' Olaf said, nodding to Solveig who came and resumed his place at the tiller, for in truth he did not much like being away from it. 'There was one hall belonging to some jarl up in Kvinnherad that every skald and story-teller used to bring up when we were beardless boys,' Olaf went on, his beard ruffling in the breeze, his eyes full of sea and sky. 'I can't recall what the argument was about but I remember the interesting bits. One night Jarl Hakon had the door of his own hall pulled off its hinges—' He frowned.

'There was something about this other jarl saying his hall was bigger than Hakon's. Anyway, one night Hakon and his crew carried this door down to his ship, took it across the Bjørnafjord and down across the Hardangerfjord, lugged it across hill and dale and came to his enemy's steading. It was pitch dark, which tells you what kind of man this Hakon is, to cross two fjords at night, and while this other jarl and his people slept Hakon nailed his door across the threshold of the man's hall.'

'They must have been woken by the hammering,' Ubba said, having like others been drawn into the story now – not that there was much room on *Sea-Sow* to escape it.

'Maybe they were too drunk to wake up,' Olaf suggested. 'Or maybe they were all deaf. I don't bloody know, Ubba!'

'I think someone would have heard it. One of this jarl's hounds even,' Ubba said.

'Whose story is this?' Olaf asked the man, glaring.

Ubba frowned, unappeased, but nodded for Olaf to continue the tale.

'Well when Hakon's lot had set fire to the place and the flames were stretching high enough to singe the Allfather's beard up in Asgard, this other jarl's people opened the door thinking they ought to escape.'

'As you would, hey,' Svein put in, a smile nestled in his red beard.

'Only they found another door more than covering the hole,' Olaf said, stretching his arms out wide. 'So this other jarl burnt to a pile of ashes knowing that he had been wrong about his hall being bigger.'

'Maybe his hall *was* bigger, but Hakon just happened to have a bigger door,' Hendil suggested not unreasonably.

'I still do not see how they could hammer their door across the other without someone hearing it,' Ubba said, shaking his head.

'Fuck!' Olaf exclaimed. 'Now I know how Crow-Song feels! That is the last time I tell you lot a good story.'

The others laughed and Olaf muttered. And Sigurd wondered

what kind of man Hakon Burner was nowadays and whether he would help him fight Jarl Randver. There had been a time, before Sigurd was born, when it looked as though Brandingi would call himself a king and accept oaths of loyalty from the other jarls, or else force oaths upon them. He had been a fierce warrior, but more than that he had become the kind of jarl to whom other men are drawn like cold hands to a bright hearth.

'He promised men plunder,' Olaf had told Sigurd when Asgot had first pulled the man's name from his memory, for no one spoke of Hakon much any more. 'And he gave it them too. They used to say his hearth warriors dripped with silver. And the more men that flocked to him the more raiding he did to keep them all in arm rings, mead and meat.'

'With awe and fear the gods observed the growing size and strength of the young Fenrir Wolf,' Asgot said, 'so it was that other jarls watched Hakon's power grow.' He had grinned then. 'But unlike Loki's monstrous offspring no one dared try to bind Hakon.'

'Aye, he made a name for himself. The kind that mothers used to frighten their children into going to bed,' Olaf said. 'But then one day a younger man with some blade-fame and low cunning – and the cunning was the important thing – changed things as surely as the tide. He got his hands on the old farm up at Avaldsnes, which as you know had once been King Ogvaldr's perch, and persuaded some karls, none of them silver-light themselves, to help him put a stranglehold on Karmsundet.' He shrugged. 'This young man's sea chest brimmed with tolls from any skipper going north up there and in time he grew far richer than Hakon Brandingi and mostly for sitting on his arse.'

They were of course talking about King Gorm, whose silver-wealth from controlling the north way put other jarls in the shade and allowed him to raise more spears and go raiding when the mood took him, which made him richer still. But Gorm had recognized Jarl Randver's own fire and rather than snuffing it out he had fanned it, helping Randver seize Jarl Harald's land

and ships in return for fighting the king's battles now that he was no longer a young man.

But despite Jarl Hakon Burner's fire fading, the man staying up in Osøyro and keeping out of the king's way after he'd unwillingly given Shield-Shaker his oath, his hirðmen, hard thegns all, stayed with him, raiding to the north and east as far as Ulfvík.

'They'll be old-swords now,' Sigurd had said to Olaf when they had considered the chances of roping Hakon in to their blood feud.

'Old but still sharp, I'd wager,' Olaf said. 'Maybe they thirst for one last good raid, one sword song to fill their ears in the winter of their lives.' His eyes had held a faraway look then. 'And they'll have sons of course,' he said, doubtless thinking of his own sons, Harek and the infant Eric, both of them back in Skudeneshavn with Ragnhild.

And so they were going north.

It was a good day to be out on the water. As soon as they came round Karmøy, passing the village of Sandve on its south-west, they had as much wind as they could have wanted running across *Sea-Sow*'s woollen sail. That same wind was whipping foam off the waves rolling north-east towards Haugesund, and Sigurd recalled the first time his father had called those waves the white-haired daughters of Rán, goddess of the sea. The knörr's swan-breasted hull ploughed these rollers effortlessly, creating hardly a bow wave, and it was clear that old Solveig was in love with the ship, despite him having in his time stood at the helms of dragons and fighting ships that would draw admiring glances from the gods themselves.

'I would trust her to take us out there if you wanted to go,' he said, nodding west, and Sigurd smiled because perhaps one day he *would* go west.

'Well you can let me off before you do,' Loker Wolf-Joint said, 'for it is hard to hang on to the edge of the world with only one hand.'

This got some laughter but Loker had a point because they

were not in the sheltered waters of some fjord now. Off their port side there was nothing but the foam-whipped ocean as far as the eye could see. Taking the safer passage up Karmsundet past King Gorm's stronghold at Avaldsnes was not an option and so now they risked the open sea. And yet not a man or woman had objected to taking the sea road and Sigurd felt proud of them for it.

'If they're stupid enough to follow us into this blood feud then I am thinking they will do just about anything,' Olaf had growled in Sigurd's ear when the decision had been made to visit Jarl Hakon at Osøyro.

Still, you did not take such fair wind and waves for granted, and any of them who had any sea-craft in them at all kept one eye on the currents and the colour of the water, and on the flights of birds, the clouds in the sky, the movement of fish beneath the surface and the runes which Asgot every now and then cast on the deck.

Occasionally they saw other craft, fishing boats mainly, hugging the shore in sheltered bays, but only the very brave or very hungry were out today, with the waves rolling as fast as a bird can fly. This thought had barely woven itself when the bird in the old pail by Asgot's sea chest gave a long gurgling croak.

'Does she still want to dig out your eyes, godi?' Sigurd called.

Asgot stopped and carefully lifted a corner of the cloak which he had put over the pail to calm the bird for they had feared it might break a wing flapping madly in that pail that was too small for it to spread them.

'We are getting to know each other now,' Asgot said, then took the cover off and picked up the raven, which pecked at his hands but with less ferocity than earlier. He brought the bird to the stern and Sigurd, who put out his hand to let the creature smell him, stared at the glossed, jet black eye that regarded him with suspicion.

'I won't hurt you,' Sigurd said, lifting his tunic's sleeve and unwinding the fine horsehair string from his arm that he had put there earlier. The string was tied at intervals with four of this bird's own wing feathers which, whilst black as night, were also somehow purple, blue and green, constantly changing as if they had some seiðr in them. Sigurd was reminded of the swirling breath in a good blade, that worm-looped pattern woven into it in the forging which seems to writhe and transform before your eyes.

'Here, do not be afraid, Fjölnir,' he soothed, judging that 'wise one' was a good name for such a creature, as he tied the string around the raven's right leg below the tufted hock. The bird fluffed up its shaggy throat feathers and made a series of deep, loud knocking sounds, and Sigurd half expected that thick beak, the bird's own scramasax, to tear into the flesh of his arm. But perhaps the raven understood that he would not hurt her, for she let him tie the other end of the fine string around his wrist and when he was done she flapped her huge wings and hopped from Asgot's hand onto Sigurd's arm, so that Sigurd winced as her feet constricted and the hook-like talons dug through the tunic's wool into his skin.

'Prruk-prruk-prruk,' the bird croaked and Sigurd held her up so that she could see the ocean and know she was one of them now, her wyrd woven into theirs. She made that strange knocking sound again then snapped her hooked beak and it was almost as though she were telling him that this boat and her crew, and the vast empty sea road off the knörr's port side, was nothing as compared with the things she had seen on her own journeys.

'This is the strangest crew I've ever sailed with,' Solveig said, shaking his head, his old eyes never leaving the shifting, spume-streaked path along which he guided Sea-Sow.

But one of Óðin's bynames is Hrafnaguð, raven god, Sigurd thought, watching the bird on his arm.

'That is a nice touch,' Karsten Ríkr said, reaching out to stroke the bird but then thinking better of it, 'turning up to this jarl's hall with your own Hugin or Munin.'

'We will see,' Sigurd said, staring into Fjölnir's right eye which had gone from black to the colour of a well-polished helmet. The wind ruffled the raven's sharp throat feathers and

smoothed those smaller feathers on her back that resembled a
fish's scales, or perhaps the rings of a brynja, and Sigurd grinned
at Olaf who had said that they would never lay their hands on
a raven and if they did it would not be tame enough to do what
Sigurd asked of it.

'I do not need it to be tame, Uncle,' Sigurd had said, when
Asgot had proved Olaf wrong on the first point by catching the
bird in a snare on the shore of the Lysefjord. The godi had set
the trap by a dead hare which Agnar Hunter had shot with his
bow and whose belly Asgot had cut open to spill its guts. Then
they had waited, scaring off an enormous sea-eagle – which
would have torn Sigurd's arm from its socket rather than sit on
it happily as Fjölnir now did – before the raven had swooped
down near by and sidled up to the kill.

It had taken time but eventually the bird caught its foot in
Asgot's noose. Knowing it was trapped, it struggled madly,
barking as loudly as Var and Vogg, Sigurd's father's old hunting
dogs, wings thrashing, beak stabbing at the twine binding it.
But Asgot had a way with creatures, a trick to calming them,
which was strange given that most of them found his knife at
their throats and their ears full of his dark invocations.

Now the bird was calm for the most part, if wary, and Sigurd
let her sit on his arm a while longer, getting to know his movements, fixing his face in her eyes, for ravens were well known
for being able to pick a familiar face out from a crowd. Then he
untied the string from the creature's foot and put her back in
Asgot's bucket, which she did not like at all, but that was partly
the point.

'She is not happy about that and I do not blame her,' Loker
said, 'for only two days ago I used that bucket to crap in.' Hanging your arse over the side of the ship was no easy thing when
you only had one hand, as Loker never tired of reminding them.

'Good,' Sigurd said as Asgot draped the cloak back over the
bird, drowning out its gurgling clamour that sounded like a
man with his throat cut but not deeply enough. 'I want her to
prefer being on my arm to being in there.'

'Well, you are lucky because you have a choice of two full arms to put her on,' Loker growled, waving his stump over which he had tied the tunic sleeve's end with a leather thong. 'Meanwhile that vicious cunny sits there sharpening her blades, probably deciding which man aboard she will maim next.'

'I have told you, Loker, she thought we had come to plunder the spring of its silver and other offerings,' Sigurd said. 'If you remember, you had your axe in your hand and I had my sword out of its scabbard.'

'If I were you I would keep my sword in its scabbard with her around,' Hendil put in, clutching his crotch and grinning.

But Loker grimaced. 'You will not find it funny when she comes shrieking at you,' he told Hendil. 'And do not ask me to pick up whatever part of you she lops off.' Hendil's smirk faded at the thought of that and Loker looked at Sigurd, the wind that played across *Sea-Sow*'s sail blowing his loose hair off his face which was gaunt and wound-haggard. 'If she were a man I would have spilled her guts by now. It is not like she has any family to take up some fifty-year blood feud by the sound of it. We'd be done with the thing.'

'She is a rare fighter from what Sigurd said and from what your own wolf-joint has told me,' Hendil warned his friend.

Loker could not disagree with that. He shrugged. 'I could open her belly while she slept. Asgot could give her to Njörd or Rán or the fish for all I care. But the scales need to be balanced for this,' he spat, waving his shortened arm again.

Sigurd glared at him now, angry to be going over this again, like a knife over skin that has already been shaved and is getting raw. 'You will not touch her,' he said. 'We came armed and un-announced to her stead and she had the right to defend herself.'

'And I have the right to my honour!' Loker snarled.

'Then come and take it, one-hand,' Valgerd challenged him. She stood in the thwarts the other side of the open hold, skinned in iron rings though she was not wearing her helmet.

'I'll gut you, whore!' Loker bellowed, hauling his sword from its scabbard, and now everyone else shared looks and mumbled curses for they knew this thing had been coming, like a cauldron of water simmering up to the boil.

'It will be interesting to see how you wipe your arse with no hands at all,' Valgerd said, pulling her scramasax from its sheath, knowing that a sword was a clumsy weapon on a boat.

'Put it away, Loker!' Olaf barked. 'You too, Valgerd. There'll be no fighting on this ship. Not today.'

Loker turned his head and spat, showing what he thought of that. 'This is not your business, Uncle.'

'It is *my* business, Loker,' Sigurd said, not needing to shout for them to hear the steel edge in his voice.

Now Loker turned to face Sigurd and his eyes were like hot embers. 'You are not my jarl,' he said. With his good arm he raised his sword so that it accused Sigurd. 'You would cross Bifröst for your vengeance. I would cross you for mine.'

Already striding forward, Sigurd pulled his sword with his right hand and his scramasax with his left, and Loker must have been unsure of himself for a heartbeat, or perhaps he was off-balanced, going to fight one-handed for the first time. His swing was clumsy, the weapon cutting into the wind wide of Sigurd's right cheek as Sigurd twisted out of its path. Before Loker could bring his sword scything back, Sigurd swung Troll-Tickler. It hacked into the stump of Loker's ruined left arm and stuck there like an axe in a wood block. Men yelled and the raven in Asgot's bucket croaked madly as Loker staggered, his eyes bulging like a red fish's, then screamed. Sigurd stepped in close and plunged the scramasax into Loker's belly, ramming and sawing the blade up under his ribs into the heart.

The screaming stopped.

Blood that felt scalding hot flooded over Sigurd's hand but he pushed the long knife deeper, grunting with the effort, Loker's beard bristles against his own face, the man's spittle-flecked breath filling his left ear. Loker's body was trembling but Sigurd took its weight and could feel blood spattering his shoes, hear it spotting the deck.

'Is this what you wanted, Loker?' he growled in his friend's ear, but Loker was beyond being able to answer. A stench told Sigurd that the dying man had fouled himself. Then the legs gave way and Sigurd pulled his hand and the long knife from the gory cauldron of his friend's guts, at the same time yanking Troll-Tickler free from the meat of Loker's stump.

Loker crumpled to the deck, blood already pooling beneath him.

'Throw him over,' Sigurd said to Svein who was at his shoulder. The big man nodded, stooped and gathered Loker in his brawny arms. Without a word he carried him to the side and dropped him into the sea.

Just like that.

'For the sake of her?' Hendil said, pointing at Valgerd. He was ashen-faced and round-eyed. Beside him Aslak stood there blinking fast, his fingers laced behind his head. Others of the crew stood slack-jawed, stunned by what had just happened. Even Valgerd had paled.

'You threaten me with steel and you had better be sure to kill me,' Sigurd said.

'He was our brother!' Hendil bawled, his hand on his own sword's hilt.

'You want to follow him, Hendil?' Black Floki asked through a wolf's grin.

'What is it to you, thrall?' Hendil spat.

Sigurd raised the bloody scramasax, which told Floki to keep out of it. He was still in the fury's maw and if anyone else wanted to fight him then so be it. But it was Olaf then who sought to throw a damp blanket over the fire of it, stepping into the space between Sigurd and Hendil.

'This thing unfurled as our sword-brother Loker wanted it to. Or near enough,' he said, looking at Hendil. Without drawing a blade he put himself there like a rock over which either of them would have to climb to get to the other. He turned then to Bjarni and Bjorn, a grimace nestled in his beard. 'Tell me I am not the only one who smelt that the wound rot had taken hold in Loker's stump. Do you think a warrior like him would have let himself die a fevered straw death, stinking like a cesspit and moaning like the wind under some old door?'

No one answered but a few shook their heads. Olaf turned his glare on Aslak and Ubba, Agnar Hunter and Karsten Ríkr. 'With that rot in his arm spreading like damp in a shoe, neither would he let himself weaken just when we needed him the most. You all know what happens in the red murder of the shieldwall.' He shook his head, as though his own memories of the shield din were hammering in his skull. 'With that stinking wolf-joint Loker would not have measured up to the man he was before. Honour would not let him put those beside him at risk.'

Olaf turned to Sigurd then, who still stood there with his gore-stained blades down by his sides and the stink of fresh blood in his nose. 'Few men would have had the courage to do what you just did, Sigurd,' he said, 'and Loker will thank you for it when you meet in the Spear-God's hall.'

'Thór's hairy bollocks!' Solveig bellowed from *Sea-Sow's* tiller, the wind whipping what was left of his white hair around his face and into his eyes. 'If you have all finished fighting like dogs over a bone, maybe you would like to reef the sail before we are tipped into the sea after Loker.'

Olaf's brows arched like the Rainbow Bridge. 'You heard the old goat!' he yelled, and with that they set about releasing the sheet, lowering the yard and taking positions at the reefing points.

Sigurd turned so that the wind was in his face. It was strong enough to billow the sail, so that taking in a reef would not be without its challenges, but in truth he doubted that the reefing was necessary in the first place. *Sea-Sow* was running before the wind as she must have done countless times before for Ofeig Scowler and his crew, and so long as Solveig steered in a direction to keep the wind off the beam there was no real fear of capsizing.

Sigurd leant over the side and put his blades into the sea, his left arm in brine up to the elbow, and watched it sweep Loker's blood off in vanishing tendrils. When he pulled them out Olaf was there, leaning on the sheer strake looking west.

'There is no need to take in a reef, Uncle,' Sigurd said.

Olaf shook his head. 'No. But it takes their minds off what you just did.'

Sigurd felt the fury and the battle-lust dissipate inside him. The wind carried it away as the sea had borne his friend's blood off his sword and scramasax. Off his hand and his wrist and his arm. He felt sick for what he had done. And yet perhaps he had had to kill Loker to show the others that he was a man with steel in his spine, a man who would not turn his back on a challenge to his honour.

And yet he thought of Loker out there amongst Rán's white-haired daughters, denied vengeance against King Gorm and Jarl Randver and the shieldmaiden Valgerd. And now against Sigurd himself. Soon the body would fill with water and Loker would make a long journey, sinking to the sea bed like an anchor broken off its rope, never again to be seen. The fishes and crabs would feed on him and that was no good end for a warrior like him.

'And there was no wound rot in Loker's stump, was there?' Sigurd asked, the wind in his ears and the sour feeling in his belly.

Again Olaf shook his head. 'As far as I saw the wound was clean,' he said. 'Frigg's tits, lad, but we have a small enough war band already without you spilling men's guts and dumping them overboard.'

Then Olaf turned and began barking orders at the crew, making sure they were doing a proper job of the reefing.

And Sigurd listened to the wind in his ears and he thought he could hear the gods laughing.

CHAPTER FIFTEEN

IT WAS A FOUL NIGHT. A CRUEL WIND WAS LASHING THE WAVES, whipping white spume from them and throwing it onto the slick shingle below the cliffs. Rain scoured the land, hissing into the thatch of Jarl Otrygg's hall and now and then coming fiercely against the plank walls like handfuls of pebbles hurled by a god. A wind-flayed, wide-eyed boy had come in telling of a whale carcass down on the narrow beach of ragged bedrock and wave-polished boulders, but was met with grunts and growls and not much else. No man was hungry enough to go down there with knives on a night like this, even if they risked some cave-dweller carving it up before the storm passed. Besides, any flames they carried would be pissed out before they'd made ten paces and there was barely enough moon to see by. As a white-haired, leather-skinned man named Gaut had said, filling his cup to show that he intended going absolutely nowhere, any man foolish enough to go down there in the dark with a belly full of ale would more likely as not end up a carcass beside the whale. 'Only, the crabs aren't bothered by wind and rain and the fool'll end up a picked pile of bones aside that beast come first light.'

'We'll go down there in the morning then,' Jarl Otrygg announced, offering his own cup to a thrall with a large jug.

'Ha!' one man barked into his ale. 'He means he'll send someone else out to get wet as an otter's arse and the skin peeled off
his damned bones.'

'Careful, Bram,' the man beside him warned, nodding
towards their jarl on his high seat against a tapestry that was
rippling and flapping from the wind eking through the cracks
in the wall. But the jarl had caught Bram's words amongst the
general hum of the hall. Not that Bram could give a fart about
that, though he tried none the less.

'Do you have something to say to me, Bear?' the jarl asked, as
a silence fell over the drinkers like a thick fur, so that the howl
of the wind out there in the night beyond the staves sounded
like the moaning of those condemned to Hel.

Bram did not even look up at the man, instead taking a long
draught of ale and dragging an arm across his mouth and thick
beard. 'I was just wondering if this wind was coming from your
flapping tongue,' he said, snapping together the fingers and
thumb of his left hand, 'for it keeps on blowing and yet is empty
as my cup.' He turned the cup upside down then held it out to be
refilled. The thrall glanced at his jarl but came forward anyway,
filling Bram's cup with trembling hands.

Otrygg's champion, a man oath-sworn to fight for him, stood
up across the bench from Bram, his face dark as a great wedge of
granite cliff jutting high above the foam-flecked strand.

'Sit down, Brak,' Bram said, with a flutter of hand, 'I have no
quarrel with you.'

Brak, a man with a reputation as a good fighter, though he
had run to fat now and was more accustomed to vanquishing
plates of boar and elk, stood there stranded like the whale on
the beach, not knowing what to do. He glanced over at his lord,
whose mottled baggy face suddenly cleared like sun breaking
through cloud, and who dipped his head, gesturing at the food
in front of his champion.

'Sit down, Brak,' Jarl Otrygg said, holding a smile on his face
that did not want to be there, 'Bram means no offence.' Beside him his wife Hallveig hissed something, her own face like

the storm outside, but Otrygg ignored her. 'We have all let our tongues slide away on the ale many times and woken to regret it in the morning,' he said.

Clearly relieved, Brak nodded to his jarl and grinned in Bram's direction then sat back down and went to work on a fleshy bone.

Bram shrugged and the hall thrummed back into life as men and women took up where they had left off and the ale flowed and the grease glistened and the lamp and hearth flames danced as though to defy the raging storm beyond the oak of Otrygg's hall.

But Bram could no more let it go than could the wind and rain out there in the dark suddenly forget its wrath and sneak away.

'This is a hall of sheep and goats,' Bram said, not loudly yet the snarl of his voice was like an iron file against the grain. Tongues went still and eyes fixed on him again. 'I have seen more backbone in an eel than I see here. When was the last time we went raiding?' he asked, his eyes raking those around him like fire irons over glowing embers. 'When was the last time you put a crew together, hey?' This was to Jarl Otrygg, whose face had drained of all colour now and turned corpse-white. 'Your ships grow worm-riddled and rot at their moorings. Your warriors grow fat and soft as Frigg's tits and where once I heard the sword song now my ears crawl with the sort of idle prattle I would expect from old women at the loom.'

At this Brak stood up again, wiping greasy fingers down the front of his tunic, and this time when he glanced at Otrygg the jarl did not look at him but neither did he tell him to sit.

'Insolent man!' Hallveig snapped, looking at her husband to do something and fast.

'You will hold your tongue, Bear, or see it cut from its roots!' Otrygg spat, his eyes bulging like boiled gulls' eggs. 'You would insult me in my own hall? You have drowned your wits in my ale, you heap of pig shit. You drunkard!'

'Aye well I'd rather be a drunkard than a hrafnasueltir,' Bram said, which got a rumble filling that hall like thunder across the roof of the world, for it was no small thing to call any man, let alone a jarl, a raven-starver. A coward.

'You forget your oath, Bram!' Brak rumbled across the ale-stained bench-boards, one greasy hand on the pommel of the sword at his hip.

'You forget that I am not oath-tied to Jarl Otrygg,' Bram said.

'*I* have not forgotten it,' the jarl said, and nor would he have, Bram thought, recalling the day, three years ago, when he had come to Steinvik to offer his sword to the jarl.

'I drink your ale and eat your meat in return for growling at your enemies,' Bram said, 'but you have no enemies because the other jarls have forgotten that you are here. To them you are worthy of no more note than the boil on their wife's arse.' He knew he had gone too far, knew that in truth Jarl Otrygg did not deserve to be so insulted in front of his people even if he was hardly worthy of a hall and a high seat. But Bram had come to the end of the rope and it was time to haul the anchor from the weeds and slime amongst which it had settled for too long. 'I drink your ale and eat your food and yet I am still hungry,' he said, downing the ale in one go and slamming the cup down. 'I am a warrior and a warrior needs silver and fame. Here, with you, there is just rust and dishonour.'

Around him men and women were climbing out from the benches, scattering as folk will from the fierce heat of a newly stoked fire. Like Bram himself they knew he had gone too far. Knew what must surely come.

An old spear-shaker called Esbern, whose fighting days were far behind him and whose long beard and braids were white as snow, pointed a bony finger at Bram. 'You insult us all. You dishonour your own name,' he said.

Bram was too drunk to feel the sting in that. 'I have long tarnished my own name by staying here, old man,' he said. 'Back to your straw death with you, unless you want one last chance at a seat in the Allfather's hall?'

Esbern showed his teeth, his hand falling to his scramasax, and for a moment it looked as though the old man would indeed end his days blade in hand like a proper Sword-Norse, but a big hand shoved him aside.

'Out of my way, white-hair,' Brak snarled, coming round the long bench to get to Bram, who felt the blood run hot in his veins for the first time in too long.

Brak's sword whispered from its scabbard and in that moment Bram respected Jarl Otrygg's champion for doing his duty even though he knew the man could not win.

Bram ducked the first wild swing, Brak's sword slicing the smoky fug above his head and burying itself in a roof post like an axe in an oak's trunk. Brak cursed and Bram hammered a fist into his stomach, doubling the champion over, then grabbed one of his braids and stepped past him, hauling the man's head backwards, and Brak was all flailing arms as Bram chopped a hand into the exposed throat. Brak went down choking, legs thrashing as his lungs fought for breath that would not come.

'Get up, you fat fool!' Otrygg yelled as other retainers went for Bram, swords drawn. The first of them thought he was Beowulf hacking at Grendel's arm, the swing so wild that it might have cut Bram in half. Had it been anywhere near him.

'Sit down, Anlaf,' Bram said, slamming a fist into the man's face, bursting his nose in a spray of blood and gristle. Anlaf dropped like a rock and Bram hauled the spear from another man's grasp, broke the stave across his thigh and pummelled his attacker with the two halves, the man throwing his arms either side of his head and retreating under the onslaught.

'Sheep and goats!' Bram bellowed as the man fell into a heap against the wall all curled up like a hedgehog before a snarling hound. A big man launched himself at Bram from behind, wrapping strong arms around him to stop his progress towards the jarl. Bram lashed his head backwards into the man's face and the arms fell away, then he turned and clutched Gevar's bloodied face between his hands and squeezed. The big man's eyes bulged and his legs gave way but Bram did not let go. 'You will all die in your sleep,' Bram snarled, 'and no one will ever know you lived.' His arms were trembling with the effort and he wondered if he could crush the man's skull, wondered if the brains would spill through his fingers. But his quarrel was not with Gevar and so he drove his knee into the blood-slick face and Gevar keeled over into the floor reeds.

The jarl was up out of his high seat now, a big boar spear in his hands and at last some steel in his eyes.

'Come then, you oath-shy son of a long-dead sow,' Otrygg said, inviting Bram forward with the spear's gleaming blade.

'I will give my oath to the man who is worthy of it,' Bram said, side-stepping Otrygg's thrust and wrenching the boar-sticker from the jarl's grasp. 'As for my mother,' he went on, spinning the spear over and driving its butt into the jarl's stomach, punching the air out of him, 'she is still alive, I think.' He jabbed the butt end into the jarl's temple and Otrygg's eyes rolled back in his head as his wife threw herself across his body, snarling at Bram to leave her husband alone.

'You have bigger balls than your husband, Hallveig,' he said, respecting her for it and staying his hand. When he turned his back on the jarl and his wife he saw a sea of faces through the smoke and all of them gripped by the shock of what had just happened.

Well that was a night that did not go as I had expected, he thought, wondering if any of them still had it in them to fight him.

'You have made enemies here tonight,' Esbern said, his lips curled, his white braids like sun-bleached ship's ropes.

Bram nodded. 'A man needs enemies, old man,' he said, and with that he stepped down and strode through the hall, folk parting before him like water before a dragon ship's bow, to where his sea chest sat beside the far wall. He bent and picked it up, settling the thing, which contained everything he owned, on his left shoulder, holding the jarl's spear in his right hand.

I'm a damned fool, he thought, knowing what he was walking out into, thinking he could have at least waited another day or two. But then even one more day as a sheep was not to be endured by a warrior such as he. By a man who would twist the deeds of his life into a reputation the way the blacksmith god Völund forges a sword that will last a hundred generations.

He stopped by Brak, who was still on his arse clutching his throat, and, leaning the spear against his own shoulder, offered the champion his hand. But to his credit Brak found enough breath to call Bram a rancid troll's fart and spit at his feet, the shame at being so easily beaten carved in his face like runes on a rock.

Bram shrugged, gripped the boar spear again, and when he got to the hall's door the boy who had found the whale down on the strand opened it for him, looking at Bram as though he had fallen from the sky.

'Remember me, boy,' Bram said. The boy nodded and Bram stepped out into the howling, rain-flayed, thundering night.

For a while he stood there, rain lashing his face, already dripping from his beard and braids, and wondered where in the world he would go now and thinking again that he must have been very drunk to leave hot food, a blazing hearth and all the ale he could tip down his throat.

Then he heard the door open behind him and he sighed because he did not like fighting in the rain as it did a man's sword no good at all to be put away wet.

He turned and saw the great bulk of a warrior standing there silhouetted by the flamelight from the hall behind him.

'Let's get this over with, Brak,' he said.

Runa could see why Jarl Randver had coveted Eik-hjálmr her father's hall, for his own, called Örn-garð, the Eagle's Dwelling-place – on account of it being perched on a hill but also, Runa had learnt, because its jarl thought of himself as a lord of land and sea – was at least ten paces shorter and the pitched roof was much lower, so that the smoke from the central hearth which did not escape through the smoke hole was slung like a pall amongst the beams and lingered there. Many of the wall timbers could do with replacing and the jarl had told her, seeming embarrassed, that he would re-thatch the roof come summer. Örn-garð was not quite imposing enough, not saga-worthy enough for a jarl who now owned a fleet of good warships, enjoyed the king's favour, and had become the most powerful man, but for the king, within some ten days' sailing of Hinderå or Skudeneshavn.

And yet despite Jarl Randver's modest hall Runa doubted his people could fault his generosity. All his hirðmen, his retainers and their women were welcome beneath Örn-garð's thatch and timber, and this night, just like so many others, the place was awash with drunken laughter, the clatter of plates and knives and the rise and fall of many voices speaking at once, like an echo of the sea hurling itself against the rocks of Hinderå's shore. The hall was smaller than Eik-hjálmr had been but the hearth was twice the size and above it now, spitted, golden and dripping fat that sizzled in the flames, were the carcasses of an elk and four plump geese. Three young thralls were tasked with turning the meat to ensure even cooking and it seemed to Runa that the care they took in their work went beyond the fear of punishment if they burnt the flesh. They were proud to do it.

The air was thick with woodsmoke and the mouth-watering aroma of the meat being turned above the fire. On the other side of her bench an old man, bent as a scythe but with eyes that still sparkled, stood playing a bukkehorn and Runa recognized the tune as she would recognize her mother's face. For the melody had been Grimhild's favourite. She had danced to it on her wedding night, she had told Runa whenever the melody played out amongst those feasting in Eik-hjálmr, though now the undulating tune was a snake coiling itself around Runa's heart and she could find no joy in it.

Oil lamps flickered in the wake of passers-by or in the gusts which seeped through Örn-garð's planks, throwing shadows across the stave walls and the tapestries woven with the images of gods and monsters, and despite the pain it brought, Runa let her mind soar back to similar nights in her father's hall, when the mead had flowed and the raucous voices of Harald's warriors had boomed like thunder and her brothers had been so full of life and ambition. When her mother and father had sat in their high seats holding each other's hands, their eyes gleaming with pride.

And perhaps it was because she had entwined herself with memories of the past that she did not at first notice the man who had come in with Jarl Randver and who now sat in a high seat on the jarl's left. Runa was sitting beside Amleth on the high seat across the hall opposite Randver's and it was he, her betrothed, who drew her attention to the fair-bearded, handsome stranger with his father. No, not stranger. She knew him well enough.

'What has Crow-Song done to be given such honour?' Amleth had asked one of his own spearmen, a tall, sinewy warrior called Ambar who had been drinking mead like a salmon drinks water.

The man had shrugged. 'I have never heard a song or saga come out of his mouth yet that would earn him that seat,' Ambar said jealously. And that was when Runa's sad dance with the past had ended and she found herself staring at Hagal the skald, whom she had last seen in her father's hall the night before the steel-storm in the Karmsund Strait. What was he doing here, as close as a blade snugged in its sheath to the jarl whose thegns had killed her mother? But then what did a skald know of loyalty? She brooded, the thought sour as old ale. Men like Hagal Crow-Song flew wherever the silver shone brightest.

'I would wager that Father sent for him because there is to be a wedding soon,' Amleth's elder brother Hrani, sitting on his other side, said with a grin, knocking his mead horn against the one in Amleth's hand, 'and Hagal will come up with some story for the feast.'

Amleth stirred uncomfortably and Runa guessed it was the thought of their wedding night that had him squirming. For whilst it was clear that Amleth wanted to take her to his bed, he had never forced himself on her nor been unkind. He cared what she thought of him, that was clear, and Runa doubted she would wield that power over Hrani if she had been doomed to marry him. He would have taken her already, perhaps on one of the benches lining the hall where she had seen him taking plenty of young girls before, all sweat and teeth and not caring whose eyes were on them.

'Of course, when I get married we shall have a better skald than Hagal Crow-Song to see us through the night,' Hrani said. He belched loudly and seemed offended by the smell. 'Still, he is good enough for you and the daughter of a dead fool, little brother.'

'Watch your tongue!' Amleth hissed, glancing at Runa, who pretended for Amleth's sake that she had not heard. The last thing she wanted was for Amleth to kill his brother in some argument over honour or insult. For Hrani had brought steel and death to her village and Runa wanted him alive when Sigurd came. She would watch her brother kill him and laugh as he did it.

'I am just teasing you, brother,' Hrani said, raising his horn to his smiling lips.

Amleth was still watching Hagal and frowning. 'He has plied his trade here many times before and never been given that seat,' he said, 'so I am thinking there is more to it than my wedding feast.' Hrani pursed his lips, thinking his own thoughts about it as Amleth stood. 'I am going to find out what Crow-Song has that my father wants,' Amleth said, hooking his leg out from under the boards.

'Can I come with you?' Runa asked, and Amleth was taken aback for a moment because Runa hardly ever spoke to him or even looked at him if she could avoid it.

He almost smiled. Then held out his hand.

As they approached Hagal looked up and when he locked eyes with Runa he swallowed hard and nodded a half-hearted greeting. She thought she saw a flush creep across his cheeks and knew he was embarrassed. And so he should be, she thought.

'Hagal, this is my son Amleth and his betrothed, Runa Haraldsdóttir,' Jarl Randver said, sweeping his mead horn towards them as they stepped up onto the raised dais beside the high seats. Then Randver frowned. 'Though perhaps you have met Runa before?'

Hagal nodded. 'I visited her father's hall on occasion, lord,' he said. 'And certainly this girl's face is more memorable than the hospitality I received there.'

'Your cup was never empty, worm-tongue!' Runa said, feeling Amleth beside her flinch. It was no small thing to insult the jarl's guest. But given the warp and weft of it all Randver simply smiled.

'As you can see, Hagal, my son will have to take his drawknife and smooth the edges of this one,' the jarl said. 'I had to do the same with his mother,' he added, his sharp eyes softening for a heartbeat. Runa recalled hearing some years ago that Thorgrima, Randver's wife, had died after some drawn-out illness, and yet clearly she was even now never far from his thoughts.

'If you think *she* is spirited you should see her brother, my lord,' Hagal said. 'Sigurd is strutting around the place crowing like a cock on a dungheap. He thinks he is a jarl already. But jarl of who or what I could not say.'

It was clear they had already talked about this, that Hagal was saying it again for Amleth and Runa's benefit.

'He should count himself lucky that he is alive,' Amleth said, scratching his neatly combed beard.

Jarl Randver leant back as a thrall put a plate of glistening meat before him. He inhaled the steam coming from it then held a piece between finger and thumb as he cut it with his fine bone-handled eating knife. The delicious smell greased Runa's mouth.

'Crow-Song has been telling me that he believes young Sigurd will never accept peace between us,' Randver told his son. 'I told Hagal that I am willing to pay the young man the bride price that would have lined Jarl Harald's chest had he still been alive.' He grimaced. 'But the skald has convinced me that Sigurd hungers only for revenge. The fool is drowning in his own blood-lust and there is nothing to be done about it.'

'Nothing?' Amleth asked.

'Nothing that will help her brother's future,' he said, glancing at Runa. 'It is a shame though, for having young Sigurd's blessing on this marriage would have been . . . useful.'

'Why doesn't Hagal just tell us where we can find him?' Amleth said. 'Better still take us there. Face to face you could convince him that this is the only way. If he still refuses . . .' he shrugged, 'then we can kill him.' He turned to Hagal. 'How many men does he have?'

Hagal grimaced. 'Not nearly enough to crew a dragon,' he said. 'Some of them are good fighters though and Olaf, his father's sword-brother, is no fool when it comes to war. There is even a woman. A shieldmaiden.'

Randver's brows arched and Amleth grinned. 'If this is one of your stories, Crow-Song, save it for my wedding night,' he said, but Hagal raised a hand.

'It is true,' he said. 'And she is a fierce fighter from what I have heard. Cut off a man called Loker's hand.'

'And this Loker is one of Sigurd's men?' the jarl asked.

Hagal nodded, a handsome smile in his fair beard.

Randver laughed. 'Then perhaps there will be no fight between us after all,' he said. 'If we leave them alone they will kill each other.'

Now Crow-Song shook his head. 'As I have told you, Jarl Randver, Sigurd is coming. As surely as night.'

'He's coming here?' Amleth said incredulously. 'Is he mad?'

Hagal's lip twitched as if to say it was possible. 'He believes he is Óðin-favoured,' he said.

'Did you know he hung in a tree for nine days to get the Allfather's attention?' Randver asked Amleth, stabbing a piece of meat with his knife. 'Knowing Crow-Song it was likely four days. Maybe five. But still. What kind of a man does such a thing?' He popped the meat into his mouth and began to chew, considering the question himself.

Runa's thoughts twisted in her head like snakes in a pit. Perhaps Sigurd *had* lost his mind. It would not be hard to believe after all that had happened to him. Or perhaps Óðin Draugadróttin, Lord of the Dead, really *was* guiding him, steering him towards some reckoning because he was a god who loved chaos.

'When is he coming then?' Amleth asked Hagal directly, his eyes still round with the shock of learning that Sigurd and his rag-tag crew had the balls to come to his father's land, where they would face a war band second in strength only to the king's. It would be a slaughter.

Hagal looked at Jarl Randver as though seeking permission to tell them.

'When is my brother coming, Hagal?' Runa said, drilling the skald with her own glare. It was to be another betrayal then, this time by a story-teller. An ambush and red murder to finish it once and for all.

Randver nodded and Hagal grinned at her, raising one fair brow. 'Why, on your wedding day, of course. When else?'

Runa thought she might be sick all over Jarl Randver's plate. Her legs threatened to buckle and she put a hand out and gripped the jarl's table, steadying herself.

'I can see why you have been given the high seat, Hagal Worm-Tongue,' she managed, and he seemed to cringe at that, as the jarl fluttered a hand at his son telling him to take the girl back to their seats across the way before she upset their guest further.

Amleth grabbed her hand and hauled her back through the smoke and fug, past the tables and benches thronged with drinkers, and when they got back to their own board there were plates of succulent-looking meat waiting for them.

'Well, brother?' Hrani said. 'Did he tell you?'

So Hrani knew, then. Amleth nodded, heavy-browed, clearly annoyed that their father had told Hrani before him.

'Good!' his brother said. 'It will make it much more fun if you know.' Bloody grease was dripping from the meat skewered on the end of his knife and he waved it in Hagal's direction. 'Hey then, little brother, it seems there will be one good performance on your wedding night after all, for Crow-Song will have a great story to tell.'

A story of treachery and blood, Runa thought, pushing the plate away from her.

Like they always were.

They came to Osøyro on a sleeping sea, the knörr barely disturbing the dark water as she slid up to a wharf whose ancient piles were encrusted with barnacles and glossy black mussels, and whose planks were slick with moss, and rotting. There was an old karvi tied up against it, but as Olaf murmured when they got a better look at it, any man stepping aboard her would likely put his foot through the hull and find himself wearing a fish for a shoe.

'She was a fine ship once,' Sigurd said, wondering why anyone would leave such a vessel unloved and sitting there to be devoured by wind and rain and time. The yard was stored on the oar trees fore and aft, and the sail furled on it was in a poor state by the looks. She had been painted long ago, lines of red and ochre above the water-stroke, but this adornment was a faded stain hinting at a better time. Now, much of the dark, water-logged oak had been painted white by the gulls, some of which took off shrieking from their roosts upon the beam as *Sea-Sow* drew up.

Olaf and Svein made her fast with ropes and Olaf nodded to Sigurd who nodded back, both of them relieved not to have made a pig's ear of the landing even in that flat sea and with less than a fart's worth of wind to worry them. For five was too small a crew for a ship like *Sea-Sow*, yet Sigurd had insisted that he would arrive at the place with no more. Not that there was anyone down on the jetty to meet them.

'And this jarl lives *here*?' Svein called, looking around the wide bay across which his voice carried like thunder across a cloud-laden sky.

'Keep it down, big mouth,' Olaf said, but Svein had only said what Sigurd himself had been thinking. As well as the karvi there were three small fishing boats roped to the jetty, but even one of these was full of rainwater, and Sigurd could not get the scene to balance in the scales of his mind with what he had heard about Jarl Hakon Brandingi, this hall-burning warrior who had given children nightmares and grown rich on plunder.

There had been houses south of here, unseen behind rocks and trees but given away by spear-straight plumes of hearth smoke rising into the still, grey sky. And it was onto a gently sloping beach near these dwellings that they had driven *Sea-Sow* that morning so that all the others could disembark leaving only Sigurd, Olaf, Asgot, Svein and Valgerd aboard.

Now, these five clambered up onto the jetty, which was no easy thing at low tide, and stood there waiting for Sigurd to decide what they would do next.

'So who is going to stay with the ship then?' Olaf asked. Sigurd swore under his breath, annoyed with himself for not bringing another two, the brothers perhaps. But he had expected Jarl Hakon's people to appear at the sight of a trader like *Sea-Sow* and they would have looked after the ship as tradition required. Not that there was anything on the ship worth stealing, seeing as the crew all had their weapons with them and Sigurd had decided to take no chances where his silver was concerned, burying all of it in a pine wood on an uninhabited island south of a place which Solveig had guessed was Røtinga.

But Sigurd had nevertheless wanted to make a certain kind of impression on this old jarl, which was why he had brought those standing with him now and them alone. For apart from himself and Asgot they each wore brynjur of polished rings that were by themselves worth small hoards. They wore belts of the best leather, gleaming buckles, shining pin brooches in their cloaks and carried impressive war gear: swords, spears, shields and, in Svein's case, a long-hafted axe. And Sigurd thought they looked like war gods.

Even Valgerd, for all her hawk-faced, golden-braided beauty, was made savage by the blade-skill they knew she possessed. Hagal Crow-Song had said that when he looked at Valgerd he saw the goddess Freyja, whose darker side is witnessed now and then in tales of her riding into battle on the bristled back of the boar Hildisvíni.

Valgerd and Olaf had their fine helmets but Svein had nothing but his mass of flaming red hair and it did not take a skald like Crow-Song to put folk in mind of the thunder god Thór when they laid eyes on Svein.

So Sigurd had come with war gods and Jarl Hakon would see it.

'You will have to stay with the ship, Asgot,' Sigurd said now, knowing full well what the godi would think of that idea. 'It is important to fill this jarl's eyes with gleaming rings and war gear,' he said before Asgot could unleash his defiance.

'I am no guard dog!' Asgot snarled.

'That is strange for you seem to have a hound's love of bones,' Olaf dared, drawing their eyes to the animal bones plaited in the godi's silver braids.

Asgot glared at Olaf, who was putting on his helmet and trying not to smirk.

'Why don't we leave the bird to look after the ship,' Svein suggested, 'for I am sure Sigurd has taught it how to sail over these last days and if there is trouble it can simply raise the yard and slip away.'

'I'd wager the creature has more wits in its skull than you have in yours, boy,' Asgot said, resigned, it seemed, to staying.

Fjölnir had been spitting mad when Sigurd had taken her out of the bucket, but now she was calming down as he let her settle on his arm, soothing her with compliments about her night-glossed feathers and deep-mindedness.

'From the looks of it we will not find what we have come here for anyway,' Sigurd said. 'This does not look like the kind of place where we will find Sword-Norse for our fight against Randver.'

'Aye, that's true enough,' Olaf said.

'Doesn't even look like the kind of place where we might find ale,' Svein put in, scratching his flaming-red beard. 'Or women come to that.' He turned to Valgerd. 'Which is a shame for you, hey!' he said through a grin.

'Did your friend say something?' the shieldmaiden said to Sigurd, nodding in Svein's direction. 'You will have to explain to him that I do not speak the language of trolls.' And with that, a blow to Svein sharper than any sword because he thought he was very handsome indeed, they set off clomping along the old jetty towards the worn track that would, if Olaf's memory served him well, lead them to Jarl Hakon's hall.

The track wound up between birch woods still dripping from earlier rain and then levelled off by rocks upon which an iron brazier sat rusting. Sigurd turned around and noted that even if the beacon were flaming like a god's pyre, no one at sea would see it for the birch trees which had been allowed to grow tall.

Two hooded crows sat *kraa*-ing near the top of an old beech tree and they started Fjölnir croaking but she did not try to fly, because she knew her foot was tied to the string wound round Sigurd's arm.

'Are you sure this is the place?' Sigurd asked Olaf.

Olaf nodded, pointing his spear at the beech whose leaves were still mostly green although Sigurd could smell the turn of the seasons on the air.

'When I came here as a boy there was a man strung up by the neck from that branch there,' he said. 'A murderer perhaps. Or a sacrifice.'

'It's a shame Asgot isn't here then,' Svein said, 'for that is just the sort of story he likes.'

'There is smoke there,' Valgerd said, pointing into the sky beyond another stand of trees. And so there was, a spreading stain of it like iron rot against the grey windless sky. Before them was a meadow of long grass, which was in itself unusual for they would have expected to see sheep on ground like that and the grass cropped short.

'Maybe this Jarl Burner died years ago,' Valgerd suggested, 'which would explain why no one hears anything about him any more.'

'Maybe,' Sigurd said, wondering if this was another wasted journey. It was not long now until the Haust Blót feast and

311

Runa's wedding to that whoreson Jarl Randver's son. But Sigurd was not ready to take on his enemy yet.

And this thought was weighing on him when they came out on the other side of the trees and saw it standing there, filling their eyes, as hard to ignore as a slap in the face with an oar blade.

'You never said we were coming to Bilskírnir, Uncle,' Svein said. They had all stopped to take in the fullness of it.

'Everything seems big when you are but knee-height,' Olaf said, as awed as the others. 'I did not think much about it then.'

For there it was, dark and poorly thatched and huge. Not Bilskírnir, Thór's own dwelling place, but a place that a god might be proud of none the less.

Jarl Hakon Brandingi's hall.

CHAPTER SIXTEEN

A THRALL CARRYING A PAIL IN EACH HAND SAW THEM AND RAN TO THE hall, sloshing milk over the pails' sides in his haste.

'Let us go and introduce ourselves then,' Sigurd said. Fjölnir croaked, one steel-grey eye boring into Sigurd's own. 'But remember, even if the jarl offers us soft furs and his best mead we will not spend the night here.'

Svein looked disappointed, then turned to Valgerd. 'We slept in a karl's hall near a place called Moldfall and this fat karl and his piss-drinking friends tried to murder us while we slept, which anyone will tell you is not good manners.'

Valgerd nodded, the whisper of a grin on her lips. 'Yes, he should have waited until you were awake and then done it,' she said.

Svein frowned at this, wondering what she meant by it, then he shrugged and told her that Floki had killed them all. 'Before I had rubbed the sleep from my eyes,' he added.

'Aye, it turned out well for us in the end,' Olaf admitted, thinking of *Sea-Sow* and the weapons and silver, and the young man who could kill without breaking a sweat, which they had got out of it. 'But I agree with Sigurd that it is better if we do not sleep here tonight.' He shook his head. 'It seems to me that you cannot trust anyone these days.'

Which was another reason why the rest of the crew were somewhere beyond the pine-crested hill west of Jarl Hakon's hall. Arriving at the place with such a small but richly armed retinue would show this hall-burning jarl that Sigurd did not fear him, and that he was a man who was either generous with spoils so that his warriors boasted war gear to make any man envious, or else the kind of man to whom great warriors flocked, much as Jarl Hakon had been in his day.

'Won't he think it is strange that you do not have your own brynja when we do?' Svein had asked earlier.

Sigurd had smiled at his friend, who was proud of the huge brynja he had got from Æskil In-Halti's dead champion at Guthorm's farm. 'He will think I am such a good fighter that I do not need one,' he said.

'Or else that your friends are such good fighters that you do not need one,' Svein had suggested, which Sigurd thought sounded just as good.

And yet it would not hurt to have more friends where Jarl Hakon could not see them. Let your enemy see the sword in your hand but not the sax behind your back, he thought now as he waited with the others a good spear-throw from the jarl's hall. As armed outlanders they did not want to go any nearer without being invited, but now that they had been seen they would not have to wait long.

'Why do I get the feeling we're walking into the wolf's lair?' Olaf said, scratching his bird's nest beard.

'It seems it is a dangerous thing being in your crew,' Valgerd said, which put a bad taste in Sigurd's mouth because it made him think of Loker whom he had killed and dumped in the sea.

'If this old jarl does not want any part in this thing we will leave him to his straw death and turn our backs on this strange place,' Sigurd said. He was watching the western woods above which two crows were attacking an eagle, taking turns to drive it off, its screech carrying across the cloud-skeined sky.

And he hoped Black Floki and Solveig, Bjarni and Bjorn and the rest of them were not too far away.

'Here we go,' Olaf muttered after what seemed like an age standing there before that looming hall like dead warriors waiting to see if there was a bench for them in Valhöll.

The longhall's great door opened and out came a knot of warriors, blinking in the day, grey as it was, and puffing themselves up like cocks as warriors will.

'Thór's arse! That one at the front looks older than Solveig,' Svein said under his breath.

'Which means he's likely seen lads like you come and go, and likely *made* some of them go, too,' Olaf growled into his beard.

'They're all old men,' Valgerd said, and she was right for many of them had white braids hanging either side of their faces and snowy beards, some plaited and tied with silver rings, others splayed from their chins like breakers smashing against rocks.

There were eleven of them and they might have been old men, two of them bent with the burden of years, but they were armed like Týr himself and proud of it. Each was wearing a brynja, most of them polished until the rings gleamed, and Olaf remarked that he had never seen so many brynjur assembled in one place before. All had spears and swords and now, as they drew close, the knot broke apart and they strode on in line, their faded, painted shields presenting a wall.

Sigurd kept his hand off his sword's grip and hoped the others did too, for all that Troll-Tickler sang to be released in the face of so many spear-armed strangers. On Sigurd's left arm Fjölnir flapped her huge wings and gave three loud *tocks*.

'Who are you?' the leader of this retinue asked. He had rings on his arms, scars too, carved into the skin like white runes.

'I am Sigurd Haraldarson. My father was the jarl at Skudeneshavn before he was murdered by the oath-breaker King Gorm.' It did no harm bringing Gorm into this from the beginning, Sigurd thought to himself, seeing as Jarl Hakon had been the fire in these parts until Gorm pissed on him.

'You are outlawed,' White-Beard said, 'for all that Jarl Randver of Hinderå is trying to build a bridge between you by marrying his son to your sister.'

'You seem to know a lot about it,' Sigurd said, 'which surprises me.'

'Why does it surprise you, Sigurd Haraldarson?' the old warrior asked, running his eyes up and down Valgerd which showed there was still a man under the iron rings, leather, scars and years.

'Because this feels like a place of ghosts,' Sigurd said.

The old warrior's lip curled in his white beard at that, though it was impossible to say whether he was amused or offended.

'Aye, well we *are* ghosts here,' he said. 'Only we've forgotten to do the dying part of it.' Some of the men at his shoulders grinned or chuckled though they did not drop their shields any lower or hold their spears any looser.

'Are you Jarl Hakon, whom men call Burner?' Sigurd asked him.

The old warrior's hoary brows arched at that.

'I have not heard that name in a while,' he said. 'For all that it was well given. And well earned.' Sigurd recognized the look in his eyes then. Here was a man remembering better times. Still, when you are as old as that any memories of being a younger man must shine like silver, he thought. 'But no,' White-Beard said, 'I am not Brandingi.' He looked at Olaf and almost nodded, the way one warrior will to another to show that he sees him and sees him well.

'I have come to speak with your jarl,' Sigurd said.

'And the bird?' White-Beard asked. 'He comes to speak to my jarl too?'

'It's a she,' Olaf put in, nodding at the raven, 'and she gets upset if you get that wrong, as any woman would.'

A few eyes flicked to Valgerd then but no one said anything, which was just as well, Sigurd thought.

'I speak for Jarl Hakon,' White-Beard said, 'and if you have come here seeking his help avenging your kin then I can tell you you have made a worthless journey.'

'Perhaps. Yet I would hear that from Jarl Hakon himself,' Sigurd said.

The man shook his head. 'I am telling you, Sigurd Haraldarson, there is more chance of my hair turning red again—' he glanced at Svein '—oh aye, youngen, it used to flame like your own.' He turned back to Sigurd. 'More chance of pretty wenches hanging off me like silver off a king, like they did when I was your age, than there is of my jarl wading into this blood feud you have with Jarl Randver and King Gorm.'

'You speak for him as you say. Do you think for him too?' Sigurd asked. 'For he does not even know I am here.' Sigurd was beginning to wonder how this man had survived to such an old age if he had riled others as he was beginning to rile him. 'Fetch him, White-Beard. Or take me to him.'

The other old retainers raised brows and shared smirks and one of them murmured something about thinking that a man with a raven on his arm would be better informed about things.

'Your hearing seems poor for a young man,' White-Beard said. His patience was wearing thin now, fraying like the hem of the tunic hanging below his brynja. 'Jarl Hakon will not come aboard this feud of yours.' He hefted his shield and tilted his spear towards the sea, which was his way of telling Sigurd to leave without saying it.

'Still,' said Sigurd, sharpening his eyes on the man, 'I have come all this way and will hear it from the jarl, I think.'

This got these men's hackles up. Their shields too, which was not lost on those at Sigurd's shoulder. Svein raised his great axe and Valgerd and Olaf tensed.

White-Beard rolled his old shoulders then and for a moment Sigurd was sure the man was going to lead his companions into the slaughter and end their lives properly. But then he gestured at his men to take up positions either side of the visitors and seemed to breathe the day's air deep into his old lungs.

'You had better come and meet him then,' he said, turning back towards Hakon's hall. And together they walked up to that looming place until they came to the door which was wide enough for three men with shoulders as broad as Svein's to walk through side by side. Not that you were likely to find three such men in a place at any one time.

Sigurd saw his red-haired friend staring at the great door and knew he was wondering if that was the door from Olaf's story, which Jarl Brandingi had taken across two fjords to Kvinnherad and nailed across his enemy's threshold to prove a point.

'Leave your weapons out here,' White-Beard said, pointing his spear at a rack under the eaves, though Sigurd doubted that rotten old thatch would keep the rain off a man's sword.

'I will go in alone,' Sigurd said.

'Aye, we'll keep hold of our blades if it's all the same to you. Or even if it isn't,' Olaf said, as Sigurd took off his own sword and handed it to him.

'The last time we gave up our weapons our host tried to kill us,' Sigurd said by way of explaining why he was leaving his retinue outside and armed.

'And he had already tried to kill us with ale that tasted like horse piss,' Svein added, though he might as well have smacked his lips together and held out a horn for the filling.

White-Beard nodded. 'I can see why you might be a man light in trust,' he said to Sigurd, then looked at Svein and Olaf. 'I'll have something brought out to wash the salt spray down.'

Olaf nodded his thanks as White-Beard told three men to come with him and the other seven to remain outside with their guests.

Svein jerked his chin towards the hall's door. 'See there, Sigurd. They must have pulled it off before it was too late. And brought it all the way back.'

Hearing him White-Beard glanced at the door, brows knitted. Then he nodded as though having hauled an old memory up from the depths, and pushed the great door open. Before he walked through, Sigurd looked at the scorch marks at its edges, black tongues of blistered wood that had licked out of some doomed jarl's burning hall. He imagined the screams of those who had burnt alive; warriors certainly, but women and probably children too. A hall burning like that was as dark a thing as a man could do. This Jarl Hakon had been a killer down to the ice in his bones where the marrow should have been.

Sigurd hoped he could be such a man again.

Fjölnir's eyes changed from steel grey to black as Sigurd walked inside the hall, his own vision swamped with darkness, his nose filling with the smells of wet wool and wet dog, the tang of hearth smoke, sweat and piss; men's and mice's. There was wood rot in the fug too and the musty smell of thatch that should have been replaced years ago. Sigurd had heard once that a rat had fallen out of Eik-hjálmr's thatch and landed on his father's plate. He looked up now, high up, his eyes fashioning the different shades of black into thick beams and ancient roof planks, and he imagined this place could rain with rats and mice and dead birds too. There were trestles and tables up there on the beams, stored for feasts and celebrations, though they looked to have become part of the roof's structure now and Sigurd guessed they had not been brought down in years.

'You should have seen it once,' White-Beard murmured, letting Sigurd fill his eyes with the place. Two rows of roof posts, too many to count now, stretched off into the gloom and along either side raised wooden benches topped with planks and sheep skins ran the length of the hall. There were two fire pits in the central corridor, though only one of them, at the far end, roared with flame and it was near this one that the benches were occupied. As Sigurd followed the old warrior, his eyes adjusted now to the place, he saw some women sitting on those benches, busy with needles and thread, or beads, or preparing food by the flamelight and that grey light filtering through the haze of the smoke hole above. These women carried on with their work, though their eyes were on Sigurd and his bird.

One, who was sitting on a stool by a loom, looked up and raised an inquisitive eyebrow at White-Beard, but her fingers kept up their rhythm amongst the warp and weft and Sigurd wondered if she was the old warrior's wife. Across from her was a low table that was cluttered with cups and plates. Sea chests were set around it and clearly White-Beard and his men had been seated upon them before they were disturbed by the milk-spilling thrall who was now lighting more of the lamps which stood about the place or hung on chains from the beams.

Then through the flames and smoke of the fire pit Sigurd saw that one of the big trestles and boards had been brought down from the beams, only it was now piled with skins and furs and being used as a bed. He followed White-Beard around the hearth, the three other brynja-clad, spear-gripping warriors at his back, and up to the bed. Upon which a dead man lay.

Then White-Beard's next words told him that Jarl Hakon, whom men called Brandingi, was not a corpse yet for all that he looked like one.

'My lord, this is Sigurd Haraldarson, the last living son of Jarl Harald of Skudeneshavn on the island of Karmøy to the south.'

Sigurd looked at the bone-sharp face, which was all that was showing above the old bear fur and sheep skins covering the rest of him, and he saw the fierceness in it. Even now.

'What are you doing, Hauk, you old fool? You know he cannot hear you any more than a turd can hear the flies buzzing around it.'

Sigurd turned and saw another man getting up from one of the benches against the far wall, leaving two bed slaves in the furs behind him. There were three more warriors standing there in the shadows though not as straight as the spears in their hands, and they moved forward with the man who now addressed White-Beard.

'Nevertheless, my lord,' Hauk replied, watching the man spill his mead as he clambered off the edge of his bench and came into the hearth's copper glow, 'Sigurd insisted on being introduced to your father and I thought to give him the honour, him being the son of Harald who all men said was a great warrior and a good jarl.'

'And yet my father even now is more alive than Jarl Harald,' the man said. 'But you forget yourself, old man,' he sneered at Hauk. 'I am your jarl and you bring guests to me, not him.'

Hauk nodded and planted his spear's butt on the packed dirt

floor which had been strewn with ashes from the fire to absorb
the damp which came in on shoes and clothes or found its way
through the old roof and the smoke holes in it.

The man turned his half-hooded eyes from the near-corpse by
the fire to Sigurd. 'I am Thengil Hakonarson and this is my hall.'
He waved the mead horn towards the shield-bearing warriors
behind Sigurd. 'These bags of old bones are my hearthmen,
though you would not know it sometimes. I like to think that
in their winter years they simply forget from time to time, their
heads full of memories. The way an old dog's legs will twitch in
its sleep, as if it is dreaming of running across the meadows like
it used to do.'

Sigurd glanced at Hauk but the old warrior's face was a sleeping sea and Sigurd guessed he was not even listening.

'But the truth is,' Thengil Hakonarson went on, 'they were
my father's men and near enough the last thing that came out of
his mouth was an order that they must swear an oath to me.' He
shrugged. 'They did not like it of course, but the old fools did it
and now they are mine.' The fat lips curled in the soft bed of their
beard, a beard that had seen no salt spray by Sigurd's reckoning.
Thengil touched the silver-inlaid hilt of the sword at his hip. 'For
some men an oath sworn on a sword still means something. It
binds them as surely as Gleipnir round the wolf's neck.' He drank
from his horn and swiped a fat hand across his mouth. 'Other
men . . . well, I don't have to tell you, hey, Sigurd.'

This was as good as bringing up King Gorm's betrayal of
Sigurd's father without actually doing it. To the heart of it then.

'I will kill the traitor king,' Sigurd said, smooth as a whetstone
run along a sword's edge. 'But first I will deal with Jarl Randver
of Hinderå.'

'And you came here thinking to persuade the fearsome Jarl
Brandingi to join you in this undertaking.' It was a statement
rather than a question. Then he laughed and Sigurd noted the
tremble of the man's soft belly and of his fleshy throat. Fjölnir
croaked at the sound.

You would like to feed on that fleshy corpse wouldn't you,

bird, Sigurd thought. It was hard to believe this was the son of the man in the bed beside them whose yellowing skin was so tight over his skull that the mouth was held open and what teeth were left were fixed in a permanent snarl.

'I had heard that your father was no friend of the king's,' Sigurd said.

Thengil's fleshy lips pulled back from his teeth and in that moment and that moment alone you could tell from whose loins he had sprung.

'My father was a friend to no man,' he said. 'Though he was generous to his hirðmen. They fought like wolves for him and never found themselves silver-light in return.' He swept an arm across the vast flame-dotted space. A mouse skittered past Sigurd's foot and disappeared under a bench. 'Look around you, Sigurd Haraldarson. You will see there are no young men here now. They have all gone.' He flickered his fat fingers up into the air. 'They flew away seeking fighting jarls and plunder. For I had to stay here and tend to my father and could promise them no plunder, only a wealth of quiet years and a straw death at the end of them.' He glared at Hauk as though the man was something foul brought in on the bottom of his shoe. 'They are my war band. They stayed for my father and now it hangs over them like a curse, as you can no doubt see with your young eyes. Are you not disgusted by them?'

'I would not want to fight them,' Sigurd said, which he knew was generous of him, but which was also true. For men who kept their brynjur and war gear as well as these men did were proud men. And pride makes men strong regardless of the years on their backs.

'They are sour as old beer, Sigurd.' He waved his horn towards the low table and the sea chests. Land chests these days, Sigurd thought. 'I hear them,' Hakon's son went on, 'sitting there talking about their friends who sit in the Spear-God's hall. Going over old battles again and again, like sheep ambling along the same path day after day. I think that sometimes they do it to get at me.' Another mouse ran across the floor and Thengil cursed and hurled his mead horn at it but the creature was long gone. The women at their work did not even look up. 'They gnaw away at me, Sigurd. They think I am a weak man who has not lived even half the life that they have lived.' He looked at Hauk and at the men at Sigurd's shoulder but none of them bit at this hook. 'But their talk is so much bleating in my ears. I have this hall and all they have is a bench and an oath forced on them by a living corpse.'

'Join me, Thengil Hakonarson,' Sigurd said. 'Bring some silver-lustre to this dark old place. Weave your own saga tale so folk will not always look for you in your father's shadow.'

Thengil scratched his soft beard then and stared at Fjölnir perched on Sigurd's arm. 'Are you mad, Sigurd?' he asked, his eyes sliding back to Sigurd's. 'Is that why you have a raven on your arm?' He squeezed his finger and thumb together. 'Jarl Randver will squash you like a louse. As for King Gorm, I'd wager he does not even know you are alive, much less care.'

'He knows,' Sigurd said.

'Aah, I see it now,' Thengil said. 'You hunger for a warrior's death because you miss your brothers and your father. You want to sit and drink with them in the Hanged God's hall.'

How had Jarl Hakon had a son like this, Sigurd wondered, then supposed that it was perhaps the jarl's disappointment in Thengil that had reduced him to that withered skull-grinning stick by the fire.

Thengil clapped his hands and the milk-spilling thrall brought him another full horn. He had yet to offer Sigurd any, which was insult enough in itself but also just another reason why Sigurd felt tempted to put the man's teeth through the back of his soft head.

'My lord,' Hauk interrupted, 'I said I would send some drink out to Sigurd's men.' He frowned. 'And the woman.'

The heavy lids of Thengil's eyes hauled themselves up at that. 'You leave your woman standing outside my hall?'

'She is not my woman,' Sigurd replied. 'She is a warrior. And a ferocious one.'

Thengil half turned his face away as if expecting Sigurd to admit the jest, but Sigurd's eyes were chips of ice and the fat man gave a great belch which rolled into a laugh as thin as piss. 'So you have roped in some women to fight for you then? And we mustn't forget that fierce bird you've got there. Such a beast will have your enemies trembling.' He fluttered a hand at Hauk to get some mead sent outside. 'A war band to weave a saga tale about, hey!'

'A hirð of white-beards and crooked-backs will hardly get you in a skald's tale,' Sigurd said, unable to stop himself biting back. 'Nor will sitting in the dark on your arse when other men are out there weaving their fame.'

Thengil winced at this and Sigurd knew his words had stung the man. They really were loyal thegns then, these ancient retainers of Hakon's, that none of them said such things to Thengil's face much less put a spear in his belly. For men such as Hauk knew only too well that their reputations, or what was left of them, were now eroded by their binding to this pale-livered, soft-living lord, like a trusted sword that is left in the rain to be eaten by the iron rot.

Thengil turned to one of the warriors at his shoulder, a man whose beard was still more brown than white and whose face gave away nothing of what he was thinking. 'This outlawed son of a dead jarl, a young man barely into his first beard, comes here to insult me in my own hall. And will I do nothing about it?' He turned back to Sigurd. 'Do I not hold my honour to be my most valued possession?' The fat lip hitched and the teeth were back again. 'Bad enough that I did not receive an invitation to the wedding of Jarl Randver's son at their Haust Blót feast.'

This was cast Sigurd's way like a challenge, like the first spear hurled from one shieldwall to another before a battle, and it crossed Sigurd's mind to pull the scramasax from its sheath strapped to his right arm beneath his tunic's sleeve. Why not open Thengil's belly? Watch his guts slither free and spill onto the floor and see what the corpse-jarl's old hearth warriors had to say about it. For did not Óðin's very name mean frenzy? Did the Lord of Death not love chaos?

'There will be no wedding,' Sigurd said. 'If the maggot Randver finds himself at the feast table that night it will be with my father and my brothers and his own ancestors.'

'You are an ambitious young man,' Thengil said, coming closer to get a better look at him. The warriors tightened the knot around them, and yet still it was the first bit of backbone Sigurd had seen in the man. Now they stood eye to eye, close enough that Sigurd could smell on him what he had been doing with the bed slaves before their arrival. It was sweet and musky and Sigurd knew here was a man with an appetite for food, mead and women, but not for war or fame.

Though as it would turn out, Sigurd was wrong about the last one.

'My father would have liked you, I think,' the man said. 'He would have torched Jarl Randver's hall for the savage joy of watching it burn. As for King Gorm, old Hakon would have enjoyed putting him back in his place. My father would never admit it but he lost some of his edge when he had to swear on Gorm's sword.' He looked back to the figure in the bed. 'I think he regretted not leading his men against Gorm when the man set himself up as a king perched up there at Avaldsnes.' He shrugged. 'But I am a different man.'

'I can see that, Thengil,' Sigurd said. 'So you will not help me against Jarl Randver and make yourself rich in the doing of it?' He was suddenly aware of Fjölnir's claws digging into the flesh of his arm. Thengil turned away, beckoning Hauk to walk with him back into the shadows beyond the head end of his father's bed. Sigurd could not hear what he was saying to the old warrior but he resisted the urge to glance over his shoulder. He knew well enough how far away the door was at the other end of the hall.

'The truth is, Sigurd Haraldarson,' Thengil called back to him as Hauk strode past Sigurd without meeting his eye and continued down the hall's flame-flickered central aisle, 'your coming here has presented me the opportunity to regain my honour.'

What honour? Sigurd thought but held his tongue.

'And I thank you for it,' Thengil went on, reaching out a hand to Jarl Hakon but holding it a finger's length from the sparse grey hair as though he dared not touch the man. He pulled the hand back and wrapped it around the other one holding the mead horn, then stepped behind one of his men, just as a shout went up from outside.

Sigurd's blood froze in his veins.

'Seize him!' Thengil yelled at his men, his eyes suddenly round, his hands trembling enough to spill mead onto the floor.

The knot of warriors around Sigurd levelled their spears and surrounded him, and he spat a curse aimed more at himself for not having somehow got Thengil outside or at least closer to the hall's door. The women on the benches stopped what they were doing now, eyes wide in the hearthlight.

'Do not kill him!' Thengil shouted. There was more shouting outside but Sigurd's ears could not untangle it and he hoped Olaf and the others were not risking a fight against eight mailed men, even as old as they were. 'You can kill that bird though, Bodvar,' Jarl Hakon's son said, and the long-bearded spearman frowned as though unsure how to go about it, as Sigurd fumbled at the string wound round his left arm, pulling it out from his tunic's sleeve so that the string and the feathers tied to it dangled from Fjölnir's foot. Yet her talons dug into his arm still, the raven eyeing those around her.

'Off with you, bird!' Sigurd growled, throwing his arm up, and Fjölnir flapped her great black wings and took off into the hearth smoke, croaking angrily. She swept up to the roof like a living shadow and for a sickening moment Sigurd thought she was going to land on a beam and perch there watching with her black-glossed eyes. But she jilted left at the last and, seeing her only escape route, pulled her wings against her body and burst out of the smoke hole into the grey beyond, the feathered string trailing after her.

'You should have speared it, Bodvar,' one of the other men said. Perhaps he had seen Sigurd's scheme in letting the bird go. Perhaps not.

'You are a nithing fool, Hakonarson,' Sigurd said. 'At the least you should draw your sword, you soft, sow-bellied shit. You troll's fart.' He spat on the man's calf-skin shoes. 'Not that Óðin's War-Riders will take you when I cut your throat, Thengil Wolf-Starver. The only thing waiting for you is a knot of worms to feed on your flesh.'

These insults slid off Thengil like pork grease off a smooth chin. He was grinning like a man who has been looking out to sea, waiting for weeks for the wind to change, and now feels it on the back of his head.

'I think I will make a journey to Hinderå to pay my respects to Jarl Randver,' he said. 'For when he sees the wedding gift I have brought he will no doubt sit me beside him at the feast table.' He fluttered fingers towards the far door. 'Take him outside,' he told his men. 'I would like to meet the fools who have crewed up with this wyrd-doomed boy.'

A man with a spear blade pointing at Sigurd's chest jutted his chin towards the door and Sigurd turned, getting a spear butt between his shoulder blades. He walked back down the central aisle, past the looms and the women with busy hands, through the biggest hall he had ever seen, which was these days a stain on the memory of the jarl who once sat in the high seat but now lay in old furs more dead than alive.

Bodvar opened the scorch-marked door and there were Olaf, Svein and Valgerd in an iron and steel knot, back to back in the middle of a bristling ring of spears.

'That did not go well then, Sigurd,' Olaf rumbled, watching Thengil's men over the rim of his shield. 'I am beginning to think you are not so good at making friends.'

Two men kept their spears levelled at Sigurd and now Thengil drew his own sword and stood behind him. The other four hirðmen from the hall joined their companions so that twelve men surrounded Olaf, Svein and Valgerd, and all of them wore ringmail. This Jarl Hakon had been as rich as Fáfnir once, Sigurd thought.

'Just give the word,' Svein told Sigurd, violence coming off him like heat from a forge.

Sigurd shook his head. 'Just stand, Svein.' He knew that the numbers meant nothing to Svein. One nod and his friend would throw himself and his great axe at Thengil's warriors and carnage would reign. But a spear or two would surely find the big man's flesh.

'Put down your blades, you growling fools, there is no reason to get yourselves butchered,' Thengil said, then gestured at Hauk and his other hearthmen. 'Even old dogs can bite. These men were killing my father's enemies before I was born.' He pointed at Svein's long-hafted axe. 'On the ground with that, red-beard.'

'Keep hold of it, lad,' Olaf growled into his beard, but it was clear Svein had no intention of doing otherwise.

'If you don't give up your weapons I will sheathe this sword in young Sigurd's back,' Thengil threatened, and though Sigurd knew the man's weight alone was enough to drive that blade into him, he knew too that Thengil would do no such thing.

'He needs me alive, Uncle,' he said. 'The white-livered nithing means to take me to Hinderå and buy himself a name there.'

'Gods but if someone gave me you as a wedding gift I'd put my foot up their arse,' Olaf said.

'I will ask you one more time,' Thengil said, the tremor in his voice betraying a rising anger now. Being Jarl Hakon's son amongst women and old men, it was likely that Thengil was not used to being defied. 'Put your blades down or my men will spear you where you stand.' The white-beards were stony-faced and ready to fight. They gripped their spears and shields with long-practised ease, as comfortably as they might hold a cup of ale, and Sigurd knew they would carry out Thengil's orders without flinching.

'Sigurd is my prize. He is the silver that will see a jarl's torc at my neck.'

'A jarl of ghosts,' Olaf said, feet planted, shield up. Ready.

Valgerd jerked her chin at Sigurd, her eyes knife points in the shadow of her fine helmet. 'What happened to the bird?' she asked.

'She flew,' Sigurd said, glancing towards the woods. A smile touched the warrior woman's lips. 'Men of Osøyro!' Sigurd said. 'Lower your spears. You are men of honour. You are far above this shit bucket Thengil Hakonarson.'

Something smashed into the back of his head and he staggered, falling to the dirt. The pommel of Thengil's sword, he supposed, feeling the blood run warm across his scalp and down the side of his neck, but he did not turn around to face the man and climbed to his feet as though it were nothing.

'Goat-fucker!' Svein spat at Thengil, straining to be let off his leash, to drown the grey day in red.

'You are proud men,' Sigurd continued, 'but you dishonour yourselves doing this man's bidding. You know full well what your jarl would think of his son. He would have wished he had drowned the nithing at birth.'

This time a hilt in his lower back that put him on his knees by the curds which Thengil's thrall had spilled. He tried to speak but could not find the breath.

'Another word and I'll cut you, Haraldarson,' Thengil barked, the bridle slipping off his fury now at being insulted before his men. Before his father's men. Before some of the women too, for they had gathered in the shadow of the hall's doorway. This was doubtless the most exciting thing that had happened in this place for years.

Sigurd could feel the bruise blooming in his flesh like a burn. He dragged a halting breath into his lungs and climbed to his feet, a spearman either side of him, their blades poised to plunge into him.

'Hakon's men, I give you this last chance,' he said through a grimace of pain. 'Back away now or die.'

'Hold your tongue, Sigurd,' Olaf said.

'Bring him to me!' Thengil barked. 'I will cut that tongue from its root! Jarl Randver will not mind that.'

'Lord!' one of his hirðmen said, lifting his spear, pointing it west towards the pine-swathed hill.

Another man spat a curse.

'Shieldwall!' Hauk roared, and he only needed to give that command once, as his men broke their blade ring around Sigurd's companions, backing off with shields raised, and spread into a line facing west. Even the two warriors guarding Sigurd hurried to join the others, at which Thengil bolted before Sigurd could take hold of him. Hakon's son slammed the hall's door shut and Sigurd heard the bar being dropped into place behind it. Then he looked west himself and the pain in his side and head was consumed by a wave of savage joy.

His men were coming. They must have seen Fjölnir take to the grey sky, the feather-tied string distinguishing her from any other bird, and now they came like wolves to the kill. Having broken from the tree line, warriors with shields, spears, axes and swords were running across the meadow, as eager for the blood-fray as Thór himself. Floki led, his hair, black as Fjölnir, flying behind him, and with him were Aslak and Hendil, Bjarni and Bjorn and the rest.

'Shieldwall!' Olaf yelled, throwing Sigurd his sword, which he caught, pulling Troll-Tickler from its scabbard. But Svein could be held back no more. He strode towards Hauk's shieldwall swinging his long-hafted axe in great diagonal circles before him, and those men braced themselves.

'Brains of an ox,' Olaf said, but Sigurd was already moving. Valgerd was fast too, at Svein's left shoulder now.

'Hold, Hakon's men!' Hauk roared. 'Hold!' As the head of Svein's axe smashed into a shield, cleaving it down the middle and lopping off the man's arm. The warrior staggered backwards, waving his half arm, the stump spraying gore over his companions. Then Valgerd plunged into the breach, knocking a spear aside and shrieking as she plunged her own through a man's neck. Sigurd was on Svein's right but he did not have a shield or spear and so he had either to keep his distance or get in close. He swung Troll-Tickler at a spear haft, forcing the blade wide, but the man behind it was strong for all his years and he strode forward ramming his shield's boss into Sigurd's face, breaking his nose. Sigurd pulled his scramasax from the sheath on his arm and stepped back, looking for the next spear thrust through blurred eyes as blood spewed from his nose onto his lips and beard.

A blade streaked from the shieldwall and he swiped it away with the scramasax, knowing he had to get in close again, then Olaf slammed his shield into the line and a heartbeat later Floki plunged into the fray, ducking low, getting beneath a shield to hack into a man's leg with his short axe. Svein was roaring like a maddened beast and Valgerd was shrieking like an eagle and then the others hit like a storm-lashed wave crashing against the rocks. Blood flew and blades sang and men began to die.

Ubba rammed his spear straight through a grey-beard's old shield and used his strength to push the shield down and this was all Karsten Ríkr needed. He thrust his sword into the man's mouth and the blade punched through his skull in a spray of blood and bone. Somehow Floki had cut his way through Hauk's shieldwall and was behind them now, dealing death with his axe and long knife, and this was enough to break the wall, for men will not hold if they have an enemy at their backs.

Sigurd saw an old warrior knock Hendil's spear aside with his shield and sink his own spear into Hendil's shoulder, but then Agnar Hunter was there with his two scramasaxes, slicing off the man's leading hand with one and plunging the other into his eye. And even a proud old warrior like that one was not above screaming in fear and pain.

'End it, Sigurd!' Olaf snarled in his ear. 'You hear me, lad? It's not worth the blood.'

Even in the grip of his blood-lust Sigurd felt the weight of this thing like a stone in his gut. He knew that Olaf was right and he bent to pick up a discarded shield. 'Back! Shieldwall!' he yelled, raising the shield to deflect another spear blade. 'Back!' For he could not afford to lose men in some meaningless skirmish. Besides which, he admired the warriors he was killing. They deserved better than dying for Thengil White-Liver.

'You heard him, Sigurd's men. Back!' Olaf roared in a voice that had carried above more battle dins than he could remember.

Solveig was bent double and panting. Bjarni was screaming insults at the white-beards and his brother Bjorn was stepping back swiping blood and spit from his torn lip. But Hauk's men, those who were still able, were striding back from the fray, back from their dead hearth companions and those they had rowed with and sung with and fought with. And there was no panic in these five men, nor any sign that they yielded.

Valgerd was on her knees opening a man's throat with her knife, his white beard blooming red in an instant. Svein brought his axe onto a fallen warrior's head, chopping it in half and burying the axe blade in the earth.

'Enough!' Sigurd roared. Blood was leaking into his throat and dripping from his beard and from the gash in his head. His lower back screamed in pain from where Thengil had punched him with his sword's hilt but all he cared about was that there were none of his warriors amongst the dead and dying. Seven of Jarl Hakon's hearthmen lay dead and two more would join their fellows soon enough by the look of the blood leaking from their wounds.

Sigurd looked up to see Asgot coming, sword- and spear-armed, his grey, bone-tied braids hanging either side of his fierce face.

The rest of his men were panting for breath from the run and the fight but they had formed into a passable shieldwall and even amidst the butchery, the stink of death and shit cloying the air, and his eyes streaming because of his broken nose, he felt prouder than if he had been wearing his father's great torc of twisted silver.

'Come, Sigurd Haraldarson, we will finish it now,' Hauk said, beckoning Sigurd with a lift of his shield, showing that the arm behind it was still strong. 'Our brothers wait for us in the Spear-God's hall. We will join them.' A grin appeared in his white beard. 'Or we will beat you and return to our mead.'

Sigurd looked the man in the eyes, feeling nothing but respect for him and those shoulder to shoulder with him.

'Jarl Hakon was lucky to have hearthmen such as you, Hauk of Osøyro,' Sigurd said, then turned his head to spit a wad of congealing blood. He dragged a hand across his mouth and beard, smearing the palm red. 'But Hakon is gone. There is nothing of the man in that near-corpse in there,' he said, thumbing back towards the hall. 'The man you serve now is a coward. He would not even stand with you for this fight but would rather hide amongst women's skirts. I say again that being oath-tied to such a man is a dishonour and you would do well to be free of such a binding.'

'We will be free soon enough, I would wager,' Hauk said.

'Aye, we can help you with that,' Svein the Red said, lifting his gore-slick axe.

'Join us,' Sigurd said. 'You have seen what kind of men I have at my side.'

'Not only men, hey!' Bjarni said, grinning.

Sigurd nodded. 'I even had a valkyrie fighting for me.'

Hauk and his men might have laughed at that, had they not seen Valgerd fight. Had they not watched her slaughter their friends.

Sigurd swept his scramasax towards his crew. His own hirð-men, he thought. Not that he had a hearth. 'We are weaving a tale that skalds will tell long after we are gone from this world. I am Óðin-favoured. Would we have beaten you so easily if I were not?'

This had Hauk thinking. The others too. It was in their faces like runes carved in old tree trunks.

'Come with us and fight Jarl Randver. Fill your old sea chests with plunder.'

Hauk laughed. 'What need have we of silver at our age?' he asked. 'We want food, mead and a roaring hearth to warm our bones. You can keep your arm rings. We rarely bother to wear ours these days.'

Sigurd nodded, accepting this. 'You must have sons somewhere,' he said. 'Daughters too and others you have known. Let them hear of you in skalds' tales and in song. Let them hear how you stood in the steel-storm one last time and earned the fame that no man can ever take from you.'

'I would have you beside me against Jarl Randver's men,' Olaf said. 'I have seen none braver than you.'

Hauk and his exhausted men stood a little straighter at that, for they were strong words coming from a warrior such as Olaf. They were mead to a proud man's spirit.

Sigurd nodded. 'Take back the honour you are owed,' he said.

Hauk wrestled with all this for a while, as Sigurd swallowed blood and the first of the two men lying with the corpses gave a death rattle and became one himself.

'You will fight a man as powerful as Jarl Randver with just those I see before me?' Hauk asked.

Sigurd nodded. 'And when I have killed Randver I will kill the oath-breaker King Gorm.'

Hauk's white brows lifted and he turned the spear in his hand, plunging it blade first into the earth.

'Then we are your men, Haraldarson,' he said.

CHAPTER SEVENTEEN

'IT DID NOT GO AS WE HOPED THEN,' ASGOT SAID WHEN WHEN HE HAD come up to them outside Jarl Hakon's hall, his eyes picking over the corpses like crows. Then he had put a claw-like hand on Sigurd's arm and looked him in the eye. 'But it seems we have some killers amongst us at least.'

'You should have seen them,' Sigurd said in a low voice, watching the others wipe bloodied blades on the hems of dead men's tunics – which Hauk did not like though he said nothing – and talking quietly among themselves. Men were often full of thunder after a fight, half of it the thrill of being alive, half of it the wild blood-lusting beast that can take its time in skulking away. But these were quiet and Sigurd knew it was a shit bucket of a victory.

He looked at the dead lying in their own filth, their skin as grey as their beards. 'These men deserved better than this, Asgot,' he said.

'Which one is Jarl Hakon?' the godi asked.

Sigurd shook his head. 'Brandingi is a living corpse on a bed by his hearth. His nithing son Thengil had it in his mind to give me over to Jarl Randver as a wedding gift.'

Asgot's lip curled beneath his grey moustaches. 'A cunning scheme, though it did not work out so well for him.'

Sigurd pointed his scramasax at the hall behind them. 'He's in there, too. He runs fast for a fat man.' Then he saw the look in Asgot's eye. That wicked sharp knife, the one that slit animal's throats and, sometimes, men's, was whispering to the godi. 'No, Asgot,' Sigurd said, 'the Allfather would not thank you for him.'

'Aye, Sigurd's right, Asgot. I've come across turds with more honour in them,' Olaf said. 'He's not worth getting your knife wet for.'

Asgot hoisted a brow. 'And these old bones died for him?'

'I doubt it,' Olaf said.

'They still fought for their jarl,' Sigurd explained. 'And because they were too proud to do otherwise lest it look as though they lacked courage.'

'And now that lot will fight for Sigurd,' Olaf said, nodding at Hauk and his four men, who had laid down their shields but were not quite ready to put aside their spears. They stood in a knot talking heatedly amongst themselves and Sigurd guessed they were arguing about what to do with Thengil.

'They are old but I am glad to have them,' Sigurd said.

'Well it is not as though this crew can get any stranger,' Olaf said, which was true enough.

Hauk looked over and caught Sigurd's eye and Sigurd nodded because he knew what the old warrior was telling him in that look. Hauk and his men would deal with Thengil in their own way.

Hauk hammered a fist against the hall's door but the women within were too afraid to open it, until he called to them by name and assured them it was he on the other side of it. The enormous door, the hero of its own saga tale, opened and Sigurd caught a glimpse of several pale faces before Hauk and the others went inside. He waited for what seemed an age, watching the snow-peaked mountains fade from sight as night's cloak fell slowly over them. And then Solveig called to him, saying that Hauk wanted him in the hall.

'I thought we'd hear him squealing for his worthless life,' Olaf said as he and Sigurd made their way across the ground which was pooled here and there with congealing blood. The dead still lay where they had fallen, because Sigurd's crew guessed that the Osøyro men would want to deal with their own. 'You think he found some backbone at the last?'

'No,' Sigurd said, as they entered the huge place which was fully formed in his eyes straight away this time because it was darker outside. He sensed Olaf's wonder at the high beams and the huge central aisle and the two stone-lined hearth pits, the roof posts like oak trees and, more than anything, the emptiness and misery of a hall that must once had been the envy of men.

'Thór's bristling bollocks but this must have been something once,' Olaf murmured. 'I am remembering some of it now.'

Sigurd did not need to reply. There would be even more ghosts amongst the benches tonight, he thought.

And then they saw Thengil Hakonarson.

His piss-dripping calf-skin shoes were three feet off the floor and he was turning slowly on the creaking rope, the bulging eyes in the purpling face coming round to accuse the men who had just entered his father's hall. For a sickening moment and by the flicker of the hearth flames Sigurd thought Thengil was still alive. But then he saw that he must have clambered up onto the headboard of his father's deathbed and that was high enough that coupled with his own weight his neck, which had never known the row bench or the shieldwall, had snapped. Though whether Thengil had chosen this rope death, or had been persuaded to it by the grey-beards, they could not say.

So the old hall-burning warrior has outlived his son, Sigurd thought. Until he saw the silver-inlaid hilt sticking out of Jarl Hakon's chest, the skins and furs carelessly thrown on the ground beside the bed. Or had Hauk done it? Had the faithful old warrior plunged Thengil's sword into the jarl's heart to send him on his way to Valhöll where he should have gone many years before now? Sigurd imagined one of Hauk's men putting his own sword in the jarl's hand and holding it there while Hauk did the rest.

But Sigurd did not ask about that, either. For it did not matter. Father and son, as different as sun and moon, were dead, and in that they were the same. The women had taken themselves off to the benches at the sides where they sat weeping and con- soling each other. Hauk and his four men looked tired enough to lie down dead beside their jarl but Sigurd knew they would be fine after a meal and a good night's sleep undisturbed by Thengil's greasy fumblings with his bed slaves.

Not that the last of Jarl Brandingi's hearthmen would rest yet. Sigurd watched as two of them took the hanged son's sopping weight while another stood on Hakon's bed to cut the rope. Why they did not simply let the troll's turd drop in a heap on the floor was beyond Sigurd, but perhaps one of those sobbing women was kin to Thengil and it was out of respect for her.

'What do you suppose they will do with him?' Olaf said.

Sigurd shrugged. 'Feed him to the crabs. That is what I would do.'

They hefted Thengil out of the hall and Sigurd caught the stench of piss as he passed, which surprised him given that his nose was clotted with drying blood.

'We will see to our dead now,' Hauk said to them, following on.

Sigurd nodded. 'We will help you.'

'No, Haraldarson, we will do it ourselves,' Hauk said.

The man with more brown than grey in his beard, who had earlier stood behind Thengil's shoulder, gave Sigurd a sour look. 'We will drink with them again soon enough and do not want them chewing our ears off for not seeing to their corpses in our way.'

Then Hauk had second thoughts and scratched amongst the long white hairs that covered his cheeks. 'You can help with the rocks,' he said. 'There are plenty under the sod on the north side of the hall by the apple trees there.'

Sigurd nodded, understanding. A pyre to burn nine men would need half the wood that had gone into Hakon's hall and even then the corpses would spill so much liquid that they would likely not burn well enough. So Hauk would dig up a swath of earth and lay out a ship with big stones. The nine dead would be laid in that ship and borne to the afterlife that way, for they had all died good deaths in the end, which was all a man could hope for from the wyrd spun him.

'Hauk!' Sigurd called after them as they got Thengil to the door. 'I claim their war gear,' he said. 'My men will have their brynjur.'

Even at that distance it was clear that Hauk did not like that. He would have laid his hearth companions in their stone ship with their swords, mail and helmets, for such things are needed in the hereafter. But he nodded curtly, for what choice did he have? He was lucky that Sigurd had left him and the others with their honour and he knew it.

'Well the stones can wait,' Olaf said, holding his hands over the hearthfire, making fists of them. The evenings were getting colder now and the hall was draughty. 'It's too late to go off digging about out there. Besides which, our lot fought well and deserve to drink it off like a proper war band.'

'Then we had better find out where Thengil keeps his mead,' Sigurd said. He was picking bits of blood from his beard and wondering what the gash in his head looked like. He was also thinking mead would be good to rinse his mouth and throat of the iron tang of blood. But most of all he was thinking that Olaf was right in that they *were* a proper war band now. They had fought together and fought well. Better still they had won. His odd crew of outlaws and dispossessed, of men – and a woman – from different hearths had shed blood and shared the sword song and there was no stronger bond than that, as his father had said many times. Gods they were good fighters! His father would have admitted that much, even if he would have made them form a skjaldborg rather than throwing themselves at the enemy like berserkers. And now they would have war gear to make the battle god Týr sit up on his bench and take notice. Perhaps only King Gorm himself could put so many mail-clad men into a fight.

'Nevertheless, he was a wolf in his time, that one,' Olaf said, the words barely loud enough to ruffle his beard. Sigurd knew he was talking about the corpse behind them with Thengil's sword pinning him to his bed. 'It is a shame we found him like this.'

A mouse scampered across the ash-strewn floor and Sigurd mused that the creatures need no longer worry about Thengil hurling his mead horns at them.

'Maybe it is not a shame at all,' he said, 'for if Hakon still had his wits then he might have done properly what Thengil tried and failed to do. I might have ended up a wedding gift at Jarl Randver's Haust Blót feast.'

Olaf pursed his lips. 'That's true enough,' he said. 'And a man like that might have known you were up to some Loki-mischief with that bird.'

Sigurd felt himself grinning. 'For a moment I thought Fjölnir was going to perch up there and dig the old wood for worms,' he said, nodding up at one of the stout roof beams. And with that they laughed, as Olaf threw an arm around Sigurd's shoulder and pulled him in to his broad chest, just stopping short of ruffling Sigurd's long hair with his other hand, as he had done countless times before when Sigurd was a boy.

'Be careful, old man,' Sigurd baited him, when Olaf broke the grip to scrape some dried blood off his brynja with a thumbnail. 'Remember the last time we wrestled? You ended up on the floor wailing like a woman in childbirth.'

'Wrestled? You distracted me and kicked me in the bollocks, lad!' He batted the smoky air with a big hand. 'Though you'll no doubt pay the skalds to weave it into some tall tale about a fight that went on all night but which you won through skill and courage and because you're fucking Óðin-favoured.'

Sigurd made a pretence of thinking about it, scratching his bearded chin as a proper jarl would do over some dispute between his lendermen which he was settling at the ting. 'No,' he said after a while. 'Kicking you in the bollocks and you shrieking like a woman . . .' he nodded, 'that will do for me.'

*

They spent the night in Hakon's hall, snugged up with furs on the benches and more comfortable than any of them – other than Hauk and his men – had been for a long time. There were nine women sharing that hearth and lamp-flickered dark, as the wind gathered outside and forced itself through the gaps in the old staves, swirling woodsmoke and sharing out the acrid stink of the fish oil burning in the iron dishes. These women included Thengil's two bed slaves, who had also performed household tasks because Thengil had long since spent his father's hard-won silver and could not afford to live as a wealthy karl let alone a jarl. But neither had he dared to go raiding to refill his father's sea chests and so he had no thralls to speak of, for the younger warriors of Osøyro who had left long ago to make their fortunes had taken their women and Hakon's thralls with them. It was not as though the jarl needed them any more, lying there as still as a warrior corpse in his burial mound, and Thengil had lacked the spine to hold on to them.

Of those eight women, from what Sigurd could piece together two were wives of Hauk's remaining men and four were now widows, and though none of them was friendly to the strangers in their hall who had killed their brave men, they seemed to have laid most of their hatred on Thengil Hakonarson. Sigurd had seen two of them spit on his hanged corpse when Hauk's men had laid it on the ground outside, for which Hauk had growled at them out of respect for the hanged man's father. Nevertheless, even with night coming they had carried Thengil down to the rocks and, with the tide on the turn, dumped him where the frothing suck and plunge would break his bones and soften him up for the crabs. They tossed his sword in with him too because beautiful as it was, no man wanted that thing for the bad luck it might bring them.

'That is that then,' Svein had said when they had watched the Osøyro men return.

'Can you think of a worse end?' Aslak had asked, which had got all of them thinking as they passed round some horns full of the mead they had found in barrels behind a hanging partition at the back of the hall.

'An arrow in the arse followed by a festering wound?' Agnar Hunter suggested, which got some murmurs of agreement.

'A knife in the groin from some cowering nithing?' Ubba offered, getting them wincing. 'With that big vein cut you will bleed white in the time it takes to curse your ill wyrd.'

'A lingering, bloodless death is worse,' Valgerd said, and perhaps many of them thought she was talking about Jarl Hakon, but Sigurd knew her mind had flown back to a cabin in the Lysefjord and a dead seeress who had been her lover. 'To be eaten by sickness from the inside. To try desperately to hold on to your life like water in your hands.' She grimaced. 'That is worse than any blade death.'

Even with the pain of that loss in her face she was beautiful, perhaps more so because of it, and so Sigurd watched the hearth flames instead. He had never known the seeress but to his mind it was Valgerd who had all the seiðr, and he had the feeling that when his eyes were on her, other men's eyes were on him, which was why he looked away now.

'None of us can say what the Norns have spun for us,' Asgot put in, and this had more or less soured the ale in their horns as each of them wondered what the Spinners had done with the threads of their lives. But they had drunk anyway, washing away the pain from cuts and bruises and the foul taste that can linger in the mouth after the killing of other men, even those that would have killed you.

And the next day they had laid Jarl Hakon on a different bed, one of seasoned timbers taken from a boathouse down by the sea, and put a torch to it, which was fitting, everyone agreed, for a man bynamed Burner. There were no tears for him either from the women or even from his hearthmen who had shared blood and mead with him over the years, for the lord they knew had been gone from them a long time already. But it was all done with honour and straight backs and Hauk and his men had dressed as though for war, their blades and helmets scrubbed until they were the brightest things, other than the jarl's pyre, on a dull day.

The wind had whipped the great, roaring flames up and northward, so that old Solveig had observed that no man could ever have been borne to Valhöll any faster, to which Floki replied that at Hakon's age he could ill afford to be slow about it if he wanted to enjoy what was on offer in the Hall of the Dead. But Sigurd had simmered during the whole thing because all he could think about was that he had not been able to give his father and brothers the hero pyres they should have had. Who knew what King Gorm had done with their bodies.

'The Death Maidens took them before their blood was cold,' Olaf said, coming to stand beside him, knowing full well what was gnawing at Sigurd as Hakon's corpse blackened in the fire, the limbs twisting into gnarled shapes and the blood bubbling and spurting, boiling up from the hole in his chest. 'There's not a chance that men like that would be passed over, hey?'

Sigurd said nothing and Olaf did not push it, for he too felt the shame of it like a wound, that he had not sent his jarl off in the proper way.

When the pyre died down and all that remained of Hakon Brandingi was a few charred bones, they made a ship of stones for the dead. Sigurd let Hauk give each fallen warrior a spear but no other weapons, these being too valuable to the living to give to the slain. Yet their old comrades did what they could, placing the dead men's other possessions in the grave, things such as combs, Thór's hammer amulets, eating knives and drinking horns. The warrior with more brown than grey in his beard, whose name was Grundar, even put a tafl board and all the pieces in there, which all agreed was a very good thing to do. No one could say how long a stone ship would take to make the journey to the afterlife were it the case that the Valkyries had not carried off every one of the fallen, being old men and long past their prime. For only the strongest warriors were assured a place amongst the chosen. But a tafl board would help make the time pass until they found their places amongst old Flaming Eye's mead benches.

'So what now?' Svein asked, coming to stand with Sigurd and arming sweat from his brow despite the chill breeze whipping across the open meadow with the whisper of winter.

'Now we wait,' Sigurd said. Men who had fought each other just days previously were now working together, digging earth and wheeling it in barrows to the stone ship of the dead and building a mound upon it. 'We wait and we prepare.' The scowl in Svein's face said what he felt about that, but there was nothing else for it. The scheme was woven and he would follow the thread of it. 'In seven days we will be in Skudeneshavn,' Sigurd told him. He had not said *home*, for with his father's hall gone and his kin dead, that place would never be his home again. 'We will meet Hagal there and see if he has been able to tempt some jarl or ambitious karl to join us.'

One of Svein's red brows arched. 'You trust Crow-Song not to have flown off to some warm hall where the lord there has him swimming in mead and singing songs about him?'

'Hagal said he would be waiting for us,' Sigurd said. 'He'll be there.' In truth he was not so certain. His whole plan was built on the skald, like ship strakes lashed to the frame, and yet he could not be sure of Hagal's loyalty because the man had never been oath-tied to any jarl and so did not know what it was to bind yourself to another no matter what. And this thought led Sigurd to the question of whether he should ask those who followed him now to swear an oath, for how could he know they would not drift away at any time if things got hard or if another man offered them more? The only thing Sigurd could promise them was blood. Without an oath holding them, what was to stop them turning their backs on him or even deserting him in the fray?

He knew that Svein and Aslak, Solveig, Asgot and Olaf would stand with him and fall with him too if it came to it. Sigurd knew that in the very marrow of his bones. But these others? He needed to bind them to him. Olaf had said they owed Sigurd their oath for giving them such booty as they now owned, each having his own brynja now for they had the nine from Hakon's dead hirðmen as well as Thengil's own which was rusted but unused and which fitted Ubba well, and the jarl's which Sigurd took for himself, wondering at the fights and adventures those iron rings had seen over the years. It was snug across Sigurd's shoulders and longer than most mail coats, reaching to mid thigh, so that Svein had said it looked as if he was wearing a dress, and Olaf had suggested that either Jarl Hakon had been a much taller man before the years had bent him, or else he had killed a giant for the thing.

'Jarls give their crewmen arm rings and blades, if they are the sort of jarls worth swearing to,' Olaf had said as Hauk had laid out the brynjur and had Thengil's bed slaves scrubbing the blood off them, 'but you, who are not yet a jarl, have given them the sort of wealth they could only have dreamt of.' He had hammered a fist into his open palm. 'Strike now, Sigurd. Make them swear the oath with the weight of these rings still settling on their bones.'

Sigurd had nodded, even though he was afraid in case they would refuse to bind themselves to him, a young man without authority, land, or a ship that would sail itself into any half-decent story. But he knew Olaf was right and that it needed to be done. So he would ask them to swear on his sword, though maybe not when they were digging earth and burying men, he thought now, as Svein swung the iron pick onto his shoulder and went back to work.

The day after that they went to those folk living west of Hakon's hall, the other side of the wooded hill, and there found two men with skill and tools enough to help them make repairs on the dead jarl's karvi, which Hauk was shame-faced to admit they had let rot at its mooring because they were old men who knew their raiding days were long gone.

'She'll never survive an angry sea or even a proper journey,' Solveig had said when Sigurd had taken him and Karsten Ríkr down to the wharf where the karvi and *Sea-Sow* were moored.

His few remaining teeth had shown in his beard then. 'You would have more chance of staying above the waves riding on the back of a seal,' he said. At least the two experienced helmsmen agreed on that, not that Sigurd had liked hearing it.

'Well, we have wood and we have time,' he had replied, though he had more of the former than the latter, 'and it will be in your interests to make it seaworthy as one of you will be at its helm soon enough.'

Karsten had growled a curse and Solveig had said he'd always known a drowning death awaited him, and from that moment the two of them seemed to form an understanding that bordered on friendship, which was at least something.

Between what they could get their hands on at the little village and what lay stored across the roof beams of the boathouse on the shore they had amassed some worked planks and enough seasoned wood, so they hauled the karvi, which Grundar said was called *Skrukka* – *Sea-Urchin* – out of the water and set to work. They replaced the worst of the barnacle-crusted strakes and the decking which was soft and worm-riddled, and scraped off the green slime and bird shit that cloaked the ship. They could not risk raising the yard with its mouldering sail because the mast looked as though it might snap if any strain were put on it.

'She'll have to be rowed,' Olaf said, so those oars up in their trees which had been most exposed winter after winter were swapped with spare ones from *Sea-Sow*.

'A little rowing will do them good,' Solveig said, which was easy for him to say seeing as he would be standing at the tiller watching them sweat.

'She just needs to get us to Hinderå,' Sigurd said, scowling with Olaf at *Sea-Urchin*, to the relentless clinking rhythm of men driving rivets home. 'After that she can end her days on the sea bed or split apart for firewood.' This time Solveig scowled because it was not clever to say such things in front of a ship.

'I think I'd rather swim to Hinderå, brynja and all,' Olaf said, and from his face Sigurd knew he was half serious. Yet it was obvious enough they were too many now to cram into *Sea-Sow*'s thwarts even with the new decking over the knörr's big hold.

And so the repairs continued, and, while Solveig and Karsten oversaw the work being done by the craftsmen from the village and their friends who, lured by Sigurd's promise of silver, had come to fetch and carry, Olaf gathered Sigurd's crew together on the flat meadow to the east of Hakon's hall.

'You came at Hauk's shieldwall that day like a pack of rabid wolves,' Olaf said in a voice loud enough for all to hear as they milled with shields and spears. 'I've seen rain hit the ground with more neatness than you hit Hauk's lot. Old Solveig struck his first blow a day later than Floki there.'

'We won didn't we?' Bjarni said. There were rumbles of agreement with that.

'Aye, we tore them apart easily enough,' Ubba said.

Olaf turned to Sigurd, shaking his head. 'Listen to the gods of war,' he said, then glowered at Bjarni and Ubba. 'They were old men!' he said. 'Men who had not had a good fight for who knows how many years!' He raised a hand to Hauk and Grundar and the others to show he meant no offence. Hauk glowered anyway, but in truth he knew Olaf was right. 'Do you think Jarl Randver's war band will be made of white-beards and men who knew the Allfather when he still had two eyes?' This got some chuckles, though not from the Osøyro men, Sigurd noted. 'Fuck no! His hirð will stand behind a shieldwall that could turn back the tide.' He thumped a fist into his own mailed chest. 'I know, I've fought them.'

No one denied that, for though only a few of them had watched the ship battle in the Karmsund Strait, they had all heard about it, heard how Jarl Harald had stood fighting to the last, his champions and two of Sigurd's brothers cut down around him.

'What's this arm for?' he asked, holding out his right arm and clenching his scarred hand.

'If you have to ask, you're doing it wrong, Uncle,' Hendil called, raising some rough laughter.

'This arm is for hacking, chopping, hewing and killing,' Olaf said.

'And drinking!' Bjorn called, getting cheers of agreement.

'This arm,' Olaf said, ignoring the interruptions and lifting his shield, 'is for pushing, deflecting and covering.' He pursed his lips and tilted his head to the side. 'Now, I know this is all very hard to follow, but are you with me so far?' No one came out with a clever answer to this and Olaf nodded. 'Good,' he said, then bared his teeth. 'But you can't smite a man if you've been knocked onto your backside, or if you are too busy letting some whoreson sheathe his sax in your ribs because the men on either side of you have broken and are halfway across some fjord, their arses flapping like a fish.' He set his feet one behind the other and gestured to them. 'You plant your feet and you stand. You stand with your brothers and you do not break.'

He jerked a chin at Aslak and Svein who lifted their shields as they had clearly been told to at the given signal, Svein's overlapping Aslak's by almost half its width as they braced themselves. Olaf lifted his leg and slammed the underside of his booted foot into Svein's shield but the two young men stood firm. Then Olaf took five paces back, hefted his own shield and charged, smashing it into theirs and leaning his shoulder into it, trying to drive forward. But against Svein's great bulk and the added resistance provided by Aslak, he made no progress, despite his growls and reddening face, and given Olaf's great brawn this was all he needed to do to prove his point.

He stood tall and came back to face the crowd. 'I want two skjaldborgar facing each other,' he barked, and when they had formed their walls, their spear blades pointing to the sky, Olaf and Sigurd took their places, one at the centre of each line. On Sigurd's right was Svein and on his left was Floki. The men either side of Olaf were Hendil and Bjorn. Two skjaldborgar of wood, iron and flesh.

'A woman in a shieldwall?' Torving said, shaking his head so that the white braids danced. 'She'll weaken the whole thing.'

Valgerd glared at him. 'The men we buried yesterday did not

find me weak, old man,' she said, and Aslak, Svein and a couple of the others cheered her, whilst Hauk and his men swore and growled.

'The man who comes up against me in a real fight will be dead before he raises his shield,' Valgerd said.

Nevertheless, even the old Osøyro men had bulk left over from their raiding and rowing days, whereas Valgerd was slender and lithe as a birch and could not hope to hold back a man three times her weight. But Olaf had already thought of this.

'Valgerd will fight behind the wall, if it comes to that. She will kill the men whose stinking breath is filling your nose and whose piss is soaking your feet, and you will be grateful to her for it. Asgot will fight there too, because I have long ago lost count of the men I have seen him kill with a spear in their eye or a blade in their groin.' Men winced at this, but the godi grinned. 'Now if you have finished wasting the day, let us get to work.' With that men loosened off necks and shoulders, hefted their painted shields up before them, and waited for the command.

'Whichever wall breaks first, those men will go hunting later and will not return without a boar for the spit tonight.'

'But the boar are all up in the northern wood a half day's walk from here,' Grundar called across from Sigurd's line.

'Then you had better hope you do not lose, Grundar,' Olaf said through a grin, as he started moving forward, the others with him, and the men yelling insults and bawling at each other.

And the shieldwalls clashed like thunder.

The next day Olaf had them practising the swine wedge, or svinfylkja, which was the best formation for driving through a mass of enemy warriors to kill their lord. As the biggest and most ferocious-looking men, Svein and Ubba made up the first rank; followed by three in the second rank, four in the third, and so on. Olaf or Sigurd would roar the command and they had to get into their positions as quickly as they could. At first it was a mess, with men crashing into each other and treading on each other's feet, and the rain-filled day seethed with insults hurled between them. But by the end of the day each of them knew their business and the svinfylkja coalesced as neatly as a skein of geese heading south.

They practised making a square of shields too, in case Sigurd should be wounded and they needed to protect him or get him away from the fray. But they must all have known there was little point in spending much time and sweat on that scheme. For being just nineteen warriors all told, they were still only half a crew and if they were being pressed on all sides so that their only recourse was to make a square, then they were almost certainly doomed. As Solveig wryly observed, that would be the sort of last stand that Hagal would love for one of his stories.

On the sixth day after they had burnt Jarl Hakon and buried his hirðmen – the seventh after they had tossed his worthless son into the bone-snapping breakers – they packed their sea chests, gathered on the rotting jetty by *Sea-Sow* and *Sea-Urchin* and readied to leave for Skudeneshavn.

The Osøyro men bid farewell to the women and said they would either be back with a tale to shake the great hall's old beams or not at all, and the older women accepted this with quiet tears but admirable dignity. The same could not be said for Thengil's two bed slaves, who clung to Svein and Bjarni like limpets to rocks, weeping and begging them not to go, which had the two men crimson-cheeked and wincing as their friends taunted them as jealous men will. For those two's benches had done some creaking in the last few nights.

Then Bjorn and Agnar Hunter hauled an old bull onto the rocks by its horns while Karsten pulled it by the halter and Hauk and Bodvar put their weight into it from behind, the beast lowing and arching its back to make itself look bigger and more threatening.

Sigurd could see in their eyes that the men and women watching were impressed by the bull and thought it a worthy sacrifice, which made it worth the lump of hacksilver he had paid a farmer in the little village for it. It was a fierce, bristling animal, pawing and horning the rock, so that it was all Bjorn and Agnar could do to hold on as Svein went forward with his long-hafted axe and stood in front of the bull and the sweating men holding it. He turned the haft and swung, bringing the weapon's thick poll smashing down onto the lowing beast's skull. It dropped down onto its forelegs stunned and Asgot came up with his wicked sharp knife and thrust it into the bull's throat and cut outwards through the thick veins there so that the blood could spill into the bowl Valgerd was holding. The bright gore spattered onto the rocks, fogging the cold morning air and filling Sigurd's nose with its richness. In no time at all the bowl was full and Asgot and Valgerd were splashing though small pools of blood whilst some of it ran off in little streams, following crevices in the rocks that led down to the sea.

Feeling that the animal was past causing them any harm now, Bjorn and Agnar let go of its horns and it slumped down to the ground with a last great snort, the lids no longer sweeping over its bulging eyes. Asgot and Valgerd fell to their knees in the crimson pools and the godi set about pumping one of the beast's forelegs, which was a trick to getting more blood out of the slash in its neck, though Valgerd's bowl was already overflowing and her hands were blood-drenched.

When it was done Asgot took the bowl from Valgerd and from his belt a bunch of birch twigs he had bound together, and went over to those watching wide-eyed and tight-mouthed. Dipping the birch twigs in the bowl he flicked the blood over their faces and even though it was warm they could not help flinching at its touch, each of them full of the seiðr of it because they knew the gods were watching. When he had finished with them he flicked the bull's blood across the bows of *Sea-Sow* and *Sea-Urchin*, invoked Óðin Sigðir, the Victory-Bringer, and then another god whom Sigurd had asked him to summon so that he might ride into this blood-fray with them. And that god was Vidar, Óðin's own son, who wise men said would slay the wolf Fenrir during the chaos of Ragnarök. And when Asgot called on this god he did so with gritted teeth and fury, so that he had more than a few men nervously touching iron.

351

But Sigurd was not afraid. He stood with his head high and his back straight, and he listened to Asgot telling the god that they were going to Hinderå, just they few against the jarl's many. And the name Vidar would be on their lips, on their young war-leader's lips in the sword song and the shield din. Jarl Randver would pay in blood for what he had done. He would suffer and he would bleed and he would die. Because Sigurd had woken the gods. The reckoning was coming.

And Vidar was the God of Vengeance.

With the bull's blood drying on their faces and Asgot's invocations still in their ears, Olaf looked at Sigurd, who did not need to ask what his friend was thinking.

A cold hand clutched Sigurd's heart. 'Now?' he said.

'Can you think of a better time?' Olaf said, one eyebrow rounded like Bifröst.

'But if they refuse? We will undo all that we have done,' Sigurd said.

'The gods are amongst us,' Olaf said, his eyes boring into Sigurd's. 'They will not refuse.'

Sigurd felt as stunned as the bull when Svein had introduced the beast to his great axe.

'We are going into a hard fight, lad. Bind them to you now. Before the slaughter's dew soaks their shoes. Before Jarl Randver's neck-ring blinds them.'

This was clear thinking from Olaf, for if things went against Sigurd at Hinderå it was possible that Jarl Randver might offer to spare his hirð, reward them even, if they came over to him. Sigurd doubted those who stood with him now would betray him like that, but having them oath-sworn to him would be further protection against any such betrayal, like a ringmail coat over wool and leather.

'What do I have to do, Uncle?' he asked.

'Nothing, lad,' Olaf said. Some of the men were making their own invocations of the gods, touching amulets at their necks and mumbling into their beards. Others were relieving them-

selves over the side of the jetty, whilst still others were climbing aboard *Sea-Sow* or *Sea-Urchin*, making their last preparations
before setting off. 'Just stand there looking like your father and
leave it to me,' Olaf said.

'And if they refuse?' Sigurd asked again. Despite all that had
happened, he felt in that moment like the young man who had
pleaded to join his father's crew and been denied in front of
everyone.

Olaf shrugged. 'If they refuse, I'll throw them to the crabs
after that fat hog Thengil.'

Sigurd felt himself smile. 'Then it'll just be us taking on Jarl
Randver and his whole war band.'

Olaf grinned, his eyes catching fire. 'Then may the gods help
them,' he said. He turned and told the crews to gather round
for there was one last thing that must be tied up neatly before
leaving Osøyro. There were frowns and murmured questions
as they came over, for with the sacrifice done and the wind in
their favour they could not see what should keep them from
heading out into the Bjørnafjord, which lay before them like
iron burnished by the dawn sun.

'Would you step aboard these magnificent ships,' he asked,
getting some chuckles for that, 'before giving Sigurd what you
owe him?'

Some frowns then. But some knowing looks too from Svein
and Aslak and old Solveig, men who had been in this with
Sigurd from the beginning when their eyes had been full of the
sting of smoke from Eik-hjálmr his father's hall.

'Would you accept such shining war gear, these well-made
brynjur, from the man who gave them, from him whose low
cunning and war-craft gave us the victory here when we needed
it, and yet not give him the very least that you owe?' This was
hard on Hauk and his men but it was true all the same.

'I know what is coming here,' Bjarni mumbled.

'You might fight for a jarl for twenty summers and grow
white-haired by his hearth and yet never win such plunder.'
Olaf pointed at Bjarni and Bjorn and at the other men who

had just weeks before been living as outlaws at the arse end of the Lysefjord. 'You must have thought your honour was long gone, like a fart in the wind. You must have thought you would never have the chance to be worthy of your ancestors and make a name for yourselves.' He folded his brawny scarred arms across his chest and his face became granite. 'You must have thought you would never see Valhöll.'

He let this sink in, let them taste the bitter draught of it.

'This man, this Óðin-favoured son of the best man I have ever known . . .' Sigurd saw a sheen in Olaf's eye and looked away '. . . has put this crew together as a good shipwright chooses the best and strongest timbers for a ship, or the way a skald weaves a story using the best kennings. I have seen enough fighters in my time to know them when I see them, and I see them standing before me now. You are all wolves. But wolves cannot bring down an elk alone. They must hunt and fight as a pack.' He glanced at Sigurd and then nodded at those before him. 'Swear an oath to Sigurd Haraldarson. Swear upon your honour to fight for him, so that we will know that our pack is strong and cannot be driven apart.'

The warriors looked at each other then, trying to measure their own thoughts on the thing against the thoughts of their companions.

'I mean no affront, Sigurd,' Grundar said, heavy-browed. He was scratching his grey-flecked brown beard. His other hand rested on the pommel of the sword at his hip. 'But you are barely into your first full beard.'

Sigurd accepted this with a careful nod, for Grundar was on the edge of an insult with that. 'And yet I beat you and your nithing lord, Grundar,' he said, and the man was sensible enough to clasp his lips on whatever reply had come to his mind.

Bodvar cleared his throat, drawing Sigurd's eye. 'Things might have turned out differently if I had speared that bird of yours,' he said, still sore about that.

'Perhaps,' Sigurd said. 'But none of you had the wits in your skulls to see why I stood amongst you with a bird on my arm.

I am amazed, Bodvar, that any of you has lived long enough to see his beard reach his briar patch.'

Some of the others laughed at this and Bodvar looked at Hauk as though he expected him to speak up for them.

Hauk frowned, chewed his lip and took a step forward so that everyone knew he had something to say, for all the look on his face said he had not yet decided what that was.

Sigurd nodded to acknowledge him. 'I would hear your thoughts on it, Hauk Langbarðr,' he said, which had Hauk frowning even more because he was not sure what to make of Long-Beard as a byname given the talking so far.

'It is true our lord behaved dishonourably. Instead of welcoming you as a host should with food, drink and hearth, he schemed to make a prisoner of you and deliver you to your enemy.' Svein spat in disgust and other men cursed Thengil's name. But Hauk had not finished yet and raised a hand to show it. 'But you were also underhand and full of Loki-tricks by hiding your men in the woods when they should have been in plain sight.'

'That raven trick was crafty,' Bodvar put in, shaking his head.

'With all your years I tricked you easily, Hauk,' Sigurd said. 'And yet you would still judge me on the length of my beard?'

'An oath is a heavy thing,' Hauk said.

'Heavier for these others who will carry it all their lives,' Sigurd said, gesturing at Aslak, Floki and Svein. He let a half smile creep onto his lips. 'I will release you from your oath in ten years if you wish to be free of it.'

Even Hauk smiled wryly at that.

The others were standing there feeling like gods of war in the booty that Sigurd had given them, so that even if they had some doubts about being oath-tied they held their tongues. Besides which, young men with fewer years on their backs will give an oath more easily than those who have seen something of the world. Olaf had told Sigurd that. 'If you have a pretty girl beneath you, you don't waste time imagining her as an old woman. You get on with the task in hand,' he had said.

Hauk turned to his friends and they talked in low voices until

Olaf said that if they took any longer to make up their minds the wind would have changed and they would be going nowhere. But Hauk ignored him and turned back to Sigurd. 'It is no secret that we Osøyro men are in our winter years.'

'Winter years? I have seen younger mountains!' Bjarni said, at which Solveig called him a loose-lipped pig-swiver, because Solveig was almost as old as Hauk's lot.

'Every man of worth knows that of all his possessions his reputation is the most valuable thing that he leaves behind when he breathes his last breath. Olaf is right. Whatever reputations we once had as Jarl Hakon's húskarlar are as faint as the moon when the sun is in the sky.' He tapped his white head. 'We keep them in our own thought chests but who else will hear of them?' He nodded at Sigurd. 'We may not live to see you become a great jarl, Sigurd Haraldarson, but we would be a part of your story. We will swear an oath . . . if you swear to put us in the heart of the fray so that men will know of us. So that skalds will sing of us when we are gone.'

That was all Sigurd needed to hear as he drew Troll-Tickler and turned it round so that it rested across his left arm, the hilt pointing towards Hauk.

And so it was that Hauk Long-Beard of Osøyro, a man who had fought for Jarl Hakon Burner in the olden days, became the first man to swear an oath to Sigurd.

They kept the words of it simple because, as Solveig was keen to remind them, the day was running away from them and the wind could change at any moment. But each man named his ancestors, if he had any worth naming, and announced their deeds as well as his own, so that to listen you would have thought every one of those outlaws and dispossessed was descended from Óðin himself. When it was Karsten Ríkr's turn he kissed Troll-Tickler's pommel, as they all must, then went on to boast that he had once sailed to the end of the sea and pissed over the edge. Then he claimed to have seen a great sea monster with arms as long as the ship he was steering.

Bjarni also unleashed a few boasts, the others' favourite being the one in which he claimed to have bedded six women in one night.

'From what I remember that night was black as pitch,' Bjorn said, scratching his cheek and frowning, 'and there was talk that at least five of our father's pigs had escaped from their pen.'

The only one who did not find this funny was his brother.

When it was Valgerd's turn the others stood there even more seiðr-struck than they had been watching Asgot sacrifice the bull, for none of them had ever seen a shieldmaiden give an oath to fight for her lord. She listed the men she had killed, if not by name then by their appearance; men who had come to plunder the spring, the seeress, or both, and Sigurd could see looks that passed between the others, because this naming unravelled like an anchor rope.

'Remind me not to get on her bad side,' Bjorn murmured.

Yet she would now fight for Sigurd and protect him with her life, which was a hard thing for Sigurd to hear coming from a woman. Even stranger coming from Valgerd, because he had the feeling he would fight the monster Grendel and his mother too, to protect her.

Olaf himself was the last of them to do it. He put his lips to the pommel of Sigurd's sword and he, who likely had the most to boast of in terms of hard fights won and ancestors who sat in the Allfather's hall, said nothing about any of that. He kept the oath short, scowling through it, and yet Sigurd knew that even though it had been Olaf's idea, the words were the hardest on him. For before Sigurd had been born, Olaf must have sworn a similar oath to Jarl Harald with whom he had been as close as a brother. But Sigurd's father was dead now, killed in battle by the traitor king, and Sigurd knew that Olaf felt his own failure to protect the jarl like a knife in his guts. Speaking a new oath to his friend's son must have put a bitter taste in his mouth.

'I will fight for you, lord, and not flee one step from the battle,' he said, his face hard as a granite cliff. 'If you fall I will avenge you and send as many of your enemies to the afterlife as I can before I am cut down beside you. I will never forget the silver and booty which you give me, or the mead and meat that we share. Sword and shield, flesh and bone, I am your man, Sigurd Haraldarson. As long as the sun shines and the world endures, henceforth and for evermore.'

When Olaf nodded to show that there was no more to come from his mouth, Sigurd told him what he had told the others, having recalled his father's words to those who had knelt before him in Eik-hjálmr. For an oath between a war leader and his húskarlar is like a sword with two cutting edges. An oath sits in the scales and must be balanced.

'I will lead you in the blood-fray and be at the forefront of the fighting,' he said, feeling their eyes on him like the weight of a brynja. 'You will find me open-handed with the spoils of war. Gjöf sér æ til gjalda.' A gift always looks for a return. 'I will be a ring-giver and a raven-feeder. As long as the sun shines and the world endures, henceforth and for evermore.'

And that was it. Gleipnir, the fetter with which the Æsir bound the wolf Fenrir, could not have held them all tighter to each other than the words they had just spoken to the lap of the fjord on the shore, the creak of the ships at their moorings and the cry of gulls in the dawn sky.

'So I have hearthmen but no hearth,' Sigurd said to Svein who came up and clapped a great hand on his shoulder, the smile on his face reaching from ear to ear.

'Who needs a hearth when you have two fine ships?' the red-haired giant said.

Sigurd laughed, relieved to shed the weight of the moment. 'And what fine dragon ships they are,' he said. 'Jarls and kings will be trembling to their bones.'

'Ships or no ships you have come a long way in no time at all, Sigurd,' Aslak said and Sigurd nodded because this was true enough. 'Your father would be proud,' his friend went on, looking at the oath-sworn rather than at Sigurd, who felt a rush of pride at having such friends as these.

'My father would be halfway to Hinderå to put his sword in

Jarl Randver's belly,' Sigurd said loud enough for the others to hear.

Olaf looked over at him and nodded. 'Right then, you wolf-feeding, widow-making sons of whores, what are you waiting for? We have a wedding feast to go to.' Although first they would meet Hagal at Skudeneshavn, along with whichever jarls or warriors Crow-Song had persuaded to join their cause.

'I hope this Jarl Randver serves good mead in his hall,' Ubba said.

'We will need something strong to celebrate getting to Skudeneshavn first without drowning,' Agnar Hunter said, for he was one of those who would be rowing *Sea-Urchin*, which they had not tested properly in the open sea since making the repairs on her.

'Trust me, Agnar,' Karsten Ríkr said, standing at the karvi's tiller and stroking the sheer strake beside him as though it were a lover's leg, 'she is happy to have men aboard her—'

'Like your woman back at Lysefjorden, hey!' Ubba said, earning himself a coarse hand gesture from Karsten.

'Even now she is remembering the old times,' Karsten went on, unwilling to let Ubba ruin the moment, 'and she is grateful to us for giving her another chance. She will not let us down.'

'She had better not,' Olaf rumbled, taking the oar which Svein offered him, as Sigurd went aboard, calling farewell to Solveig who stood by the tiller at *Sea-Sow*'s stern.

'It is not my wyrd to have ships sink under me, Uncle,' Sigurd said.

And neither was it. For there were men that needed killing.

And the gods were watching.

CHAPTER EIGHTEEN

WHEN KARSTEN AT THE TILLER CALLED OUT THAT THE NORTHERN TIP OF Karmøy was coming up off *Sea-Urchin*'s port side Sigurd felt a wave of relief roll across the men at the benches. The rowing had been hard and the muscles in Sigurd's lower back and stomach thrummed with hot pain. It would have been hard going even with a full crew of twenty-four at the oars, but with only twelve rowing and one bailing – the other five being needed aboard *Sea-Sow* – it had been slow and exhausting and recklessly dangerous. For they had taken this old, patched-up ship into the open sea and the water had spilled in between the strakes and sloshed about in the thwarts as they took turns to break their backs bending with a bailer to fling sea back to sea. But Karsten had proved his sea-craft, hugging the coast and the sheltered waters but avoiding the rocks and using the currents where he could to make the rowing easier.

His own back to the whale's road and blind to the skerries submerged by the high tide, which could have ripped the karvi apart, spilling them into the brine like guts tumbling from a belly-wound, Sigurd had watched the helmsman like a hawk. And he had been impressed by what he saw, for Karsten had never once looked unsure of himself or *Sea-Urchin*. He stood up there on the stern platform with the pride of a jarl in his high seat, which was hardly surprising given the strange twists of his wyrd. For he had been steering a ship full of raiding Danes when Jarl Arnstein Twigbelly from Bokn had swept upon them with sword and slaughter. Twigbelly had taken Karsten prisoner and in revenge for the raid on his lands would have taken Karsten's eyes so that he might never again look upon the fjords. But Karsten had jumped overboard and, in his own words, swum like an otter, the Norsemen's arrows plunging into the waves around him. Once ashore he had stolen a little boat and rowed east to Jørpeland, there learning that if you wanted to disappear and yet stay within spitting distance of the sea, then the Lyse-fjord was for you. He had hidden there with other hunted men and might have ended his days there if Sigurd had not sailed up that fjord looking for the brothers whose sword-fame had reached his ears. But now here was Karsten with a tiller in his hand and the sea air in his nose, and who could ask for more?

They had caught up with *Sea-Sow* the previous dusk and spent the night in a sheltered cove, which gave them the time to properly bail out and plug the worst of the leaks with twists of resin-soaked horsehair. Then another hard day's rowing had brought them to Karmøy and this was when Olaf barked at them to pull harder and longer because the sea was turning rough and they could not risk pulling in close to the shore to moor for the night so near to Avaldsnes and the lair of their enemy King Gorm.

'Why don't we kill that lump of troll snot while we are pass-ing?' Svein called from his row bench as though it would be as easy as that.

'Because I do not want to be seen in this worm-gnawed ship when we come face to face with that toad-fucking traitor,' Olaf said, earning himself a mutter and frown from Karsten who, like Solveig, believed a ship could hear such an insult and take offence. 'And also I do not mind rowing here and there like our ancestors did,' Olaf went on, 'but coming to a fight tired and aching is not a far-sighted thing to do if the man you are fight-ing is a king and has more spearmen than a dog has fleas.'

It would have taken weeks to find a tall, straight oak and fashion it into a new mast to replace the rotting one, and they had not had the time. Instead they had left the rotting one stepped, with the yard and furled sail cradled in the oar trees, because it would be better if any other crews they came across did not know that *Sea-Urchin* could not be sailed. For all that, they might wonder why the crew-light ship was struggling under oars when the wind was whipping spume off the waves.

'Biflindi will still be sitting there on his pile of toll-silver when we are ready to pay him in steel,' Sigurd said, 'but first he will hear what has befallen his friend Jarl Randver. It will worm into his head and he will begin to wonder if the gods have turned their backs on him because he is an oath-breaker.'

'Well if he is at Hinderå for the wedding we will kill him then and be done with it,' Svein said, and the others laughed at that despite their aching muscles and sore bones. But Sigurd shared a look with Olaf because they both hoped that King Gorm would not be at Hinderå. Dealing with Jarl Randver and all his thegns would be hard enough, but if the king was there with his retinue then Sigurd's ambition would be sluiced away in his own blood and that of those now oath-tied to him.

'He won't be there,' Olaf had assured him when they were weaving their plan and Sigurd had brought up the possibility of it, thinking that Randver would see the value of having the king there as a guest at his son's wedding. 'The king holds his own Haust Blót feast and you can imagine what a mead-soaked night that is.' Olaf had shaken his head. 'Biflindi will not sit in another man's seat in another man's hall when his own people expect to raise their horns to him and stuff themselves with the wealth of his table.'

Sigurd hoped now he was right, as they laboured with too few oars in the water, gulls wheeling and shrieking above them, and Karmøy slid slowly past.

Through sweat-stung eyes they watched the sun fall over the edge of the western sea and Olaf barked at them to row even harder until by the last of the light still clinging to the day

Karsten threaded them between the islands off Karmøy's ragged south coast and they came to Skudeneshavn.

Sigurd murmured a curse when he twisted round to see that there was only one ship tied up to the jetty and that was *Sea-Sow*.

'Óðin's arse!' Olaf said, 'where has that damned skald got to? He should have been here by now.'

'Maybe he means to make a big thing of it by coming across the Boknafjord at the prow of some jarl's longship so we can all see him and cheer,' Aslak suggested through a wry smile.

'Aye, he'd like that,' Olaf agreed.

'I would like it too,' Sigurd said, 'the jarl part of it anyway.'

In moments those on the port side had pulled in their oars, whilst on the other side they backed water and Karsten brought *Sea-Urchin* up to the mooring with the tenderness of a father's kiss on his child's cheek. Then Agnar Hunter and Bodvar were throwing ropes to Solveig and Valgerd as the others came down the hill to greet them.

Sigurd could not help but picture his mother standing there on the grass-tufted rocks and his stomach lurched at the memory, the pain of it drowning the ache in muscle and bone.

'There is Crow-Song,' Svein said, grimacing as he pushed his big hands into the small of his back trying to get his bones right after all that rowing. 'And that is not the way you told it, Aslak.'

For Hagal was stumbling down the worn track in the least heroic way and there was no torc-wearing jarl with him. Though there were two men Sigurd had never seen before.

'Who are they, I wonder,' Olaf murmured, standing on the jetty and offering Sigurd his hand. Sigurd grabbed hold and Olaf hauled him up out of *Sea-Urchin* and put out his arm for the next man.

'Hagal, I am glad to see you,' Sigurd said as the skald came up and they clasped each other's arms in greeting.

'And I am relieved to see you, Sigurd,' Hagal said, frowning as he looked over Sigurd's shoulder at the men coming ashore.

'But it is a shame what happened up there at Osøyro. I heard it some days ago.'

Sigurd pursed his lips. 'Yes and no,' he said. 'Every man has a brynja now, which is like having twice as many men.'

'Three times as many,' Olaf put in.

Hagal nodded, unconvinced, then turned to the two men waiting behind him. Both were big men and fighters by the looks, and Hagal seemed wary of them the way a man is wary of another man's hunting hounds.

'This is Kætil Ivarsson whom men call Kartr,' he said as the one with the thatch of fair hair and ruddy cheeks stepped forward and nodded at Sigurd respectfully.

'Why are you called Kartr then?' Sigurd asked.

'I am a blacksmith but in my life I have moved around from place to place,' he said, and the man's trade did not surprise Sigurd because he had a smith's brawny arms and big shoulders. He shrugged those big shoulders now. 'I would push my tools before me in a cart,' he said, which was answer enough.

'And I am Bram whom men call Bear,' the other said, keeping his feet rooted to the spot as though he expected Sigurd to come to him. He was a beast of a man, not as tall as Svein but broad and solid-looking with a face that was all beard and a nose that looked to have been broken a dozen times.

'Hagal tells me you are a fighter, Sigurd Haraldarson,' Bram said before Sigurd had the chance to ask him why he had come to Skudeneshavn with Hagal.

Sigurd looked at both men and nodded. 'I am going to kill Jarl Randver of Hinderå. And then I am going to kill King Gorm,' he said, seeing no point in watering the thing down. 'I expect I'll have to do some fighting to get these things done.'

Bram nodded. 'I was up in Steinvik for the last three winters and the jarl whose mead I soaked my beard in had forgotten how to be a raiding man. Like an overfed hound he was happy to sit by his fire, farting the days away. I could stay amongst him and his sheep no more.'

'He released you from your oath?' Sigurd said.

'I never swore to him. He was not worth my oath.' He stared at Sigurd, his teeth dragging beard bristles over his bottom lip as he appraised the younger man.

'I was at Tysvær in Jarl Leiknir's hall when Bram came to the place asking if the jarl would raid again before winter,' Hagal said, then grinned. 'I told him to forget about Jarl Leiknir and that I knew a man who was weaving a great saga tale.'

'You will swear an oath to me, Bram Bear,' Sigurd said, then gestured at the mail-clad warriors around them. 'All of them have done it.'

'Three things,' Bram said. 'For three things I will oath-bind myself to you.'

'Three things for one oath?' Sigurd said. 'To my ears that does not sound like a fair trade.'

The big man smiled at that. 'If you had seen me fight you would be scratching your head wondering why I ask for only three things.' He jerked his bushy beard in Svein's direction. 'Want me to turn that big ox inside out? What about him?' he was pointing at Olaf who was making sure that *Sea-Urchin* was secure. 'I'll put him on his arse if you like.'

Sigurd batted the offer away with a hand. 'Ha, that is easy, I have done it myself,' he said. Bram cocked an eyebrow at that, for Olaf looked like a god of war in his brynja, its rings straining across those shoulders of his. 'So what three things do you ask in return for your sword?' Sigurd asked.

'Fame, silver, mead,' Bram said. 'Give me those and I will cut your enemies down like barley before the scythe.'

He was a boaster this one, and yet there was something about him that made Sigurd believe it was more than just bluster. There was a bristling violence about him, not as dark as that which welled in Floki, but no less dangerous for that, Sigurd suspected. And then Sigurd recalled his ordeal and the visions that had come to him as he hung between worlds in that stinking fen. He had met a proud bear and that king of the beasts had gone for some honey even though it sat within a black cloud of angry bees. *Perhaps they will kill you*, Sigurd had told the bear. And the bear had laughed.

'And you, Kætil Kartr?' Sigurd said, turning to the other man. 'Do you want fame, silver and mead?'

The blacksmith scratched his fair beard, frowning. 'When I am dead my name will live on in the blades I have forged. That is enough fame for me. As for silver, I am tired of going from place to place and would put my roots down before I am too old to swing my hammer.'

'Kætil happened to be passing through Tysvær,' Hagal said. 'You would be impressed with his work.'

'I will find a good anvil stone and set up a proper smithy,' Kætil said. 'Hagal tells me there is bog iron around here running down in the streams.'

Sigurd glanced at Hagal who gave a slight shrug and Sigurd nodded, deciding it was Kætil's own fault if he believed what a skald told him.

'I will need silver,' Kætil said. 'And forging blades is thirsty work, so I will never turn down ale and mead.'

'And are you a good fighter?' Sigurd asked. 'For those big arms of yours make you slow, I'd wager.'

'I have had my share of fights,' the blacksmith said. 'Why else do you think I move from place to place?' He shook his head. 'There is usually some argument about payment for a knife or spear head.' His lip curled in his fair beard. 'It is funny how men easily forget what they agreed to pay.'

'And you'll swear an oath to me, Kætil Kartr?' Sigurd said.

The man nodded. 'I will,' he said.

'Who else have you brought me, Crow-Song?' Sigurd asked, making a show of looking around and up towards where his father's hall used to stand.

The skald flushed red. 'I tried, Sigurd,' he said. 'But—'

'But you could not find a jarl drunk enough to join me in this fight,' Sigurd finished for him.

'It is hard to find raven-feeders these days,' Bram muttered.

But Sigurd was still coming to terms with the hard truth that he had just twenty men and no time to find more, for in two days Runa would marry Jarl Randver's son Amleth.

'It will make a better tale, anyhow,' Hagal said, 'the fewer of us there are.'

'I will not deny it,' Sigurd said. 'Let us just hope one of us is left at the end to tell it.'

Bram Bear was grinning, his cracked lips spread within the great mass of his beard, which Sigurd thought was strange given what he had just said.

'I think I am going to like you, Sigurd Haraldarson,' Bram said.

'We'll see about that,' Sigurd said.

Then he drew Troll-Tickler and laid it hilt first across his left forearm.

'My father would have paid your brother the mundr,' Amleth said, 'and twice as much as the usual bride-price. Twenty-four aurar, the worth of ten cows. As well as oxen and a horse and bridle, or a good sword and a shield if that was what he preferred, which I suspect he would.' A thin veil of rain was falling and Runa clenched the cloak tighter at her neck as they watched two of Jarl Randver's men untying the small boat. 'Sigurd was a fool to turn this down.'

Across the fjord from the tree-thronged island upon which they waited she could see Jarl Randver's guests lining the stony beach and gathered on the wharf against which three of the jarl's longships, including *Reinen* and *Sea-Eagle*, her father's ships, sat at their moorings. In accordance with local tradition Amleth would row her across the water in an act symbolizing their journey as husband and wife from this day forward. She knew those guests across the water were eagerly awaiting them so that the ceremony could begin and the festivities could follow in a wash of mead and feasting. Perhaps they did not know that their host had planned another spectacle for their enjoyment, though this one would be drenched not in mead but in blood.

'As for your morning-gift, you will find me very generous,' Amleth said, looking west across the sound and then towards the bigger of the two islands between them and the mainland, behind which four more of his father's warships waited hidden from the sound. 'Beautiful clothes, jewellery, slaves. Whatever you want, I will give it if I can.' He smiled but it was stiff as a new scabbard.

Runa tried to swallow but felt as if she had something caught in her throat. Talk of the morning-gift filled her with dread, for what was it if not the price of her maidenhood? All too soon the night would come, her brother would be dead and she would be lying beneath the man standing with her now. Perhaps he would put his seed in her belly and she would be trapped, doomed to spend her life amongst those who had killed her mother and her brother. Those who had their hands bloody up to the elbow in the ruin of her former life and all that her father had built.

Her other brothers would not bear it were they alive. Sigurd would not bear it, which was why he would come for her this very day, as Hagal had betrayed to Jarl Randver. And when he came, those ships waiting behind yonder island would swoop like an owl from a branch and Sigurd would die.

I could throw myself into the fjord, she thought. I could end it now. But Sigurd would still come, she knew. Even if Amleth did not row them across the water, Sigurd would come. Crow-Song had told the jarl that Runa's brother meant to have his revenge that day, a feast of blood before the dark months. And though Runa knew her brother could not win against so many and with them expecting him, perhaps he might see her jump into the cold water and know that she died still holding her honour. Perhaps he would see this before they cut him down.

'It is time, Amleth,' one of the men called up from the slick rocks that bristled with mussels and slippery red weed. He was on his haunches holding the boat which was rocking gently on the calm sea.

Amleth nodded, offering Runa his arm so that they might

walk down to the boat together, but Runa did not take it and so he began to walk down alone.

Runa did not move. She looked up at the dark clouds, letting the rain fall softly on her face. This was not the wedding day she had talked about with her mother. As a jarl's daughter she had always known she would be a peace-weaver, but even her father, ever with one eye on strengthening alliances, had promised her that she would not marry any man she did not think she could come to love.

She clenched her teeth together at these memories of her parents. Their words had been of no more substance than the misty air. They had left her alone. All of her kin had abandoned her. All except for Sigurd.

'Come, Runa,' Amleth called up to her, an edge to his voice now. He was nervous, too. It was all over him. His father had set him up as the bait on the trap, for all that he was getting a bride out of it, and his eyes were up and down that rain-murked sound like shearwaters across the waves.

'My brother will kill you, Amleth,' Runa said, wanting to twist the knife in his fear. Wanting him to know that it was not over yet.

He looked past her up towards the rocks and trees of the deserted island, as if he expected Sigurd to suddenly appear there, as if the last of Jarl Harald's sons had moored unseen on the other side of the island and was coming to kill him.

'Sigurd is Óðin-favoured,' she said. 'Your father was a fool to make an enemy of him. He is coming and he will not be stopped.'

She watched him fiddling with the silver mjöllnir at his neck, the little hammer glinting between finger and thumb. Perhaps he would not dare climb into that boat with her and row them to the shore where some two hundred guests waited, no doubt slick-mouthed at the thought of the beasts their host had slaughtered for the celebration.

'I will pick you up and put you in that boat if you do not come now,' he said, a flash of tooth in his beard that reminded

369

her of his father the jarl and his brother Hrani. Hrani who was waiting now in his ship *Hildiríðr* – *War-Rider* – for Sigurd to appear from behind one of those islands, and that thought sent a shiver through Runa because Hrani was a killer and wore it like a cloak.

'Come,' Amleth said, 'let us be done with it,' and with that he walked back up the rock, grabbed Runa's arm and hauled her down to the boat.

'The wind and current will take you that way,' the man not holding the boat said, nodding south-westward, 'so you'll want to aim at that naust.' He was pointing at a boathouse on the water's edge a good arrow-shot along the shore from Jarl Randver's wharf.

Amleth nodded. 'I will be happy to get to the other side, Thorgest,' he said.

Thorgest grinned. 'But tonight will be a feast to shake your father's hall, hey.'

Amleth pushed Runa into the boat and she stumbled over the row bench, falling down into the forward thwart at the bow. Amleth sat himself down with his back to her, and picked up the oars, putting them into the rowlocks. Then the man holding the stern pushed off and Amleth began the stroke, his broad shoulders and back swelling with the effort.

Herring gulls shrieked and tumbled through the misty grey above them. A guttural croak drew Runa's eye to a cormorant flying eastward, low across the water and black as a shadow. She lifted the thin leather thong with its silver pendant of Freyja over her head and held the precious thing in her hand, her fist closed so tightly around it that it would take more than death to wrest it from her. And she invoked the goddess.

But whereas most women on their wedding day would seek Freyja's help in the begetting of a child, for one of the goddess's names is Gefn which means Giver, it was to Freyja's darker side that Runa now appealed. For Freyja was also called Skjálf: Shaker. She was a goddess of battle and Runa asked her to ride into this fight beside her brother. But if the gods abandoned them now as they had abandoned her father and her mother and her brothers, then Runa would throw herself over the side and drown in the sound. Let Rán Mother of the Waves have her. Rather that than live here amongst these men, with the furs and jewels of a jarl's daughter but the honour of a slave.

Amleth looked over his shoulder and growled a curse. Thorgest had been right about the current. The little boat was being borne west into Sandsundet, which was not where Amleth wanted to be, Runa knew. Because if Sigurd was coming, that was the direction he would be coming from, having put himself behind an island or one of the bluffs or promontories along the mainland's ragged coast.

'The gods do not want this marriage,' Runa said. 'Oðin has commanded Njörd to stop us reaching the other side. You cannot deny that we have barely made any progress at all, even with your strength.'

'Hold your tongue, girl,' Amleth snapped over his shoulder, putting more effort into the pull, his oar blades plunging and dragging the sea past.

'You will have to row harder, Amleth!' Thorgest called from the shore, which was advice that Amleth needed like a sprung strake.

He was puffing with the effort but at last it was paying off and they seemed to be getting somewhere, though Amleth was still having to put more muscle into the left oar to counter the tide.

A peal of thunder rolled across the northern sky and Runa chose not to say anything about that because Amleth could hear it for himself and had enough fear in him to take some bad omen from it. Instead she looked out across the channel, cinching the cloak tighter around her shoulders and pulling it across her legs to keep the rain off. Then she smiled bitterly in spite of herself for worrying about staying warm and dry when she had already decided to drown herself in the cold dark if things went as they surely must.

And then she drew a sharp breath and Amleth muttered some invocation to his gods. Runa felt her stomach sink like a rock to the sea bed. It was as though a cold hand squeezed her throat, choking her, starving her of breath. The hairs on her neck were raised and her bowels had turned to water.

Because Sigurd was coming.

She wanted to stand up and wave her arms. To warn her brother that Hagal had betrayed him to Jarl Randver and that they would be upon him like war hounds on a lone wolf. But Sigurd must already know that because *War-Rider* and the other three ships had already slipped their moorings and were edging around the big island off the mainland.

She could see Hrani standing up at the prow, could tell it was him by his beautiful silver-panelled helmet which seemed to shine, catching what little light there was on that grey, rain-veiled day. All four ships had the wind in their favour and their sails were round-bellied, their sides lined with painted shields.

'Go back, Sigurd,' she said under her breath, willing him to save himself, and in that moment the love she felt for him rose in her chest and had tears spilling from her eyes. 'Go back.'

'He must want to die,' Amleth said, still pulling the oars, his eyes riveted to the swan-breasted knörr.

'Please, Sigurd. Please live,' Runa said, the words lost amongst the rolling waves of fear and sadness that swamped her. She was on her knees now, one hand clutching the little boat's top strake, the other fist clenched round the Freyja amulet, staring at her brother's ship as though she could make it turn around. It *was* turning, but only to make the most of the wind and cut across the sound towards them, and Runa knew with freezing dread that even though Jarl Randver's ships were released to the kill, her brother refused to give up and save himself.

Amleth was leaning right back in the stroke, close enough to Runa that she could smell the mead sweat on him and the juniper and camomile with which he had washed his hair. 'No man will say he lacked courage,' he said, grunting with the effort of rowing. They were over halfway across the channel now and *War-Rider* and the other three ships had already crossed before their bow. Runa could see their thwarts bristling with men and spears, and perhaps the sight of these men in their war gear hauled a memory into her mind of her father and brothers going off to fight King Gorm in Karmsundet. Suddenly she was flooded by another feeling and she knew it to be pride. Sigurd had seen his enemy coming for him and had known it was a trap. But he came on anyway because he was his father's son. Runa knew then that he would be drinking with their father and brothers in the Allfather's hall that night and she would have him tell them that she was brave, too. That her honour was no less a thing than theirs.

She put the thong with the Freyja amulet back around her neck and clambered to her feet, balancing against the rock of the boat on the waves. Then she put a foot up onto the top strake, took one last look at the swan-breasted boat, hoping that her brother could see her.

And jumped.

'Turn, damn your old bones, turn!' Olaf growled.

With the rest gathered behind them out of sight, Sigurd and Olaf lay amongst the sea-lashed rocks on the western shore of the headland, looking out across the sound. To the east beyond hills and woods stood the highest ground upon which Jarl Randver's hall sat. They could not see it from where they had put ashore, having done some more hard rowing to bring *Sea-Urchin* to a safe, secluded mooring, but they could see the hall's hearth smoke hanging like a brown stain in the grey sky. They could be there in the time it takes to whet a good knife, as Kætil Kartr had said. Or drink two horns of mead, Svein had added.

'Turn now, you stubborn goat,' Olaf hissed.

Because if old Solveig did not turn *Sea-Sow* now, the first of Jarl Randver's ships would be upon him. And those men would see that there were only two men aboard the high-sided ship. But even with the clever preparations they had made with *Sea-Sow*'s yard and sheets it was no easy thing for just two men to turn her so that she might run with the wind.

From the height of the rocks Sigurd could see Solveig running from tiller to bow and he hoped that the distance was yet too far, and his enemy's dragons too low in the water, for the jarl's thegns to see the knörr's helmsman going up and down that deck like a washer-woman's elbow.

And there was Runa. She was at the bow of a small boat, her golden hair shining through the thin rain, bright as a lamp's flame against the grey fjord, and the sight of her had Sigurd's heart pounding like a blacksmith's hammer against the anvil of his breastbone. His belly was a snarl of coiling serpents rolling over each other and just like at the slave market he wanted to call out to her, to let her know he was there.

I'm coming, Runa. You are not alone, sister, his mind whispered, as though the words could glide across that water like a stiff-winged fulmar and nest in Runa's ear so that she would no longer be afraid.

'Ah, there he goes and not before time,' Olaf said, drawing Sigurd's gaze from Runa to *Sea-Sow* as her yard came across and the ship rolled with the shock of it, looking dead in the water. But Solveig and Hagal would be working furiously, hauling ropes and tying them off, doing the work of five men. And yet, Jarl Randver's lead ship, which was full of spearmen, was now less than three arrow-shots away from *Sea-Sow* and Sigurd could hear those men's war cries amidst the gulls' yowls and the surging sea.

Then *Sea-Sow*'s sail cracked as the wind caught it.

'This is going to be as close as two coats of grease,' Olaf said, as the round-hulled ship lurched forward and cut westward through the rain-shrouded sea, 'but if anyone can give them the slip it's Solveig.'

'He's done what we needed him to do,' Sigurd said, proud of the old helmsman. 'They both have.'

Thinking that Hagal had betrayed Sigurd by telling him of Sigurd's plan, the jarl had spun his web and Solveig was the fly that had tugged the strings. Now perhaps as many as one hundred of Randver's warriors were heading away from their lord's hall, away from the jarl himself if he were not aboard that fine, dragon-prowed ship leading the race.

Sigurd and Olaf crawled away from the bluff and stood, their backs turned to the sea and their eyes on the faces of those gathered around them, warriors and oath-tied all. They looked like war gods in their brynjur with their gleaming spear blades, shields and some of their faces half hidden behind helmets. 'Now we remember our fathers and honour those of our line going back to the beginning,' Sigurd said, going from eye to eye, lingering a while on each to remind them of the oaths they had taken. 'Now we weave a yarn for skalds. We will kill this ill-wyrded jarl and make ourselves rich in fame and silver.'

There were wolf grins in their beards and they would have beaten their spears against their shields, except that there was no point in letting their enemies know they were coming.

'Hit them fast and hit them hard,' Olaf said, tying his helmet's strap beneath his chin. 'I am thinking of Thór hurling his hammer at some big farting giant.'

Svein liked that from the grin splitting his red bristles. 'We are the Tumult-God's hammer,' he said.

Hauk and his men stood as proudly as they must have done in their prime, their white or grey hair tied in tight braids and their beards plaited with silver rings. Floki was their opposite, taut-skinned, black-haired and just coming into himself as a man. His dark eyes gleamed like a predator's with the prospect of killing. Svein and Bram Bear looked like warriors of legend, the kind of men whom jarls put at the prows of their ships and skalds put at the heart of their tales. Valgerd was pale and beautiful and deadly. Her fair hair hung in two ropes either side of her face, as did Sigurd's own, so that it would not blind her when the blades were flying.

He wanted to tell her to be careful, to stay clear of the heart of the fray if she could. But he knew that would be like telling a fox to sit on its own tail in the chicken coop and so he said nothing.

They were more than ready, they were eager to be let loose to the fray. Sigurd could see it in their eyes. They wanted to prove themselves to him, and that staggered him, though he would not dwell on it now. 'Whoever falls this day will drink the Æsir's mead with my father,' he said.

'Save some for the rest of us,' Bjarni said to no one in particular.

His brother lifted his spear to draw eyes to him. 'And if you see our father Biarki . . .' he stopped, frowning. 'You will know him because he will be the one wearing the expression of a man who has been thrown from a cliff . . .'

Bjarni scowled and nodded.

Bjorn continued. '. . . then tell him that we are busy avenging him like good sons should,' he said.

Sigurd turned to Olaf and they touched their spear shafts together. 'Let us go and save Runa, Uncle, and give this jarl what we owe him.'

Olaf nodded and with nothing more that needed saying Sigurd hefted shield and spear and set off at a loping run across the rocks and tufts of tall grass, cutting across a boulder-strewn hill and following a flinty path up the rising ground.

Towards Jarl Randver's hall.

CHAPTER NINETEEN

THEY WERE PUFFING BY THE TIME THEY HAD CLIMBED THE BIRCH-THICK reverse slope of the hill upon which Jarl Randver's hall sat like some giant eagle's eyrie.

'Óðin's arse, but all that iron puts ten years on you,' Bram said when Sigurd joined him at the hill's crest. 'I've seen water go uphill faster.'

Sigurd would have bitten right back if he'd had the breath. Instead he dragged the back of his spear hand across his eyes, wiping the sweat from them. Besides which he knew Bram was saying it mostly because he and Kætil Kartr were the only ones not wearing a brynja and the Bear was the kind of man who would have you think that was by choice rather than anything else.

'I am saving my strength,' Sigurd said as Floki came up on his left shoulder. He had the sense that the young man would be at his side throughout what was coming. 'Have you seen anyone?' he asked Bram. The air up there was thick with the resinous tang of the woodsmoke leaking from the hole in the thatch below them.

Bram shook his head. 'Looks like anyone who matters is still down at the wharf waiting for the young lovers.'

'They will be across by now,' Sigurd said, recalling how

Randver's son Amleth had been putting all his muscle into the rowing, the water being against him.

'Aye,' Olaf put in, breathing hard, hawking and spitting into the rain-soaked grass. 'So if you want to do this the way you told me then we need to move fast. They'll be back to soak their beards in Randver's mead any time now,' he said, nodding towards the path that led off from the hall's south side and over the ridge down to the sea.

'Floki, Valgerd, come with me. You too, Aslak,' Sigurd said, telling Olaf to stay there and await his signal. Backs bent, keeping low, the four of them hurried down the hill between rocks and ancient tree stumps and hurled themselves against the west side of the longhall. Sigurd peered round the edge. All clear. He made his move and the others followed, so snug against the hall's old staves that their cloaks snagged now and again and Sigurd could smell the resin in the wood. He stopped at the southern edge and this time when he looked around he cursed inwardly. There were two spear-armed guards, one either side of the hall's pillared entrance way.

He turned to Floki and gestured for him to go all the way back around the hall and wait for his move. Floki nodded and loped off, hunched like a wolf following a scent. Sigurd looked towards where the worn path led over the hill's edge, holding his breath to give his ears the best chance of hearing voices or feet coming up the trail. He knew he was taking a risk, that Randver's people could appear at any moment. And if they saw him and his men they might retreat back down to the ships taking Runa with them. Which was why he wanted to lay a trap for Randver as Randver had done for him.

When he thought Floki must be in place on the hall's other side, for he would not be able to see him because of the entrance way, he counted four long breaths.

Then he ran.

The guard turned, eyes bulging in shock as Sigurd's spear plunged into his belly and burst from his back. Valgerd's spear ripped his throat out before he could scream and Sigurd saw

Floki doing a much neater job, burying his short axe in the other guard's head, dropping him in the blink of an eye. Then they were inside, their eyes adjusting to the flame-orbed gloom, and a dozen thralls holding trenchers and jugs stood frozen as though turned to stone by some powerful seiðr.

'Keep your mouths shut and you will live,' Sigurd told them, as Valgerd herded them to the back of the hall which was partitioned off by a thick hanging of woven wool that had once been a ship's sail.

Sigurd turned to Aslak and told him to fetch the others and dump the bodies out of sight. 'And see what you can do about the mess we made,' he said, for his and Valgerd's spear-work told its own story in the blood that spattered the rain-glossed mud outside.

Valgerd and Floki were already coughing and Sigurd tried to swallow the snag of it in his throat as he looked around his enemy's hall. The walls were draped in pelts and skins and the benches around the edge were piled with furs.

'Gods, this is as smoky as a dragon's cave,' Floki sputtered, lifting his shield through the grey pall, smoke billowing in its wake.

'My father's hall was bigger. The roof was higher too,' Sigurd said, striding over to Jarl Randver's seat, thinking it strange that Runa had been living in this dark-timbered place, beneath that old thatch. 'I had expected something better from Randver.' Something more imposing, he thought, from a man of the jarl's ambition. No wonder the man had had his eye on Eik-hjálmr.

'Still, he is a generous jarl by the looks of all this,' Floki said, wide-eyed in appreciation of the three long tables, all of them so laden with platters and bowls of food, some of it still steaming, that had they been ships they would have been in danger of sinking. 'It will taste good after the fight,' Floki said, grinning.

Sigurd would not agree aloud about Randver's generosity but it was true enough, he thought grudgingly, his mouth watering at the sight and smell of the huge pig, spitted and glistening above the central hearth. Its fat was beginning to drip into the flames with a rhythmic hiss that sounded like a serpent's breath from some tale told to frighten children.

It will burn on one side with no thrall to turn it, he thought, stepping up and seating himself in the jarl's high seat that was halfway along the east side where the stave walls bowed out so that the middle was wider than the ends. He blew out the fish-oil lamp hanging beside him and leant his shield against the seat's left side where he could grab it quickly.

'He will not like that,' Valgerd told him, eyes glinting within the holes in her helmet's guard. That was understating it, Sigurd thought, laying the spear across his knees and trying to appear as self-possessed and at ease as you could in another man's seat in another man's hall. The hall of a jarl who led the raid in which your mother was murdered.

'Good of the rancid badger's arse to lay on a feast for us,' Olaf said, striding into the hall, not coughing like the younger ones. 'Everyone in the back there,' he barked at the others, pointing his spear to the back of the hall where the old sail hung from the beams. When he drew level with Sigurd he stopped and locked eyes with him as the rest flowed past like water around a boulder. 'You sure about this, lad?' he asked in a low voice.

Sigurd nodded. 'Keep them quiet back there, Uncle,' he said and Olaf dipped his head, hefted his shield and went to join them. It was a risk, Sigurd knew, sitting there as far away from the partition as he was from the door. Randver's hirðmen could rush him or fill him with spears before Olaf and the rest had a chance to join the fight. It was reckless. Foolishly so. But it was also impudent and bold and would make a skald grin in the telling of it, and Sigurd could not resist it.

And then he waited, seemingly alone in his enemy's hall as the wood in the hearth crackled, pulsing grey and gold and bursting into flame with every splash of fat from the spitted pig. And the oil lamps flickered, sending snakes of soot curling up to the low roof where the smoke hung thick as sea fog. And the trenchers of food steamed on the table, giving off scents that made Sigurd's stomach growl.

And Jarl Randver returned.

First came warriors, still laughing at what they had seen down at the shore.

'They will be passing Taravika by now,' a broad-shouldered man with a beard rope halfway down to his belt was saying, cutting a swath through the smoke of the place with two others.

'They'll be food for the crabs is what they'll be,' a shorter man whose flat nose took up most of his face said. 'Which is a shame as I would have liked to see this mead-mad boy.'

They had not thought anything of the absence of the spear-men at the entrance then, Sigurd thought, keeping as still as he could as more folk came in, their excited blather flowing through the hall like a frothing wave.

'This will be a feast to remember, hey!' someone said.

'But where are the damned thralls?' a man said. 'This meat is burning.'

Sigurd could feel the sweat between his palms and the warm beechwood arms on the jarl's seat, but he kept them there, clenching the wood, resisting the screaming urge to pick up his shield as more sword-armed men came in. Most leant their spears against the wall near the door but many had swords at their hips and all had scramasaxes or short knives and Sigurd's mouth was so dry that he feared nothing would come out when he did try to speak.

It was incredible that no one had seen him yet. But then, he was mostly in shadow and their eyes were on the food. Besides which, the last thing they would expect to see was another man sitting in their lord's seat, especially the man who they thought was being chased west, if he were not already a spear-gored corpse.

A woman, a guest by the look of her brooch and rich gown, came so close that he could almost have reached out and touched her as she took hold of the spit handle and began to turn the pig. He thought his heart would beat a hole in his breastbone and he was silently invoking Óðin because he hoped the god was watching now, when the woman looked up, their eyes meeting

381

through the herb-scented smoke. Her mouth fell open but the sound came from another.

'Who in Heimdall's hairy arse are you?' the warrior with the flattened nose said. Other men and women turned and nailed their eyes to Sigurd though none did any more than that, probably because in his brynja and helmet Sigurd looked like a god of war and assuming he were not a god then he must be someone important.

'Where is Jarl Randver?' Sigurd asked, his voice as even as a sleeping sea.

'Who are you?' Beard-Rope asked, beginning to smell trouble, right hand moving across to his sword's hilt.

'I asked you a question, you swine-headed troll,' Sigurd said.

Beard-Rope pulled his sword from its scabbard.

'What is this?' someone bawled, the voice smothering all others like a pail of water flung over a fire. The throng parted to let Jarl Randver approach, men's and women's eyes jumping from him to Sigurd and back again like fleas across a fur. Randver's son Amleth followed in his wake, one arm around Runa and both of them soaking wet beneath other men's cloaks. When she saw Sigurd, Runa's face lit up, eyes wide, hands stifling the gasp that came to her lips, but then she was lost to Sigurd's sight as the ugliest man he had ever seen moved in front of her. He knew this must be Skarth, the jarl's champion and prow man, and he stood now at his lord's shoulder.

'Who are you?' the jarl demanded of Sigurd. His eyes held two parts fury to one part curiosity, and he looked like Baldr the Beautiful standing beside Skarth. The champion was not a tall man but he had the shoulders of an ox, a neck as thick as a man's thigh, and arms like gnarly oak boughs. His head was scabbed and bald but for one braid of white hair that hung from the right side to his shoulder, but none of these things prepared you for the face. An axe, Sigurd had heard.

'I am Sigurd, Jarl Randver,' Sigurd said, tearing his gaze from Skarth and fixing it on the man whose seat he had made himself comfortable in, for he did not want to miss the jarl's expression then. 'Sigurd Haraldarson.'

The jarl flinched as though struck by an invisible hand. Swords hissed from scabbards but Jarl Randver had the presence of mind to hold up his hand to stay theirs.

'*You* are Sigurd?' he said, as a murmur went through the assembly. The jarl's handsome face seemed to clench like a fist as his mind tried to get a grip on what was happening.

Sigurd nodded and Skarth's mouth did something that might have been a grin. 'I have come for my sister,' Sigurd said, letting his eyes bore into his enemy like a shipwright's auger making rivet holes to clench down the strakes. 'And I have come to kill you, Randver.' He grinned.

Some of Jarl Randver's warriors laughed at that. Amleth told a man to watch Runa, then came forward, sword drawn.

'Your skull must have sprung a leak, Haraldarson,' the jarl said, tilting his own head to one side.

'And when I have killed you and your sons, you ill-wyrded murderer of women,' Sigurd said, 'I will spit on your corpse and throw you to the fish.'

The jarl frowned, knowing that there was more to this than what his eyes could see and his ears could hear.

'Let me gut him, lord,' Skarth growled.

Sigurd showed his teeth then. 'I am waiting, you swine-headed troll.'

Skarth drew his own sword, the serpent in that fine blade alive then in the flame-licked smoky air of Randver's hall, and Sigurd heard the jangle of war gear and the scuff of feet on the rush-strewn floor. Women screamed, men cursed, and the lamp flames flickered with the tumult of it.

'You will have to go through me to get to him, Skarth son of Skamkel,' Olaf boomed. He stood there at the far end of the hall, shield- and spear-armed, his eyes piercing Jarl Randver's champion like the spit through that glistening pig. Either side of him was a wall of limewood, iron, flesh and blades and all of it strengthened by an oath.

'Kill them!' Jarl Randver yelled, spittle flying, eyes bulging.

And Sigurd snatched up his shield and spear and threw himself at his enemy.

But Flat-Nose flew at Sigurd and Sigurd twisted left, getting his spear shaft up to catch the scything sword which bit into the wood, jarring Sigurd's arm up to the shoulder joint. Flat-Nose drove in with his right shoulder, the solid meat of it punching into Sigurd's chest and throwing him backwards so that they both landed in a heap, the air driven from Sigurd's lungs and the stinking spittle from Flat-Nose's snarl spattering his face.

The man rammed his head down into Sigurd's eye and Sigurd got his own hands up and dug his thumbs into Flat-Nose's eye sockets, trying to drive the fibrous balls into the man's skull as thunder filled the hall. Then Flat-Nose was flying, being hauled up off Sigurd who saw Svein's teeth and wild eyes as the giant lifted Flat-Nose like a barrel and, roaring, hurled him against the wall. Sigurd rolled over and saw Floki hack a face in half and Ubba drive Rope-Beard back into the press with his shield and Randver's people were falling before Sigurd's Wolves like tall barley before the scythe, their death screams like the voice of Hel herself.

'Runa!' Sigurd yelled, scrambling to his feet, blinking blood from his right eye. Olaf was fighting Skarth but there was little room for sword work in the press as Randver's warriors sought to stand and the women tried to flee, crawling over the tables like desperate animals, scattering food everywhere in their panic. 'Where is Runa?' Sigurd called, picking up his spear and jumping up onto Randver's seat to see above the seething, clamorous chaos. He saw Agnar Hunter open a man's neck with his long knives and Valgerd gore a big, black-bearded man with her spear. Then he saw Runa being hauled towards the door. She was fighting and the man seemed unsure how to deal with her for he could hardly haul the would-be bride out by her golden hair. Sigurd lifted his spear to cast it but decided against taking the risk.

'The other door, Sigurd!' Svein said, gripping his long-hafted axe by the throat, its massive blade glinting hungrily.

Sigurd nodded and together they ran to the back of the hall beyond the old sail partition where the thralls still huddled, shining-eyed and trembling like sheep, and Sigurd lifted the small door's iron latch and they burst out into the wet day, haring the length of the hall.

'Runa!' Sigurd called and seeing him she broke free of the warrior's grip and the man seemed relieved to be rid of her, turning now to face his enemies and do a man's work. Runa ran to Sigurd and threw herself against him and he held her in his arms, putting his face into her sweet-smelling hair. As Randver's man held his ground, sword raised, Svein looped his war axe twice through the air and brought it down from a great height into the man's head, cutting him in half from skull to groin, where the blade slid off his arse bone and came out bloody.

Women were running off up the rocky bluff or down to the sea and now Randver's warriors were spilling out of the hall like blood from a wound, roaring encouragement to each other, trying to face the wave of steel-edged death that was rolling over them. Out came Randver but he had a knot of brave thegns around him including Skarth and for a heartbeat Sigurd's blood froze in his veins but then he saw Olaf come out, all teeth and beard, his sword dripping.

'Stay back, Runa,' Sigurd barked, then hurled his spear and it flew at Randver but somehow Skarth saw the streak of it and swung his sword, knocking the thing out of the air before it could skewer his lord. Sigurd watched his Wolves emerge and launch themselves at what remained of Randver's hirð. He saw Torving dart forward, his white braids swinging, and sink his spear into the soft flesh beneath a man's raised sword arm, and he saw Bram hack off a man's leg and then turn to Rope-Beard who hammered his sword against Bram's. Bram took the blow and turned his shield, swinging it edge first into Rope-Beard's face to send him staggering. Then Bram shouldered Bjarni and Grundar out of the way and hewed into Rope-Beard's skull, which burst open in a splash of blood, bone and grey brains.

'Randver!' Sigurd roared, hauling Troll-Tickler from its scabbard and pointing it accusingly at the jarl who was in the thick of it now, sending splinters flying from Hauk's shield. 'Randver, you grasping arse welt! The gods have abandoned you!' Fighting for his life the jarl had no time to trade insults, as another of his warriors went down under Bjarni's axe and Floki ducked under Amleth's wild sword swing and opened his shoulder to the bone. Amleth shrieked and Skarth threw himself at Floki, knocking him back into Karsten and Bodvar.

Sigurd was reluctant to leave Runa but the battle-thrill was in him up to the eyeballs and he craved to sink his sword into his enemy's flesh like a blood worm. 'Stay with Runa, Svein,' he said, and the big man nodded grimly, but then Valgerd yelled Sigurd's name and launched her spear high over the seething knot of fighting men and Sigurd saw that warriors were coming over the rise from the sea.

'Thór's arse! Now we have a fight,' Svein said, striding towards the newcomers, his axe looping through the rain-veiled air.

'Skjaldborg!' Olaf bellowed, but Sigurd was still going for Randver. The jarl had only four bloodied and desperate men with him now including Amleth and Skarth and if Sigurd could kill Randver it might finish it.

'Skjaldborg, Sigurd, damn your eyes! Here! Now!' Olaf yelled.

And Sigurd spat a filthy curse because he had been so close to his vengeance but now he would have to wait. Yelling at Runa to stay between his men and Randver's hall, he and Svein strode up to join the shieldwall as these new men, who must have been the crew from one of the jarl's other ships which had returned, hurried to stand with the battered survivors facing Sigurd and his Wolves. These fresh men came with shields and spears and some wore mail, so that the scales was beginning to tip, at least in terms of numbers.

Olaf knew this all too well, which was why he roared at those with him to move forwards and close the distance which the jarl and his men had put between them.

'They're still coming, the whoresons,' Ubba growled and so they were, more and more men spilling over the crest, full of fury at seeing their lord beset and so many companions cut down outside their hall.

'I'm glad of it,' Bram said. 'It was too easy before.' His thick kyrtill slick with blood, he began to beat the inside of his shield with his sword's hilt and the others took up the rhythm, advancing step by step towards the enemy at whom Jarl Randver was barking his own orders, trying to get them into something resembling a skjaldborg. The axe wound in Amleth's left shoulder was spilling blood down his side and his face was ashen, but he was still there beside his father, clinging to the wreckage of that day.

Then the shieldwalls struck with a dull thud of wood against wood and the ring of steel on steel, and Sigurd found himself shoving against a newcomer who was mail-clad, thickly bearded and strong. Sigurd swung Troll-Tickler high, twisting his wrist to turn the blade and strike the warrior's back, but the man's brynja and the leather beneath took the blow and Sigurd pulled the sword back over swiftly lest someone lop off his arm.

'You'll have to do better than that, lad,' the man spat, shoving his shield into Sigurd's so that Sigurd had to re-plant his back foot and use all his strength or be shoved backwards. On both sides men were stabbing spears and swords over the tops of shield rims and between them, seeking faces and unguarded shoulders.

Behind Sigurd's iron and flesh rampart, moving up and down the line like wolves seeking a way into an animal pen, Asgot and Valgerd smashed skulls, opened groins and pierced bellies. But weight of numbers was starting to tell now and Sigurd's skjaldborg was no longer gaining ground as more of Randver's men joined the fray, making his shieldwall two men deep.

Sigurd reached behind him and thrust Troll-Tickler into the ground, then pulled his scramasax out of its sheath.

'Valgerd!' he yelled, and the shieldmaiden, who was behind

him, knew what he intended for she snugged up to him and jabbed a spear over his shield at the man he was shoving against. Sigurd heard her blade point scrape off the man's helmet and then Randver's man brought his shield a little higher, which was all Sigurd needed him to do. Keeping the pressure on his opponent's shield he suddenly dropped to his left knee and brought the scramasax up and across with all the muscle his right arm and shoulder could give it, and the blade's point burst through iron rings and leather, skin and fat.

'Óðin!' he yelled, tearing the scramasax through the man's belly until he felt the hot gush of gore spill over his hand. Then he stood, putting his shoulder back into the shield, and tried to step forward but his foot was slipping on the man's slithering gut rope and it was all he could do to stay on his own feet.

'Kill them!' Olaf bellowed. 'Gut the pig-stinking, whore-born nithings!'

The din was deafening. Blood and spittle and curses flew. Men shrieked in pain and bled and died, cloying the air with the stench of their opening bowels, and Sigurd looked up just in time to see Torving go down, his neck opened by a spear. The Osøyro men around him clamoured, rousing each other to avenge their fallen sword-brother. But they were tiring.

Skarth was screaming at Olaf to come and fight him and Sigurd knew there was nothing in the world Olaf would rather do than face Randver's champion, man to man, but he would not break up the shieldwall to do it.

'Fight me, Olaf!' Skarth roared, hammering his sword against Hendil's shield, sending slivers of wood flying. 'Fight me, you pale-livered cunny. You raven-starver!' Then his next blow cleaved Hendil's shield in two and Sigurd's man bellowed defiantly, raising the remaining half, but it was not enough and Skarth struck his arm off at the elbow, the stump spraying blood across his teeth and lips. Hendil stood his ground and swung his own sword at Skarth but Randver's champion sheathed his great blade in Hendil's face, a full foot of it erupting from the back of Hendil's skull.

'Close up!' Sigurd roared, a sword scraping off his mail-sheathed shoulder and a spear blade clanging off his helmet. Beside him Bjorn grunted as a blade found its way past his shield, but he stood firm, teeth gritted, trading blow for blow. But they were being pushed slowly backwards and Sigurd hauled his sword from its soil scabbard lest he lose it as their shieldwall gave ground.

Hauk fell back, his cheek opened by an arrow shot by the lurkers at the back, and Sigurd felt his shoulder come up against the wall that was Olaf.

'We can stay here and do this,' Olaf growled without turning to him, 'and die for it, or we can make a break for the ships and finish this another day.'

Half blinded by other men's blood, his ears ringing with the hammer and anvil din of it, Sigurd did not know what to do. His thoughts writhed like snakes in a fire. 'We can beat them,' he spat, his mouth full of the iron taste of blood and his arms burning with the strain of sword and shield work.

'No, lad, we can't,' Olaf said, ramming his sword over his shield and pulling its gore-slick length back as quick as lightning.

Sigurd could hear Jarl Randver screaming at his men to keep surging forward, to keep their blades plunging. He heard the jarl reassure his hirðmen that his son Hrani would soon come to join the fray and with him would come another four crews. When they came Sigurd knew his own crew would die in a terrible red slaughter.

And so he knew they had to make a break for it. If they could get down to the jetty maybe they could take the nearest ship and escape the murder.

Or maybe they would be cut down one by one before they even reached the sea.

'Wheel right!' Olaf yelled, and the left side of the skjaldborg began to give ground. Keeping their shields up and their sword arms working, they shuffled back together, shields overlapping as tight as a ship's strakes, whilst Sigurd and those to his right refused to give ground, yet turned slowly but surely left. Round came the line, inexorably but as yet unbroken, Randver's thegns pushing on where they could, thinking they were doing their jobs. And Sigurd knew he had Olaf to thank for getting this skill into them all before they ever set foot in Hinderå, for they now had their backs to the sea.

'Move over, lad,' Hauk said, and Sigurd and Bjorn turned their bodies sidewards to let the Osøyro man wedge himself back into the line between them.

'I'll wager this takes you back, hey, white-beard?' Bjorn said. Not that the man's beard was white now, with the arrow-gouged flesh of his cheek hanging there spilling dark blood into it. His beard braid was wicking the gore and was now dyed almost completely.

'Aye, lad, we did have one or two brawls like this,' Hauk said. 'When we were not busy having proper fights.'

Bjorn and a couple of the others laughed at this, which was a good thing to hear given the deepening mire they were in. Sigurd risked a glance over his shoulder and was relieved to see Runa still there, gripping a spear she had found, her eyes round, glutted with the carnage of that day.

'Keep it steady, Sigurd's men!' Olaf barked, but they did not need Olaf or Sigurd to tell them what the plan was now, and as one they began to move backwards across the rain-slick muddy ground, muscles full of searing pain, mouths too dry to talk and eyes full of stinging sweat. Back towards the bluff. Towards the sea.

'Runa, you are my eyes!' Sigurd yelled, and as much as he wanted her to stay close to him, he needed even more to know if they were going to walk backwards into another of Randver's crews. Knowing what she must do, Runa ran off along the path, disappearing beyond the escarpment, and for what seemed like too long she was gone, so that Sigurd's battle-lust was ice-tempered by the fear of losing her again.

'Hold here!' someone in Randver's skjaldborg bellowed, and the weight against Sigurd's shield was suddenly gone and there was ground between the two shieldwalls again. Men were hauling damp air into their lungs and spitting thick saliva. They armed sweat from their eyes, checked their shields for damage and invoked their gods.

'We're doing well,' Olaf said, rolling his shoulders and working a crick out of his neck. 'But we can't stay.'

Sigurd knew his friend was right. They had killed many of Randver's men and had even come close to killing the jarl himself, but they had failed and now the tide of this fight had turned. Even with the advantage of their brynjur and their blade-craft, they could not now hope to turn it back, and Sigurd knew he owed his newly forged Fellowship a chance to live beyond that bloody day.

'Whoresons know their business,' Hauk said, his beard rope dripping blood now, for Jarl Randver was using this respite to rebuild his shieldwall, putting the best-armoured men, those with brynjur or helmets or good leather armour, in the front line and those without behind them. He had more than forty men there now and he was also ordering some of them into another skjaldborg, an eight-man wall of shields and spears which Sigurd guessed he would send round the next clash to come at his seventeen from behind.

Then Runa was back at his shoulder and he thanked the gods for that as she caught her breath and fixed him with her blue eyes which looked like their mother's more than ever in that moment.

'There is no one between us and the jetty, brother,' she said, which was to Sigurd's ears like ale to a parched throat.

He nodded, the plan weaving in his mind even as he spoke his next words.

'Uncle, can you give these Hinderå men a good reason to piss in their breeks?' he asked.

Olaf frowned but soon enough caught the thread of what Sigurd had in mind. He nodded. 'I can keep the sons of swines thinking of other things, Sigurd,' he said, 'but it'll unravel soon enough and then it'll be every man for himself. Bloody chaos.'

Sigurd grinned. 'The gods love chaos, Uncle,' he said, then

called for Valgerd and Karsten Ríkr who slipped from the shield-wall and came over, blinking sweat from his eyes. When Sigurd told these two and Runa what he wanted from them they nodded and shared a determined look amongst themselves.

'Ready, Uncle,' Sigurd said and Olaf nodded again, spat on the ground and thumped his sword against his shield.

'*Svinfylkja!*' Olaf yelled in a voice that the freezing dead themselves must have heard down there in Niflheim. Olaf did not move but everyone else did, the shieldwall breaking up, war gear jangling as they arrayed themselves behind Olaf in the wedge-shaped formation that resembled a swine's head. And while they did this, Randver roared at his men to brace themselves for what was coming, and those men beat spears and swords against their own shields for courage and to rouse themselves to the imminent clash.

And they were too concerned with the bristling, ringmailed swine-wedge facing them to care about the three who had made a run for it towards the sea.

'Move, Uncle,' Sigurd said.

'Not a chance, lad,' Olaf said over his shoulder.

'Step aside, Olaf,' Sigurd said. 'They have held good to their oath and I will hold good to mine.' Olaf glowered and shook his head. But then he growled a curse into his bird's nest beard and moved aside, letting Sigurd take his place at the point of the wedge, for Sigurd had sworn to fight before his men and he would have them see him do so now.

Olaf was off his left shoulder and Svein muscled Bjorn out of the way to stand off his right, his crescent-shaped axe blade slick with gore and his red beard split with a grimace. Behind stood Floki, Bram and Bjorn and behind them the rest made up the formation, and knowing the men that stood with him then, Sigurd almost pitied those in the shieldwall before them.

He wished his father and brothers could see him now, that they would know how he faced their enemy with courage and in the sight of Óðin One-Eye and Vidar God of Vengeance. Not that Sigurd did not feel the worm of fear gnawing at his guts.

It was not a fear of pain or even death, for in death he would surely drink mead in the Æsir's hall with his brothers, though he did not wish to leave Runa alone in the world. But rather that writhing worm was the fear of failing to quench the fire inside him in the blood of this reckoning. He had done everything he could to get the Allfather's attention. Now he would honour the Spear-God by living up to Óðin's name, which means frenzy.

'Now,' he said, lifting his battle-scarred shield and dipping his head just in time, as an arrow glanced off his helmet and flew wide. They strode with him, staying close to one another, keeping the wedge tight and strong, and they roared as they covered the ground. And on Sigurd's first swing Troll-Tickler bit deep into a man's shield and Sigurd forced the shield down so that Bram could bury his sword's tip into the man's eye and pull it free, spattering Sigurd's face with hot blood. Sigurd hauled his blade free of the splintered wood and drove on. Svein rammed the head of his long-axe into a bearded face, staving in the skull, then turned and hooked the crescent blade behind another warrior's neck and pulled the man towards him and Floki knocked his shield aside and sheathed his hand axe in the man's forehead.

On they drove, right through Randver's skjaldborg like a rivet driven through green spruce, and men died beneath their blades. But the Svinfylkja formation could not hold with the enemy all around them now and spears coming from every side, and in ten thumping heartbeats there was no more wedge, only a knot of men fighting for their lives against more than twice their number.

Sigurd found himself at the heart of the knot then, as though his hirðmen had gathered around him, putting their own bloodied, battered bodies between him and their enemies, and for a moment he stood there as the deafening chaos whirled all about.

He saw Ubba smash a face with his shield boss then hack the dazed man down. He watched Bjarni duck a scything sword and thrust his own blade up into a man's inner thigh and he heard that man's scream above the battle din. Sigurd spun and saw Agnar Hunter and Kætil Kartr fighting back to back, Agnar catching a sword swing in the cross of his two long knives and turning the blade aside then slashing a knife across a face. Kætil was bleeding from three wounds, the worst a deep bloody cleft in his shoulder that looked like the work of an axe, yet he fought like a hero from some old tale, roaring challenges at his enemies.

Those old warriors who had once fought for Jarl Hakon Burner fought side by side once more and it was only their long experience of doing so that was keeping them alive, Hauk standing there grim-faced between Bodvar and Grundar, the last of their old hirð, men from a bygone age.

'We must fly, Sigurd!' Olaf said and Sigurd turned, instinctively looking for Randver, trying to lay his eyes on the jarl amidst that maelstrom. 'He's safely out of it,' Olaf said, knowing what was on Sigurd's mind. 'His boy took a wound and Randver hauled him off. We can't get to him now, Sigurd, and we'll never get to that whoreson king if we die here.'

'To the sea!' Sigurd roared, and his Wolves replied with a last great effort, trying to put their opponents down to give themselves a chance. With Randver out of the snarl of it the rest did not know what to do and Sigurd's hirðmen were able to draw together again, presenting a loose wall of shields to a badly mauled enemy that seemed relieved to catch their breath.

Their eyes on the jarl's men, Sigurd's crew shuffled backwards towards the ground they had previously occupied near the edge of the bluff, but for Hauk and his two companions who stopped and planted their feet, their blood-spattered, ragged shields overlapped. They looked exhausted, yet held their heads high and tried to straighten their backs.

'Here, Hauk!' Sigurd barked.

'No, lad!' Hauk called over his shoulder. 'We've never run. Not from any fight. And we will not run today.'

'We can make it, Hauk!' Sigurd said.

'You had better, lad,' the old man said. 'I expect you to come back here and finish what we started.' He hammered his sword hilt against what was left of his shield. 'Osøyro men!' he bellowed, his voice dry and cracked as old leather. 'Tonight we drink with our sword-brothers in Valhöll.' Grundar and Bodvar thumped their own shields and spat challenges at those coming to kill them. One last proud show of defiance in the face of death that had Sigurd's crew thumping their own shields, more than a few of them looking like they would rather stay to finish it one way or another. 'Now go!' Hauk yelled over his shoulder. 'We will wait for you in the shining hall, Sigurd Haraldarson!'

Sigurd shook his head but a big hand gripped his shoulder. 'Better they end it like this than with spears in their backs,' Olaf said, nodding towards the pitiful shieldwall. Sigurd knew this was true enough, for Hauk and the others would not have the legs to run. Yet the thought of leaving them there to be slaughtered was like a blade in Sigurd's chest, as Skarth began bellowing at the jarl's warriors now, rousing them to one final effort as he strode towards the Osøyro men.

Sigurd took one last look at those brave three, their old legs rooted to the ground so that only death would move them.

And then he turned and ran to the sea.

CHAPTER TWENTY

THEY RAN DOWN THE SLIPPERY PATH WHICH LED TO THE SHORE, THE Osøyro men's last sword song lingering in Sigurd's ears like smoke in woollen clothes. And when they clattered down to the wharf his heart leapt like a salmon in his chest, for Runa, Valgerd and Karsten were aboard *Reinen*, his father's old ship, and the dragon had slipped her moorings.

'Are we leaving then?' Karsten called from the mast step, a grin in his beard. Men were clambering aboard, some going to help with the sheets while others brought the oars down from their trees and threaded them through the ports. They would need wind *and* muscle to put as much water between them and Jarl Randver as they could.

'Does me good to see her,' Olaf said, taking hold of the oar Bram gave him, the two of them getting ready to push *Reinen* away from the wharf.

Breathing hard still, Sigurd found his nose filled with *Reinen*'s scent: the pine resin and the tar-coated ropes, the wet woollen sail and the brackish seep water in the bilge around the ballast stones.

'We would have set fires in them but it was too wet and there was no time,' Valgerd said, nodding at Jarl Harald's other ship, *Sea-Eagle*, and Randver's favourite ship, *Fjord-Wolf*, which were crewless and drifting off from their berths, their mooring ropes cut.

'You have given us a chance,' Sigurd said, nodding to Valgerd in thanks then looking up to where Jarl Randver's men were spilling over the hill and cursing at what they saw – two ships adrift and *Reinen* slowly easing away from the wharf.

'Well no one can say we have not ruined their feast at least,' Olaf shouted and this got some belly laughter even from men sheeted in blood and still thrumming from the fight, as they pulled their oars through the slate-grey, wind-stirred sea, most of them standing and bending deep because there were no sea chests aboard.

'There were sea chests on *Fjord-Wolf*,' Runa said, coming to stand with Sigurd, 'and that man said we should take her.' She nodded towards Karsten behind them at the tiller. 'But I told him you would rather take *Reinen*.'

Sigurd saw that her whole body was trembling and he put his arm around her, wincing at the many pains in his own body, though he did not think he was cut deeply anywhere. 'Do you think Father would have left her to that pile of goat turds?' he asked, watching Randver who was on the jetty now, roaring commands at his men who were milling on the boards, unsure what to do next, though a knot of them had found a small boat and were already rowing towards *Fjord-Wolf*.

With a shaking hand Runa pushed her still damp hair over her ear and asked if she should row, too. Sigurd shook his head. 'We will catch the wind in a moment and Karsten is a good helmsman.' He took off his cloak, relieved to see that there was not much blood on it, and put it around his sister's shoulders on top of the one she already wore in case she was cold. 'Rest while you can,' he said, pointing to a place in the thwarts on the port stern. Then he turned to look at his ragged, grim-faced crew.

Kætil Kartr was not rowing for he was white as bone from leaking so much blood, though he stood even so, watching the shore rather than sitting in the thwarts and saving what strength he yet owned. Bjorn was grimacing from a cut in his side where his brynja was torn and bloody, and if Agnar Hunter's head were a hull, its crew would have been busy bailing for it had an ugly gash in it.

Still, they had left five of their sword-brothers up there on the hill and Sigurd knew that was the deepest wound of all.

'Have their bollocks shrivel up and drop off, Asgot!' Ubba called to the godi, who stood up at the stern, his arms raised to the sky as he crowed a galdr at their enemies on the shore. His keening voice was enough to chill the blood even if you did not know the spell he was weaving with that ancient seiðr. But Sigurd's ears could unravel enough of it to know that Asgot was singing Jarl Randver's doom. No hero's pyre for Randver, just a cold blade and a colder grave, and every man or woman aboard *Reinen*, no matter their wounds, was glad that that dark, baneful curse was not being sung at them.

'That will do. Bring them in, lads!' Olaf called, pushing his own oar all the way out through the port and bringing it back over the sheer strake. There was wind in the sail and with so few men rowing would gain them nothing now. He came over to stand with Sigurd who was still at the sternpost watching Randver's men bring *Fjord-Wolf* back to the jetty where the rest waited, their spears pointing to the low heavy clouds rolling in from the east. Gulls keened wildly overhead, perhaps in answer to Asgot's old spell, and Rán's white-haired daughters were appearing here and there, racing across the sound as though they too fled from the jarl's wrath.

'I wonder what happened to old Solveig and Hagal,' Olaf said. Sigurd knew his old friend was trying to take his mind off what might have been. There was no sign of *Sea-Sow* or those of Randver's ships that had chased her west. The crews that had come and saved the jarl's skin must have been lying in wait behind another island in the sound and Sigurd smiled grimly at the lengths his enemy had gone to in trying to catch him.

'Listen,' Svein said, cupping a hand to his ear. 'I think I can hear Crow-Song's arse squeaking.'

Olaf grinned. 'And I wouldn't blame him, what with four crews snapping at their heels. But if you really listen hard you can hear old Solveig laughing. Those whoresons will starve to death before they catch up with that old goat.'

'Then let us hope we do not run into them when they give up and turn for home,' Karsten called from the tiller.

'If we do we will see what kind of a helmsman you really are, hey!' Olaf said, which did not seem to worry the Dane.

Sigurd stood there with Olaf beside him, the wind ruffling their beards and drying the gore that crusted on skin and in the iron rings of their brynjur. And yet an ominous silence spread between them like a bloodstain as, far behind them now, their enemy's ship harnessed the easterly gusts and ploughed a spumy furrow through the sound. Randver, it seemed, was as eager to kill Sigurd as Sigurd had been to kill him.

Eventually it was Olaf who hauled the thing to the surface. 'We had no choice, Sigurd,' he said, scratching his beard.

'There is always a choice, Uncle,' Sigurd said.

Olaf pursed his full lips. 'Even a wolf will slink off when the farmer brings all his hounds out.'

Sigurd turned to him now. 'But we are more than one wolf,' he said, sweeping an arm across the deck and those catching their breath at last and seeing to their wounds or else working on the sail to keep it catching the wind. 'Did I make myself known to old Blaze-Eye just so that he could watch me fly from the man I have sworn to kill?'

'Well he is not the only one that needs killing,' Olaf said, meaning that they still had to deal with King Gorm which seemed beyond impossible now.

'And you think I will have Óðin's favour after this?' Sigurd asked.

More beard-scratching now as Olaf chewed on that.

'You want to finish it?' he asked, though it was not a question. Not really.

Sigurd held his eye, in that one fjord-deep look saying more than words ever could.

'Frigg's arse,' Olaf growled, then turned to Karsten. 'Bring her around!' he called. 'You see that piece of dog shit ship back there full of men who want us dead? Aim for that.' Karsten's mouth unhinged but Olaf had already turned to the crew, to Svein and Floki, Bram, Bjarni, Bjorn and the rest, who were gingerly getting to their feet. 'Did you really think you could sit on your arses for the rest of the day?' he bellowed. 'Did you think that little scuffle back there proves you're good men in a fight? That you're worthy to share the same saga tale as Olaf Smiter and Sigurd Óðin-Favoured?' Most of them were wide-eyed and taken aback, but Svein and Bram shared a predator's grin. Floki was looking at Sigurd and nodding slowly as though he had been waiting for this moment all his life. 'Your ring-giver has something to say.' This was clever on Olaf's part for it reminded them of their oath without calling Sigurd a jarl, which was a thing he could not claim yet.

Sigurd stepped up onto the raised platform and stood beside Karsten who was already getting his mind around turning *Reinen* into the wind.

'Look!' he said, pointing off the bow towards *Fjord-Wolf*. 'This jarl *wants* to fight us.' He caught Runa's eye and that was a thorn in him but there was nothing he could do about that now. 'Svein, your father Styrbiorn was a fearsome prow man. I have no doubt he would be proud of you today for you will stand at *Reinen*'s prow.' The red-haired giant grinned like a man with two mead horns.

Sigurd knew Olaf would have expected to be the prow man, but Sigurd needed his battle-craft and could not risk a wound putting him out of the fight early on.

'I will not run from this jarl,' Sigurd said. 'Instead I will kill him and the gods will watch me do it.' He grinned at them then. 'If any of you does not want to fight him with me, you are free to walk away, I will not stop you.'

They laughed at this, even Kætil Kartr, who had less blood in him than on him.

'Well then, let's get on with it!' Olaf said, as Karsten drove the tiller hard to port, turning *Reinen* into the wind until it caught the sail, at which time Bjarni and Bjorn released one corner of the sail and the others released lines at bow, midships and stern. Sigurd and Olaf pulled hard on the ropes that stretched to each end of the yard to draw the sail over to the other side of the ship and catch the wind again. It was a fury of muscle and rope and barked commands, but when it was all done and Karsten had turned *Reinen* onto course they did not trim and tighten the sail again as they normally would.

'Drop the yard,' Olaf said, which had them looking at each other with furrowed brows. 'And get the anchors in. It's shallow enough here, I'd wager.'

Sigurd looked at him. With the sail down they would be helpless. Olaf shrugged, nodding at the froth-crested waves dashing across the sound. 'Lashing the ships together in this will be like trying to catch a fart. If we want to fight that worm-arsed shortwit, the least we can do is try to lie still as a new bride on her wedding night.'

He flushed then, glancing at Runa, who half smiled to put him at ease.

'I am not married, Uncle,' she said, as the anchors fore and aft splashed into the sea. 'Some uninvited guests ruined the wedding.'

Sigurd grinned at Olaf and grabbed his helmet, the leather lining of which was still sweat-soaked. 'This will be a hard fight,' he said, tying the thong beneath his chin, the marrow in his bones beginning to thrum again, 'and some of you will never look upon the sea or the sky after this day.' They were putting on their own helmets, gathering spears and shields and shrugging some life back into tired limbs. 'Whoever falls today will be honoured with a pyre and sent to the Hall of the Slain with all their war gear. You have my word on this.'

Sigurd could offer them no more than that and he turned to watch *Fjord-Wolf* ploughing its furrow through the sound towards them, her prow already bristling with men and steel.

The anchors seemed to be holding and the ship's bows pointed more or less north-east, the sea pushing past either side rather than hitting her abeam which would have had her rocking enough to turn a land man green.

'As good a place as any,' Karsten said, looking over the side and following the line of the stern anchor rope. The water there was at least partly sheltered by the Nilsavika headland and if there was to be a ship fight there were plenty worse places for it.

Svein fetched *Reinen*'s figurehead and fixed it in place at the prow, then slotted the antlers into it and those who were new to *Reinen* seemed satisfied with the beast.

'She is better looking than most of the women my brother has been with,' Bjarni said admiringly, which might have been true for Bjorn did not disagree.

'Keep away from Skarth if you can,' Olaf said as Sigurd and his hirðmen, just thirteen warriors, gathered in line either side of *Reinen*'s prow.

'You only say that because you want him for yourself,' Ubba said, gripping the throat of his long-axe whose haft rested on the deck.

Olaf did not deny it. 'We have unfinished business,' he said.

'Well I will kill whoever comes within reach,' Bram said, 'so if you want this Skarth on the end of your spear you will have to hope you get to him first.'

Agnar Hunter and Valgerd took up bows and tested their draw. They could not shoot far with their strings wet as they were but it would not matter for this would be an intimate affair, as Svein remarked to Valgerd while she was tying the arrow-thronged quiver to the shield rail on *Reinen*'s sheer strake.

'And the worst part of it is that we are downwind of them,' the red-bearded giant said. 'When they shit in their breeks at the sight of us we will be choking on it.'

'Here they come!' Olaf said as their enemies' war cries carried across the water and Sigurd looked at Asgot who nodded, lips hitched back from his teeth. Some men touched amulets at their necks for luck but most had enough iron all around them and touched brynja rings, spear blades, helmets or sword hilts.

'It's time, Runa,' Sigurd said and she nodded, their eyes riveted on each other's for a moment, then she hefted a shield and went to stand by the mast. Sigurd wished she were further away than that, but had to content himself with the hope that Randver would not hurt her if he won. Then he remembered that she and Randver's son Amleth had been soaking and shivering when they came into the jarl's hall and he was struck by the idea that Runa had tried to drown herself.

'Now then,' Olaf bellowed, 'remember to let them get the hooks in and the ships kissing before you start killing the ugly sons of sows.' He looked at Valgerd and Agnar Hunter. 'That doesn't go for you two. If you can thin them . . . give one or two of them an eye problem before we snuggle up, that will be no bad thing.' They nodded, nocking arrows to their strings because in twenty heartbeats *Fjord-Wolf* would be in range even with wet strings.

'Let's make them feel welcome, hey!' Bram roared and they all began to hurl insults at those coming to kill them.

'I wish Crow-Song was here to see this,' Aslak said.

'Don't you worry, lad,' Olaf said, 'when he tells it Randver will have four ships and we'll have Thór himself standing with us swinging his bloody great hammer.'

And he had barely got this out when Agnar and Valgerd let fly their first arrows and men lifted their shields to overlap them and form a bulwark above the sheer strake.

When *Fjord-Wolf* struck *Reinen*, men on both ships were sent reeling but Svein had one brawny arm round the prow beast and as Randver's ship glanced off *Reinen*'s bow and scraped along her steerboard side he swung his great axe and took a man's head off his neck. The man dropped to his knees, his neck stump spraying blood six feet into the air, and Randver's crew hurled their grappling hooks into *Reinen*'s thwarts. Those on *Reinen*'s port side ran over to join the others and no one cut the ropes, Bjarni even holding out a hand and yelling at one of Randver's men to pass it over, which the man did, the two of them hauling on it to bring the ships together.

Olaf ignored his own command about waiting for the ships to be securely lashed before killing their foemen. He hurled a spear which punched into a man's chest, throwing him back into his companions, and this unleashed the rest to the slaughter. Agnar loosed an arrow which streaked into a face, the shaft going through one cheek and out the other, and Valgerd put one through a beardless stripling's arm as he raised it to cast his spear.

Ubba was roaring curses and jabbing his long-axe at shields and Asgot was a fiend with his spear, cutting and ripping, and Sigurd could already smell fresh blood in the air. A sword glanced off his helmet and thumped into his shoulder and he sank his spear into the man's shoulder so that the sword fell from the man's hand and splashed into the sea between the ships. Then *Fjord-Wolf* and *Reinen* came together with a bump and Randver's crew tied off the ropes which was brave of them – working on knots when men were trying to kill you.

Another of Randver's warriors, a big mail-clad man Sigurd remembered from the earlier fight, stepped up onto the sheer strake and swung his long-hafted axe, smashing Bjorn's shield to splinters. His next swing would have killed Bjorn but Kætil Kartr was there and plunged his sword through the big man's thigh, making him bellow like an ox. But those legs were like trees and somehow the big man kept his balance and swung the axe again and the blade sliced Kætil's sword arm off at the shoulder. Bjorn hurled himself forward, driving his spear into the man's belly, and Sigurd saw the moment that the rings burst apart and the blade sank into the flesh. The big man doubled over and with another great shove Bjorn tipped him back into *Fjord-Wolf* and Randver's men roared to see the big man down.

Another brave warrior tried to come aboard, chopping the end off Aslak's spear as he put one foot up on the side, but a heartbeat later that foot and most of the ankle were lying in *Reinen*'s thwarts thanks to Floki's hand axe, and perhaps the man might have grieved for it had Floki not cracked his skull open with his next swing.

But Sigurd could see what the enemy had in mind, for if they could come aboard *Reinen* their advantage of numbers would likely win the day, with Sigurd having barely enough men to put a skjaldborg all the way across the deck.

'Vidar be with me now,' he growled under his breath, and with that he stepped up onto the sheer strake, roaring like a berserker and jabbing his spear at every man before him, and two swords hacked into his shield, splitting it across the middle, so he shook it loose and hauled his scramasax from its sheath.

And he jumped. The weight of him in all his war gear was enough to force a space amongst the thronging enemy like a rock dropped into water. Even so he should have died then, gutted and spear-gored, ripped and hacked, but before he could even set about him he was knocked to the deck by another mail-sheathed warrior with black braids flying. Floki had no shield, just a short axe in either hand and those weapons were a blur as he parried blades with one and struck with the other, opening bellies and necks, butchering men as though they were carcasses lying on the board. Randver's men raised their shields and shrank back from him and this gave others a chance to come over from *Reinen*. Sigurd drew Troll-Tickler and put his back to Floki, catching a blade on his sword and slashing the scramasax across a man's eyes. Bram was there too, and all along *Reinen*'s side men were plunging into *Fjord-Wolf*'s thwarts, which was so shocking to Randver's crew that they were already giving ground across their deck.

Sigurd turned and saw Svein swinging his axe, creating great arcs of room for other *Reinen* men to pour into. Randver stood on his ship's mast fish, sword and shield in hand, yelling at his men to stop being cowards and drive their enemy into the sea, which was easy for him to say standing there watching other men die.

Ubba dropped a barrel-chested warrior with a well-placed thrust of his axe's head into the man's face and this left him facing Skarth who had until now been guarding his jarl. Ubba grinned and jabbed the long-axe into Skarth's shield by way of a greeting and Randver's champion cast the shield aside, knowing it would not take much punishment from a long-hafted axe wielded by a man of Ubba's size. Then Ubba brought the axe up and round and down but Skarth had not become Randver's prow man by losing out to a wood-cutter's strike like that and he twisted out of the blade's path as it thunked into the deck boards. He brought his big, worm-looped sword down and cut through the axe's haft, which was a thing worth seeing, then he stepped forward and hacked aside the stave Ubba now brandished as a club. Ubba spat in Skarth's face as the champion's sword scythed into his neck with a wet chop that Sigurd heard above the battle din, but Ubba's neck was stronger than his axe's haft and at least he died with his head still on.

'Olaf!' Skarth roared. But Olaf was busy fighting two men on the steerboard side.

'Sigurd!' Runa screamed and Sigurd saw that one of Randver's men had gone over into *Reinen* perhaps thinking to end the thing by threatening to kill Runa. There were too many bodies between Sigurd and Runa and he knew he could not get to her in time.

'Valgerd!' he yelled, and the shieldmaiden looked up, her eyes following where Sigurd's scramasax was pointing. She moved like lightning, hamstringing one warrior and knocking another aside before getting to *Fjord-Wolf*'s side and casting her spear. The shaft flew straight as a shipwright's plumb-line and took Randver's man in the back so that he staggered into Runa and she squirmed free of him, letting him slump to the deck where he thrashed like a fish.

'Sigurd!' Aslak called and Sigurd turned, getting his sword up in time to block a wild swing from a pock-marked, yellow-skinned warrior who stank like death. Sigurd stepped in and punched the long knife up into the man's guts and held it there, using the man as a shield as he hauled foul breath into his lungs and looked for the next man to kill. Then Aslak went down from a blow that dented his helmet and Karsten took a spear in his shoulder just as another man hacked into his leg with a hand axe. The helmsman roared in pain and fury but the sound stopped as the spear came again, this time bursting from his chest.

Floki was walking death, seemingly untouchable as he worked his craft and thinned Randver's crew. Beside him Olaf, Asgot and Bjarni were working side by side, pushing Randver's men back towards the stern where the jarl had put himself now. On the other side Svein, Bram and Bjorn were making a slaughter for ravens for it seemed Randver had no men in brynjur left standing. Valgerd had gone back aboard *Reinen* to protect Runa, but the shieldmaiden was now working along the side with her bow, shooting arrows into men who were too busy fighting for their lives to do anything about it.

'Leave him for me!' Olaf clamoured at Agnar Hunter who was scything his two long knives at Skarth. He managed to cut the champion's forearm but then Skarth lopped off one of his hands and before Agnar knew it was gone Skarth took the other hand too. Agnar raised both spurting arms and glared at them as though unable to believe what he saw, as Skarth plunged his sword into his open mouth, twisting the blade in a mess of blood and broken teeth.

'Finish it!' Sigurd yelled. Men shrieked and bellowed and *Fjord-Wolf*'s thwarts ran with blood that pooled by the ship's ribs. And Sigurd's Wolves would not be stopped now. They hacked and ripped until their arms felt as though they were on fire and still they slew their enemies even as those men saw their doom and some of them threw down their swords.

'I am coming for you, Randver!' Sigurd bellowed, pointing his blood-slick sword at the jarl who stood up on his stern deck. Sigurd's men moved with him like a wave of death sweeping over his enemy's deck. 'Are you ready for me, Randver? You white-livered nithing!'

Hearing this and seeing the day was lost Skarth strode back to join his lord and the two of them watched as the last three of Randver's hirðmen were slaughtered where they stood. Sigurd turned and looked back across *Fjord-Wolf*'s deck. Bodies lay everywhere. You could hardly see the oak boards for them.

Then he turned back to the bow and told his men to hold, which they did, gasping for breath but holding themselves straight and tall, chests heaving like forge bellows, sweat dripping from beards and running down sleeves to cascade from wrists.

Then Bram shrugged his broad shoulders and stepped forward.

'Don't even think about it,' Olaf gnarred, and Sigurd knew there was no point in trying to stop Olaf now. Skarth grinned, if it could be called a grin in an axe-holed face like that, and shook his head to rouse himself, his one blond braid whipping his scab-crusted head.

'I will enjoy killing you, Olaf,' Skarth said, and the only answer he got was a clash of blades that must have rattled his big bones. There was no more said between them as their swords rang out and they circled each other like two great wolves, each seeking the opening.

But then Olaf seemed to tire of the game. He took Skarth's next blow on the strongest part of his sword near the hilt and forced the other's sword up high then stepped in and smashed his helmet into Skarth's face. Skarth stepped backwards and scythed his blade down but Olaf blocked it again, this time sending it wide and hammering a fist into Skarth's jaw and it was a blow that would have stunned a bull. Skarth staggered, lifting his blade to block the sword he thought was coming. But Olaf stepped up with a clenched fist and hammered him and this time Sigurd heard the jaw bones crack like knots in wood when the fire eats into them.

Skarth went down onto one knee and Olaf stared down and shook his head as though disappointed, then swung his sword and took off Skarth's ugly head.

'You've improved his looks anyway, Uncle,' Svein said with a grin, standing there with one arm resting on his long-axe.

Jarl Randver looked to the south-west as though he thought his son might suddenly appear with four ships full of men. But there was nothing out there other than Rán's white-haired daughters running across the wind-rippled sea. Sigurd thought the jarl would throw himself over the side then, rather than beg for his life. But Randver was a still a jarl, even with none of his hearthmen left around him, and he had not got his torc by being a coward.

'I will wait for you in the Allfather's hall, Sigurd Haraldarson,' he said, then cast his shield over the side, raised his sword wide and strode forward. Sigurd avoided the first three cuts, catching the fourth on his own blade, then plunged the scramasax into the jarl's neck and hauled it across, ripping the throat open in a snarl of flesh and windpipe and glistening white bone.

'You will see your sons there first,' Sigurd snarled in his ear, throwing his blades down and picking the jarl up by his sword belt. Then Svein was there and together they lifted the jarl, whose eyes bulged with the things he could no longer say, and dumped him over *Fjord-Wolf*'s side. Then they leant on the sheer strake and watched as Randver's fine brynja dragged him down into the dark depths and the waves covered him as though he had never existed.

Olaf came and stood beside him and for a long while they looked out across the grey sea as the gulls shrieked overhead like they do when fish guts are thrown overboard.

When Sigurd turned back he saw Runa standing there amongst the bodies, staring at him, her golden hair loose to her shoulders and her face white as new snow, so that he blinked at the vision of her, wondering how something so beautiful could live amongst the stinking, butchered corpses.

'We should leave, Sigurd,' Aslak said, arming blood from his face. Floki was cleaning his axes. Asgot was slumped against the side panting like a dog. Bjarni and Bjorn were looking for plunder amongst the dead, and Bram and Valgerd were watching Sigurd. 'We don't want to be caught out here tied up when the jarl's other ships return,' Aslak went on.

Sigurd nodded but did not move. He looked up at the sky, half expecting to see a raven flying there, one of Óðin's birds perhaps. Some sign that the Spear-God was present, that he had seen what had just taken place.

But there was nothing but the bruised clouds and the wheeling gulls.

'So that is that,' Olaf said.

Sigurd looked at him and nodded. But then he went back to the side and looked west, because west lay Avaldsnes.

And the king who lived there.

ACKNOWLEDGEMENTS

My hearty thanks to the following:

Bill Hamilton for his sage advice and for steering me through the skerries upon which I would otherwise no doubt founder. Simon Taylor for never doubting (at least not openly) that I could summon the tale and deliver it on time, and for his well-honed editorial eye. Elizabeth Masters whose Viking-like enterprise and energy ensures that this saga spreads its wings, and for bringing new backsides to the row benches. And to Steve Mulcahey for designing a jacket which is, to my eyes, stunningly beautiful and should, I hope, draw the eye like rich plunder. To Phil Stevens for rowing a Viking ship with me and for making up stories over mead. To Conn Iggulden who read an early version and kept me entertained by quoting lines he enjoyed via text and, though it must have pained the ex-teacher in him, only pointing out the odd error here and there. My HWA friends for their generosity and for organizing some brilliant 'office' parties. I would also thank you, far-wandering reader, for coming on this adventure with me and for your unyielding Viking spirit. What a crew we make!

ABOUT THE AUTHOR

Family history (he is half Norwegian) and his storytelling hero, Bernard Cornwell, inspired **Giles Kristian** to write his first historical novels, the acclaimed and bestselling *Raven* Viking trilogy – *Blood Eye, Sons of Thunder* and *Odin's Wolves*. For his next series, he drew on a long-held fascination with the English Civil War. *The Bleeding Land* and *Brothers' Fury* follow the fortunes of a divided family against the complex and brutal backcloth of a conflict that tore this country apart and ended with the killing of a king. In his new novel – *God of Vengeance* – Giles returns to the world of the Vikings to tell of the beginnings of Sigurd and his celebrated fictional fellowship. Giles lives in Leicestershire.

To find out more, visit www.gileskristian.com